SUZANNAH ROWNTREE

Dark & Dawn

Miss Dark's Apparitions, Volume IV

Chapter I.

I have always known that I am likely to run mad. People with the sort of gift I have—the ability to see and, on occasion, to converse with, the spirits of the unquiet dead—often do end up in strait-waistcoats in lunatic asylums. I had met one of these unfortunates myself, once, as a girl in England; and I had resigned myself to my fate. There was nothing I could do about it except try to render my family financially secure before the blow should fall, and lay up a quantity of white satin in which to go mad, like the Bride of Lammermoor.

But I was not ready to go mad *yet;* and so I told my father's ghost that morning when I awoke far too early to find him hovering aimlessly in a corner of my Ekaterinburg hotel room.

In my defence, I had had a trying few days. A visit to Moscow during the coronation of the new Tsar—or Cousin Nicky, as *one* of our party knew him—had resulted in calamities of various different sorts. For one thing, it had seen Grand Duke Vasily Nikolaevich—for reasons which remained completely incomprehensible to *me*—choosing to abandon his friends and undertake an ill-advised marriage to a spoilt young princess, from which he had already fled once. It is true that Vasily was offered obscene wealth and unfettered power, should he return to the bosom of his monstrous family.

1

It was true, too, that more than one of the vampire Grand Dukes of the Russian Empire hungered, very literally, for his blood; and they were now quite likely to get another taste of it before the year was out. I was pretty sore about it, for I had had the poor judgement to have fallen quite inadvisably in love with the disastrous Grand Duke. Perhaps that in itself was a sort of madness.

Far more serious, however, had been the awful disaster at Khodynka, which had resulted in so many hundreds—if not thousands—of deaths. As a result of that tragedy I had been briefly overwhelmed by a flood of fresh shades, all of whom had carried with them the most frightful sensations of suffering and despair. Ever since, my spiritual faculties had been sharpened, so that I could not help seeing a great many more imprints about me than usual. But the most troubling result was that my father's imprint now followed me about wherever I went. It was now some two or three days since we had fled Moscow; and in all that time I had been unable to escape that silent, ghostly presence. Was this how my madness began? The woman at Hanwell Asylum so long ago had also been in the habit of conversing with the spirits of her dead relatives.

I did not *feel* as though I was going mad, however; at this moment, my mood was distinctly one of exasperation.

My father's improvident choices during life had left my mother, my three sisters, and myself in a condition of genteel poverty which doomed us to go through the world scrimping and saving to keep body and soul together—and now it seemed that he was no longer content with haunting only my waking hours. That morning, he had also stolen into my dreams. I was at home in Brixton. The afternoon sunlight fell slanted and golden through the front hall of the house, where I and my sisters waited with Nanny to bid our father farewell before he left us and went away to Hong Kong. Something had happened, however. A letter, with a postmark in beautiful and peculiar hieroglyphics, was handed in and ooh'ed over by the parlour-maid and Nanny before being hurried away to Papa's study, where he had been bidding farewell to Mother. Nanny said that the postmark was from somewhere in China, and then she told us all sorts of wonderful things about that country—how their Emperor demanded that everyone, even civilised Englishmen, should greet him by pressing their faces against the ground; how their little girls went about on tightly-bound-up feet, so that when they were old they could scarcely hobble; and how many of the people were hopeless idlers who loafed about all day smoking opium until all their substance had been consumed and their strength decayed. It was a long lesson, because Papa, whose cab had been waiting in the street for his imminent departure, remained in his study for an endless time and we could hear his voice speaking to Mother in some agitation. At last he emerged from the study looking very solemn and a little bit pale. It was then that he came to me and kissed my forehead and told me to be good; and then he said farewell to Katie and the twins; and then he went away and we never saw him again. Nanny and the parlour-maid did not last much longer. From that moment, the fortunes of the House of Dark were ruined.

I awoke from this dream—or, rather, from this long-forgotten memory—to find my father's imprint seated in a wooden chair in the corner of the hotel-room, placidly reading the newspaper. I knew he was only a memory, but I could not help speaking to him anyway. "I wish to heaven

3

you'd go away and stop haunting me," said I in a voice nearly choked with tears. "I don't mean to run mad. I haven't the time. And I haven't got any white satin to do it in."

Of course the imprint made no response to this. I could not make myself stop remembering, merely by wishing to do so. That was the worst thing about it. The shades of the dead do not, as a general rule, remain in this life very long; they are moved on very quickly to a different world. What remains when they depart is only a memory imprinted upon the places and people left behind. I knew very well that if I was being haunted by my father, it was only because I could not relinquish my own unfilial feelings. Yet as I pulled the bedcovers more tightly around my ears—for the Russian nights are often cold, even at the threshold of summer—I felt myself awash in fresh resentment. If only Papa had behaved with greater forethought, then we should not have lost our fortune, and he would not have died of the plague in Hong Kong, and I should not have been obliged to leave my home and go out into the world. Nor would I be waking up in a cold hotel-room deep in provincial Russia, with a chilled nose and a broken heart, and with secret-policemen and vampire Grand Dukes no doubt hot on my trail.

It was not a reasonable thing to feel—I see that now, of course. But I was having a wretched week, and in that moment I blamed my father for all of it.

I was not quite sure what had brought the old memory floating back to me, for it was many years since I had thought about the letter from China. Perhaps Nijam, outlining our plan of escape from Russia upon the previous evening, had brought the thing to mind.

"The main thing is to get well on our way to Vladivostok

before anyone realises we have gone east, rather than west," she had said, adjusting the steel-rimmed *pince-nez* upon the bridge of her nose, through which she was examining a map of Siberia which she had purchased in Kazan. "From there we must catch the first steamer to Hong Kong, or whichever British colony is nearest. Don't you have connections on that island, Dark?"

"Yes, and I'm anxious to avoid them!" I had retorted. My father's former business partner, Sir Humphrey Seton, had recently returned to oversee the Hong Kong trading empire which my father's carelessness had once brought to the brink of ruin. Nor was this the only reason Sir Humphrey had to view the Dark family with suspicion. "Don't you remember quite recently relieving Sir Humphrey of a diamond worth two million pounds?"

Miss Nijam gave me a blank look. "Naturally I remember it," she said. "If there's no one else who can be of assistance to us in Hong Kong, then we must just keep our heads down and not allow Sir Humphrey to discover us. We shall be perfectly safe otherwise: the plague has died down lately."

The theft of the fabulous Noor-Jahan, I hasten to remind the gentle reader, had been carried out in a spirit of the purest altruism. No doubt you will feel that this was still very wrong of us. Indeed, sometimes I was not quite easy about it myself. Sir Humphrey had always stood as a benefactor to my family. It was he who had paid for me to attend Saint Alphege's Seminary for Young Ladies, thereby qualifying me to earn my keep as a governess in the dreary old days before Miss Nijam had invited me to join her in stealing the fortunes of the rich and monstrous.

At Nijam's words, Mimi Laine had made an indelicate sound.

"Who cares about Hong Kong?" she asked. "If things go on as they have, we won't make it any further than Ekaterinburg. Schmidt says we're getting low on money, and if we telegraph Schloss Frohsdorf for more the police will be on us like a chicken on a bug."

To Alphonse Schmidt, golden-haired and golden-hearted, had been entrusted the common purse. It was Nijam who had made this arrangement, saying that I was too scatter-brained, and Mimi too mercenary, to be trusted with it. As for herself, she did not want to be bothered with the responsibility. She had enough to do plotting our escape from the net which threatened to ensnare us.

Nijam did not make indelicate sounds, but she had an excellent line in withering looks, one of which she now sent Mimi's way. "We shall just have to sell some things, that is all. —*No*, Mimi, for heaven's sake, no larceny; I know you are very good at it, but we can't afford to be in any more trouble with the law than we already are." She had checked her watch. "We shall arrive in Ekaterinburg in half an hour; let's split up now, and find hotels and pawnbrokers and whatever else we need in pairs. If the police are after us, they'll be on the lookout for a group of four."

That was how Mimi and I had found ourselves registering at a hotel under assumed names—and that, I suppose, was how I came to dream of Chinese postal-marks. I never did find out what was in that long-ago letter, which had so furrowed my father's brow; but it now put me in mind of another letter. Venturing out of bed, I opened the valise which stood in the corner. The pearl *collier de chien* which had been given me by an American admirer had gone to the pawnbroker's with Mimi on the previous evening, together with the black-and-white dress which I had worn to the French embassy ball that last eventful night in Moscow. I was not sorry to see either of them go, for I could never wear the pearl collar without recalling the sensation of Mr Vandergriff's hands about my neck; and as for the dress, it was a weight off my conscience, for I do not think that Mimi had come by it honestly in the first place. Besides, the sight of it reminded me wretchedly of the last time I had seen Vasily—on the balcony of our stuffy little Moscow apartment, asking how I meant to repay him for abandoning his monstrous family, together with all the riches they offered him!

At least there was now a good deal more room in the valise. My hand immediately fell upon Vasily's sketchbook. For a moment I hesitated, wondering whether I might not be better off burning the thing, for the sight of it only caused me pain. Two days on the train from Moscow to Ekaterinburg had left me feeling no less hurt and confused by the Grand Duke's unaccountable behaviour. Vasily *knew* that remaining with his family meant, at worst, his death, and at best, his marriage to the self-centred Serbian princess who had betrayed us to the police. What could he be thinking? and why, if he was so hard-hearted as to abandon the only people who still cared for him, had he filled the sketchbook with drawings of *me*?

I laid the book carefully aside. I could not merely toss it into the fireplace, for I could not yet bear to destroy the only evidence I had that Vasily might in some way return my feelings. Instead, I reached into the valise again and at once found the letter from my mother, which was postmarked three weeks ago in London. Heavens! this, too, reminded me of Vasily. On the day we left London, when my mother promised to write to explain why I had her blessing in stealing the Noor-

Jahan diamond from Sir Humphrey Seton, Vasily had been standing at my side… The missive had evidently been sent to Schloss Frohsdorf, our Austrian headquarters, before being forwarded to Moscow; and since then had lain unopened in my valise, quite forgotten amidst sundry upheavals of the heart.

Everything reminded me of Vasily. Morning sunrise reminded me of Vasily. Barley-sugar hawked by urchins at the train-station reminded me of Vasily. Every dark-haired, bearded passer-by in the street caught the tail of my eye and made my heart leap in expectation of Vasily. If this was love, it was a shockingly uncomfortable experience.

I opened the letter and perused it. Then I perused it again, because it quite upended all my ideas. The passage in question read as follows:

Since it seemed cruel to raise vain hopes, it was never my intention to breathe a word of what I am about to write to you; but now I can scarcely withhold an explanation. You are aware of the sad business which blasted our fortunes and took your dear father from us. He died, of course, in possession of a certain interest in the shipping company. This share of the business was, under the terms of the will, held in trust by Sir Humphrey to be divided between his daughters when they should attain the age of twenty-one, or be married: whichever should occur first. That share still belongs to you girls, since it was never legally transferred to Sir Humphrey; and with the subsequent success of the business, I cannot see any reason why your share should not now be worth a great deal more than it was eleven years ago. In any case your part of it ought to have been made over to you four years ago, on your twenty-first birthday. Indeed, upon that occasion I wrote to Sir Humphrey to remind him of his obligations as trustee; whereupon I received an account which quite surprised me. By this account, the shares owned by your father were fewer in number than I at first supposed: one-tenth of the number your father mentioned in his final letter to me. Sir Humphrey seemed to think that the number mentioned in the letter was a scribal error, and suggested that since the real number was so small, and their value so negligible, they should remain in his care in hope that they may someday appreciate in value. With only your father's word against Sir Humphrey's, and the company records being kept in Hong Kong, I could see it would absolutely take a lawsuit to compel him to render me a true accounting and disburse the money; and then, how could I be sure that the fruit would be worth the toil? You know that we have never had money to spare, and the only certainty in the matter was that the solicitors must be paid. Perhaps it was wrong of me, but I considered the money lost, however much—or little—it may be.

Even now I am persuaded that it would be unwise to take Sir Humphrey to court. You have chosen to take the law into your own hands, and to do so would be to risk exposing yourself, as well as him, to censure. Still, in my opinion the loss of the Noor-Jahan is not a great deal more than he deserves.

I do not know which shocked me more—the admission, from the woman who had raised me strictly according to the Ten Commandments, that she considered my theft to be justified; or the accusation levied against Sir Humphrey himself. Was it not the likeliest thing in the world that my ne'er-do-well father had in a fit of forgetfulness or absent-mindedness affixed an unwarranted zero to the number of his shares? Sir Humphrey, on the other hand, was not the sort of person to make such an error. His father, now—*him* I knew to have been a thoroughly bad sort, for he had made his fortune in India during the mutiny, and I myself had witnessed an imprint of the elder Seton shooting down the Begum of Bengal in cold blood. But Sir Humphrey himself had always been our benefactor. True, upon inheriting his father's estate he had not taken the step of returning the Noor-Jahan diamond to its rightful owners; but that was a fault I could sympathise with. I am not sure that I could have parted with such a diamond under similar circumstances. I knew that Mimi Laine could not.

No sooner did this thought cross my mind, than there came a soft tapping at my door and I opened it to find Mimi herself on the threshold. The sight of her momentarily drove all thought of the letter from my mind. Her fine, heavy, ashen masses of hair had been cropped close to her head, leaving her gamine face looking more like a boy's than ever.

"Mimi!" I gasped. "Your *hair!*"

"What about my hair?" she demanded. "Come downstairs; we must get breakfast before the train leaves."

"But your *hair!*" I repeated. "Why?"

"Isn't it obvious? It was worth a great deal, so I sold it. I did not have a great many other things to sell; not after I gave Anna everything I collected at the embassy ball."

Now certainly there is nothing so *very* shocking about a lady selling her hair—only I knew how many pieces of herself Mimi had sold in the course of her life, and I had taken some comfort in the thought that as part of my crew, she should never need to do so again. Now, beholding the wreckage, I could not help the tears springing to my eyes. I had failed her.

"Mimi, you shouldn't have done it! We could have found something else to sell!"

"Well, I would have sold my blood, except that no Grand Duke would let himself be found dead in this town."

I could not venture to ask if it had occurred to her to sell anything else. I could only say, feebly, "Mimi, my dear, don't you think that there are some things that *shouldn't* be sold?"

"No, I don't," she said, rather stubbornly. "It's all business, isn't it? What are you reading, there?"

I did rather badly want someone else's opinion of this extraordinary letter, so I handed it over to her and begged her to tell me what she thought. Having read it, rather slowly, Mimi's brows rose in surprise.

"What good fortune that we are going to Hong Kong! We must steal the money, of course."

She said the thing with such airy certainty that I felt almost dizzy. "Steal it?" I whispered, sending my father's imprint a rather guilty look. "But we've already stolen the Noor-Jahan from Sir Humphrey—and then we made him pay for the fake, to boot!"

"That American, Vandergriff, paid for the fake," Mimi corrected me, "and we gave the money *and* the Noor-Jahan back to the Indians; and you never saw a penny. Come, Dark! *Do* let us steal the fortune."

I could not help laughing at the wheedling tone in her voice. "But I really can't," I objected. "Depend upon it, my father made a mistake in writing down the number, and—"

"We can find out," Mimi said with a wave of her hand. "The company office will contain the records; how hard could it be to steal a few old sheets of paper that no-one wants?"

I bit my lip. "I'll think about it," I said, but as I bundled the remainder of my belongings into the valise and followed Mimi downstairs, I felt quite certain that my answer ought to be no. Thieves we might be, but strictly philanthropic in nature: it was our task to redress the wrongs of others, and not to enrich ourselves. Then I recalled, with a pang, that my sisters also had equal shares in the inheritance. How lucky for them, if it turned out that the legacy was a sizeable one after all! What I would not give to see them established for life, no longer dependent upon myself for their bread! But no, this was still too self-interested for me to feel quite comfortable. I ought not to waste any time—or Franz Haber's resources—on such a selfish cause.

The hotel was a humble establishment intended for those who required modest and economical lodgings: a dingy but rather charming place built, like many of the smaller and older houses in the town, of wooden logs stacked upon a brick foundation. The establishment did not provide its guests with food at this early hour, so Mimi and I ventured out into the street and bought meat-stuffed pastries from a street-vendor. The morning was dark and overcast, the heat-wave of the past week having given way to a thick blanket of clouds and a scouring north wind. It felt as though it might be about to rain.

Since the train station was not far away, Mimi and I hurried through the streets towards it on foot. Everyone knows the name Ekaterinburg now, of course, on account of the ghastly events which were to take place there some twenty years later, but at the time I knew it only as an out-of-the-way place on the edge of Siberia, at which we should leave Europe and start our journey across the boundless plains of Asia. I was surprised to find the town quite prosperous, containing no more than the normal urban population of imprints—suicides, carriage accidents, police atrocities, and the like. Amidst the charming wooden houses at its centre there were a great many ornate neoclassical confections. These, a traveller's brochure at the hotel informed me, had been built with local gold, for at one time—long before Ballarat or the Klondike—half the world's gold was mined in Siberia. As for the station itself, this was a long, low, fairytale building in red brick with white architraves and a gaily painted, steeply-pitched red and white roof. There were scattered pedestrians on the pavement at its entrance, and Mimi tugged at my elbow as we approached.

"Look, there's Nijam and Schmidt," she said.

A grimy urchin was busy hawking newspapers in a loud, piercing, rather melancholy cry. Schmidt had evidently purchased one of them, for he turned towards me clutching it in a shaking hand. That, and the look on his face, told me at once that something was wrong. In a few steps I reached his side: then I saw the newspaper and my heart quite congealed within me.

It was printed in Russian, of course, and made no more sense to me than did Greek to Julius Caesar. But the portrait of Grand Duke Vasily Nikolaevich spoke for itself—as, too, did the black border of deepest mourning which surrounded the image.

"Miss Laine," Schmidt implored, holding out the paper to her. "You can read this, can't you?"

But that morning I did not require Mimi's help in reading anything. I always knew it would happen. For days I had been bracing myself for the news. Vasily had returned to his monstrous family, and now he was dead.

Chapter II.

There was, after all, not much that Mimi could tell us about what had happened to Vasily. The paper only said that he had died "yesterday, suddenly, at Moscow", mourned by his family and fiancée.

"What an excellent thing that there is *one* of the party who understands Russian," Nijam said, briskly, when the paper had been read. "Come along, then, Mimi, there's no time to lose; you must help me to buy our tickets to Vladivostok. I see you cut your hair."

With that she strode off in a very heartless manner. Mimi followed her. Schmidt and I could not possibly have moved a foot: we gazed at each other, thunderstruck. Schmidt had gone very pale, and I felt almost numb.

"It can't be," Schmidt said after a moment. "It's a hoax. He can't really be dead. Sir is much too clever for that."

If only I could believe him! I shook my head, reflecting that sir was, on the contrary, a fathead. Had he not been a fathead, he would never have gone back to his family, and they would not have eaten him. "I only hope he did not suffer," I began, and that was too much for me. I was compelled to stifle any further sounds with my handkerchief.

Vasily, dead! The mind recoiled from such a thought.

Not Vasily, whom Mimi had once called the scandal of Christendom! *He* could not die—so young, and so bad. After the first moment of shock, I began to feel quite angry about it. In all the improving fiction I had read, it was the bad young wastrel who *did* die young, cursing his unlucky fate, together with the drinking and dancing which had been his downfall. (The improving fiction is of course too proper to mention anything *worse* than drinking or dancing.) And now it seemed that the improving fiction had spoken truly! It was absolutely insulting, and I wished very much to have a word with the Author. Vasily deserved better than to be a moral lesson for impressionable young ladies. Fail though he might, he had *tried* to be better; he had, for however brief a time, *wanted* to be better. And at that I broke down entirely.

Let us not dwell upon the following quarter-hour. I was nearly late for the train, for I retired to the ladies' room and ruined a handkerchief before I managed to get hold of myself. After that an express came in from Petersburg and I skulked in my cubicle until the rush of passengers abated sufficiently to allow me a chance to wash my face in private. Still, I am afraid that I crept aboard the Trans-Siberian train in rather a sorry state, just as the whistle was going, with a reddened nose and watery eyes.

The morning, as I have said, was dark. Rain had begun to pelt from the heavens, and in the bare, austere corridor of the carriage, electric lamps burned with a low hum. Everyone else had by now ensconced themselves within their compartments, and the corridor was cold and empty save for a dark and rather indistinct figure at the opposite end—a man who, like myself, had climbed aboard just as the whistle went. As the train laboured out of the Ekaterinburg station to begin its long journey, I dabbed at my eyes again, although it is doubtful that my horrible handkerchief could possibly have absorbed any more tears. Blinking at my ticket, which Nijam had passed under the cubicle door with the injunction not to delay, I saw that even in my haste I had boarded the correct carriage. Indeed there was only one passenger carriage on the train, the remainder consisting of freight. As I began to inspect the compartment doors for the number on my ticket, the hum of electricity began to stutter, and the lights to flicker. I looked up and saw my fellow-traveller turn towards me.

It was then that I knew Vasily was really dead. Alive, he could never have been so dishevelled—blackened with soot, daubed with blood, and emanating the sickly-sweet scent of dynamite. The lamps flickered in long, sobbing gasps that echoed my breath as he came noiselessly towards me. One moment he was just a shade of darkness; the next, a pale and staring apparition in the light. I could not speak—I could not move. "Vasily," I whispered through my tears.

The next moment, I felt a thrill rather like electricity itself as his arms closed about me—for they were warm, solid, and living! For a moment I resisted in pure shock. "You're alive?" I whispered, but Vasily wasted no time on words. I found myself being kissed in a manner which banished once and for all the idea that I had strayed into a work of improving fiction. Having offered a silent word of apology to the Author of my existence for having doubted His beneficent Providence, I abandoned myself to the experience entirely. The lamps, having laboured for a moment in vain, gave up altogether, plunging us into a gloom in which every sense was swallowed up by Vasily, and the soft, desperate sounds that he was making against my lips and skin.

At length the lamps came back up with a hiss, and it was partly the glare of light, and partly the need to draw breath, that made me draw back to look up at him. I touched his cheek, needing more than his desperate grasp on my waist to reassure me that it was true—that this was not some wild dream. "You're alive," I said again, bereft of any words more eloquent. "The newspaper—I thought you were dead."

"Nijam was right," he murmured, still hungrily watching my mouth. "I ought to have arranged my death long ago. It was the only way to keep you safe." With that he leaned towards me again.

The interval, however, had seen the return of Reason to her throne—at least where *I* was concerned. We were in a public place, after all; and my father's imprint lingered pensively at my elbow. It is difficult to abandon oneself to passion with a deceased parent looking on, and beyond that I felt myself utterly at a loss to account for this behaviour. Why, the last time I saw Vasily, the wretch was vowing to marry somebody else!

"Wait," I protested, attempting to fend him off. "What do you mean by all this?"

He blinked. "What do I *mean* by it?"

"Did I give you leave to kiss me? What sort of woman do you think I *am?*"

"What—? Be reasonable! What else am I going to do? I've nothing else to recommend me—no fortune, no connections, no name—"

"—and a fat head," I said, attempting to remove myself to a safer distance as he sought to redouble his attentions. By now I had regained my wits. I thought there was some odd desperation in his bearing: and you can't tell me that he was

17

simply overwhelmed by his own feelings, when I was close enough to see his eyes, which were quite clear and calculating. All of a sudden my stomach turned. None of this was real: he was playing a part with me. *Molly Dark's Lover; Or, The Prodigal Returns.* "And why should you think you can recommend yourself to me like *this?* —No! I swear I'll bite you if you kiss me again! Answer the question, Vasily Nikolaevich, and look me in the eye when you speak to me!"

Dragging his attention away from my mouth, he sent me a wrathful look. "You said you loved me," he said, accusingly. "You minx! If you'd said it a moment sooner I would never have agreed to marry Zlata!"

"Well, I never!" I cried, when I recovered the ability to say anything at all. "You expected *me* to speak—to declare my feelings, when *you* had not? Do you think me completely lost to decency? Release me at once!"

"I shan't," he said at once, and I fear that he might have been about to recommend himself to me more strenuously still, had not the door to compartment number nine opened, almost at Vasily's shoulder.

"I *knew* I heard Vasily's voice," Mimi declared. There was an exclamation from Schmidt, who burst out into the corridor with a bang.

"Sir!" he gasped. "What on earth—!" but then, perceiving that I was presently clasped to sir's bosom, he subsided into a mortified silence. Nijam and Mimi followed him more sedately; and Nijam took off her *pince-nez* to look Vasily up and down.

"I see you took my advice," she said calmly. "Could you not have done so sooner? You have cost Miss Dark a very tempestuous morning."

18

"Tell him to let go of me!" I said, before Vasily could answer that question with a disclosure that might have been as embarrassing as it was maudlin. I was by no means sure that I wished my friends to know the full extent of my folly—that I had confessed to Vasily that I loved him!

Schmidt having turned reproachful eyes upon him, Vasily complied at once; and I followed him and the others into the compartment in great indignation. How dare Vasily kiss me in that cavalier manner—a manner with which, I reflected, no gentleman ought to kiss a lady to whom he was not absolutely married! and having done so, how could he then reproach me for not speaking sooner? I had never heard anything so foolish in my life. It is bad enough that young ladies are brought up expecting to regard ourselves as failures if we are not married by the age of twenty-five, but heaven help us if we make any attempt to bring this happy state of affairs about! Did Vasily not know that the one thing more disgraceful than an old maid, is a flirt? Wild donkeys ought not to have drawn the words from my lips; they had been forced from me under great duress, and now he had the nerve to ask why I had not said them sooner!

It was Vasily all over, in fact: for as long as I had known him he had been fencing with me, desperately trying not to let his guard down, not to be seen or known. I recognised it because in some measure, all this time, I had been doing the same. But really! if he cared for me, he ought surely to tell me!

And then there was the kiss, which made me more indignant by the minute—the kiss which he said was the only way to recommend himself to me, as though I had no sense or judgement of my own; the kiss which was as false and theatrical as it had been on that first occasion in the Schloss

Frohsdorf, when he was pretending to be the long-lost husband of Marie-Caroline. If Vasily had an ounce of real, honest regard for me, how could he treat me in such a way?

It was in this simmering mood that I crowded into the compartment with the others to hear Vasily's explanations.

"In the end it was quite easy," he said, throwing himself upon the bench-seat in an attitude of splendid self-satisfaction. I remained standing, stiff with outrage. Mimi and Nijam, who have no delicate feelings, obliged themselves instead. "All I needed was a ticket on the express train from Moscow to Ekaterinburg, a quantity of explosives, and a corpse. None of them were very hard to come by. I saw to the explosion yesterday and alighted from the express this morning just in time to catch a glimpse of Miss Nijam's trunk being hoisted aboard. I followed, naturally, and here I am. Was there much about me in the papers?"

"No," I said repressively.

"But on the platform they were selling papers with my face on! Didn't they mention the explosion? No? What about the mouse?"

"Which mouse?" Schmidt asked, his brow furrowed in confusion. I bit my lip, unwilling to enlighten him.

"Why, the Fabergé mouse I gave to Miss Dark," Vasily said plaintively, "which she told me was too costly a gift for her, and which she fished out of the waste-paper basket again the night she left, even though she swore she did not want to have it. Ha! You didn't expect me to notice *that,* did you, my dear? I planted it upon the scene of the explosion expressly to serve as a message! You ought to have read about it in the papers and known that all I did, I did for you."

"How should I have done so, when Mimi is the only one of

us who can read Russian?"

"She would have read it aloud—oh, what does it matter? All's well that ends well!" He beamed indiscriminately about the compartment. "Grand Duke Vasily is dead—that's a load off my mind! And now: Miss Dark," he added, sliding from the seat and falling to his knees before me. "Little did you know when you professed to love me, that you pronounced my death sentence. Now I approach you, a new-born man. I love you to distraction, and I have died to prove it. Say you'll be my wife?"

My mouth opened, but for a moment or two nothing came out. "I *beg* your pardon," I said at last.

"I have nothing with which to endow you," he added, seizing my hand, "except a stolen Meissonier painting, which I presume Mimi has not allowed to depart from beneath her watchful eye. Trusting that she will return it to me, however, I bestow it entirely upon you! Speak, my love—make me the happiest of men!"

With a repellently mawkish expression, he kissed my hand. More theatrics—more forced ardour! I snatched it away.

"You're mocking me! How dare you!"

With that he looked so taken aback that I was forced to believe him when he said, "My dear! Never in my life have I been more truly in earnest! Where's the difficulty? I love you, and you love me. Say the word—"

"Absolutely not!" I squeaked in fury. What! having first scolded me for not declaring myself, did he now presume that I had fallen into his lap? "What, you say you're in love with me? This is news!"

"Well, I could hardly make you an offer without a proper dowry, could I? Miss Dark, I've always known you must marry money. Honour obliged me to remain silent until I had something with which to endow you."

It was not his silence which infuriated me—it was the manner in which he now spoke. "And now you think I will be yours for the price of an oil painting? If I was that sort of woman, I would have married Warren H. Vandergriff!"

With those words, I could stand it no longer. The compartment had grown warm with the sheer number of people— Vasily and I in histrionics, and the others agog with curiosity— so that I felt I could scarcely breathe. Flinging open the door, I burst into the empty corridor. Outside, rain from a lowering sky lashed the train windows and the green, verdant forest country beyond. I paced the corridor, tossed upon my own storm of emotion. The morning's events had quite broken up my self-command, and I was torn between desperate gratitude that Vasily had lived and found his way back to us, and the overpowering temptation to wring his neck. Marry him? How could I? I did not even think I could stand to take a train journey with him!

That thought sobered me, for I realised, with a cold shock, that I was going to have to have it all out with him. I *do* dislike to make a scene! But there was nothing for it. A scene there must be, or else I could never speak to him again—and since it would take us weeks to reach Vladivostok, not speaking to Vasily in these cramped quarters would surely be impossible.

For a moment it occurred to me that I might simply get off at the next stop, fleeing back to Moscow and whatever awaited me there. But then I remembered Zlata and Missy and the ghastly, fanged Romanovs; and that decided me.

I marched back into the compartment, surprising whatever hushed conversation had begun in the aftermath of my departure.

"No," I told Vasily without preamble, "I *won't* marry you. How could I do so?"

"Very easily," he told me, the light of battle once again dancing in his eyes. "I have you now, my dear—you admitted yourself that you love me!"

"Let me speak!" I demanded—shaking with nerves, but aware that if I did not speak now I might never have another chance. "Having concealed your own feelings, you scolded me for not confessing mine sooner—and when I did, you presumed I could be bought! Well, I'm not for sale!"

Mimi laughed—at least *she* was enjoying herself. "Don't argue, Vasya! We all heard it!"

"And that isn't even the main thing," I added. "No doubt you mean to flagellate your dirty linen in public again and tell me that I can't expect anything better from someone as irreparably bad as Vasily Nikolaevich Romanov. Well, I don't believe you are sorry at all! You're only trying to make everyone else feel as sorry for yourself as you do. If you really wanted to do better, you'd stop wailing about your sins and *do* better. And if you really wanted to be unselfish, you wouldn't have sacrificed yourself to *Zlata Milanova,* of all people! You'd make amends to all the people you really did hurt, no matter what they could give you in return!"

"Hear! hear!" Mimi exclaimed. Vasily looked indignant— well, if nothing else I had quite shattered his complacency. For a moment he seemed unable to speak.

I drew a deep breath and lifted my chin. "There," I said, "now you know that I'm in earnest. I can't do it. Just as I couldn't marry a bad man for his money when it was Mr Vandergriff, I won't marry you, either—for love *or* money."

Vasily found his breath. "Do you hear this?" he exclaimed to the compartment at large.

"Yes," said Nijam, who—strange to say—had watched all this with a tight-lipped smile. "It's about time someone said it."

"Schmidt!" Vasily appealed, but Nijam's Alphonse reddened.

"I agree with Miss Dark," he said, and after that it was so silent that one might have heard a needle drop. Or is it a pin?

In time, Vasily recovered his breath. "Never in my life have I been spoken to like this!"

"And it's been ruinous to your character," I said, deciding that I might as well be hung for a sheep as a lamb.

"Every time I ask you to marry me I get the most frightful scolding! If you felt that way, why did you kiss me just now?"

I was about to protest, with burning cheeks, that he had kissed me first; but Nijam said, with incisive brevity, "Because she cares about you, naturally. Pay attention."

I could have kissed *her* for that. "Precisely," I said, tears coming to my eyes. "If I didn't care, why would I bother to say such things? But I won't marry you, Vasily. I don't trust you enough."

"No, of course you do not!" Vasily got up, managing to strike a nobly tragic attitude even within the cramped confines of our compartment, and flinging out an arm which came within an inch of knocking off Mimi's hat. "Well, I ought to have known! I have betrayed everyone who has ever loved me. Why should Miss Dark be any different? I ought to have stayed in Moscow, that loathsome place! At least there I had a name, and comfort! Now I have nothing—nothing. Well, I beg your pardon, and I shall relieve you all of my company at once!"

"Sir!" Schmidt protested, blocking his way not so much by design, in those cramped quarters, as necessity. "Where will you go?"

"To the devil, I suppose, since I am already a dead man!"

"Oh, for heaven's sake," Mimi erupted, grasping him by the sleeve. "Don't be an idiot, Vasya."

"What more could I have given?" he asked, and I was astonished to see the sheen of tears in his eyes. A moment ago he had been so sure of himself, and now he was absolutely caving in. My heart bled for him. "I've thrown away everything I once held dear! What more do you want?"

To tell the truth, I hardly knew what I wanted. I wished he would stop treating me like something to be bought, like a dainty, or manhandled into submission, like a ninny. I wished I could believe that I could trust him—that he would go on loving me even after the first flush of possession faded, and selfish desire no longer bound him to me.

I wished, desperately, for things to go back to the way they were before we went to Russia—before Vasily began dreaming of repairing his fortunes, and I found that my own life was less precious to me than his. But there was no going back to those days; and I could not yet see any way forward. My heart bled for him, yet I knew that to show any softness might ruin us both.

"What I want," I said with a catch in my breath, "is some peace and quiet." With that I fled into the corridor again, feeling wretched about the whole affair. I had spoken, and it had done no good at all, and we were no further forward.

Trust him! Well, I might not want to marry the man, but of course I trusted him to some extent. I had no choice. Vasily knew all my secrets—one by one, he had stumbled across all of them; even the secret that I loved him. Yet *that* did not worry me at all. Some part of me knew instinctively that my secrets were safe with him. Then, he claimed to have betrayed me—but what made him say such a thing? Why must he continually paint himself blacker than he was? We were not affianced, that his betrothal to Zlata should have been treachery. Nor had he given us over to the police, that night at the French Embassy ball. He had, in fact, sacrificed himself in the most idiotic way possible to get the rest of us safely out of the country. No: for as long as I had known him, Vasily had never been treacherous—merely self-centred and inconstant, and *that* was why I could not trust him. What! courting me for so long, paying me attentions, flirting and teasing, and swearing the whole time that it meant nothing at all—just because he was too great a coward to let me see the true depth of his feelings? In all that time, he had only tried to protect himself.

Yet I must acknowledge that I, too, had tried to protect myself in the same way. I let out a sigh. I did not think that my fault was as great as Vasily's, for I had been reared never to let the true depth of my likings show; and even now the intensity of my feelings terrified me. I had kissed Vasily in a manner that was perfectly abandoned, and I felt how terribly easy it might be to abandon myself yet further. Perhaps I *ought* to marry him, lest I ruin myself entirely! But no: that was the way to ruin, not merely a reputation, but a life. Vasily did not see where he had gone wrong, and if I did not withstand him now, how would he learn better?

It was true that he had abandoned Zlata, his family, and the money at once the moment he understood that I loved him; and that was not nothing. Still, my heart told me that marriage to Vasily would be a disaster if he could not learn to *do* right and not merely to bewail his wrongs; if he thought the only way to get my regard was to kiss me until I lost my wits. One day I might not feel like being kissed, or he might feel like kissing someone else, and then where should we be?

All this was running through my head when the door to compartment nine opened. Nijam emerged and said, "I engaged two compartments, of course. You're bunking with me in eight."

"Oh, thank goodness," I said, following her into the tiny chamber. The amenities on the Trans-Siberian train were a good deal less elegant than those on the Petersburg-to-Moscow train. The cramped quarters were upholstered in a faded and sensible material, and panelled with rough pine. The little potbellied stove, however, looked quite as serviceable.

"You have four weeks to sort things out with Vasily," Nijam said, not unkindly, but without preamble. "Possibly more, if there are many delays on the way to Vladivostok. Take your time deciding what to do. Mimi and I will back you up, of course, and if you decide he must go, go he must."

The assurance that my crew would take my part, whatever else happened, was tremendously comforting. All the same—I bit my lip. "Oh, Nijam! What can I do? I can't send him away—he'll do himself an injury. And I certainly can't marry him; not unless I can trust him better."

"I don't object to Vasily doing himself an injury, on principle," Nijam said. "But there's another possibility—you might give him the chance to *prove* himself trustworthy."

"How?" I asked blankly. "He'll keep dangling after me for as long as I refuse him; it's what happens after I say yes that frightens me! We can't seduce each other for the rest of our lives. How I wish I had some money! Then at least I would be assured of keeping him!"

Nijam tilted her head as though she wanted to stare at me over the top of her *pince-nez,* and only the accident of not wearing them prevented it. "Apparently Vasily's trustworthiness, or lack thereof, is not the sole problem," she murmured. I did not quite understand what she meant by this, but she went on briskly: "Trust Vasily, or don't—personally, *I* wouldn't, for the man's as weak as water. But don't blame him for *your* anxieties. That would be a very stupid thing to do. Have you finished with volume two of *Can You Forgive Her?*"

I had not. Still, Nijam is not the sort of person to whom anyone says no—except Alphonse Schmidt, which is a matter of endless marvel to me. Having acquired the book, she bustled off again, leaving me quite unable to rest. What could she mean by saying that I blamed Vasily for my own anxieties? She agreed, herself, that he could not be trusted!

It was all very well for Nijam to tell me I should let him prove himself—*she* was not being asked to entrust him with her hand and future. By now, however, I had come to see that Nijam had her own variety of insight into the human condition, and if I took her advice I should at least be putting off the evil day, in which I might be obliged to send Vasily away forever. The time, too, would give both of us a chance to reflect. Perhaps Vasily would eventually tire of dangling after me, if not as quickly as he would tire of being married to an obscure bourgeois!

In the meanwhile, it struck me that I had no objections to working with Vasily on the old footing. Although I had long presumed the Grand Duke's primary motivation to be monetary in nature, he had now twice given up a very significant fortune for my sake. Even his behaviour in Moscow, which had been so perplexing to the rest of us, could now be explained. He had indeed been chasing after imperial favour and imperial fortune; but not merely for his own profit. In fact he was doing it for me—because he thought me the sort of woman who could be bought.

That last thought made me bite my lip. I did not then understand why it made me so formlessly angry.

In time we reached our evening stop. Our fellow passengers—who appeared to be thin, tired, and mostly of the peasant class, presumably immigrants travelling east in search of new lands to farm—were able to alight from the train to stretch their legs and buy a little dinner from the vendors on the platform. I followed them more slowly, for despite my anger I had come to a decision.

I would take Nijam's advice. Now that I had been honest with Vasily, I would give him another chance to prove himself. I told myself at the time that I owed it to him; I look back now and see that I did it perhaps most of all for myself, for I was not strong enough to send away the man I had come to love.

When the others returned with their dinner—Schmidt trailing Vasily very watchfully, as though he really thought sir might fulfil his threat to go to the devil—I followed them to compartment nine with my mother's letter in my hand. I was still not quite easy at the thought of expending our precious resources upon repairing my own family's fortunes, yet mature consideration had convinced me that a little investigation might be wise. I owed it to my sisters to determine what might be owing to them; I owed it to Sir Humphrey to clear, if I could, the cloud of suspicion my mother had cast over him; and if there was any hope of finally laying my father's ghost, it was in Hong Kong that I must seek the reason for his failure. Most of all, however, I thought that we all badly needed some job of work to occupy us and smooth over the recent upheavals. The thought of travelling all the way to Vladivostok and back without some scheme to distract us was enough to give anyone the willies.

I was very much taken aback to find Vasily half out of his shirt. The explanation was evident. I had noticed that the aforesaid garment was besmirched with both grime and blood; now it appeared that a piece of shrapnel had left a gash across his shoulder, which Nijam was now inspecting through her *pince-nez*.

"This will need stitches," she announced. "Wait a moment and I'll fetch my kit."

Vasily's attention had been fixed on me. Nijam's words, however, made him quiver like a jelly. "I don't want you stitching me up! I'll have a proper doctor, or no stitches at all!"

"I've installed prosthetic transmitters in people's brains, Vasily," Nijam said inexorably. "I'm quite capable of stitching up a trifling scratch."

"Yes, but must you do it while *I'm* trying to eat?" Mimi demanded.

"My shoulder will wait," Vasily declared, easing the shirt on again. He stole another, almost furtive glance at me. "It looks as though Miss Dark has something to say to me."

"I have something to put to you all," I said tremulously. "A job, in fact. Read this."

I put the letter into Vasily's hands. He looked surprised and uncertain, but obediently read the indicated passage—aloud, so that everyone could hear.

Nijam raised her eyebrows. "Sir Humphrey Seton!" she exclaimed. "Will we be *able* to trick him a second time?"

"Why not? Mimi asked. The light of battle was kindled in her eyes. "It worked the first time."

"It's not that I want to *steal* from Sir Humphrey," I assured them all. "My father might very well have made a mistake. Only I ought to find out what happened in Hong Kong eleven years ago, when he died. His imprint has haunted me ever since, and I tried waiting for it to fade, but it never did. And ever since the Khodynka Field disaster, it's followed me *everywhere.*"

"You mean he's with us now?" Mimi inquired.

I nodded towards the window end of the compartment. "At present he's sitting in the washbasin reading a book. Imprints almost never get *stronger*—not in my experience. I don't like to ask for help, but something is wrong, and I need to know *what.*"

Mimi clapped her hands. "Let's steal a fortune!"

I bit my lip. "No! The fortune isn't the point!"

"What nonsense," Nijam said briskly. "Of course the fortune is the point. It could make all the difference in the world to your sisters, and there's no reason to believe your father would have made that sort of mistake about his own shares."

That was because she never knew my father, but it would not have been very filial to say so. Nijam went on:

"Now, let me think. Sir Humphrey still believes he has the real Noor-Jahan; he knows you are his partner's daughter, he knows that Vasily is a Grand Duke who attempted to steal the diamond, and he knows me as the Begum of Bihar. That means much of the job will be up to you, Dark, with the help of Schmidt and Mimi. If he gets a glimpse of me or Vasily, the game will be up. Tell us about your father's business with Sir Humphrey, Dark."

The speed with which her brain worked left me feeling almost dizzy.

"Are—are you sure?" I stammered, glancing at Vasily and Schmidt, who had until now remained silent. "You don't want to think it over?"

Vasily said nothing: he only looked pale and subdued. I wondered whether Nijam had been giving him the same sort of ultimatum she had given me.

"Oh, for heaven's sake! Let us have *some* entertainment," Mimi said.

Sighing, I launched upon my story. At the time of my father's death, the shipping company was a fledgling venture of just three years' duration, carrying tea from the south coast of China to Sir Humphrey's warehouse in Hong Kong—or plain Mr Seton as he was then—and thence to England, where my father received the merchandise and sent the ships back loaded with items of manufacture from English factories. Most of these were sold in India, before the ships continued to China again to collect a new load of tea; and thus the trade flowed around the world.

"And did they ever ship opium from India to China?" Nijam asked, quite point-blank.

"Dear me, no!" I said. The problem with the China trade always had been, of course, that the Chinese were quite uninterested in English manufactures, so that a river of English silver was always flowing into China for tea and silks and porcelain; but none flowed out—not until some unscrupulous merchants discovered a ready market in China for Indian opium, and then the deficit righted itself. "Papa quite abominated that trade. Seton & Dark was among the first Hong Kong trading firms never to have dealt in opium at all."

"I see!" Nijam said. "Go on."

The blow had fallen eleven years ago. It began with a letter from Hong Kong: the old baronet having fallen ill, Mr Seton would be returning to England, and my father was requested to travel to Hong Kong to supervise the China end of things while Seton settled his father's affairs. In fact, the old baronet was to live another ten years, but it was on this voyage that the present baronet had met and courted his wife, the American heiress Adelaide Vandergriff, with whose prosthete nephew the attentive reader is acquainted. Meanwhile, in Hong Kong, my father quickly ran into difficulties. The exact details escaped me; but I gathered that the business had suddenly and disastrously begun to lose money. My mother began to go about the house with a drawn face, and once Mr Seton had visited us and remonstrated with her for perhaps an hour in my father's study. After that he took passage on a fast steamer to Hong Kong; but when he arrived, my father was already dying of the plague, and the business had nearly failed altogether. Only Seton's foresight in having secured himself an American heiress with a fabulous dowry had kept the venture afloat until my father's depredations could be repaired.

After that, the Darks had been quite ruined. One by one my mother let the servants go, and only a generous gift from Mr Seton had enabled me to attend school, so that I might become a governess and contribute something to the family's upkeep. That was the story as I had always known it.

A thoughtful silence descended upon the compartment.

Outside, the long Russian evening had begun. The rain having cleared somewhat, the Siberian forest gleamed in the light of the setting sun. The landscape looked clean and new and freshly-washed. Plucking up my courage, I turned to Vasily.

"You asked," I said timidly, "what more I want from you. I want to know that you are someone I can trust, not just for great dramatic sacrifices, but for small and daily things, too. Help me, Vasily. Help me expose Sir Humphrey the way we exposed your father, and perhaps a time will come when we can discuss—everything else."

Throughout this speech he kept his eyes lowered with quite unusual meekness. Now, at last, he looked up at me. I had never seen Vasily look like this before—chastened and a little frightened. Nijam, I decided—Nijam *had* given him a talking-to.

"You will allow me to stay by your side?" he asked. "You will not send me away?"

I wanted to kiss the lines from between his worried brows. I restrained myself with a great effort. "I'm offering you another chance," I told him gently. "Let's turn over another branch."

"A *leaf*," Nijam muttered.

"I'm pretty sure it's a branch," I told her, eager to restore the conversation to something like normality. "An olive branch, in fact."

Nijam shook her head and went to fetch her needles, muttering something about me calling myself a governess. Mimi and Schmidt, rather too loudly, began to discuss the ways in which we might expose Sir Humphrey's evil deeds. I am fairly certain that Vasily sent me a look of pathetic, dog-like gratitude; but I was doing my best not to notice.

Chapter III.

In the end it was a whole two months before we arrived in Hong Kong, most of which was spent trying to reach Vladivostok. It turns out that the Trans-Siberian Railway is a rather shoddy affair: a single set of tracks laid out across an endless wilderness, bumpy and poorly constructed, with hairpin turns and vicious inclines which cause the wheels to shriek and the engine to groan with effort. Since there was only one set of tracks, at nearly every stop we were obliged to wait in order to allow a freight train loaded with wheat to pass us as it made its way towards the great cities of the west, and Europe beyond. Several times we were obliged to stop for several days in some remote village, waiting for a broken rail or washed-out bridge to be repaired.

Still, we got to Vladivostok in the end: a burgeoning European town on the edge of the Sea of Japan, where faces and languages from East and West mingled in the streets. Here—although I am not sure that it was right to do so—Mimi was permitted to do a little thievery, and the result was five second-class tickets on a very third-class steamer which pitched and yawed abominably all the way to Hong Kong.

I employed the Siberian journey in writing down an account of our adventures. I am not the author of my family. My spelling is abominable and I always did tend to go off on tangents, rather than sticking to the main point. Moreover, I could never think of anything very interesting to write *about*. Of late, however, my life had become interesting enough to provide material for any number of books, and now that my occupation as a sort of philanthropic thief was no longer a secret from my family, I very much wanted to tell them about it. Moreover, the work served to distract me from the peculiar sensations—the thoughts of Vasily—which plagued me. At times my stomach would become tight, and my heart took to leaping and swooping in ways that were not at all justified, and I felt the oddest compulsion to burst into tears. I felt both languid and expectant; sick, and euphoric. Most of all I could scarcely pass Vasily in the corridor without wishing to repeat that kiss.

In order to stave off these feelings, I set to work, and by the time we reached Vladivostok I was ready to dispatch the first version of these memoirs to Brixton—brief as they were, with some of the less respectable details omitted, and with every bump and swerve of the Trans-Siberian Railway recorded beneath the nib of my wandering pen. Perhaps, I thought, my sisters would be sufficiently entertained by my misadventures to type them up and correct the spelling.

On the steamer I did not write at all. I spent too much of the voyage being sick.

But of course you want to know what the former Grand Duke was doing during this time. At first, Vasily kept to himself, and when we did meet he was almost painfully polite. This was excruciating, but I did not like to give him encouragement of a sort I could ill afford. After about a week, when I could endure it no longer, I stopped him as we passed in the train corridor and said plaintively, "I cannot bear this constraint between us; can we not call a truce and go on being friends, as we once were?"

"We shall be whatever you like," he said, very readily, "so long as I may go on dangling after you in this deplorable fashion."

After that, things were a deal friendlier. If I wanted a cup of tea, or a door held open, Vasily was there to do it; but otherwise he neither teased nor flirted with me, and neither of us mentioned the kiss again. I could almost have gone back to thinking us mere professional acquaintances, except that I sometimes found Vasily watching me with an almost calculating look, like a general pondering his next campaign.

It was a hot, humid afternoon in August when we reached Hong Kong. My first impression of Victoria Harbour was of a broad sweep of blue-green water, great looming green mountains, and heaped upon the thin strand between peak and water a city of tall white warehouses and tenements, very graceful and pretty with red tiled roofs and arched balconies. Steamers, picturesque Chinese junks, and a profusion of smaller vessels plying the waters between the island and the nearby mainland completed the picture, which was as pretty as a postcard. I should have liked it immensely, had it not been for the weather, which was atrocious—hot and muggy, with a thick grey blanket of clouds sealing the heat close to the earth. All day the atmosphere had been almost stifling, with constant distant thunderstorms flickering on the horizon amidst curtains of rain. My white dress, having given up on English decorum somewhere around the thirtieth parallel, was quite soaked with perspiration. None of my clothing had been properly dry in days.

"You look tired," Vasily said in a low voice, as we stood on the deck watching the great colony approach.

"You aren't supposed to say that to a lady," I told him. The first seasickness of the voyage had passed off, but the journey had been a long one. "I am only weary, that's all, from the journey and the weather."

"You would feel better if I kissed you," he suggested, with a sidelong glance.

I remembered what it had been like to kiss Vasily. I remembered also what it had been like afterwards, to see the look of calculation in his eyes. "Please don't press me like that," I said. "It isn't gentlemanly."

"But I *want* to press you," he said plaintively, "in all sorts of interesting ways. No, hear me out!" he added, as I sent him a look of displeasure. "I know I did wrong—I ought to have known that you didn't want money—but I'm going to lose my wits if I can't speak to you the way I used to. Things have been so stiff between us lately."

They *had* been stiff between us, but was that my fault? "I don't like it either, Vasily, but at present I can give you nothing more than friendship, and I won't have you ask for more."

"But I don't want your friendship," he protested. "I don't *mean* to have your friendship. No man can be witty, or tender, or passionate, as a friend."

It was perhaps heartless of me to laugh, but he did sound so aggrieved! "You might try it, before you declare it to be impossible."

"I might have tried marrying Zlata!" he said indignantly. "You don't want me—you want some ghastly bourgeois with a greengrocer's shop and a temperance pledge."

"I never said I wanted you," I reminded him. Somehow, I

was now feeling more cheerful than I had in weeks. I had to admit to myself that I had missed our sparring.

At that, there came a dangerous gleam into his eyes, and he leaned a little too close. "Ah, but you and I both know that you do."

He drew back a little, just enough to see the effect of his words; and for that I said to him, "We all want a great many things that are not good for us."

"Gospodin!" he said. "You're not the first to tell me that… Come, my dear. A man like me is almost completely useless as a friend. Better try me as a husband. You won't regret it."

"If you can't be a friend, then you can't be a husband either," I told him. "They require many of the same qualities, you know."

"Reliability, I suppose." He shuddered. "Respectability. Well, I have tried my hand at a great many things; I suppose I can try my hand at this. Nijam has explained to me that I have a great deal of ground to make up after what happened in Russia, and not just with you. But tell me you'll give me something in return?"

"I won't kiss you," I said again.

"Because you're afraid?"

"Because I pine for your touch," I said in my most melodramatic voice, to make him think that the truth I uttered was a jest, "and I'm afraid of losing my reason altogether if I get it."

"Oh, *bozhe moi,* please don't say that," he said, laughing, "it doesn't suit you at all. No, I won't kiss you, but do for God's sake let me flirt with you a little, and I'll try to be as reliable and respectable as you please."

"It's a bargain," I said, and felt lighter and happier. If Vasily could accept our strictures, then surely there was hope for him.

"Must you go to Sir Humphrey tonight?" Vasily asked presently. "Wouldn't you rather face him in the morning after a decent night's sleep?"

I shook my head. In one way the endless journey had been a welcome relief: there are not many ghosts either in Siberia, or at sea, which is too fluid to hold an imprint of any sort. Hong Kong would be a different matter. A city teeming with life is always full of remembered tragedies.

"No," I said. I had just caught a glimpse of my first Hong Kong imprint. Just beneath the surface of the water, a pale and desperate face was looking up at me, its arms flailing in a fruitless attempt to swim; and I knew that somewhere in the relatively shallow waters beneath us, the bones of the dead still ached with longing to live and breathe. "Sir Humphrey has a house on the other side of the island. I will rest better there."

"Besides," Nijam put in, approaching the rail where we stood, "if Sir Humphrey chooses to verify Miss Dark's story, it will look very suspicious if she doesn't go directly to the castle from the docks."

"Let's not waste any time," Mimi agreed, following Nijam. "Look at all those balconies! I haven't had a good climb in *months.*"

"*I* haven't had a good *wash* in months," Schmidt said mournfully, "and neither has the laundry, and everything's getting mildewed in this humidity."

I sighed, for indeed I was also longing for a good scrub in a bathtub, and the luxury of bleach and iron for my clothing. Starch, too, would be nice, although I did not think that any amount of starch would hold for long in this stifling weather.

Within the hour we had docked and spoken to the customs officials; and Nijam, with her usual ruthless efficiency, obtained directions to a boarding-house on Queen's Road between the market and the post office.

As we emerged from the customs-house, I think all of us heaved a sigh of relief. "Back on British soil!" I said; and with that, Mimi took out the internal passport and other documents which she had been obliged to carry through Russia—tore them into a quantity of small pieces, and scattered them into the wind. We watched them go with quiet satisfaction, for all the way across Russia we had never been quite confident we were not being watched by the police, or by one of their numerous spies and informers.

"Not that it's British soil, any more than Finland is Russian soil," Mimi pointed out, as we followed Nijam—who had taken advantage of Mimi's little ceremony to engage a rickshaw to carry our luggage—into the narrow, steaming streets of the city. I had to admit that Mimi was correct, for despite the serried neo-Gothic arches and mock-classical pillars which adorned the noble facades of the buildings, many of the signs and awnings were written in Chinese and perhaps only one in ten of the pedestrians were European. Some of the latter were hard-looking foremen and sailors, who hurried through the streets on foot; but most were prosperous-looking merchants and their ladies, whose ostrich-feathered hats stirred languorously in the hot and fitful breeze as the sweating, sandalled rickshaw-men wheeled them through the streets. I could not help shuddering at the thought of a whole city where the predominant mode of transport employed human beings as beasts of burden!

As for the other pedestrians, I rather think that I heard

tongues chattering in Portuguese and Arabic, and once I saw a pair of Hindu policemen strolling by in turbans and gold-braid tunics. But by far the greatest proportion of the population were Chinese. I had met Chinese, of course, in London: serious, Anglicised clerks and students, with beautiful manners and neatly cut hair. Perhaps some of them had come from Hong Kong. They had certainly returned here, for here they were, hurrying to and fro with briefcases and umbrellas under their arms, and going in and out of offices. In addition to these were splendid old gentlemen in long robes and pigtails; sweating labourers pushing carts or dragging rickshaws in broad pointed hats; even busy-looking maids or brightly-clad young misses with downcast eyes, hurrying by in twos or threes in enviably thin, loose garments that seemed far better suited to the climate than my own. I was surprised to see that their feet were quite a normal size. Perhaps Nanny's lessons about China had not been perfectly accurate, at least where Hong Kong was concerned. Certainly nobody looked like an opium fiend.

"Look at these charming little stalls," I said, quite enchanted, as we passed a bustling market. "Shouldn't we try some of the food?"

"Not unless you want a stomach-ache," said Nijam; adding, in a voice that suggested she thought it rather a shame, "Besides, we haven't time to study the effect of local bacilli on unacclimated digestions. You and Mimi must set off for Pok Fu Lum at once if you want to arrive before dark. Ah! here is our boarding-house." Schmidt paid the driver, who unloaded our luggage from his cart and headed off at a surefooted lope. Nijam peered into the purse and raised an eyebrow.

"We'll need to wire Herr Haber for more money," she

observed. "I can see to that once we're settled. Now, Dark and Mimi: off with you to Seton Castle. Don't forget your story, and don't forget to keep your transmitters on."

"What, you'll send them off alone in a strange city?" Vasily said. "It's not to be thought of. I shall attend them."

"Sir!" protested Schmidt, and Nijam said, "You will do no such thing. If Sir Humphrey catches a glimpse of you our plan will be useless."

"If Sir Humphrey catches a glimpse of him," I added, "then Grand Duke Vasily will be brought back to life, and all our trouble will be for nothing!

"But I shall disguise myself with the utmost cunning!"

"You said that in Russia," Mimi reminded him, "several times, and not once did you keep your word! Don't worry about us. If we run into any trouble, I have my tiger claws."

Vasily looked mutinous. "You can't expect me to spend the entire job hiding in a third-rate boarding-house for fear of being seen!"

"Why not?" asked Schmidt. This was so unexpected that Vasily almost choked, and even Nijam opened her eyes very wide at him. Schmidt reddened and added, "I mean to say, I am sir's bodyguard, and it is my opinion as a matter of professional pride—"

"Oh! very well, very *well*," Vasily said, throwing up his hands. "By all means, Schmidt, let us not impede your brilliant career! But I don't see how I am to be of any use to you skulking about in a boarding-house. I am a Grand Duke! I was not meant for such things!'

"You're plain Mr Basil Nicks now," I said, and Mimi added, "You might try doing the laundry."

With that we hailed a passing rickshaw, and Vasily was

obliged to stifle his indignation. The driver readily agreed to take us the three and a half miles to Sir Humphrey's estate on the other side of the island. My head spun at the rapidity with which I was being transformed into another of the complacent English ladies being wheeled about the streets like princesses; but there was manifestly no other way to get about. "Please don't feel obliged to hurry," I told the driver, but he set off at the same speedy lope the others adopted.

We had come ashore in central Victoria, and in order to reach our destination must circumnavigate the western end of the island, where the roads became narrower and the floods of pedestrians and rickshaws more numerous. This must be one of the Chinese neighbourhoods—we later learned that it was called Tai Ping Shan—and it was much shabbier and more crowded than the central district. On the slopes and crags above us rose serried ranks of cramped little houses, and once we were stopped and made to take a detour by tired, sweating infantrymen in white flannels and pith helmets.

"This street is closed, miss," their luxuriantly mustachioed corporal told me in a broad Shropshire accent. "Governor's orders. No one's to go in or come out until the place has been inspected and whitewashed."

I heard loud protests from a nearby house as three or four Chinese women were herded out into the street by another of the pith helmets. They clung to each other in a piteous way, quite clearly terrified, while soldiers ran to and fro with buckets and brushes, or loaded household items into a cart.

One woman does not like to see another in distress, and I could imagine how I should feel in their place, with an occupying power forcing me into the street and pawing through my belongings. "Good heavens," I said, "what is happening? Is this a sack or a siege of some description?"

The corporal bristled in the way of offended bureaucracy everywhere. "Governor's orders, miss. It's the plague. The Chinks can't keep themselves clean and healthy, so it must be done for them."

I felt sorry for our driver, who understood English quite well and was compelled to stand and listen to this calumny. I had heard people say the same sorts of things to Nijam and was so mortified to have incited similar comments that I did not know what to say. Mimi was far quicker off the mark.

"Someone should be appointed to keep *you* clean," she retorted. "Don't you know that you're sweating like a pig?"

"Look now—! Look now—!" the outraged corporal sputtered, turning an outmoded shade of puce. I leaned forward and suggested to our driver that we might proceed, and he was all too happy to oblige.

In time we emerged from the city altogether and climbed up a muddy road into a steaming jungle. Trees arched over the narrow road, and their tangled roots sprawled into the undergrowth. Many of them were also festooned with what at first I took to be vines, but closer inspection proved to be aerial roots dangling from the branches.

As the road grew steeper, it also became more winding. Our driver slowed and began to pant, until Mimi and I could bear it no longer and relieved him of our weight. No doubt our luggage was quite enough for such a road. We went on foot for a little while, and between the moisture crawling down our throats with every breath, and the perspiration running down our temples and other unmentionable places, it was difficult to tell whether we were swimming or walking.

My plan to arrive at Seton Castle in a state of pitiable

disarray thus made excellent progress; and in due course, having wound our way between two peaks across the western tip of the island and come to the southern aspect of the mountains, we arrived at the gates of Seton Castle itself. These stood open, and our driver began the last torturous ascent up a zig-zag path to the house, which was hidden from the road by the steepness of the eminence upon which it was built, as well as by the thick vegetation which surrounded it. At last, having ascended two or three terraces, we turned the last corner and beheld the crenellated battlements of the castle, which loomed above us like a pale shade against the darkling sky.

Mimi stopped in her tracks, and I followed suit, repressing a sudden wild desire to laugh. Sir Humphrey had built himself a great white house with battlements, turrets, and huge traceried Tudor windows. There was a carriage entrance in the sunken ground level, but to ring the doorbell the ordinary visitor would be obliged to climb a great sweeping staircase to the grand entrance above. The house was every bit as splendid as Schloss Frohsdorf, the home of the last of the Bourbons, and far more ostentatious; but there was something wildly discordant about it, too. Such a house did not rightly belong on this hot, tropical island amidst the banian trees, and the shrilling insects, and the stifling breezes. Nevertheless, a castle is a castle, no matter how inappropriate. I shivered with pleasant anticipation, imagining secret passages, werewolf princes, or mad wives in the attic.

"Don't you feel exactly like Jane Eyre?" I asked Mimi, when I had paid the rickshaw driver and we stood together with our valises at the foot of the steps.

"Who is that? A thief?" Mimi asked.

I sighed. Mimi had even less poetry in her bones than Nijam. "That would have been quite a different book," I murmured, and tapped my transmitter to switch it on. "Nijam? Can you hear us?"

For a moment, all I heard was a chattering, whirring sound; and then amidst the interference, Nijam spoke. "Barely. Have you arrived?"

"Yes, and we're about to knock on the door. Let us hope that the harbour-master was right about Mr Vandergriff having taken ship for California." My prosthete ex-fiancé, who had excellent reason to suspect me of the theft of the Noor-Jahan diamond—a theft which had cost him a Roumanian castle worth every penny of two million pounds, which is a story I haven't the time to repeat here—had recently travelled to Hong Kong with his aunt, Lady Seton, in order to conclude some sort of fabulously profitable trade alliance with Sir Humphrey. Upon our arrival in Hong Kong, the harbour-master had assured us that Mr Vandergriff had taken ship for America the previous day. He had been warned not to do so, for all signs indicated that a storm was brewing, possibly even one of the great typhoons which make navigation in the China seas so hazardous in the summer months. Nevertheless, since the great business interests of Vandergriff and Son could not be thwarted by something as trifling as a little weather, Griff had weighed anchor.

"How could the harbour-master be wrong?" Nijam asked testily. Indeed, it would have been rather awkward had Griff still been on the island, for he was now aware of our transmitters, and no doubt quite capable of adjusting his own in order to listen in. "Next time try to find a higher place from which to transmit, Dark; the interference is intolerable." With that the chattering sounds subsided.

"Wait—" I objected, but it was far too late; she must have switched her transmitter off. I had only wished to remind her to inform Vasily of our safe arrival, so that he should not be unduly worried. "Just once," I murmured, "it would be nice if Nijam said *how do you do* or *all the best,* instead of popping in and out like a Jack-in-the-box!"

Mimi did not hear this complaint. She had found the doorbell—which was operated by means of a thick rope hanging to one side of the door—and was tugging on it with childlike satisfaction. Some minutes passed, and the door opened to admit a ray of electric light which made the night behind us seem suddenly very dark. Here another discordant image presented itself: for the footman who answered the door was liveried just like an English footman, and like an English footman had evidently been selected for the sake of his strikingly handsome looks, which were not English at all.

He bowed and bade us a good evening in heavily accented English. I gave my name and added, "Is Sir Humphrey at home?"

The question seemed to confuse the footman, who sent an uncertain glance behind him. "I am not sure—" he began, but then, quite suddenly, he was pushed aside by a grim and very short person with steel-grey hair and disapprovingly pursed lips. From the bunch of keys that hung from her belt, I supposed her to be the housekeeper.

She looked us up and down. "No soliciting," she snapped in broad Scottish accents, before going to shut the door in our faces. Mimi swiftly interposed her foot to prevent it from closing.

"We are not solicitors!" she objected. This was undoubtedly

true, though not quite what we had been accused of.

"We're here to see Sir Humphrey Seton," I added, as the housekeeper opened the door again. "My name is Mary Dark. You might have heard of my father, who was—"

"I know who your father was," the housekeeper said in vinegary tones. Her thin lips pursed even more tightly for a moment; her gimlet eyes pierced straight through me, and for a moment I thought that she must with one glance have divined all my purpose and history, and knew the errand upon which I had come to this house. "Well, you'd better come in," she said at last, not at all as though she meant to make us feel welcome. With a few equally acid words, she sent the footman about his business.

Mimi picked up our bags and stepped across the threshold. For a moment I lingered on the step, and something—certainly not the cold, for on this island even the breezes were hot—made the fine hairs prickle on the back of my neck. I glanced over my shoulder into the gathering dusk. My father's imprint stood, as ever, by my side—but with a start I found that there was another dim shape at the foot of the white stairs, silently watching me. This figure was clad in light European-style flannels; its hat cast its face in shadow, but all over the pale jacket and shirtfront were horrible, glistening patches of dark wetness.

For a moment the imprint and I stared at each other, and then the housekeeper asked, "Are you coming in or not, Miss?"

Her words made me jump. The door stood open before me, glowing with light; yet for the first time that evening I wondered whether I might not be better off remaining outside with the ghost. There was no time to hang back, however; no time to ask myself what secrets might lie buried within the white walls of Seton Castle. If I hesitated, this peremptory woman might shut me out. Then I would have no chance of laying my father's imprint, nor of mending the rift in my crew. I stepped over the threshold into the light; and in my last glimpse of the stairs before the door was shut and bolted by the grim little housekeeper, I saw that the imprint in the bloodied flannels had vanished.

Chapter IV.

Mimi and I were ushered into a study and told to wait. Illuminated only by the green-shaded lamp on the desk, the room was full of shadows. Great punkah fans hung from the distant ceiling, listlessly stirring in a draught I could scarcely feel. The walls were lined with leather-bound books, although when I took one out it proved to be blighted with mildew, and I could see at a glance that none of the pages had been cut. Evidently Sir Humphrey did not read; but the gleaming sweep of the great mahogany desk and the worn surface of the blotter were covered with a clutter of papers and ledgers, pens and pen-wipers and stamps, which showed how he spent his time. The desk was also fitted with two stacks of drawers; but these were locked. Mimi, of course, discovered this at once.

"Stop that, Mimi!" I hissed. "You can't walk into someone's house and rifle through his desk. Wait until he's off his guard and we're properly settled in the guestroom."

Mimi grumbled, but she moved away from the desk. It was as well that she did so. In another moment the door flew open and Sir Humphrey entered. For a moment he blinked at us in the dim green light; and then with a trembling hand he put on his spectacles and blinked at us again.

"Sir Humphrey," I said, allowing my disquiet to show in my voice—for the murdered man I had seen on the stairs had left me suddenly less sure of my old benefactor's beneficence. "It's me—Mary Dark."

"It *is* you," he exclaimed, seeming to recover himself a little. "I wonder at your boldness, Miss Dark, in showing your face in *this* house."

"Please don't be angry!" I took out the handkerchief which has done me such excellent service over the course of my career, and shook it so that the new black border about the edge was clearly visible. "I would not have come, only I am in *such* dreadful trouble, and I could not tell who else to ask for help!"

"Oh! you've come to me for help, have you? I should have you thrown out. You baggage! Didn't you and your friend the Grand Duke steal from me a diamond worth two million pounds?"

I had expected this, of course. Sir Humphrey could not know for certain that Vasily and I *were* the ones who had stolen from him the fabulous Noor-Jahan; he only knew that we had undoubtedly *attempted* to do so. The diamond certainly *had* vanished, and Sir Humphrey had then been obliged to make his wife's nephew hand over a property worth two million pounds to an Indian Begum in order to obtain what she swore was the real Noor-Jahan.

But he was not going to throw me out; not when he thought there was a chance he might be able to recover the original diamond. I moaned into my handkerchief. "Oh! I have been a wicked, wicked girl, Sir Humphrey! I know that now!"

"Then you *did* take it!" he said, almost triumphantly. That seemed to decide him, for he came over and seated himself magisterially behind his desk, clasping his fingers together over the expanse of his white waistcoat. His evening-dress was immaculate, but I did not think that he could have been having a very bright evening, for the house was as silent as the grave, the hot air was suffocatingly still, and the great traceried window looked out onto an abyss of darkness, unrelieved by the faintest light. "You had better tell me all about it," he added, with a return of his usual avuncular air.

I twisted the handkerchief between my fingers—summoning up my story and my courage together. I had come here half believing that Sir Humphrey was innocent, but the sight of the imprint had roused the liveliest suspicions. I must tread carefully.

"He's dead," I blurted, the way I had practised on the boat, to a discriminating audience of one who declared himself incapable of not attending his own eulogy. "Vasily—the Grand Duke, I mean. We were married, you know!"

Sir Humphrey raised a sceptical eyebrow. "Were you indeed?"

"Very quietly, in Vienna, just a little over two months ago." I dabbed at my eyes. "I knew that he was a Grand Duke, and me only a governess, but I loved him! Perhaps it was foolish of me!"

"Perhaps it was," Sir Humphrey agreed, very drily. I wondered whether he was in fact deriving some pleasure from my distress. It seems a hard thing to say of anyone, but there was a distinct look of satisfaction in his eyes. "I don't suppose you signed a certificate of marriage?"

I opened my eyes very wide. "Oh, I do remember signing *something*, but I'm afraid I don't have it now. I couldn't find the certificate, you see, when it was time to flee—but I swear it was all legal and correct! It must have been!"

"Other Grand Dukes have done more foolish things than marry governesses," Sir Humphrey said with a shrug. "Go on."

"We went to Moscow," I went on, "for the coronation, you understand. Vasily thought that he might mend matters with his cousin Nicky—with Tsar Nicholas, I mean. He didn't tell Nicky that he had married *me,* because that would not have helped at all. Only then, Nicky wanted him to marry a Serbian princess…"

I gave a little sob, poorly stifled with my handkerchief. Sir Humphrey's satisfaction became still more marked. "I see!"

"Oh, no! You misunderstand! Vasily didn't want to marry Princess Zlata at all!" I assured him with affected naïveté. "Only he had to pretend he would, so as to placate his cousin. But then, one morning—you know that Russia has a great many anarchists. A man came with a bomb, and…Oh, Vasily!"

I disappeared once again behind my handkerchief. After a moment I came up again and fluttered the hanky at my white lace dress. "No one would recognise me as his wife! I could not even afford to buy a black dress in which to mourn him! And then there was trouble with the police about his luggage. I had to run away from them, or else they might have put me into one of those horrible Russian gaols one hears about."

"So you came East?"

"You were the only person I knew who might help," I whispered. "And they were watching the European trains…"

"Naturally." Sir Humphrey waved a dismissive hand. "What is wrong with you women? Always making fools of yourselves over men! Your Grand Duke would have married the princess, of course."

I gasped with indignation. "Never!"

"He was a rogue," Sir Humphrey insisted. "A spy. A thief! The sort of man who will pretend to marry a foolish girl as a pretext for debauching her."

He had not offered me a chair, making me stand before him like a prisoner at the bar. Now, drawing myself up to my full—considerable—height, I fixed him with a glare. "Sir Humphrey! How can you expect me to listen to such things? The Grand Duke might have been a very bad man *once*, but now—" Mimi aimed a stealthy kick at my ankle, and I caught myself on the very brink of a mistake. *Now*, Vasily was supposed to be dead.

No, I thought in the echoing silence, as I sought the safety of my handkerchief—no, I didn't think that Vasily *was* the sort of person to marry a woman under false pretences, with the intention of abandoning her at his first convenience.

But I did not know whether he was able to stand by her through broad and narrow; or whether in times of trouble and temptation, he was better accustomed to running away than to standing his ground.

"Now he is dead," Sir Humphrey said, with mock kindness. "We may congratulate ourselves that he was exploded before he was able to put his villainy beyond all doubt, by deserting you on the streets of Moscow. What? Don't pretend that you didn't know the sort of man he was. You helped him to steal the Noor-Jahan, didn't you?"

It was useful, in a way, that he clearly thought me an innocent baby deceived by a plausible villain. Raising my face from my hanky, I fixed him with piteous eyes. "He said that it was stolen property in the first place."

That made Sir Humphrey turn quite red. "What nonsense! You can't expect an idler like Grand Duke Vasily to know anything about the just spoils of war. What did he do with my diamond?"

I shrank in on myself. "I don't know," I whispered. "I never saw it again after he died. It wasn't in any of his trunks."

"And of course you looked for it."

I did not much care for the jeering tone of his voice. "I knew I must flee to you, and I thought that if I brought it back—"

"But you didn't."

"No. I couldn't find it. I think—I think he must have sold it."

"In secret," Sir Humphrey agreed, "and without giving you any legal claim upon his property." He joined his fingertips together in that magisterial way of his. "In fact, you have been quite thoroughly taken in. Having assisted the blackguard in stealing the Noor-Jahan, you have been left without the smallest share of the proceeds. You were tricked into a marriage of dubious legality, which has left you destitute and barely respectable, and now you have come begging to me for help. Is that correct?"

"Oh, Sir Humphrey, *please* help me—for my father's sake, if not my own." I clasped my hands. A hard look came across his face at the mention of my father, but he mastered himself and forced a compassionating look.

"Well," he said, "at least I am none the worse off for your meddling, my dear, for my wife's nephew has replaced the diamond with another equally good, at no cost to myself! I suppose that after all—"

What he supposed I shall never know, for he broke off as a sudden commotion of running feet and wailing voices drew near. The next moment, the door to the study burst open and Lady Seton herself entered.

This is to put it altogether too mildly. I had met Lady Seton before, one evening at the British Museum, at which date she had struck me as a kind, handsome, and naïvely self-absorbed American woman in a fabulous Worth gown. Tonight it took me a moment to recognise her, for she was clad in a trailing white *négligée;* her hair tumbled down her back in wild, uncombed masses; and her face was distorted in terror. No sooner did she appear than I was seized by overwhelming agony, which shot through me with sharp pains from neck and armpit. At once there followed her into the room oh! such a crowd of imprints—poor Chinese men, women, and children. Their hands and faces were blackened, as though dipped in ink; blood dribbled from their mouths and some of them had hot red swellings upon their necks. I had never before laid eyes upon a plague victim, but I knew at once that this must be the dreaded Black Death!

Lady Seton burst into the room, I say, attended by this crowd; and upon seeing me she recoiled as though I had struck her. "Oh!" she screamed, pointing wildly at me, "there is another one! Oh, Sir Humphrey, what have you done now?"

In the confusion of the moment I heard, rather than saw, Sir Humphrey leap from his seat behind the desk. "Adelaide! Collect yourself!" he bellowed, and I knew that he must be rushing forward to seize his frantic wife. Only one thing at that moment mattered to me. I staggered forward, hampered by the ghastly pangs of the dread disease which the imprints broadcast directly to my nerves, and seized Lady Seton by the shoulders.

"Lady Seton," I begged her—and I must have appeared half-mad myself, for the air was too thick to breathe and I was gasping dizzily for breath— "Lady Seton, for heaven's sake tell me—*who are all these people?*"

For a frantic moment she looked upon me with wildly rolling eyes; then the handsome footman, and a very tall woman in the uniform of a nurse, descended upon her and snatched her from my grasp. The imprints flocked closer about me. I lost sight of Lady Seton and her minders, and even of Mimi amidst the crowd of the dead. Utterly overwhelmed by their despair and agony, I succumbed with relief to unconsciousness.

Chapter V.

I came to myself a few moments later under the impetus of a glass of icy liquid, which Mimi thoughtfully emptied down the front of my dress. Sir Humphrey was regarding me sardonically from the great mahogany desk; the Grim Housekeeper stood nearby with a sweating jug, and to my great relief there was no sign of any imprint but my father's. The utter silence of the house, save for the distant rumble of thunder, had returned. Of Lady Seton there was no sign either to be heard or seen; so that one might almost suspect she had been a dream.

With the return of consciousness came an awareness of my position—helpless on the Persian carpet of a man I might soon be engaged in defrauding. I pulled myself quickly to a sitting position. How grateful I was that Mimi had come with me!

"I do apologise for Lady Seton's indisposition," Sir Humphrey said, which was perhaps the first time I had heard him apologise for anything. "You must have had a great shock! Why don't you take Miss Dark to one of the guest rooms, Mrs Lister, and we can finish our conversation in the morning."

Thus, with an avuncular smile, he indicated that the interview was finished. So dismissed, Mimi and I followed the

Grim Housekeeper into the hall and up the great stairs to a bedroom in the upper storey. With the windows open, the room might be light and airy, with a high ceiling to allow the warmth to rise away from the inhabitants. Tonight, the windows were shut tight, so that I felt like a beetle trapped in a jar. The white spaciousness of the room was weighed down by dark mahogany cornices, bottle-green carpet, and heavy mahogany or perhaps walnut furniture. The luxury of this house, I thought, was not the baroque froth and ornament of the Schloss Frohsdorf: it was a peculiarly stodgy, English sort of grandeur, heavy and austere, like a bad Yorkshire pudding.

Mimi went at once to the French doors opening onto the loggia or balcony, only to discover that they had been locked.

"Don't meddle with anything that's locked," Mrs Lister said, in tones that brooked no argument. "It isn't safe."

She withdrew, and thus did not see the saucy tongue which Mimi stuck out as she departed. A hairpin and a few moments of tinkering and scratching did the trick: Mimi threw open the French doors and we looked out into the loggia, which was arcaded with mediaeval pointed arches and lined with some very pretty inlaid tilework. A distant flicker of lightning illuminated the delicate wrought-iron spiral staircases that linked the loggia not only with the ground floor, but also with the roof above; and Mimi gave a sound of satisfaction. "That will let us onto the roof to transmit more easily."

"Or onto the ground, to run away," I said. The knowledge that I could quite easily leave the house, if I wished, was distinctly a comforting one. "Come away from the door before they catch us snooping."

The imprints I had seen must belong to Lady Seton, for they had vanished together with herself. I could not forget them, however, any more than I could forget the bloodied man upon the stairs. Imprints did not cluster about innocent people: was I wrong about Sir Humphrey, after all?

Or perhaps it was all some silly mistake, and I might find myself ruining an innocent man!

"I wish we had not come," I murmured, as Mimi tinkered with the locks on the windows, throwing open the casement to allow a little movement in the air. I wished I could unbutton my frock, for the clothing which would have been light and airy in an English summer felt in this climate like so many damp and heavy blankets. "We would have been better off searching the company records in Victoria—*oh!*"

There was a standing mirror in one corner of the room, and as I glanced into it I thought I saw a flicker of movement in the room behind me. With my heart in my mouth, I whirled about to see what stood there, but there was nothing. Mimi observed me with a wry smile.

"Another ghost?"

"I don't think so," I confessed. "It's Lady Seton who's seeing most of the ghosts; she came in with a whole train of them."

"I know. You shouted out *Who are all these people?* and Sir Humphrey made a face like *this*," Mimi offered, narrowing her eyes with a very calculating expression. "Don't you think he was strangely calm for a man with such things going on in his house?"

I could not help a shudder as I switched on my transmitter.

"Nijam? I asked. "Can you hear me?"

"I can," Vasily said at once. The higher vantage-point of the second story allowed his voice to reach us somewhat more clearly. "Miss Nijam!" I heard him call, and a moment later with additional crackling and some heat, she asked, "Dark,

61

did you take my book?"

She had been working through the second volume of *Can You Forgive Her?* slowly for some weeks without finishing, and so I had taken the liberty of purloining it from her cabin before disembarking. If I was going to expose myself to the trouble and danger of Castle Seton, I wanted to do it in the company of the disastrous Lady Glencora.

"I wasn't aware that it *was* your book," said I, taken aback. "Besides, I thought you had lost interest. You're always telling me how you consider novels to be inferior. Why don't you amuse yourself with *Metals in the Service of Man?*"

For a moment Nijam was silent. "We'll discuss this later," she said at last, in an ominous tone. "What news?"

"Well," I said, "for one thing, this isn't a castle; it's a mausoleum."

In a few words I informed them of the evening's events. The murdered man on the stairs; Lady Seton roaming the house in distraction; the crowd of Chinese who followed her about—and Sir Humphrey sitting in the midst of all this, Mimi added, perfectly cool and collected.

"As though the canary wouldn't melt in his mouth," I said, seized by another fit of suspicion.

"It's butter," Nijam said, upon hearing this last observation. "The canary is what the cat got—oh, why do I bother? It sounds as though Sir Humphrey had something to do with the plague outbreak, and Lady Seton knows it."

"I must find an excuse to speak to her in private," I agreed with a sigh. We had agreed to search both Sir Humphrey's house, and his offices in town, for company records and any word of my father's doings in this island. "But that will mean staying at the castle a day or two longer."

"Of course you must stay, now that you are well ensconced. Vasily can run the job from here in Victoria."

"I beg your pardon!" I said. "Why Vasily? Why not you?"

Vasily murmured something about how flattered he felt. I flushed.

"I know I ran the job in Moscow," Nijam said, "but things have changed, and there's no point in my sitting at home all day listening for one of you to run into trouble. Don't you know that Vasily's face is in the papers here, too? Even our landlady noticed the resemblance."

I did not know it—it had never occurred to me that Vasily's death might reverberate in newspapers around the globe.

"If he shows himself in public everything will be over," she added. "We shall simply have to change rôles. Until things calm down a little, I shall assist Schmidt, and Vasily must stay at home and direct matters from there."

"Good Lord, you're serious," Vasily said, voicing my own thoughts. "Miss Nijam, I beg you will reconsider! There could hardly be a worse man for the job!"

"And whose fault is that?" Mimi wanted to know.

Naturally Vasily was averse to the idea: he never had been the sort to sit quietly at home, doing what was needful, while others took the spotlight and the world's attention. I did not like to be harsh, but I knew that having begun down this road with Vasily, I must go on.

"Nijam is right," I said stoutly. "If you want to be a man we can trust, then you must *be* the man we can trust. I told you that I don't need grand sacrifices; I only want you to do what is needful. And don't tell me I don't trust you sufficiently for the job," I added, as he made a sound of protest. "I'm not in the least worried about you double-crossing us. Apart from anything else, Nijam will have you torn apart by wild horses if you do."

"I would never do something so uncivilised," she objected.

"Nijam will inject you with the plague," I amended.

"What I wouldn't give for a look at that bacillus," she murmured wistfully. "It was discovered right here in Hong Kong, you know; by a Japanese physician! If there wasn't the job… Well, Vasily?"

"I'm a Grand Duke," Vasily muttered. "You should address me as *your grace.*" This was evidently not a serious request, and none of us treated it as such.

"It's settled, then," Nijam said. "Schmidt and I will pay a visit to the Seton & Associates offices here in Victoria. Mimi will interrogate the Seton servants, and Dark, you will see what you can learn from the Setons themselves."

"And me?" Vasily asked mournfully. "What is there for me to do, besides sit at home and listen to transmitters?"

Schmidt announced his presence with a deprecating cough. "There's a button missing from one of sir's shirts," he said. "You might like to try sewing it back on. And perhaps polishing your shoes. I would see to them myself, but I shall be out with Miss Nijam, visiting—"

"Visiting the offices of Seton & Associates," Vasily said gloomily. "I know! Oh, to think that I should have sunk so low as to polish my own shoes!"

"It's the best thing that could possibly happen to you," said Mimi. With that everything was settled; she and I bade the others good-night and switched off our transmitters.

Chapter VI.

Sometime in the night a dream came to me. I hurried through the endless loggias of the house, too frightened to run, but desperate to evade a horrible train of ghostly attendants. Rain lashed at the shutters and puddled on the patterned tiles. The air was not air—it was some noxious gas that constricted my lungs and made every movement slow and laborious; it was a hand closing about me, about the house, crushing and choking. I knew instinctively what the matter was. The house and I alike were strangers here: the island wanted us gone.

My father's imprint walked ahead of me, never turning his head to look back; and I followed, desperate to warn him of some impending danger. My breath was loud in my own ears, panting and shallow; yet no matter how fast I went, he was always ahead, always walking in a slow and measured stride. From the upper storey, I followed him down the spiral stairs and into the lower loggia. In the storm-racked garden, the banian trees tossed their heads beneath the white flicker of lightning, their dangling roots rippling eerily in the wind. Nevertheless, on my father went, raising his lantern over his head to shed light upon the way. A flight of steps at the rear of the house led in turn to a muddy path that plunged down the slope and through a dark tunnel of trees. At the end of that path, far away, a door opened and light flowed out through a pointed arch, illuminating the man who stood within, a black outline against the light. My father stepped into the downpour and went towards him. I seemed incapable of following. I stood on the edge of the verandah with a spray of raindrops on my face, trying and failing to call out. My heart was in my throat, choking me.

Then a door quite close to me slammed, and someone took my shoulder in a pincerlike grasp. "Miss Dark!" said a harsh voice. "Miss Dark, what are you doing here? Didn't I tell you not to wander the house after dark?"

With a cry I awoke to find myself standing precisely where I had dreamed myself to be—at the verandah's brink, my face wet with the rain that wept from the skies. At my elbow, Mrs Lister scowled up at me. Wrapped up in a grey dressing-grown of what appeared to be repulsively hot and itchy wool, she flashed her lamp directly into my eyes. I recoiled and would have fallen down the steps had she not caught hold of my arm.

Lightning flickered overhead, and in that glaring light I saw that a path did indeed lead away from the house just here, vanishing into the tangled undergrowth! But then—was my dream indeed a common nightmare, or was it a matter of far greater significance?

"Well?" Mrs Lister demanded, when I failed to speak. "Answer me! Why did you come here?"

I cast a despairing glance about me. "How should I know? I was asleep!"

"Then you ought to be in bed," she said.

At that moment someone screamed—and such a scream! Even amidst the muttering of the thunder and the rushing of wind and rain, it was quite loud and clear—somewhere near at hand within the house. I leapt with fright. "Is that Lady Seton?" I blurted out.

Mrs Lister responded only with a tightening of her thin lips, and a narrowing of her beady eyes. "That's none of your business," she said. "Come along." And she pushed me towards the spiral stairs.

"But didn't you hear that scream?" I demanded, hesitating with my foot upon the first step.

"Lady Seton is like you," said Mrs Lister, "she sometimes has trouble sleeping. You must have disturbed her just now when you cried out."

Muddled though I was with sleep, I knew it behoved me to use caution. I must show exactly as much curiosity as might be expected from a person in my situation; but I must not press so hard, as to make my true intentions clear.

I followed the housekeeper meekly back to bed, therefore, and crept beneath the sheet wondering what she might mean by her words. I did not see how Lady Seton was like me at all, except in being able to see certain of her own imprints. She had gone quite mad, and had done it very correctly, in white lace; but I was only sleepwalking.

In fact this was a sign of things to come, but that I only learned the following morning.

* * *

I was awoken in the morning when Mimi entered with a cup of tea. This in itself was not remarkable—I had played the fine lady before, and one of the little benefits of such a position is to be awoken by one's maid with cups of tea in the morning.

Mimi, however, had gone beyond the call of duty.

"The door was locked," she said, shutting it behind her. "I had to use my lock-picks."

"Just to bring me tea? Mimi, you're by far my favourite lady's maid. Nijam never put herself to so much trouble." I sat up with a yawn and, pushing the hair from my eyes, saw that Mimi had entered by the internal door to the hallway. "What about the loggia doors?"

"Also locked," she replied, rattling the handle. "Someone was anxious to keep you in your room all night."

"It must have been that housekeeper," I said. The fears that had plagued me last night in the dark felt very far from reality, now the morning had come. "The Blister caught me sleepwalking last night and gave me a scolding for it. I think it's for fear I should stumble upon Lady Seton again." I took a meditative sip of tea. "You'd better go, Mimi, before someone finds you where you shouldn't be—and be sure to lock the door behind you."

"What if the Blister doesn't let you out?"

"Then you had better come to get me, and we'll visit Lady Seton together. In the meantime, don't forget your task is to question the servants. —No! Leave the tea; I want it."

Mimi departed, and I continued the acquaintance of my tea-cup, which contained a very hearty oolong. The morning wore on without much change in the weather, which was if anything more sultry and thunderous than yesterday. Having managed to dress myself unaided, although even my finest cambric shirt felt hot and prickly, I went to sit in the cane armchair. In the heat and humidity, and after my interrupted sleep, I felt tired to death. To keep my fatigue at bay I took out Vasily's sketchbook—which he still had no idea was in my possession, and I certainly did not mean to enlighten him now—and spent a wistful hour in perusing its contents. Vasily had drawn me in a host of different attitudes—asleep on a train with a very serious face; stitching a button onto a cuff with my mouth all pursed up; laughing over some joke I could no longer remember. Many of the sketches, however, had caught me with an impish smile. If Vasily's sketches were anything to go by, I must be ripe for any mischief. I gazed at them with a feeling of guilty comfort. Here I was, insinuating myself into the house of a man who had always been my benefactor, in the suspicion that he had embezzled a great deal of money—when after all, my father and I had already nearly ruined him twice. And there on the other hand was Vasily, who had seen all my faults and *liked* me for them. It struck me that he must really be fond of me, and I did not quite know what to do about it. He seemed determined to marry me, and I felt increasingly fearful that he would get his way, even against my own better judgement. I closed the sketchbook with a snap.

At last a knock came at the door. At my invitation, it was unlocked and Sir Humphrey entered, followed by a doctor. Leaping from my armchair, I faced them with what I thought was the appropriate amount of outrage. "Sir Humphrey, what do you mean by having my door locked, so that not even my maid could assist me?"

"Good morning, my dear," he said, scrutinising me through his spectacles. "I do apologise, but it's safer to keep your door locked if you are likely to be sleepwalking at night."

"But it isn't night," I pointed out. "The sun has been up for hours, and I've had nothing to eat!"

"No doubt that's the servants' fault, for I can't imagine Mrs Lister meant to leave you immured like this. I'm afraid the native character is a bad one, and hopelessly addicted to opium! This gentleman, my dear, is Dr Sewell. After your fainting-fit last night, I thought he had better come to take a look at you before he visits Lady Seton."

I was not sure I liked the idea of having Lady Seton's doctor take a look at me, but Sir Humphrey did not wait for my assent, and neither did the doctor, who came forward and shook my hand with an obsequious bow. "I heard we had an upset last night," said he. "Did something happen in the study with Lady Seton?"

"She startled me, that was all," I said. I did not like to explain my fainting-fits to a doctor I did not know and had not asked to consult. "As for the fainting, I'm not used to this tropical heat, and I had already walked half the way from Victoria Harbour."

The doctor made a grunt of assent, not at all as though he had heard a word of my explanation. "And what precisely did you mean, Miss Dark, by asking Lady Seton *Who are all these people?*"

I do not think I can have perfectly concealed my surprise. Not only had Sir Humphrey brought in a doctor to look at me—but he had also discussed the episode with him in my absence! Well: Sir Humphrey had always been a little disposed to interest himself in things that were not strictly his business, and had he been otherwise my mother and sisters might have done without more often than they did.

Stifling my annoyance, I said, "I don't remember saying any such thing. Although I do recall being rather horrified to see Lady Seton being manhandled by a pair of servants."

At this, Sir Humphrey reddened. To the doctor he said, "What do you think, Sewell? Mrs Lister found the young lady sleepwalking in the loggia last night, and she has recently been disappointed in love, you understand. Is it possible that Lady Seton's hysteria could be communicable?"

"But I don't have hysteria!" I cried, startled entirely out of countenance at this suggestion that I might share Lady Seton's madness. The doctor peered at me through his spectacles again, with a judicious air that made me inclined to put him down as one enamoured of his own authority.

"She does seem rather agitated, Sir Humphrey."

"I've never felt better in my life," I protested. "Really, doctor, there's nothing wrong with me that a spot of breakfast couldn't fix."

"Very likely, my dear Miss Dark—but you forget that so long as you are under his roof, Sir Humphrey has a duty of care towards you. Here, allow me to take your pulse."

I permitted him to do so, and then in obedience to his wishes stretched out my arms, wriggled my fingers, and repeated *She Sells Sea-Shells*—to what purpose, I could not and cannot perceive.

"And where is your home, my dear?" he asked.

"Brixton," I said. I was quite disinclined to tell this officious man anything, but I supposed Sir Humphrey would answer for me if I refused.

"And have you ever been married?"

Just in time, I recalled that I was here under false colours. "Yes," I said, "very briefly, but now he is—dead." I did not like to say more, because a young woman under suspicion of hysteria does not like to tell a mad-doctor that she has been married to a Russian Grand Duke.

"And have you ever had any lovers?"

"Indeed not! I am a respectable woman!"

71

"Naturally; but as your doctor I must ask such questions, as they may shed light upon your case. You received a great shock, then, when your husband died? How long ago was it?"

"Two months," I said, seeking out my handkerchief again. With each new question, my heart was sinking. All his questions tended to suggest that there was something wrong with me—and none of them had to do with my physical health.

"The blow is very fresh, then; very fresh," the doctor said with perfunctory sympathy. "Now, do you ever see faces about you—on the walls, for instance—which you alone can see?"

"I cannot say that I do," I said, which was strictly true. I was hardly in a position to admit to the fact that, for instance, my father's imprint was even now writing a letter at the small desk in the corner of the room. Even the best of friends would be inclined to question your sanity under such circumstances.

Perhaps looking in that direction was a mistake, for the doctor's eyes narrowed. "Or voices—do voices ever speak to you?"

"One is asking impertinent questions even now," I said tartly. The doctor's laughter was as perfunctory as his sympathy had been. I do not think he relished the cut.

"Perhaps that's what she meant by asking Lady Seton about *all these people*," Sir Humphrey told the doctor, before I could object. Even if he had *not* taken my father's shares and lied about them, he was terribly officious! "It isn't the first such episode Miss Dark has experienced, you know. There was one in March, at the British Museum."

The doctor tutted and shook his head. "You've had a very great bereavement," he told me, "and it's my opinion that you need absolute rest and quiet, or I will not be answerable for the consequences. I shall give you something to help you sleep, and you must not trouble your mind about anything at all for a little while."

I disliked all this thoroughly: it sounded rather like I was being declared insane. "Something to help me sleep? What, precisely, do you mean?"

"Something you had best not trouble your mind about. Sir Humphrey, I am sure you are willing to provide what is necessary?"

"Of course. You are to put your mind at ease, Miss Dark, and allow me to make all arrangements for you," he said, patting my hand in a fatherly manner.

"You think, then, that my condition is serious?" I asked, for I began to fear that they would not even inform me of my own diagnosis. "I assure you that I feel perfectly well!"

"Well, we do not want to precipitate a brain-fever, do we?" replied Dr Sewell, and I sighed, perceiving that this was all the sense I was to have from him.

"Then may I go downstairs and have breakfast?"

"Of course you may," Sir Humphrey said; but when I had removed myself from the room, I lingered a moment in the hallway to listen at the door.

"What do you think?" Sir Humphrey asked.

"Very bad," the doctor said, with a soft tutting noise. "The worst sign is the insistence that she is quite well."

"Lady Seton made the same remonstrances, if you recall," Sir Humphrey said with a sigh, "and you say that *she* is quite hopeless. Well, let's not waste any time. Come downstairs and help me draw up the guardianship papers."

With that I fled.

The reader may well believe that, as keen as my appetite had been, this distressing interview had quite taken it away.

The breakfast-room was well-stocked with kippered herrings, steak-and-kidney pudding, and kedgeree, but these appetising aromas only turned my stomach. Apart from the food, the room was quite empty: my host had evidently breakfasted already, and I had the liveliest doubts as to whether Lady Seton was at liberty at all.

Given the luxury of solitude, I paced the room a prey to troubling thoughts. Guardianship papers! This went beyond mere officiousness—Sir Humphrey meant to have me declared incapable at once! But *why?*

I remembered my nightmare, and the doubts that had beset me in the dark, amidst the imprints. I sat down, pressing a hand against my beating heart, and for a moment thought I might faint from the relentless heat. Despite the morning's fitful rain the gracefully traceried window stood open, providing a glimpse of the sea beyond the rugged coastline of the island and allowing free passage to the sluggish breeze, which lumbered wetly about the room and crawled down my throat like a sort of gaseous millipede. I took one or two gasping breaths and switched on my transmitter.

"Is anyone there?" I ventured, praying that no one would notice the tremble in my voice. Vasily, however, heard it at once.

"You sound frightened, little mouse. Say the word, and I'll come hiss at the cat for you."

It was the first time he had called me that in a while, and the old endearment steadied me. I managed a laugh. "You'll do no such thing. Only, I seem to have wandered into a Wilkie Collins novel. Isn't that ridiculous? Sir Humphrey has just brought in a doctor to see me, and he says I am a hopeless case, and now they are downstairs drawing up the papers to have me declared legally incapable!"

Mimi's voice cut in, clearer than Vasily's. "Is Sir Humphrey not content with *one* madwoman in the house? The servants say that Lady Seton has no trolls in the valley, and has to be kept locked up. What does he want with another one?"

"But he hasn't *got* another one," I protested. "I'm not mad!"

"Kind of you to clear that up," Nijam said drily. "Wait a moment and I'll switch on this antenna—there! What's this about you being mad?"

Her voice had suddenly become beautifully crisp and clear—no doubt she had spent half the night hard at work on some amplifying device for the transmitters.

"I told you last night that Lady Seton is overwhelmed by imprints," I said. "But why should Sir Humphrey want *me* to be mad, too? He had quite clearly primed the doctor with tales of my fainting and sleepwalking and goodness knows what else, and now I am thought to be mad, only because I say I am not!"

"It's the money," Vasily said at once. "If you are mad, you cannot inherit your father's money. Sir Humphrey keeps control of it."

A silence followed, crackling only faintly with radio-static. "We don't know that for *certain*," I protested weakly. "What if we ruined him, and it turned out that he was innocent?" Even as I said the words, I heard how they must sound to the others. Why else should Sir Humphrey say he had no time to waste in securing my guardianship? And then there was the murdered man I had seen upon the stairs! and the plague dead who tormented Lady Seton!

Nijam gave a sigh. "Dark, we have reason to suspect the man of having falsified your father's share holdings and

75

contributed to multiple plague casualties; you must admit that it's highly suspicious."

Of course it was horribly suspicious. Why did I feel like the most ghastly ingrate, merely for entertaining the thought?

"I know," I said weakly. "Promise me we won't do anything without evidence."

"We don't mean to," Nijam said coolly. "Pay attention, Dark. That is why we are conducting this investigation at all. Evidence we shall have, in just a few days."

A few days! Meanwhile, what would happen to *me?* With a shudder I remembered the woman I had seen in the strait-jacket in the lunatic asylum at Hanwell. For the first time I wondered whether she had really been mad!

"I can't stay in this house much longer," I whispered. "They'll lock me up!"

"Don't worry, Miss Dark," said Alphonse Schmidt. "We stole the Noor-Jahan from the British Museum. We can fetch you out of any asylum in the world."

"There's no reason on earth to think it'll come to that," Nijam said testily. She never did manage to be as comforting as Schmidt. "There are legal formalities to be observed, and Sir Humphrey will be very cautious as to how he goes about that—he won't want to draw too much scrutiny, especially since you aren't really mad. No; I think he's more likely to keep you at Seton Castle, which, in the circumstances, is ideal. Now, if you'll excuse me, the antenna's working nicely, and Schmidt and I have that evidence to gather."

"Wait," I protested, but Vasily said:

"It's too late; she's off. You must simply assure yourself that it will take a great deal more than a lunatic asylum to dissuade me from marrying you."

Since I had always expected to end up in a lunatic asylum sooner or later, this was rather comforting—although I would rely upon Vasily's word only if I actually *did* end up in an asylum, and no sooner.

"Have you learned anything else from the servants, Mimi?" Vasily added.

"Most of them don't speak English very well," Mimi said, sighing. "Only the butler, the housekeeper, the lady's maid, and the valet are English; and they look down on the rest and think me hardly any better than the Chinese."

"But you must have learned *something*," I prompted.

"Oh, yes," she said. "I tried seducing the butler." I was so startled that, having taken up a serving-spoon to prod listlessly at the kedgeree, I nearly flung a spoonful of it across the room.

"He said," Mimi added, oblivious to my consternation, "that Lady Seton is locked into a room on the ground floor. She hasn't been herself since she and Sir Humphrey arrived in Hong Kong a month or two ago; she's been waking in the night to scream. Even some of the servants say she's haunted."

"Meet me in the loggia after breakfast; we'll pay her a visit this morning," I said. With these words I made a clatter with the lid of the herring-pan, and that, perhaps, is why I did not hear the door open behind me. "The servants are right about one thing: she is certainly being haunted. This house is thick with ghosts, and not merely—"

I do not know what warned me that I was no longer alone. Perhaps it was the feeling of eyes fixed upon me. Perhaps it was the merest breath of air as the moist currents within the room ran towards the open door. With a gasp I turned and met Mrs Lister's grim stare.

"There's no such thing as ghosts," she said with withering

Scottish contempt, "there's only diseased minds and reprobate hearts. Have you not finished your breakfast?"

"Not yet," I stammered, hardly knowing what else to say. The Blister fixed me with a grim smile and departed, leaving me to sink shuddering into my seat at the breakfast-table. If Sir Humphrey wished to have me declared mad, I could scarcely present him with a better opportunity than to be caught discoursing to thin air on the prevalence of ghosts in his house.

My appetite, which had returned somewhat during the conversation with my crew, now took flight entirely.

Chapter VII.

Seton Castle was roughly rectangular in shape, with a two-level loggia surrounding it on all sides save the front. Three little octagonal towers had been added to a front corner and both the long sides, no doubt with a view towards repelling attack from some quarter or another—which I found a rather odd attitude towards an island as evidently peaceable and industrious as that of Hong Kong. The black clouds, and the atmosphere of dense and suffocating heat, threatened *something,* to be sure—but what, I was not yet quite sure.

I sought to rally my spirits with the half-guilty reflection that in any given predicament, the danger which threatens is always at least partly *me!* Had I not stolen one fortune from the melusines of Schloss Frohsdorf, and another from the skeleton-infested British Museum, out from under the nose of the celebrated prosthete detective Vandergriff himself? Had not my friends stood by my side through the ballrooms and gaol-cells of Imperial Russia, and would they not stand by me still, no matter what Sir Humphrey might take it into his head to do?

Having forced down a little breakfast, therefore, I ventured outside to circumnavigate the lower loggia, or peristyle, or whatever such an arcaded walkway is called when it is upon the ground. At the very back of the castle, a pointed arch led to the same steep stairway by which my father's imprint had departed the castle upon the previous evening. From the foot of the stairs, the path descended the terraced hill upon which the castle had been built, vanishing within a snarled tangle of banian trees. If there was indeed a door at the end of that path, it was hidden from the house. Turning away from the stairs, and from the magnificent prospect they commanded, I continued in my peregrinations to the northwestern aspect of the castle, where I found a service entry.

The Chinese servants bustled in and out of the kitchen on sundry errands, but there was a still point in this flurry of activity: a beggar, who sat cross-legged by the door gnawing upon a crust of bread. His clothing, and the stained knapsack by his side, looked as though they had once belonged to a labourer or sailor. At first these ragged accoutrements, together with a pair of bare feet and one of those quaint, cone-shaped Chinese hats, were all I could see of the man. When he looked up, however, I was surprised to see that beneath the tangled black mass of beard and hair was a European. Such an indigent would have been a common sight in London, of course, but in Hong Kong I had not yet seen any white man lower down the social scale than the upper servants in Sir Humphrey's house.

This one looked very wild and beggarly, and when he smiled at me I saw that his teeth, while strong and even, were repulsively yellow. Not liking either the smile, or the half-crazed look in the man's eyes, I hesitated for a moment, wondering whether I should switch on my transmitter and ask Mimi to meet me somewhere else. But even as I hesitated in the face of this *bête noir*, Mimi herself emerged from the kitchen and hurried to meet me.

"There you are," I said gratefully. "Come away and talk to me. Who is that?" I added in a lower voice, as we hurried away from the beggar.

"That? A beachcomber," Mimi said, casting a glance over her shoulder. "The servants give him food—the Chinese servants, that is. The English servants say he's gone native and throw things at him. Why do you want to know?"

"I don't particularly," I told her, "only I thought that if Sir Humphrey was going to concern himself with lunatics, he might begin with that man!"

"Ah, but that would bring him no profit," said Mimi.

She might very well be correct, of course, but I meant to have my little moan. "It isn't fair! What about Vasily's father? There is Grand Duke Nicholas, quite clearly as mad as a goose, but in order to get *him* locked safely away we were obliged to provoke him into biting someone on the stage of the Bolshoi Theatre, right in front of the Emperor and the whole civilised world! Meanwhile here am I, Molly Dark of Brixton, perfectly sane—but no, I am to be condemned as a lunatic merely because I have been disappointed in love and fainted once or twice. Is that reasonable?"

"Nothing in life is reasonable," Mimi said, "no matter what Nijam thinks; and it certainly isn't fair. You must simply make the best of it."

"Perhaps so, but I always expected to be locked up for *genuine* insanity, and not because I seem to have strayed into a Wilkie Collins novel!"

Mimi, meanwhile, led me to the pair of French doors on the ground floor at the back of the building, opening upon the same rear stairway I had been admiring a moment before. To

81

one side of the double doors, bars had recently been fitted to the windows—an inexpressibly sinister sight! I knew at once what they were for, and trembled.

"This is where the butler said we would find Lady Seton," Mimi said, "although, seeing these bars, I do not think that we needed the directions."

I shuddered again. "Are the doors locked?"

"It will be no trouble at all if they are," said Mimi, taking out the little leather pouch in which she kept her lock-picks, and scrubbing her hands across her skirts in an attempt to dry them.

The sound of our voices must have been swallowed up by the frequent thunder, which had hardly ceased to growl and mutter since our arrival in these seas. The wind, too, had begun to gather strength, and the entire loggia underfoot was wet from the squall of rain which had visited whilst I was choking down my breakfast. The harbour-master had been right: we were clearly in for a storm.

Just as another squall came hurtling from the sky, the doors opened and admitted us to a wide, dark corridor running the length of the castle, ending at a big door of green baize which sealed this part of the house from the front. Beneath the whistling of the wind, and the stampede of raindrops across the pavement outside, there came for a moment a thin high keening sound that could only have been made by a human throat, but shortly faded away.

I shivered and attempted a joke. "What a sinister place this is! I half expect some frightful bounder to appear and deceive me into an ill-advised marriage!"

Mimi snorted. "I don't think you've been paying attention." She closed the door behind us and we wiped our feet upon the mat before continuing—it would be no good giving ourselves away by leaving wet footprints in the corridor. Inside this part of the house, the air was hotter and stickier even than it had been outside, filled with the scent of mildew and decay. A door to our left, at some distance from the one by which we had entered, must be the entrance to Lady Seton's apartments. We had just stolen up to it, and Mimi was feeling in her pockets for her lock-picks, when the handle rattled and we heard voices on the other side.

"It's the Blister," I hissed. For a moment we stared at each other in a panic; and then Mimi tried the door opposite—it opened—and we slipped into a dark sitting-room, whose furniture was shrouded in white sheets. Little did I know what a close acquaintance I was to have with that room before all was said and done! Of this, however, I had no notion at the time. On the other side of the door which concealed us, the Blister emerged from Lady Seton's apartment. The tall, Amazonian nurse followed her into the hallway and together, still talking, they went towards the door leading to the front of the house.

Lady Seton's door stood open—no doubt the nurse meant to return—and now Mimi left our hiding-place and flitted soundlessly across the corridor towards it. The housekeeper and the nurse, who stood with their backs towards us at the green baize door, seemed quite absorbed in their conversation. This seemed to concern a relative of Lady Seton's, with whom the lady wished to communicate in defiance of her husband. Both servants seemed determined to thwart this understandable impulse.

From the room opposite, Mimi beckoned me to follow her. My whole body was sticky with nervous perspiration, and such was the heat that I half expected to keel over halfway across the dangerous corridor. Consigning events to my Maker, however, I forced myself to move with deliberate, measured lightness across the carpeted passage and in at Lady Seton's door.

This led to another sitting-room that might have been very pleasant had it not smelled of mildew and cheap cigarettes. The latter were part of a litter of belongings that evidently belonged to the nurse. A closed door beyond must lead to Lady Seton's bedchamber. Going to a black case that stood upon a side-table, Mimi went efficiently through the bottles there, clicked her tongue with happy surprise, poured out some of one bottle's contents into an imperfectly laundered handkerchief, and greeted the nurse when she returned to the room a moment later with a face full of what, inspecting the bottle Mimi handed to me, I found to be chloroform. The whole thing had taken no more than two minutes, and since we positioned ourselves stealthily to either side of the door, the Amazonian nurse had not caught a glimpse of either of us.

"Well done," I whispered, glancing into the corridor to reassure myself that the Grim Housekeeper had really departed.

Mimi, struggling beneath the weight of the tall nurse, lowered her to the ground—but the woman's limp arm swung out and knocked a teacup from an occasional-table, causing the most shocking smash. At once, a shriek of terror echoed from behind the bedroom door. Mimi and I waited, our hearts in our throats. But the nurse did not stir, and Lady Seton's voice faded to an unhappy whimper. The house settled back into its sticky, brooding silence.

Pushing the fine hairs back from my perspiring forehead,

I tried the handle of the bedchamber door. "I'll need you to open this door for me, Mimi."

She shrugged. "Are you quite certain?"

I knew what she meant—for all that I knew *I* was not mad, the sounds Lady Seton had made were of a nature likely to arouse the liveliest suspicion. Nevertheless, what other choice did I have? I thought Lady Seton might converse with me; I knew Sir Humphrey would not.

Seeing my nod, Mimi began tinkering at once with the lock. This elicited a startled movement from within the room, and then, as I took hold of the doorknob, an indignant cry.

"Don't you dare come in!" Lady Seton shouted. "I don't want a nurse! I want a solicitor!"

"It's only me, my lady—Molly Dark," I said, opening the door a crack. At once something crashed against it. There was a distinct smell of kedgeree. I inched the door open still further to find Lady Seton brandishing an enamel tooth-mug, preparing to send it after the tin bowl of kedgeree—for naturally they had removed any sharp or breakable objects from the room. The sight of me arrested her movement, and for a moment she gazed at me with wide eyes and parted lips.

Lady Seton looked dreadful—gaunt and weary, as though she had neither eaten nor slept in weeks. Her hair was in disarray, her fine figure had withered away, and dark circles ringed her eyes. As for the white draperies in which she was clad, they were limp and stained. Either no one had cared, or dared, to provide her with fresh garments.

She recoiled a step, and the tooth-mug fell from her nerveless fingers. "Molly Dark!" she wailed. "Are you a ghost? Has he killed you, too?"

Has he killed you, too—how shall I describe the shudder that ran all through me at those words! Motioning to Mimi to remain in the sitting-room, I ventured into the bedchamber, holding out a hand as though approaching some trembling animal. "Good morning, Lady Seton," I said soothingly. "Indeed I'm not a ghost—take my hand and see!"

She reached out to touch my hand, and then seized it in a sort of desperation when she found it to be solid and real. "Molly Dark!" she repeated. "Here, of all places! You should not have come!"

"What do you fear?" I asked her gently. And who did she think had killed me? Sir Humphrey? —but of course I could not ask the question outright; she was too agitated for that.

Even this was too much for her. She recoiled another step, shaking her head. "I mustn't say."

I glanced about the room, seeing the disorder that reigned there, and the kedgeree that was but one of the many stains adorning the door, many of them already white with mould. There were spots of mildew, too, on Lady Seton's white robe. I swallowed hard: I could not help imagining myself locked into such a room, with its barred windows and doors, and the noxious stew that confinement had made of its atmosphere.

"I don't like to see you in this state, ma'am," I said, thinking of how she had sent her carriage for me on that memorable night at the British Museum, and had then fetched smelling-salts when I needed reviving. "Would you like me to help you comb your hair? Should I send for some food?"

Lady Seton shook her head in an overwrought way. "No! No food. They put drugs in it to make me sleep!"

"All right," I said. I must get her to trust me before she would accept food at my hand. "Sit down, then, and I'll comb your hair."

From the look on her face I could see that she was eager to be tended; yet still she hesitated. "I want Warren," she said. "If Warren was still here Sir Humphrey would never have dared to lock me up like this."

Warren? Why, this must be my former fiancé Warren H. Vandergriff, the same relative who the servants were plotting to keep away from her. "I regret to say that Mr Vandergriff has taken ship for San Francisco," I told her, and was surprised to find that, for her sake, I did regret it.

"I know that!" she said, wringing her hands. "I want to send a telegram after him. I've been locked up ever since he left!"

"But your trouble did not begin then, I think. You've been seeing the dead for longer than that, haven't you?"

Lady Seton trembled. Until now the room had been clear of imprints, except for my father's silent ghost, which was enjoying a cup of insubstantial tea at the window, gazing out upon the rain-lashed sea. His presence had not bothered Lady Seton at all. Since he was *my* ghost, I did not think that she could see him.

At my foolish question, however, shadowy figures began to appear—the Chinese sufferers who had accompanied her last night in the study. Speaking of them had brought them to mind. The poor woman's trembling increased. My own heart began to labour as their sensations bled into my own—their suffering, their grief, the appalling pangs that had racked their bodies. Perhaps Lady Seton felt it too, for she uttered a keening cry and put her hands over her face, sinking to the floor in an attempt to escape the intruders.

The dead were dead, and there was nothing I could do to help them unless I could get Lady Seton to speak to me. Nearly staggering beneath the weight of their suffering, I knelt beside her, gently touching her shoulder.

"Here," I said. "Feel my hand. I'm real—I'm alive—and *I can see them too.*"

She raised her head, shuddering. "What do you mean? Who can you see?"

"The ghosts," I whispered. "Look, that one is a scholar with a drooping moustache. That one is a little girl with ink-black fingers. That one—"

But Lady Seton burst at once into floods of tears. Her hands clasped almost convulsively upon mine. "I thought I was mad!" she wept. "They told me I was mad, but I'm not! I'm *not* mad! You believe me, don't you?"

"I believe you," I said—and it was the truth, although I thought that she was in a fair way to being driven out of what wits she did have by the treatment she had received. Any woman, locked up by her husband in idleness and squalor, with no company but that of the restless dead, might quickly run as mad as a glover. I shuddered, feeling more certain than ever that this was what had happened to the woman at Hanwell—that this was what might very well happen to me, if Sir Humphrey had his way!

"Why," I asked presently, when Lady Seton's sobbing calmed somewhat, "are they haunting *you?*"

"I wish I knew!" she whispered, glancing about her, and gripping my hands more tightly. "It was Sir Humphrey, not me, who brought the plague to Hong Kong!"

"He *brought* the plague? Impossible!" The moment I spoke the words which rose instinctively to my lips, Lady Seton flinched away from me, and her eyes shuttered up, as though she suddenly saw me as another of her persecutors. I could have bitten off my tongue. Why was my first impulse to defend the man, when he had attempted to have me declared insane?

I added, more carefully: "What I mean to say is that my father died of the plague here ten years ago—surely *that* wasn't Sir Humphrey's fault."

But Lady Seton shook her head. "Your father inspected a ship from Yunnan before it had been quarantined, and when he caught the plague he also quarantined himself. But two years ago, Sir Humphrey stopped paying attention to the quarantine altogether because he didn't like to delay his shipments. That's how the Black Death got into Tai Ping Shan. It spread like a wildfire—and all so that we could eat caviare! You tell me to eat—but how can I, when I am surrounded by people who died for the sake of my dinner?"

When I glanced about I saw that the imprints had faded away again, perhaps momentarily exorcised by Lady Seton's confession. All the same, my heart bled for the poor woman, haunted as she was by a guilt her husband evidently did not share. "It wasn't you who cut the corners," I told her.

"No, but it *was* Sir Humphrey! Your father knew better!"

I bit my lip. "I know almost nothing about my father's death. Is there nothing else you can tell me?" —She shook her head. "Do you know where he is buried, then?"

"Oh—that I do know." Now that her confession was made, Lady Seton seemed calmer. "Sir Humphrey built a chapel near the road for the use of the people of Pok Fu Lum. Your father is buried there. Take the steps at the back of the house, and the path will lead you to it."

At once it struck me that this was the same path down which I had seen my father's imprint walk last night, in my dreams. I shuddered again, a prey to nameless suspicions. It seemed significant, somehow, that I had dreamed of my father going towards his grave—although *how* significant, I could not at that moment have guessed.

I patted Lady Seton's arm again and asked her whether, if I had Mimi bring a piece of unmarked fruit, or a whole loaf of bread from the kitchen, she thought she might be able to eat something. To this she assented, and then, with a promise to help her if I could, I left her. Mimi was standing over the nurse with the bottle of chloroform, but she shook her head when I asked her whether the woman had stirred. Leaving the fallen Amazon to make what sense she could of her unexpected fainting-fit, the two of us locked the doors behind us and retreated cautiously into the loggia.

"What did you learn?" Mimi asked in a low voice.

For answer, I simply collapsed into one of the wicker chairs that stood in the loggia, pressing a hand to my labouring heart. Our adventure had left me feeling wrung-out, like a dish-cloth. Mimi must have been feeling the heat, too, for she plopped into the chair beside me and wiped listlessly at her forehead.

I could think of no fate more horrible than to be shut up, dosed and neglected, until I went mad in earnest. At the Schloss Frohsdorf the worst that could happen was death or mesmerism. Death is an escape from the ills of this world— *to be absent from the body is to be present with the Lord*, after all—and mesmerism is only a fleeting madness. Although neither was a very appealing prospect, I would choose death a thousand times rather than to go mad by inches during a long and hopeless captivity.

Malicious or not—and after seeing Lady Seton's lodgings I found it harder to believe he was not—Sir Humphrey had not spared his own wife. Why should he spare me?

I reminded myself again that, compared to Lady Seton, I

had the advantage not merely of present friends, but also of *low cunning...* Having recovered my breath, as much as was possible in such a fuggy heat, I pulled myself together and rose from my armchair of distress.

For the moment it was not raining, and a glimmer of sunlight escaped the thick, dark clouds overhead, illuminating the wisps of steam that rose from the jungle. The ground glistened with puddles and runlets of water, however, and the sound of the dripping from the trees was nearly as loud and steady as the rain. I glanced towards the clouds, thinking that another squall would almost certainly be along in a moment. I should not inspect the chapel until I could do so without getting wet and betraying where I had been.

"Come, let's make our report together," I told Mimi, hastening towards the nearby spiral staircase, which I had traversed the previous night.

The staircase led us to the upper loggia, but did not end there; so, out of curiosity, and because the fitful gleams of sunshine seemed to be getting stronger, I climbed a little higher still and found myself upon a widow's walk which ran the perimeter of the tiled roof. From here the views were magnificent, overlooking much of the western tip of the island. Through a cleft between two mountains one could even catch a glimpse of Victoria to the north, and the mainland beyond. Towards the east, before a grey smudge of rain closed off the horizon, there stretched a sea as dark and storm-tossed as the sky itself. The only sign of life upon that vasty deep was one solitary steamer, although whether it was arriving or departing I, with my inexperienced eye, could not tell.

Mimi uttered an exclamation of delight and leaned out over the white battlemented parapet to drink it all in. My own enjoyment of the view was tempered by the knowledge that the rain must shortly drive us inside again; and so I switched on my transmitter.

"Vasily? Are you there?'

"Fear not! I hang upon your lips."

"How inconvenient," I said. It *was* inconvenient that I should be made to remember the occasions upon which Vasily had been in contact with my lips.

"Well, it isn't as though I have anything else to do, except— good Lord! does Schmidt expect me to *prepare dinner?* Was it not enough that I must wash the breakfast dishes?"

"I will pray for you," I said, "and for Nijam's palate. Stop laughing in that heartless manner, Mimi, or if you must, switch off your transmitter. I have a report to make."

In a few quick sentences I informed Vasily of the morning's interview, and of what we had learned from Lady Seton. "I must say that it's looking worse and worse for Sir Humphrey. I don't believe that Lady Seton is any more mad than I am— and she assures me that Sir Humphrey is at least partly to blame for the plague epidemic!"

Mimi clapped her hands. "Let's steal you a fortune, Dark!"

"Hold your ponies, Mimi," I protested. "Stealing his money would only benefit *me.* But if we were to expose him—the way we did to the old Grand Duke—it might be the only redress the people of Tai Ping Shan are ever given. And now we have the leverage to do so. It's as Aristotle said: *give me a place to stand and I will move the world.*"

"Really, Dark!" Nijam cut in, her voice sorely distorted by the distance. She must be away in the town on her own errand, but something I had said forced her to join the conversation: "That wasn't Aristotle; it was Archimedes. I shudder to think what havoc you must have wreaked in the schoolrooms of Vienna—but apart from that, I doubt it *is* the right leverage. The plague would have spread to Hong Kong in any case; it was already making its way across the mainland."

Mimi scowled. "Why should Sir Humphrey take all the trouble to lock up his wife, unless he wanted to keep it a secret?"

"Mimi has a point," Vasily said. "The British justify their empire through virtue—they claim with some justice to be better and more benevolent rulers than the likes of Russia, or Germany or China."

"And what a lot of effort *that* takes," Mimi muttered with sarcasm.

"Naturally; but not even Sir Humphrey would dare to explode *that* illusion, by confessing to having set the plague among the natives."

"The plague has already caused a scandal in England," Nijam put in. "For years the colonial authorities have taken a *laissez-faire* policy towards the Chinese on the island—leaving them more or less to run their own affairs—but now questions are being asked. Why didn't we make sure the slums were less crowded, and more sanitary? The answer, of course, is that the thing was discussed, and it was thought best to leave the Chinese to their own devices, and not to impose upon them. You've done well, Dark, but it will be difficult to make Sir Humphrey responsible for the outbreak, and even harder to ruin him in that way—not when he is such a respected man on the island."

"If Seton is the sort of man to cut corners on quarantine and then lock up his wife as a madwoman, rather than risk exposure," Vasily said, "then he has certainly sinned in other

93

ways as well. Leave Lady Seton for now, Miss Dark; try to find out more about the circumstances of your father's death, and the administration of the resulting trust. If there was foul play there, we shall have him."

I did not like this suggestion, for I would far rather have done something for the plague victims than myself. "Sir Humphrey may have embezzled the Dark inheritance, but there are hundreds of people dead because of his greed! It hardly seems fair!"

"No, it isn't fair," said Vasily, "but if there is nothing else we can do to hold him accountable—"

"Let us not abandon the idea," I begged. "I will keep investigating here at the castle, but tell Nijam to find out what she can about the origins of the plague. *Do* say yes; you know how much she loves a good bacillus."

"Miss Nijam's happiness is always foremost on my mind," Vasily said dryly. "Very well—since Nijam wishes it!"

I switched off my transmitter, and Mimi said, "You might also consider your own happiness, Dark."

I blinked, somewhat at a loss. I *did* consider my own happiness; constantly. It was one of the reasons I must always work so hard to put others before myself. "I'm not here for my own enjoyment, Mimi. Don't you understand that we have work to do? We had better get into Sir Humphrey's study and go through his desk—there may be evidence. Do you think you could get one of the servants to tell you the whereabouts of his safe?"

Mimi shrugged. "The English servants are like oysters, but perhaps I can pry something out of the butler."

I gulped, not quite knowing what to say. I felt quite sure that I did not want to know the answer to my most burning question; but in the end I thought that if I was to be Mimi's friend I could not remain silent. "Mimi—when you say that you seduced the butler—did you really mean it?"

At first Mimi only looked at me in incomprehension—but upon seeing my face, which had become hot with embarrassment, she understood and laughed. "Oh! you mean, did I go to bed with him? No, but why does it bother you? I've gone to bed with a lot of people for things I need."

Her hair had not grown by much in the two months since she had cut it off and sold it to help buy us passage to safety; and my heart wept for her. "Mimi," I said as gently as I might, "to me you are not a commodity, to be bought and sold for my convenience. You are worth ever so much more than that."

Mimi reminded me of Vasily in some ways: she never liked to betray that she was affected. She was, however, far less capable of hiding her emotions: she stared fixedly past me for a moment, and blinked a great deal, before saying gruffly, "A thing is only worth what people are willing to pay for it, and how could I afford morals? I am the only thing I've ever had to sell."

"It will be all right if we fail to bring Sir Humphrey down. No one is forcing you to do this—"

Perhaps this was the wrong thing to say. "No one forced you to sell yourself to Griff, either," Mimi said, a trifle resentfully, "so don't look down on me for doing the same! We women must all be bought and sold sooner or later. At least, I mean to be the one to profit from it."

Chapter VIII.

While Mimi and I were having our conversation on the roof, Nijam and Schmidt ventured out of their lodgings in the direction of the waterfront, where they hoped to pay a visit to the offices of Seton & Associates. As they walked, Nijam kept an eye on the clouds. Despite the brief sunshine, they were very dark and heavy, and she did not wonder that a typhoon had been forecast. She could only hope that this everlasting heat and humidity would be relieved by the storm, for despite her Indian blood, she was London born and unaccustomed to tropical climates.

"You have our story straight? You are the prospective investor, and I am only your stenographer, so you will need to do most of the talking." Nijam paused for an answer, but there was none. "Schmidt?"

She had been walking briskly in a straight line, ferociously intent upon the job at hand. Now, collecting that she had neither seen nor heard from Schmidt in a little while, she cast a glance behind her. He had fallen behind, likely distracted by the market they had just passed, where a woman with baskets of peonies and camellias was selling flowers to the passers-by.

"Don't dawdle," she told him, as he strolled up to her with both hands clasped behind his back. Did he think they had all the time in the world? "It will rain again in a moment."

"I know," he said, bringing a hand out from behind his back to show her what it held. "I have an umbrella."

Looking at the umbrella, Nijam ruthlessly quashed the softness welling up somewhere in the internal region of her ribcage where tender emotions might dwell, if hearts were not machines designed primarily for the circulation of blood. Schmidt could not be encouraged to care for her—not with his memories gone. It would not be honest. "That's all very well for *you*," she said, purposefully tart, "but *I* would like to remain dry too, you know. Keep up." With that, she turned abruptly and continued walking.

He *did* keep up with her, too—he absolutely gave a little skip and put himself next to her, opening the umbrella with a flourish and holding it over her head. "Look," he said, "it's big enough for both of us. Do you like flowers?"

"No," said Nijam. It was true that she was in a bad mood and being unreasonable, but it was also true that she did not like flowers. The news caught Schmidt absolutely by surprise. His blue eyes opened so wide that, had she been in a better mood, she might have found the sight rather comical.

"Why not?" he asked, after a moment's utter disarray. Evidently his question had not been a serious one.

"They're bright," Nijam said, "and smelly."

"Oh," he said, very quietly. Too late, Nijam realised that he was still concealing something behind his back. There came a flash of pink as a big, blowsy peony fell discreetly into the gutter and lay there, ignored. Nijam's circulatory system gave another flutter, but she exercised her customary self-command and walked on. She did not like peonies. She did not *want* a peony. And she could not have Alphonse Schmidt.

"What *do* you like?" he asked after a moment. "What would you buy to treat yourself? Jewels?"

Nijam shook her head. "Peppermints," she said. "Or bull's-eyes. Or barley sugar. You can't eat an emerald, and they're shockingly expensive."

Schmidt laughed, shaking his head. "Surely there is *something* you like, beyond sweets."

You, she thought despairingly—*I like you, I want you.* She cleared her throat. "Socks."

"Socks," he repeated.

Nijam shrugged. "I like to be warm and comfortable. And I like to have tools for my projects. That's all. And here we are."

She had never stopped walking, and now they came out onto the promenade—or *praya,* as it was called here—which lined the waterfront: a broad stone-fronted road from which a great number of little jetties protruded, providing room for the Chinese to tether their fishing-boats while they were in harbour. Today the whole waterfront was crowded with junks and sampans, all of them battened down for the approaching storm—which indeed now seemed ready to begin in earnest. Despite the comparative shelter afforded by the harbour on this, the leeward side of the island, wind, rain, and spray gusted in from the water, making the promenade a rather uncomfortable place to be.

Nijam accepted Schmidt's proffered arm, which brought them closer together beneath the umbrella. He smelled of rain and heat and very faintly of Vasily's pine-scented cologne—Nijam grimaced. Of course he smelled like his master!

Before long they identified their target: a two-storey building with an arcaded porch of white blocks, which bore the legend *Seton & Associates.* Once having taken shelter within its walls, they soon found themselves in the presence of a polite young Chinese clerk with impeccable English who introduced himself as Li Ling. Schmidt introduced himself in turn as Herr Schmidt ("of the Cologne steam-engine Schmidts") together with his secretary, Miss Nijam.

"Steam-engines?" young Mr Li inquired, raising an eyebrow in polite wonder. "What brings you to Hong Kong, Herr Schmidt? Is it the Kowloon Railway?"

Nijam, scribbling diligently, gave her putative employer a stern look over the top of her *pince-nez*.

Schmidt swallowed. "That is only the family business," he added, with an effort dredging up the story he had been ordered to produce for the benefit of Seton & Associates. "My own business is different. I wish to import tea from China to Germany, and I was told Seton & Associates was the company to approach."

The clerk nodded. "You really ought to speak to Sir Humphrey Seton himself," he said. "As it happens, Sir Humphrey is not in the office today. Have you made an appointment?"

Schmidt sent Nijam a glance. "Did you not receive a letter from Vladivostok?" he inquired, which was not a direct lie. It was better, Nijam knew, when Schmidt did not have to lie; his face would go as stiff as a playing-card, and his eyes would become a little glassy. You had only to look at him to know that he was being very awkwardly deceptive.

"I can ask the secretaries, but I think your letter must have been delayed. We can make an appointment for you in the next day or two?"

"Please do," Schmidt said, "but can't you tell us anything about the business today? I am contemplating a large investment, and there is much to discuss with my partners in Germany, even before I meet with Sir Humphrey."

"Of course," the clerk said. "Please, follow me."

The tour of the offices was a brief one—limited to a view of the stenographers' room and introductions to some of the company's leading officers. It was easy enough to identify the office where the shareholders' records must be kept, although Nijam thought that Mimi might be required for the job of actually locating the records. The best mode of entry would be by the window, which was some distance from the ground.

She observed with interest that all the rank and file, and much of the management of the firm, were Chinese. A number of others, she judged, were of mixed descent like herself. As Nijam observed them bowing to Schmidt she could not help wondering whether they, like herself, felt continually caught between two worlds, native to neither and alien to both—but her business left her no opportunity to question them.

The company, Mr Li informed them, had been founded to export tea from South China via Hong Kong to London and Sydney, and was thus one of the first of the great Hong Kong trading-houses to keep its hands clean of opium. Soon, a new link across the Pacific to the Americas would be opened up, transporting South China tea and textiles to San Francisco and labourers to Mexico. The addition of a German branch to the business, one of the officers assured Schmidt, would not be difficult to accomplish if the Cologne steam-engine Schmidts were able to provide steamers to work the passage from London to Hamburg. Schmidt quite confidently informed the gentleman that this would be no trouble at all.

Very soon they had been conducted once again to the front room, where Mr Li asked if they had any further questions. "Just one, in fact," Schmidt stammered. "I take it you have docks and warehouses somewhere along the harbour? Perhaps we could see those?"

The clerk hesitated with a glance towards the rain-lashed windows. "Perhaps you would like to wait for Sir Humphrey, some finer day?"

"We don't mind the rain," Nijam said at once. "Mr Schmidt brought his umbrella."

"Perhaps we might visit on our own," Schmidt added. "There is not much else to do on a day like this; one might as well get all one's business done."

"No, no," Mr Li said at once. "You must not visit the docks without an escort—the Typhoon Gang considers them part of their territory. Their Mountain will not want trouble with the authorities, but some of the Forty-Nines—the younger brawlers, you know—may make trouble. If you wish to visit today, I will attend you."

"The Typhoon Gang?" Schmidt prompted, once Mr Li had collected hat and umbrella, and led them out into the lashing rain. "They sound like a gang of outlaws."

"You have not heard of the triads?" Mr Li inquired. Nijam had, but she held her peace, for she did not know whether her information was correct. "They are only a little like an outlaw gang, you understand. They are more like what you would call a mutual aid society, providing food, housing, and protection to the poor."

"Don't the English authorities see to such things?" Schmidt asked.

"We prefer to take care of our own affairs," Mr Li said.

"But isn't it true that the triads have been outlawed in Hong Kong?" Nijam asked.

Again, Mr Li answered diplomatically: "Well, it is hard to keep the triads in order. There is sometimes trouble—extortion, robbery, trafficking in black-market goods and women. Everyone is doing their best to live."

Schmidt frowned, and in the mildly exasperated tone Nijam knew and loved, said, "So, the triads were created to provide the Chinese with basic necessities of life; and the authorities responded by outlawing them? How will that solve anything, besides driving them deeper into a life of crime?"

For the first time, an unguarded gleam of emotion seemed to escape the clerk's eyes. "If life was too easy in Hong Kong, then all of China would wish to come here," he said. "That is what the English said."

Schmidt digested this in blank amazement, but Nijam said, "What about you, Mr Li? Did you come from China?"

"I came from Canton for my education as a boy," he said. "Things are not always peaceful in China. After the uprising last year, I brought my parents to live in Hong Kong too."

Nijam had read about this in the papers—an abortive uprising against the Chinese emperor in Canton had led to hundreds of arrests and executions. She observed Li Ling with new respect, wondering whether he was one of the many Hong Kong-educated Chinese, with their democratic ideas, who had come to swell the ranks of revolutionary societies on the mainland. The question might be an intrusive one, however, particularly if the Li family had fled the empire for political reasons. British education might foster democratic ideals; but British authorities were far too anxious to retain their foothold in Hong Kong, to risk offending the imperial authorities on the mainland by actually promoting those same democratic ideals.

Instead, Nijam quietly followed Schmidt and Li along the waterfront to the dockyard operated by Seton & Associates, where a number of steamers were snugly docked. Big, black, serviceable cargo vessels, with short masts bracketing a blocky wheel-house and a thick steam-chimney, they had evidently been hawsered here to wait out the storm in comparative calm. Even in this wet, hot weather the work went on at a feverish pace. Soaked to the skin, labourers hurried to and fro between ship and warehouse, bent double beneath the weight of chests, sacks, and boxes. Some of them, Nijam thought, did not look very well: bone-thin, they had vacant stares, and their breath came slowly and shallowly despite the exertion of their labours.

"The ships must be unloaded before the storm worsens," Mr Li explained.

"How much are they paid?" Nijam asked.

"Not a great deal," Mr Li said, naming the figure. Nijam frowned, doing sums in her head as Schmidt asked to see within the warehouse. Here it was dark, but blessedly sheltered, and there was some relief from the rain which the umbrella could no longer fend off. The warehouse was heaped with boxes. None of the ships in dock had been loaded, Mr Li explained, because with the storm expected to worsen, the cargo would be safer in the warehouse. "Tea," he added, "must be kept dry."

"And where is the tea grown?"

"In Yunnan, miss."

"Yunnan," Nijam repeated. "Isn't that where the plague originated?"

"I have heard it said so," was the evasive answer.

After taking them over the warehouse, Mr Li finished by

serving them tea in the overseer's office. Here Nijam, having gleaned a deal of information herself, prepared to bring the day's business to a close.

"I have read a great deal about Yunnan's exports," she said. This was nearly true—the morning had been spent plundering the City Hall library. "Tea, tin, and—so I am told—a great deal of raw opium, which is shipped to northern China by sea." She sipped her tea before administering the *coup de grâce.* "I've heard that much of this Yunnan opium comes to Hong Kong."

Mr Li, over the course of the afternoon, had come to regard Nijam with a distinctly wary expression. "Some of it may travel through Hong Kong, but it cannot be unloaded here. It is against the law to import opium to Hong Kong if you do not hold the government monopoly."

"Naturally," Nijam said with a smile. Mr Li was proving to be a foe worthy of her steel. She did not attribute his careful evasions to some racial defect in his character, as a more hasty person might. She understood all too well what it was like to yield to authority when you could not defy it, and to save one's resistance for the times when it might count—as, for instance, when the whole Revive China society should attempt to capture Canton from the emperor. After a moment she went on: "All the same, I believe that many of the labourers at this dockyard are showing signs of opium addiction. I'm aware that the government monopoly on opium keeps Hong Kong prices high—so high that I don't see how the men are able to afford it on the income you described. So, there are only two possibilities. Either your labourers have some other source of income beside what Sir Humphrey is paying them— or they are getting opium cheaply on the black market. Who knows what might be coming in from Yunnan among all these tea-chests?"

Mr Li had gone absolutely still, beholding her with a look of blank astonishment and not a little wrath. Nijam's transmitter crackled in her head. "Miss Nijam! Miss Nijam!" Vasily protested from his room at the boarding-house, where Nijam devoutly wished she had stayed. "What are you thinking? This is a confidence-trick, not a court-room! You can't throw around accusations—you have to keep your cards close to the chest!"

Vasily needed her in the field, Nijam thought resentfully, so he would just have to get used to her way of doing things. Happily, Schmidt stepped in and saved her the trouble of saying anything at all.

"What Miss Nijam *means* to ask," he said, very earnestly, "is—does Sir Humphrey treat his workers well? I can't help noticing that apart from one or two overseers, the entire labour force is Chinese. The business may be *named* Seton & Associates, but it is your people who do all the work."

So Alphonse had noticed this, too! Nijam thought, with another circulatory episode.

Mr Li did not speak, but his face changed, and Nijam could sense his unspoken agreement. Schmidt's words of sympathy, it was clear, had succeeded where her own chain of logic had failed. And then, she must remember that all the Indians she had hitherto seen in Hong Kong had worn the uniforms of British policemen: to Mr Li she might be simply another of the white man's lackeys. She cleared her throat and tried again.

"We know that Sir Humphrey broke quarantine. You must have lost a great many men to the plague."

Mr Li glanced about the office as though he feared being

overheard, but then he became direct. "Why are you asking these questions?"

"Because we want to help," Schmidt said earnestly.

"Do you?" he asked. "Because it sounds as though you only want to hurt Sir Humphrey. How can you help us? You don't know us. You don't know what we want."

Nijam drummed her fingers against the table. "That's a fair point. We *don't* know what you want. But perhaps one of the things you want is to hold Sir Humphrey accountable." She watched Mr Li's face closely. "There are monsters in London as well as in Peking. My people know that, the same way yours do."

He sent her a long, piercing look, and relaxed sufficiently to take a sip of his tea. "The Government cares about the plague only because it's made them lose face. They don't care about opium at all, except insofar as they can turn it to their profit." Having drained the small bowl of tea, he rose to his feet. "You are wasting your time here. If you want to hurt Sir Humphrey Seton, you must prove that he has injured Englishmen. Now it is time for me to return to the office. When you have finished your tea, a foreman will guide you out of Typhoon territory."

The door closed behind him, leaving Nijam with much to occupy her thoughts. Schmidt regarded her in puzzlement, but it was not until the foreman had escorted them to Queen's Street and the more well-to-do environs of the city, that he broke his silence.

"Do you really think that Sir Humphrey is importing black-market opium from Yunnan?"

"It would make sense, wouldn't it?" Nijam retorted. She began counting points on her fingers. "We know that he deals in the Yunnan trade, and they're the primary Chinese producer of cheap domestic opium—its quality is not as good as the opium grown in India, so it's more affordable for the masses. We know that he doesn't just ship tea to London, but also to other ports like Canton, Sydney, and San Francisco, where there are large markets for opium. We know that he treats his labourers like wastepaper, or he would have taken steps to protect them from the plague. We know they are paid barely enough to keep body and soul together. We can see that they're showing signs of opium addiction, which shouldn't be possible on their wage, with the price of legal opium being what it is. If Sir Humphrey was supplying them with black-market opium, it would explain their symptoms—and why they continue to work for him." She took a deep breath. "It might explain more things than that—such as, why Sir Humphrey didn't want public health officials inspecting his ships."

"It is difficult to believe such villainy," Schmidt said after a moment, with an uneasy laugh. "First setting the plague loose in Hong Kong, then imprisoning his wife as a madwoman, and now forcing opium upon his workers to keep them compliant?"

"Not all monsters drink blood," Nijam said, "and besides, I never said he had *forced* opium upon the dockhands. Sir Humphrey is a villain, but *they* chose to work for him—in just the same way they chose to become addicted to opium. There will always be people weak enough, or foolish enough, to allow themselves to be exploited. Mr Li is not in their predicament, as you might have noticed."

"Mr Li is evidently in a more advantageous position," Schmidt pointed out. "He has an education, decent wages, and every chance to better himself. He need not turn to opium to ameliorate his condition."

"Neither must the labourers," Nijam said, exasperated. "Of course they have greater *reason* to do it, but you can't really think that their addiction would disappear if only Sir Humphrey was held to account!"

"I never said that," Schmidt protested. "I just don't think it's helpful to blame people who have so little ability to better themselves."

"And I don't think it's helpful to ignore the choices they *do* have," Nijam snapped. Schmidt's soft heart was sometimes accompanied by a soft head. "It's patronising. They aren't *babies*, you know. Sometimes you *can* be complicit in your own exploitation, Schmidt, and that *is* a moral failing."

After that, they walked home in silence. Nijam felt herself bristling with irritability. She longed to prove, with devastating logic, that Schmidt himself was the perfect example of someone habitually complicit in his own exploitation. It was due to this complicity that she had been forced into this agonising position at all, doomed to watch over his safety, but never to love him. Under such circumstances, his unthinking defence of the dockhands rankled like a personal insult.

She had softened towards Schmidt lately, but that was a mistake. He could not know that his confidences wounded her; but with nothing to be gained by this pain, why should she endure it?

"You're walking too slowly," she said at this juncture. "Give me the umbrella." He looked puzzled, but complied; and, angling the makeshift shelter against the rain, Nijam strode away without looking back. She did not run, much though she would have liked to.

Chapter IX.

"Sir Humphrey—trafficking *opium?*" I gasped that evening from the privacy of my room, when Nijam, via transmitter, had laid out the day's findings. "I can't believe it!"

"Why not?" Nijam demanded. "It seems that he's done everything else you can think of."

"But it's ridiculous," I protested. "The opium trade is not *respectable,* and he and my father were always against it. Why, only the other day he was complaining of the difficulty in finding Chinese servants who were not addicted."

"Respectability, my dear," Vasily murmured, "is about appearances, not *truth.* Consider the demimonde balls I used to hold in Soho: they always were attended by a great many very respectable Englishmen."

"But Sir Humphrey isn't—"

"Had those men not been respectable, they would hardly have had to attend *secret* balls," Vasily said, and I sighed.

I did not know how to explain how ridiculous it all seemed to me—that Sir Humphrey should be playing the part of a pantomime villain, doing every bad thing that could be imagined. At this rate, we should soon learn that he had been in the habit of strangling kittens and taking sweets from babies. The evidence might be there; but how could I manage to believe it without feeling like the most frightful gull? It all reminded me of that suspension of belief which my sister Lilias talks about, in books of fiction. My suspension of disbelief was at that moment under a very great amount of strain.

"The penalties for selling black market opium are enormous," Nijam went on, oblivious to my discomfort. "Of course anyone may sell opium outside Hong Kong with Her Majesty's goodwill—even in other colonies, where the damage is only likely to injure a small proportion of the workforce. But to sell or distribute it within Hong Kong, one must bid on the government monopoly, which no respectable Englishman would do now-a-days. If it could be proved that Sir Humphrey had sold black-market opium, it might just be enough to ruin his reputation, if not his fortune."

"There's our angle, then," said I. "It's as I said earlier: the money doesn't matter to me. It will be enough to see his evil deeds laid bare."

"It may not be enough to achieve either," said Vasily. "All the evidence we have so far is hearsay. Miss Nijam will need to investigate further. Miss Dark, you and Mimi must remain at the castle. Keep looking for information regarding your father, his shares, and any records of opium shipments. Meanwhile, Schmidt must pursue his investments in Seton & Associates." He paused for a moment. "Let's wire Herr Haber for money."

"Again?" Nijam asked. "So soon?"

"Not for our wages this time," Vasily said, a note of vulpine delight in his voice. "We're going to make that sizeable investment in Seton & Associates—or at least, just enough to have Sir Humphrey eating out of our hands in hopes of more."

* * *

Uneasy lies the head that wears the crown, they say, although never having worn a crown I cannot say for certain whether I agree with them. I can assure the reader with absolute certainty that being suspected of insanity is no joke either. The prospect had preyed upon my mind all day, and now, in the witching hours, I found that I no longer wished to be alone with my thoughts. My room was unbearably hot, forbidding sleep. The windows had to be closed to shut out the wind and rain which scoured them; and despite the protection of the loggia, there was a monotonous *drip, drip, drip* somewhere within the walls. Every time I opened my eyes in the room's darkness, I caught the faint glimmer of my father's imprint pacing to and fro, to and fro, until I thought the constant flickering movement would drive me to distraction. I turned away from the imprint and began to think of Vasily instead, but this was worse. The thought of those two kisses! and his wiry arms about me in the carriage after he had faced his family! and his gentle hands applying arnica to the bruises which Griff had left on my throat!

There was only one cure for this fever. With sleep apparently out of the question, I fitted my transmitter to my ear, connected it with its battery, and switched it on.

"Is anyone there?"

For a moment there was no reply, and my heart sank. Then, as I was giving up hope, the transmitter in my ear rustled to wakefulness.

"Miss Dark?" Vasily asked softly. He had not called me by my Christian name once since the kiss on the train two months ago, and it left me feeling somewhat bereft. "What is wrong?"

How could I admit that I only wanted to hear the sound of his voice? "Nothing, really," I said. "Did I wake you?"

"Not at all, little mouse."

He had not called me that very often lately, either. I smiled into the darkness. "Couldn't *you* sleep, either?"

He was silent a moment. I wished I could see his face, all the way over in Victoria. At length he said, "I don't like to think of you and Mimi alone up there at Pok Fu Lum. Don't tell Nijam. She'll only explain how irrational I'm being, and that's no help at all. Why are you awake?"

I could scarcely tell him that I was tormented by the memory of his touch. At best, it would make him yet more intolerably conceited. At worst, it would inform him that his wiles had succeeded. Half the truth must do.

"I don't like it, either," I told him. "I don't like being thought mad, and I don't like being alone in this house, locked into my room with only my father's ghost for company." I hesitated. "And the worst of it is, I can't help but feel that I am making a horrible mistake."

"A mistake?" Vasily asked blankly. "How?"

I bit my lip. "It's me," I said. "I know that Sir Humphrey is a bad man, who has caused Lord knows how many plague deaths, and has locked up his wife as a lunatic, and will do the same to me if he gets the chance. And that is without even considering the opium, or the fact that he may very well have stolen bread out of my sisters' mouths. So why do I feel *so* very wrong for deceiving him?"

Vasily said nothing; but it was an inviting kind of silence. Darkness and distance lay between us, and on this topic I felt that I could be absolutely honest with him.

"Until now—in Vienna and Russia—I've always felt quite certain that I was doing the right thing. But this is no pantomime villain—it's *Sir Humphrey*, who used to hold me on his knee when I was a baby." My explanations were somehow insufficient, even to my own ears. "He paid for me to go to school, you know!"

"With money that should have been your own," Vasily said, very quietly.

"Well, we don't know that for certain." I sighed. "What if we're wrong? Think of what's at stake! If he really *is* a villain, and I let him get the better of me, he'll shut me up to die by inches in the dark. But if I act hastily, we might ruin an innocent man. And I know you'll say that he can't possibly be innocent, but I keep imagining things... Maybe he really thinks Lady Seton and I are mad. Most people don't believe in ghosts, after all. Maybe he doesn't know anything about the opium—maybe it's his captains smuggling it from Yunnan without his knowledge, and then selling to the dockhands on the quiet. Maybe the plague, and the disagreement about the shares, were just honest mistakes and not even his own."

"Maybe," Vasily said very quietly, "the company began losing money eleven years ago because Sir Humphrey was smuggling opium even then, and your father tried to put a stop to it."

I bit my lip. The same thought had occurred to me. "I know that it's not rational, I know it's all awfully suspicious, but I still feel like the most terrible ingrate. Sir Humphrey used to say such wise things, every quarter-day, whenever he visited to pay my school fees—*wealth consists not in having great possessions, but in having few wants.* Or, *an investment in knowledge pays the best interest.* He was always full of sayings like that. How I always used to look up to him! That is, until

113

the Noor-Jahan affair."

"It sounds to me as though he was very careful to bring you up to do so," Vasily said. There was a note of disgust beneath the laziness of his voice. "It is easy for a thief to say such things to the one he has robbed—and politic, also, to give her the notion that she should be grateful to him."

I considered this in silence. The notion was creeping upon me that if Sir Humphrey had done half the things of which we now suspected him, then all along he had conducted himself with the most brazen hypocrisy it had ever been my lot to see. I did not quite know how I ought to respond to this. There seemed no words for it that a lady should utter.

"Was that all that was worrying you?" Vasily asked at length, lightly mocking. "Or did you call me only to hear my voice?"

"I didn't call you," I said with great dignity. "I asked if *anyone* was there. What have you been doing with yourself all day? Did you stay in the house as you were told?"

"Ugh!" he said. "I have washed dishes and swept floors, my dear. The indignity! Could Nikolasha have seen it I should never live the thing down. I had no notion that such a tedious lot of work went into keeping a place tidy! Not that it was in a very good condition when we came. Our landlady," he added, with ineffable disgust, "had left the sheets unironed."

"Un*ironed?*" I echoed.

"Indeed! At least they were clean, I suppose."

I do not suppose that I had ever slept between ironed sheets in my life—unless those at Schloss Frohsdorf had been ironed. But then, it had never occurred to me to ask. Who had the time to iron sheets, unless they were being paid to do so?

"Vasily," I said in a voice that quivered, "do you mean to tell me that you ironed the sheets?"

"Well—it wasn't as though there was much else to do, once I'd finished the other tasks and sent the boy out for dinner. Schmidt showed me how to use the contraption."

I would never have described an iron as a *contraption,* but evidently Vasily was missing an important part of his education. "And dinner?" I asked. "What did you have?"

"Champagne and caviare," he replied promptly.

I couldn't help myself. "Caviare!" I shrieked, and burst out into laughter. "Oh, Vasily! Where on earth did you find *caviare?*"

"Oh, *I* didn't find it. I sent a boy for it. That was only meant to be *entrée*—but it's as well that I did so," he added moodily, "for when the boy came back with the duck, there was evidently no point in trying to turn *that* into dinner."

"Why? What was wrong with the duck?"

"It was quacking," Vasily said glumly. "I *expected* a properly dressed fowl. What was I supposed to do with a live one?"

I hugged myself with glee at the image that rose to mind. "I don't know, but—you were a vampire once, surely?"

"My dear! How should *that* give a man any idea of the proper method of butchering a water-fowl? If I'd had a rifle and an acre of wood, I might have tried shooting it. But after that it ought to have been Schmidt's job."

"I'm surprised you didn't ask him. Or Nijam, once she got home."

"Schmidt took one look at the creature and went out for bird-seed, or whatever it is ducks eat," Vasily said, "and Nijam has given it a name—Bill, naturally."

"*Nijam* gave it a name?"

"I gather she has a weakness for the creatures, which will be the first weakness I've detected from *that* direction. Anyway,

'Bill's' cage is presently contaminating the bath-tub. I don't know how I've been eating all these years, if this is the help I have to rely upon."

"Schmidt does roast beef half the time," I said, "as anyone with sense would." I was struck, quite helplessly, by the vision of a domestic life with this man. I imagined a little loft in Paris or Vienna somewhere, wallpapered with sketches of me, in which Vasily lounged comfortably in bare feet and a dressing-gown of figured silk, by turns sipping champagne, ironing sheets, ordering duck, and complaining about the landlady. I found to my horror that this vision was desperately appealing to me. It was not the respectable bourgeois marriage I had always imagined, in a staid house in Brixton with the children tidied away into the nursery and myself and my husband tidied away into study and drawing-room, respectively. It was warmer than that; it was desperately untidy; it was *home.*

I lay alone in the darkness of Sir Humphrey's big, empty castle and felt as though I might break my heart for wanting that little loft in Paris.

"I feel that I've done barely anything, apart from purchasing an ill-advised duck," Vasily went on, petulantly. "Nijam and Schmidt, and you and Mimi, are doing all the real work. Well! We will find a way to bring Sir Humphrey down, no doubt, and after that…"

"Yes?" I prompted him.

"After that," he said, with an oddly vulnerable note in his voice, "I hope to God you'll let me beguile you into making the most foolish decision of your life."

There was that talk of beguiling me again—as though I was some beast to be trapped, instead of a rational creature to be honestly wooed. "Vasily," I said hopelessly. "Why must you

116

beguile me?"

"Don't you know, my dear?" Once or twice he had over-whelmed me with kisses: now, unexpectedly, he overwhelmed me with a flood of words. "I told you I had never been interested in princesses. You've met Zlata and Missy—you know what they are like. They cannot help being cruel and self-centred, even when they mean *well. Bozhe moi!* I know I am no better. But I can't help myself. I seem to have set my heart on *you,* and I mean to have you. I may no longer be a vampire, but I'll try if I can still mesmerise a woman."

"But I don't *want* to be mesmerised! You aren't a vampire anymore; why must you try to be one still?" I sank a hand into my hair, and yanked at it in chagrin. "I know that I'm not a princess to you, but why must you treat me like a dainty? If you want one of those, you can hire one!"

"A *dainty?*" he repeated, so startled that his voice grew louder. "A *dainty?* Why would I—how do I treat you like a dainty?"

In my mind, a thousand answers clamoured for articulation in vain. I hated all this talk of *beguiling* and *having*—but I did not quite have the words to explain why. "Well," I said, "you think I'm the sort of woman who'd succumb to a little meaningless seduction!"

"If you were a dainty I'd only have to fix a price," Vasily protested. "It's precisely because you *are* a respectable woman that I'm having to do such a weary lot of beguiling!"

"You *did* have your price fixed on me!" I said. "You meant to buy me at the cost of that painting!"

"And shall I ever hear the end of it?"

In the silence that followed I wished—*how* I wished I had not called out to him! The darkness, the distance, the friendly conversation—all of it had conspired to lead us into this trap.

After a moment, Vasily said more calmly, "I beg your pardon. I ought to have said that I regret the presumption. I ought to have known better. And I don't care how much beguiling I must do, if you'll consent to be my wife. But it's as my wife that I mean to have you, not my *dainty*."

That much was true—had I not witnessed Vasily dealing with a dainty, two months ago at the Maryinsky Theatre? He had only wanted information, of course, but at the time the bald, businesslike manner of the transaction had shocked me.

I remembered Anna in Moscow urging me to give in to Vasily, to become his mistress. I remembered thinking that I could almost do so, if not for the prospect of sharing the man I loved with another woman. Ever since I had known Vasily I had presumed that if he wanted me at all, it was as his mistress, not as his wife; that even if he took me as his wife, he would expect me to share him with others. I never gave him credit for having the least bit of his own self-command—never thought of him as a moral agent, who might of his own free will choose to be bound to one woman forever. I felt that I had done him an awful wrong.

Words of contrition hovered upon my lips, but I could not speak them—not now, while he spoke to me with such over-weening self-assurance. If I had overheard a man speaking to one of my sisters like this, I would have been fit for murder... I groped for the words.

"You can't speak of beguiling me, Vasily, as though I had no mind or judgement of my own; as though I were no better than a dumb animal."

There was a blank silence. He said in quite a different voice, "I never meant—"

"You've said it many times by now." In the hot stillness, I gulped for breath and tried again. "And you can't speak of *having* me, either, as though I were a pair of cuff-links, or—or a cup of tea. I won't be bought, and I won't be *had.* I'm a person, too."

This time the silence went on so long that I might almost have thought that he had gone away, if not for the transmitter's soft crackling. The longer this went on, the more afraid I felt.

"Why don't you say something?" I asked at last.

"I don't know that I should," he replied—and his voice was very subdued. But he did go on, after all: "To me, you've never been a cup of tea. I esteem you more greatly than any other woman I've known."

I knew precisely what Mimi would say to that: "And what a great deal of work that must take," I echoed, with an audacity that surprised even myself. "Don't you see that it makes no difference whether you think I'm a cup of tea, or a masterpiece in oils? Either way, you still think of me as a thing you can have. All your grand sacrifices are to say: if I pay a high enough price, then I'm sure to have what I want. That's part of what I mean, when I say I don't want to be treated as a dainty."

"Then I won't," he said, again with that note of desperation in his voice. "What's the other part?"

I closed my eyes, let out a sigh, and told him my greatest fear.

"The truth is, you want me now," I said. "But if I let you have me, what then? How could I possibly keep your attention? All your life you've gone from one woman—or man—to the next. Why should I be any different?"

Again, the silence was so profound that I feared he would never speak again. Perhaps this was the moment at which I would make him angry! But no—at last, he sighed.

"I told you it would be the most foolish decision of your life," he said bleakly. "Once, I might have tried telling you that you're different to the rest—but the truth is, you aren't. You're right: you oughtn't to be treated like a dainty; you ought to be loved. You ought to have a man you can trust, who would never betray you. All of them deserved that, and none of them got it from me. I'm still not sure I know *how* to do any better." There was another silence; this one shorter than the first. Then he went on:

"There's nothing different about you. The difference, so far as there is one, is in me. I would have been happy once to go from one woman to another—never truly loving, always on my guard; a creature of appetite, wanting only to devour. Then…"

He had never really told me about the events which had led him to shed his fangs. He told me very little more, now. "It's a long story," he said, covering the tremble in his voice with a laugh. "I met a woman, and she was the death of me. I didn't love her; I see that now. I only wanted to use her, and perhaps one of the things I wanted to use her as was the instrument of my own salvation. But she said *no*. She wouldn't be used, and she refused to be my salvation. Instead, she had the nerve to offer me her forgiveness—and the opportunity to relinquish my fangs. In a moment of weakness, I succumbed…Molly! Are you there?"

He broke in on his own story with such an anxious note in his voice that I wanted to laugh in spite of myself. "Was she the one for whom you stole Missy's diamonds?"

"Yes, but that's not important." He took a deep breath. "I had no fangs. I had no salvation. I had no woman to dull the pain of everything I had lost. I went to Paris and tried to pick up my life where I had left it off, with Mimi. But I couldn't bear it any more. I could never forget that I had paid for every caress. I saw how I was endured with contempt, and I knew I deserved it. If I still wanted that, I could have it. Now I think I'd sooner shoot myself. Then I met you." He drew another deep, ragged breath. "You've never despised me, Molly; you've never endured me, and you've never tried to sell me anything. I'm not man enough to resist such a thing; I'll confess to that."

He stopped speaking at last.

"You're silent," he said, when I could find nothing to say. "Tell me you're still there. Tell me you heard me."

"I heard," I said. Perhaps I felt the same way as he had, a little while ago—speechless, and with a great deal to think on. "Only I don't know what to say."

"Then don't," he said. "But know that no argument, no plea, will sway me. Little mouse, I'm too great a villain to let you graciously alone. Perhaps I'll make you love me, or perhaps I'll make you hate me; but don't ask me to leave you, because I won't do it. You'll have to shoot me first."

There came the unmistakable click of his transmitter switching off, and I found myself alone in the close darkness of my room. It was a hollow threat, of course: he must know how much he was at my mercy. He must know that if I truly came to hate him, I could with a word betray him to his enemies.

I nearly screamed when another voice suddenly echoed in my ear.

"Oh, what a villain I am!" Mimi mocked. *"Your pleas are useless! If you do not marry me, I will punish you horribly! I will dangle after you like a lovesick puppy, and then you will be sorry!* Dark, if you want him shot, I shall be *more* than happy

121

to oblige. But perhaps that will not be necessary. It's always possible he'll learn to cook duck."

From which I divined that Mimi had been listening in on the whole thing. In a way, it was rather a relief to have someone I could scold.

Chapter X.

I awoke the following morning from unsettling dreams. I saw my father with a pale, set face going through the locked drawers of Sir Humphrey's desk, searching for something with a kind of mute desperation which communicated itself to me, so that I watched with my heart in my throat to see what he might do when he found it. At length he did find it: a ledger book wedged into the very back of the very lowest drawer. He did not open it. He only sat down behind the desk, buried his face in his hands, and remained there a while in a posture of abject despair. I felt, as clearly as I ever have in the presence of an imprint, the sick resignation that swept over him at the mere sight of the hidden book, and even in my dream I knew that what I saw was some truth sunk deep into the bones of the house.

My room was darker than the lateness of the hour would suggest, and outside the wind howled and rattled at the house like a wild beast trying to get in. Even in my room, sheltered as it was by the loggia, its hot, moist breath stirred the syrupy air. When I rose and opened the curtains I found that a thin puddle had crept beneath the locked French doors and was oozing across the tiled floor. Outside, leaves and twigs scurried past my window. The sea was no longer visible, nor the city. The house stood alone, cut off and beleaguered by cloud and rain: on the hillside all around us the banian-trees rippled in the wind, reaching out their fingerlike roots as though they would have liked to seize upon the castle—sink in their teeth, and crush and devour until there was nothing of the alien structure left but rubble!

The scene was utterly wild and desolate; the day fit for treasons, stratagems, and spoils. What if Sir Humphrey chose this day to immure me, like his wife, in some noisome hole? What if he spirited me away to some place where my friends would never find me? Was it possible that this storm would cut me off entirely from all aid? Hastening to my pillow, I drew out the transmitter that dwelt beneath it, fitted it to my ear and switched it on. At once I heard Nijam saying with some asperity, "—can't even sleep between unironed sheets, and you want the duck to go without fresh, dry bedding—Is that you, Dark?"

"Y-yes," I panted. "It's nothing. I only wanted to see whether the transmitter would still work in all this weather."

"It's low-frequency, Dark; it can manage a bit of rain. —Let me know if you have any difficulty finding what we need, Schmidt."

Reassured, I left Nijam to arrange Bill's bedding and turned my mind to my dreams.

What had troubled my father so much in his final months? I never remembered seeing him worried, agitated, or despairing. I had always imagined him drifting about this house with the same detached serenity I recalled from him at home, in life—until the business with which he was entrusted, failed and died of sheer neglect. But that was not how the castle remembered him. Now, I saw him acting with decision and vigour towards some definite goal…no: towards some truth, which terrified even as it compelled. And I had never known!

No, my father had not drifted through life in sloth and ease. Whatever he had done with his affairs, he had not entirely neglected them.

I sighed, thinking of the dream in which I had seen him go down the path towards the chapel—and of the vision I had had before that, of the man covered in blood. I did not know what to do about *those* apparitions, but it was evidently time I had a look through Sir Humphrey's desk myself.

This morning, the Blister appeared in due course with a key to unlock my door, and Mimi followed on her heels with the teacup. I found Sir Humphrey at the breakfast-table in high spirits. "I shall be spending the day in Victoria," he announced, cracking open a hard-boiled egg with a swift, decisive blow of his spoon. "I have a new investor to meet with."

I knew he must be referring to Schmidt, so I only opened my blue eyes very wide and said, "In *this* weather? Will you be safe?"

"I should like to see the bit of wind and rain that can keep me from discharging my duties," Sir Humphrey said, with a nobility of resolution which quite defeated me. In the course of the morning he set out; and an hour later, while Mrs Lister was busy making her morning visit to Lady Seton, Mimi and I gathered at the study door. This—like every other door in this house, it seemed—was locked.

"You keep watch," Mimi told me, "and I'll pick the lock."

I leaned against the wall beside her, grateful for the sombreness that ruled over this house if it meant that we would be left to our own devices this morning. The servants must be busy tidying the rooms, for the entrance-hall in which we worked was for the moment deserted.

"I'm sorry I snapped at you last night," I told Mimi. "I suppose it doesn't matter if you heard everything. Only I know Vasily would have hated it."

"Of course he would," Mimi said with a sniff. "He should accustom himself to it, though, if he wishes to pretend he is sorry. People who are really sorry for their sins don't try to hide them."

She was right, in a way; but I resolved not to induce any more midnight confessions via transmitter. Even former monsters are entitled to their privacy.

"Was he telling the truth, then?" I asked. "About you and him, I mean; in Paris."

Mimi shrugged. "To me it did not sound like a lie."

"I suppose I ought to thank you," I said at length, with a self-conscious laugh, "for bringing him to repent his wicked ways."

That surprised her. "Me?"

"Well, you are always telling him such a lot of hard truths; I presume that you must have done so in Paris, too."

"Oh, that?" Mimi gave an unladylike snort. "When it profits me, I *do* know how to bite my tongue and tell a man what he wants, Dark; give me credit for that. Nor am I a fool, to throw away an imperial Grand Duke! Every man who pays for a woman knows—or suspects—that she only loves him for money, and that is enough for most of them. Vasya ought to have been happy with me—he *would* have been happy, if he hadn't already been eaten up with guilt, and with longing for something better. Ah! Here we are."

The lock clicked, and I caught the door-handle to turn it. Our way into the study was open. Mimi straightened. "What he told you about Paris was the truth," she added, "but he hasn't told you everything about the other woman, the one who came before. He never told me, either, but I think the truth of it was a little less pretty than *I wanted her and she said no.*"

I was not sure what to say to that. Mimi crossed the study to the French doors onto the loggia, and set to work picking that lock, too. "Keep watch in the hall," she told me over her shoulder. "I am going to crack every lock I find in this room."

I settled onto the sofa with the second volume of *Can You Forgive Her?* just in case Mrs Lister should emerge from the depths of the house to demand why I was loitering in the hall. I stared at the words without quite seeing them, however. All I could think of was Vasily—Vasily, who had listened with astonishingly little demur to all the demands I had made of him on the previous evening, who had admitted that he ought to have done better, and who had at length told me *something* about the past of which he was so ashamed, even if it was not the whole truth.

Vasily, who was still keeping *something* of it back from me. Surely Mimi was right, that people who have repented for their sins don't try to keep them secret.

Yet Mimi had still been quite definite that she had done her best to charm Vasily, and the failure had been on his part, not hers.

I returned to the study door. Mimi was within, attacking the drawer locks one by one. "Do you think it's true, then?" I asked her. "That he's really changed? That he isn't just doing this for *my* sake?"

Mimi barely spared a glance from her work. "I've said so, haven't I? More than once."

127

I bit my lip. "Do you think he has changed *enough?*"

"Why are you asking *me?* You should make up your own mind about that." Mimi finished her work with a grunt of satisfaction, and stood. "Vasya said something very odd to me on the train. *I know how to make a woman want me, Mimi, but how do I make her trust me?*"

In a way, it was comforting to know that I plagued Vasily's thoughts as inescapably as he plagued mine. "And what did you say?"

"I told him, *Why do we trust anyone, you tallow-head? Why do you trust Alphonse Schmidt?*" Mimi watched me through narrowed eyes. "But it's more complicated than that, isn't it?"

"What do you mean?"

She shrugged. "I don't know. Sometimes I wonder whether it's Vasily you don't trust; or whether it's yourself." The words reminded me of something Nijam had said not so long ago, but Mimi gave me little time to ponder them. She gestured towards the desk. "It's all done. If someone comes, I'll warn you over the transmitter, and you can go out by the door to the loggia."

Wrenching my attention back to the job at hand, I handed my book to Mimi, slipped into the study, and allowed her to close and re-lock the door behind me. I slid into the big leather chair that stood behind the desk and paused to consider my main objective. Perhaps this ought to be the ledger I had seen in my dream, but in any event I must go over every scrap of paper I could find, seeking answers to all the questions we had, between us, collected.

I had got no further than this when I glanced up to see my father's imprint.

He stood on the far side of the desk, both hands planted

stubbornly upon its surface; he had gone quite red in the face, and was absolutely shouting at me! I recoiled in astonishment. The reader knows that I cannot claim to have been a *good* child; but never in my naughtiest moments had I seen my father angry like *this*. Indeed I could not remember having ever seen him angry at all—yet here he stood with flashing eyes and lips drawn back in something almost like a snarl.

Of course I could not *hear* what he was saying in so agitated a manner, any more than I could tell to whom he was saying it. I knew to whom the desk belonged. But my father had already been dying of plague by the time Sir Humphrey had returned to Hong Kong, and the man before me was clearly in the best of health.

I think that I must already have had a premonition of what was to come; but it was a premonition, no more. Had I guessed the awful truth, I should have rejected the thought out of hand, wondering whether my mind really was diseased.

"Dark," Mimi called softly, over the transmitter. "The Blister just came up from the back of the house. You had better hurry."

I startled, and the imprint, which had loomed over me so angrily, dissipated altogether. I reminded myself that although the housekeeper was unlikely to intrude upon her master's locked study, she had been required to keep an eye upon *me*. If she could not find me, she was bound to become suspicious.

I reached out, therefore, and began to go through the big mahogany drawers which had been unlocked for me by Mimi. They contained papers, mostly—sheafs of letters, bills of lading, and so forth. In the bottom-most drawer I found something truly odd: a jewel-box. Opening it, I drew out the first of the little velvet pouches which came to hand and found a handsome aquamarine-and-pearl collar which I had

129

last seen in London adorning Lady Seton's neck. I must have made a sound of surprise indicative of pearls, for over the transmitter, Mimi's practised ear detected it at once.

"What is it, Dark? what have you found?"

"Lady Seton's jewels," I answered, staring at them in fascination. "Why should he have *these* in his desk?"

"He means to prevent her running away with them, of course," Mimi said. "Strange! I should sooner expect him to keep them in his safe."

I glanced about the room as I paged through the sheaf of letters, being sure to glance at each one. "Did you find the safe?"

"Not yet," she said with a sigh. "The butler is a clam, and I suppose I am too fine a lady, now, to retrieve his secrets in the customary manner. Have you found anything interesting, beside the jewels?"

"Nothing," I said with a sigh, smoothing the letters once more into their native habitation. "I'm afraid that Sir Humphrey is entirely respectable. No gambling debts, love letters, risky speculations, or embarrassing preoccupations." And no ledger, either! I pulled open the next drawer and elicited the bills of lading. "All his correspondence is with his lawyers and agents and the captains of his ships, and his bills of lading…" I ran a finger down the first, and then began checking them against the next. "Tea, raw silk, herbal remedies, and occasionally some porcelain, all packed into chests. I can't imagine what—"

"Dark," Mimi interrupted, in a voice of concentrated agitation, "get out of there at once. Sir Humphrey has come home."

I stiffened; the blood seemed to congeal in my veins. "He's

back? Already?" I glanced at the clock, and then at the French doors, which opened onto the leeward side of the house and were thus sheltered from the driving rain. I could not imagine what might have brought Sir Humphrey hurrying home in such weather, barely within three hours of setting out.

Then Mimi spoke again, her voice little more than a hoarse whisper.

"Get rid of your transmitter," she said. "Vandergriff is with him."

With that, the connection fizzled and went dead as she followed her own advice.

From the entrance-hall of the castle, with its echoing white marble and dark lintels, I could now hear male voices, and footsteps treading nearer. Sir Humphrey seemed in a good mood, his booming voice discussing his new German investor. For a moment I sat numb and motionless at the desk. Vandergriff must have returned to port, no doubt as a result of the inclement weather. My former fiancé was a man who wielded the power, not only of untold wealth, but also any number of prosthetic enhancements. Having cut away everything soft and humane and replaced it with cold steel, Griff heard everything—saw everything—knew everything. I knew a great deal better than to hope that he had forgiven me for my attempt upon the Noor-Jahan, or the two million pounds it had cost him to replace it, or the fact that in the end I had turned down his offer of marriage.

It was this man who now approached me in Sir Humphrey's company—I could not tarry. With a movement of my foot I closed the drawer at my side; meanwhile, I switched off my transmitter and wrenched it from my ear, praying that Griff's own transmitters had not somehow detected the ones Mimi and I had used. The French doors stood unlocked behind me. Even as Sir Humphrey's key rattled in the lock behind me—how I blessed Mimi for having the presence of mind to lock that door between us!—I wrenched open the French doors and slipped out into the stifling wind. The loggia, at a glance, was mercifully empty. The verandah looked out upon a hillside that had become one sheet of running water. I took three steps to the brink, opened the hand concealed within my skirts, and let my transmitter fall, together with its battery, into the nearest runnel of water. It was swept into the undergrowth, and I never saw it again.

Now I was truly cut off from my friends!

I turned from the rail with an idea of running up the nearest spiral staircase to the upper loggia, where I might seek refuge in my room. That, alas! was not to be. From behind the stair a wild figure appeared, giving me such a start that I choked on my own indrawn breath. It was the beachcomber I had noticed on the previous morning. His tangled beard fluttered like a flag in the wind, showing a gleam of yellow teeth. If this was a smile, I liked it even less than I had liked the last. Surely he must have seen me emerge from the study!

He moved forward again. It was only at that moment that I saw he held an axe crosswise before him. A sick wave of nausea swept over me at the sight; I gave way one step, and then another, as he approached. For a moment all I could think was that the man who had seemed so pitiable and frail yesterday gazing up at me from the verandah looked a great deal more wiry and threatening today.

Then I gathered up my wits and considered how best to preserve myself. I might try showing him a clean pair of ankles. But if I fled—no. I did not dare to turn my back on the man. Instead, I gave way another step, and said in the steadiest voice I could summon, "Put down that axe at once!"

To this he paid no heed, only advancing again. My retreat brought me once again abreast of the French doors to the study. The beachcomber reached out and wrenched them open—an operation which the wind assisted with a bang, so that to the men inside, we must have been revealed quite suddenly, like the actors on a stage. For a moment the blood fled to my heart, so that I felt dizzy with fear as I looked from Sir Humphrey to Mr Vandergriff, and the papers which the wind sent flying about the room. Then the beachcomber extended his axe with a threatening motion, and I yielded, not without some calculation, to my terror.

"Sir Humphrey!" I shrieked. "Griff!" —and I rushed into the study, putting myself behind them. "Oh, thank heaven! Who *is* this madman?"

"I caught her," the beachcomber told Sir Humphrey in a voice like the rasp of an unoiled hinge, "sneaking out of the study just as you came home."

The two of them turned to gaze at me—Sir Humphrey with genuine puzzlement, but Griff with a cold grey stare that made my heart sink, recalling that he was celebrated as a detective. After a moment of this scrutiny, my erstwhile fiancé turned to Sir Humphrey.

"Are those French doors ordinarily left open?"

"No," Sir Humphrey said, puzzled. "I keep them locked as a general rule."

"And your desk?" Griff pressed. My heart sank further still as he bent and drew out first one drawer, and then another. Observing this, Sir Humphrey's face darkened.

"What is the meaning of this, Miss Dark?" he demanded.

I was prepared for this possibility, of course; I had spent an anxious half-hour over breakfast dreaming up my defence, when I ought to have been choking down cold toast and kippered herring. "I *saw* something," I whispered. "The shadow of a man passing through the loggia and into the study. It spoke to me, Sir Humphrey. I—I had to follow. I was too frightened to refuse."

"The doors," Griff said coldly, "were locked."

"Oh, no," I told him with an earnest shake of my head. "The ghost unlocked them."

"How can a spirit unlock a door?" Sir Humphrey asked, but I simply shook my head with the most innocent air I could muster. I was playing a dangerous game, of course: there was a reason I had dreaded being caught. Sir Humphrey had gone to some pains to convince the doctor, if not also himself, that I was mad. Now, acting the lunatic was my only hope of convincing him that I was not also malicious. I repressed a shudder, wondering whether I might merely be trading a gaol-cell for a lunatic asylum!

In one sense my gambit was a success: Sir Humphrey turned to Griff and said, "It's no use questioning her. She seems to have caught whatever has been ailing your aunt. Evidently someone has been intruding where they shouldn't, but Miss Dark is surely incapable of managing it."

"Perhaps Miss Molly is more capable than she looks," Griff drawled. "Things tend to disappear when she gets into places she shouldn't. Don't you keep the Noor-Jahan in this room somewhere?"

Sir Humphrey absolutely gaped at him for a moment. "By Jove!" he gasped. He darted across the room to a small, hidden cupboard over the side-board and opened the small safe within. This was obliging of him, and on Mimi's behalf I felt quite grateful. The safe was not a large one, as I have said. It was quite empty, apart from the great, gleaming jewel which Nijam had created as an imitation of the Noor-Jahan.

The reader may remember that Nijam herself, in the guise of the disinherited Begum of Bihar, had sold the ersatz diamond to Griff as a replacement for the real stone, which had disappeared from the British Museum shortly after receiving a visit from Vasily and myself. At the sight of the great imitation diamond, Sir Humphrey let out a sigh of relief. "Safe!" he said. "For once, my boy, you've let your imagination get the better of you."

"Better test it," Griff said laconically. He had not moved from my side; and even if he had, the beachcomber stood before the closed French doors, still grasping his axe. Escape was impossible.

"I've never been so insulted in my life," I said, but perhaps I did not speak loudly enough to be heard over the wind.

Sir Humphrey patted his pockets. "Have you a pocket-knife?" he asked Griff; but that gentleman shook his head. For a moment they both seemed at a loss; and then Sir Humphrey made a sound of satisfaction, and drew out Lady Seton's jewel-box from the open desk!

At once I knew that *that* part of our game, at least, was up. Nijam's success in passing off the artificial stone as the Noor-Jahan lay entirely in the fact that, being harder than the glass which is commonly used to impersonate diamonds with the unwary, it was strong enough to resist being scratched by anything softer than corundum. Hitherto, the artificial diamond had stood up to Sir Humphrey's pocket-knife with ease. Now, however—he drew out a flashing diamond ring, and my heart fell.

There was a breathless silence, and I am afraid that Sir Humphrey made an indelicate exclamation. His face reddened. "False, by Jove*!*"

"Show me!" Griff demanded. A light shone cold and blue in the depths of his right eye, illuminating the imitation diamond as he raised it for inspection. It took him no more than a moment to satisfy himself that Sir Humphrey told the truth; there was an absolute silence as he put the stone down, and I wondered whether he had really expected to find that the Begum's gemstone was the real Noor-Jahan.

"I spent," he told Sir Humphrey in a voice of concentrated fury, *"two million pounds* to buy this! And now you tell me it was a fake?"

"It was real when we bought it from the Begum!" Sir Humphrey protested. "That hussy has exchanged it for a bit of trumpery glass!!"

"I *beg* your pardon!" I cried, divining that the *hussy* he referred to was myself. "How could *I* have stolen your diamond, when I have scarcely been in this house a full day, and I've been locked into my room for most of it?"

"It wouldn't be the first time you've tried to get your hands on the Noor-Jahan," Griff said, more calmly. After the first outburst, he seemed to have recovered himself. "This diamond has now disappeared on two different occasions, and *you* have been in the vicinity both times."

I thought that this was extremely unjust. Just because I had been caught sneaking about the room where Sir Humphrey kept his safe, I was to be accused of stealing the Noor-Jahan a *second* time? Griff had a careful mind, and his prosthetic eye saw further than most. He must see that this Noor-Jahan was something rarer and brighter than mere glass. He must recall—as Sir Humphrey did not—that the diamond sold by the Begum had only been tested with steel, and not with another diamond. He must at least *suspect*—if he really had any respect for my abilities—that the first theft had succeeded!

Then, with a shudder, I recalled the man telling me—in his peculiarly bloodless fashion—that he amused himself hunting down criminals. I now had ample evidence that he did not much care whether the methods he used were cricket, and it occurred to me that, having failed to catch me once, he did not mean to allow me a second chance to escape.

Griff's cold, grey eyes were fixed upon me, missing no detail of my expression.

"You are persecuting me," I whispered, raising my chin with tremulous defiance. "You are angry with me for rejecting your suit, and so you will prosecute me as a thief, when you know very well that I am only a poor weak woman! Well, I am at your mercy! Have me searched, if you can be so ungentlemanly—ransack my room, and see whether I have the Noor-Jahan hidden anywhere about me!"

"Thank you; I will," Griff said promptly.

"Mrs Lister will see to it," Sir Humphrey put in, ringing the bell. I perceived that my touching speech had not touched them in the slightest.

"Is there anyone who might mount a watch on her?" Griff added in a low voice. "One of the footmen, perhaps?"

"I don't think so: they're Chinese, and lazy fellows."

"What about *him?*" Griff asked with a jerk of his head towards the beachcomber, who all this time had been hovering much too close with his axe. "He's a white man."

"He's a beachcomber, and has gone half native himself," Sir

137

Humphrey said with a contemptuous look. "Who knows what else might disappear with one of his sort in the house?"

"*Quis custodiet?*" Griff murmured, but there was a gleam in his eye now of pure speculation. He turned to the beach-comber. "I can make you more than human, boy, and give you a paying job. You'd like that, wouldn't you?"

The beachcomber, who was surely too old to be addressed as a *boy,* sent Griff a look half of terror and half of longing. More than human—what was *that* to mean? his look seemed to inquire. *I* could have answered that. Evidently Griff meant to make a prosthete of the man, with a view to controlling his actions. I did not know whether to be sorry for the fellow, or relieved that at least I should not be wholly at his mercy.

Just then, however, Mrs Lister entered. She raised her brows at the sight of our odd assembly—the beachcomber with his axe, Sir Humphrey grasping the false Noor-Jahan as though it might be as precious as the real thing, and Lady Seton's jewels lying in a tumble of black velvet bags upon the blotter—but said nothing.

"Ah, Mrs Lister. Take Miss Dark to her room and search her and her belongings," Sir Humphrey ordered, wheezing a little with emotion. "The Noor-Jahan has disappeared and been replaced with a fake!"

"As you say, sir," Mrs Lister replied, sending me a look of pure venom. "If she has it, I'll find it. Come along, miss."

"One moment," Griff added. He came to stand before me, and his fingers tapped a little pattern upon his temple. For a moment he stared fixedly into my eyes—trying, no doubt, whether he might pick up a radio signal. I returned a fervent prayer of gratitude to the Author of my existence that I had rid myself of my transmitter, and in so unobtrusive a manner that the beachcomber had not seen it fall. When no success greeted Griff's attempts, he made a soft *tch* and actually searched me— touching first one ear, then the other, and finally probing my coiffure. I shuddered, recalling a previous occasion upon which this man had touched me, and the dreadful strength of his hands around my neck.

"Take her away," Griff told Mrs Lister at last. To Sir Humphrey, as I was hurried from the room, I heard him remark, "It beats me what she's playing at. But she's got no confederates, at least."

Nor did I. I kept an eye open as Mrs Lister marched me to my room, but of Mimi there was no sign.

Chapter XI.

Having one's person and belongings searched by a grim-faced Scottish housekeeper is not the pleasantest of experiences, and I don't recommend it to the reader. Of course the Blister did not find the Noor-Jahan: that was long gone, handed over to the agents of the rightful owner—for if anyone could be described as its rightful owner, the real Begum of Bihar best fit that description.

Mrs Lister departed, locking the door behind her, and I was left alone to pace and worry. Sir Humphrey and Griff clearly held me in great suspicion—and although Lady Seton was likely to welcome the latter with open arms, it was Griff who posed the greatest danger to my crew. Until his return, Sir Humphrey had been content to consider me merely mad, and not malicious.

How were we to carry out our plan beneath the very nose of a prosthete detective? The whole scheme had been built upon the presumption that Griff would *not* be in Hong Kong. Now, I speedily reviewed the situation. Griff knew that Vasily and I had colluded to steal the Noor-Jahan in London. He must recall finding us in the exhibition room housing the Seton Collection, the safe open and the diamond missing—until I had forced it into his hand. The real Noor-Jahan being quite catastrophically haunted by centuries' worth of depravity and bloodshed, and Griff being entirely unprepared to face an onslaught of agony-stricken imprints, the effect must have been absolutely shattering. Vasily and I had elected to leave the Noor-Jahan behind in order to secure our escape, but Mimi, happening along a little later, had retrieved the stone from the unconscious detective's grasp before passing it on to its rightful owners.

As far as Griff knew, therefore, I had been in the vicinity of the stone's disappearance, but he could not say for certain that it was I who had taken it. I had certainly *returned* it to him. The ultimate thief might equally well have been Vasily, or anyone else—a museum guard, for instance, who had stumbled upon the scene while Griff was having fits. In the immediate aftermath, any natural instinct Griff may have felt to hunt down the culprits must have been quenched by the shock he had received from the imprints, and by Sir Humphrey's desire to cover up his embarrassment by quickly purchasing the false diamond from the false Begum, as performed by our own Miss Nijam. Now, not only did Griff not know who had taken the real stone; he also did not know whether the stone purchased from the purported Begum had ever been real to begin with, or whether it had been stolen at a later date.

It was entirely too much to hope, thought I mournfully, that a man as coldly calculating as Warren Vandergriff would allow himself to be dazzled by all this uncertainty. Now that he had recovered from his shock, he seemed ready to pursue me with all the ruthlessness in his nature, never mind if I was guilty or not.

I attempted to console myself that at least, if Griff put me behind bars, I was unlikely to go mad in a lunatic asylum. But this was scant comfort. I did not like the thought of going mad in a gaol, either.

In the meanwhile, what could I do? My fingers strayed to my ear out of sheer habit, but my transmitter was gone, washed down the hill. Even if it could be found, and—still less likely—made to work again, how could I risk using it, when Griff might be listening in? From now on, the only safe way to conspire would be in person, and then only with the greatest care, lest Griff should have concealed one of his little listening-bugs on our persons, or in our surroundings. Even if Mimi was still in the vicinity, how could we collude under these circumstances?

Was the plan still good? After all, Griff knew very little that Sir Humphrey did not, and indeed we had constructed our plan upon the presumption that they had been in close communication. Since Griff's presence impeded our communications, from here, if I went on at all I must go blindly, abandoning myself to the machinations of Sir Humphrey and the foresight of my friends. I thought of the mistakes we had made in Russia, carrying on with our plan even as Vasily became more deeply enmeshed within his family's dreadful power. I did not wish to do as he had, and allow my personal desires and animosities to decoy the whole crew into useless danger—certainly not when the primary beneficiary of such danger would likely be myself.

Again I found myself more inclined to withdraw at once, than to go on. Perhaps, only a day or two previously, I might have. But I had now come to suspect that Sir Humphrey was a bad man in ways that went beyond whatever his conduct might have been towards my own family. How much suffering could have been avoided, had he not given himself over to careless greed? How much more suffering might ensue in the future if I ran away at the first setback? If I was the only person who could investigate Sir Humphrey's misdeeds, let alone hold him accountable, then it did not matter how minor those misdeeds were compared to what he had almost certainly done to his labourers and the other poor people of Tai Ping Shan. It was surely my duty to them, to pursue him as far and as fast as I could.

Perhaps, I thought, my father had come to a similar conclusion.

There was more to my father's final days than at first I had suspected. He had been at odds with *somebody* before he died. Could that person have been Sir Humphrey? Had my father taken ill *after* Sir Humphrey's return? If Sir Humphrey was a bad man *now*—and my crew were convinced that he was— then was it not the likeliest thing in the world that he had also been a bad man in my father's day?

For many long years my feelings toward my father had been ones of muted resentment, but now I found myself looking at matters from another point of view entirely. Again I thought of all the things Sir Humphrey had said, the subtle barbs painting my father as lazy, improvident, foolish and idealistic. Perhaps, all along, it was Sir Humphrey who had been wrong, and my father who had been right! Perhaps, all along, he had cultivated that resentment to keep me from developing any curiosity about my father's final doings!

Again, I felt that no words were bad enough for his hypocrisy; they stuck in my throat, a heavy mass that made it hard to breathe.

I had a weary long day of it, shut up in that stifling heat with only my own unhappy thoughts for company. There was no sign of Mimi, and I could not even inquire of the Chinese servants, since Mrs Lister brought my midday meal. Even had my door been unlocked, I would scarcely have been at greater liberty, for the storm had now reached its height. The house shuddered in the ceaseless blast of the wind and the driving gusts of rain, an island in a grey and watery world. Never have I ever felt more desperately alone. I could not make myself read, and it was unwise to write or plan. All I could do was think—of my predicament, which was bad enough, or of Vasily, which was equally agitating. There he was in Victoria directing the job, and I was now utterly reliant upon him and the others.

At length darkness fell, and to my surprise, Mrs Lister brought up Sir Humphrey's request that I should join him and Mr Vandergriff for the evening meal. My suspicions told me that this was most likely with a view to getting me out of my room so that Griff could fill it with transmitters. Indeed, upon descending to the dining-room, I was met by Sir Humphrey alone.

"Miss Dark," he said with a kindly smile, as though he had not very recently accused me of stealing a diamond worth two million pounds, "do be seated. I'm glad you felt well enough to join us."

I did not know whether I would be able to stomach any dinner in the present company, but it was incumbent upon me to collect as much useful information as possible. The room was all white plaster and high, vaulting timber beams with punkah fans swaying to and fro, moving the hot air. There also appeared to be a genuine fifteenth-century tapestry hanging upon the wall, although I felt certain from the smell that this, like so many other things in the castle, would prove to be infested with mildew—as indeed one might expect of an item designed for Flemish winters and transplanted, regardless of need or suitability, to a Hong Kong summer. The table was a long one, made of some dark tropical wood, and was so enormous that it must have cost very little less than the tapestry itself.

Observing this echoing mediaeval splendour, I asked: "Where is Mr Vandergriff?"

"He'll be with us in a moment," Sir Humphrey said blandly. No doubt—as soon as he had finished laying traps for me!

"Mrs Lister must have told you she found nothing in my room," I told him, with very little effort putting a soft quiver into my voice. "You can't still believe I came into your house to rob you! Why are you keeping me shut up? What do you mean to do with me?"

He answered this question as easily as the last—and I shivered a little, reflecting that he was a good deal more composed than I liked him to be. "Well, of course, my dear, I'll take care of you. You are in some sort my responsibility, and I'm afraid you haven't been yourself lately. Of course I apologise for the suspicion that has fallen upon you, but you must see that when a jewel worth two million pounds goes missing, one cannot rule out any possibility! That is all behind us now. You did not have the jewel. Someone else must have taken it. Or perhaps we were cheated by that virago of a Begum. Griff will look into it."

I was quite certain he meant to do so. "And my maid?" I asked, equally piteously. "I haven't seen her all day."

"I have discharged your maid," Sir Humphrey said with an air of judicious resolution. "You need greater care than she can give. She has been paid and sent away."

145

"Sent away—in *this* weather?" I protested, really aghast.

"There's shelter in the hamlet down at Pok Fu Lum," he said. "Pray don't worry about her. I shall engage someone else to look after you—the best to be had on the island."

I wondered whether the hamlet down at Pok Fu Lum was still standing, or whether it had, as seemed likely, been swept away by floodwater. Then I wondered again whether it was wise for me to remain in this house; and a third time, whether it would be possible at all for me to escape, if I wished to. The storm had abated a little since its heights this afternoon, but was still blowing moist draughts through the great hall. In the meanwhile, it seemed clear that Sir Humphrey had returned to treating me, not as a thief, but a madwoman.

"Thank you, but truly I'd rather have Mimi back," I protested. Sir Humphrey smiled in a pitying sort of way, as though I couldn't be expected to know what was best for me. Griff entered the room.

"Ah, here's our final guest," Sir Humphrey said with ponderous cheer. "And how is that beachcomber fellow—Bone?"

"Bone will be as good as new in a day or two," Griff told him. Nor was I left to wonder what this might mean, for he turned to me to explain. "Bone has been given a prosthetic eye, which ought to be in good working order in a day or two, if everything heals well. I am not a surgeon, so it's possible that I have made some little error in the procedure."

I could make no reply to this. Oh, yes! it *was* just possible that tearing out a man's eye and cramming in a new one might disagree with him! I did not particularly like what I had seen of the beachcomber, but I found it absolutely deplorable that he should have been subjected to amateur surgery. Nevertheless, I accepted with clenched teeth the chair which Griff drew out to offer me, and was thus settled very decorously at the table. The two of them had, in the past six hours, accused me of madness and theft, dispatched the housekeeper to search me and my belongings, locked me into my room, and sent away my only friend and servant—but let it never be said they were not gentlemen!

"What brings you back to Hong Kong, Mr Vandergriff?" I asked, when I had recovered my equanimity sufficiently to speak.

"Please," he said, "call me Griff." I could make no reply to this either, and he added: "I turned back because of the storm. It was my idea to sail directly for home, but the skipper swore our course would take us directly into the typhoon, and so we were compelled to return to port. I've been here, you know, doing business with Sir Humphrey."

"Oh, yes," I said. "You told me that you meant to begin shipping goods from San Francisco to Hong Kong."

"Something like that," he said, evidently pleased with my apt recall. "Manufactures from American factories, Californian wheat, and anything else we could sell on this tiny island."

"And what will you bring from China to America in return?" I asked, out of genuine curiosity and perhaps a little suspicion.

"Labour, mainly. We have about as many coloureds as we want in the U.S., of course, now that the post-war labour shortage has been filled." It took me a moment to understand that by *post-war labour shortage* Griff was referring to that gap left in the economy of his country by the freeing of the slaves. "We put a stop to the coolie trade with the Chinese Exclusion Act of ten years ago—but they aren't so discriminating in Mexico, where there's still a hungry market for Chinese labour. Enough of the coolies still imagine that life will be

147

easier on a foreign plantation to sign indenture papers for as many years as it may take them to work off their passage. …Apart from labour: textiles, of course, and a quantity of tea, since the coolies drink it."

"I've heard they also consume a quantity of opium," I said, looking as innocent as possible.

"I'll ship no opium," Griff said with a decided shake of his head. "We've put a stop to that, too, in the U.S. Filthy, enervating habit!"

"Hear, hear!" Sir Humphrey said, raising his wine-glass. I wondered whether he was sincere, given the habits of his own workers.

I marvelled at the mind that could sneer at the opium trade but thought nothing of decoying living human beings into risky voyages across the sea to a land where they would be friendless and helpless, practically slaves, and unfamiliar with the language. Even if the United States government had now placed a ban on Chinese immigration for the future, there must be thousands of "coolies", as Griff so contemptuously called them, still working out the long term of their indentures on plantations across the continent. "And *is* life easier for the labourers on a plantation?"

Griff shrugged and laughed. That he was content with such an answer told me everything the unfortunate Chinese might expect in their new lives. I had heard something of the conditions suffered by the blacks on Caribbean and American plantations before the abolition of slavery, and could not imagine the Chinese being treated any better on those same plantations, by those same masters.

"Oughtn't they to be told what to expect?"

"That's their lookout," said Griff. "We don't sell them any

puff or nonsense. They know the terms, and it isn't up to us to make sure they are imagining correctly."

"But when they might so easily be exploited—"

"Exploitation," said Sir Humphrey majestically, "is the essence of trade! The free market allows certain forms of exploitation, and if people are foolish enough, or uncivilised enough, to indulge themselves in idleness or squalor, then they cannot expect to get ahead in life. We must not forget that the market may work for a man, as well as against him."

That might be so; but it struck me that there might also be other forces than the market at work: such as, for instance, venality and prejudice.

"I'm not in favour of exploiting anyone," Griff said—which was more than Sir Humphrey was prepared to say. "It's a free world, and nobody is forcing the coolies to make the journey. If they have any sense they must not expect things to be easy in a foreign land. But it's a better chance than they'll get here in China: they'll be free men if they can stick it out to the end of their term. If a Chinaman can't get rich in the Americas it is his own fault."

"I'm sure you know more about it than I do," I said meekly, for there was evidently no use in arguing. And if the unfortunate Chinese were unable to "stick it out", where should they be then? Laid in a shallow grave in a strange land, no doubt. Feeling fit for a few treasons, stratagems, and spoils of my own, I covered my indignation with an ingratiating smile. "You look a great deal better, Griff, since your attack in London."

He frowned at me. "Attack? What attack?"

"Oh! I heard that you'd received some sort of nervous shock, perhaps connected with the Noor-Jahan…"

149

"You *did* have a rather nasty turn," Sir Humphrey told him, helpfully. "Left you quite wobbly, too, for a few weeks."

"That had nothing to do with the diamond!" Griff snapped. Then he changed the subject altogether and asked Sir Humphrey a question about the German investor, and his interest in shipping goods from India as well as from Yunnan. So much for any hope that the Noor-Jahan might have left Griff a better and wiser man!

From there the conversation roamed at large until the gentlemen's cigars were brought and Mrs Lister informed me that she was ready to escort me back to my room. At this, I shrank away and cried out, "Oh, must I go back to my room already? I have been locked up there all afternoon!"

"Now then, Miss Dark," Sir Humphrey told me, "you know that you have been sleep-walking, and we only lock the doors to keep you safe."

"It's for your own good," Griff added. "I won't have my fiancée breaking her neck on those spiral staircases in the dark."

I inhaled a cupful of the damp air wrong and went into a coughing-fit. "I beg your pardon," I whispered, when I was able to speak. "Your *fiancée?*"

He raised an eyebrow. "Surely you cannot have forgotten your promise to marry me? *I* certainly have not."

Did he mean that to sound so very ominous? "But all that is at an end," I squeaked. "I told you so, that last evening at the British Museum."

"*I* don't recall any such thing," he said, dismissively. Quite likely that was true: at the time at which I had informed him of my change of heart, Griff had been writhing about under the influence of the Noor-Jahan. "Since you've cleared yourself

150

of the charge of theft, I don't see why we shouldn't pick up where we left off."

I was utterly at a loss. "But since then I've been married to someone else—to Vasily Nikolaevich, in fact."

"Who has since died," he said, with a dismissive wave of his hand. "You can't really mean to refuse me. There are girls in New York who'd kill for a chance to marry the Vandergriff millions. Besides, if you want to call it off, you had better return my gifts."

He was referring, of course, to the pearl *collier de chien* he had given me before Vasily's ball, as though to mark me as his own. That little toy was gone, sold in Ekaterinberg to assist us in our escape, probably for a fraction of what it was worth. I felt an almost hysterical laughter crawling up my throat at the thought that Griff should think me eager to marry him, after attempting to blackmail me with a pearl necklace!

It is probably too much to say that Sir Humphrey came to my rescue—but at that moment I should almost have been glad to see Missy of Roumania. "Don't press her," he told Griff. "It's as I said—Miss Dark has had a terrible shock lately, and is not quite herself. Ladies, God bless them! You must allow her a decent amount of time to mourn."

"Not quite herself! I can believe *that*," Griff muttered. "Has she seen a doctor for it?"

"Yes, and he has prepared a certificate to say that she is— ahem." —He whispered something behind his hand. Griff's brows rose.

"It's hard to believe. First Aunt Adelaide, and now Miss Dark!"

"I congratulate myself that if not for Lady Seton's doctor, Miss Dark's subtler symptoms might have gone undiagnosed for some time." At that, Sir Humphrey sent me a look that was almost gloating in its sense of triumph. I was sitting there with hot cheeks, feeling humiliated to be the subject of their discussions; but I saw that look and quite forgot my confusion.

"I would have imagined her to be quite sane, myself," Griff said meanwhile, with a mournful shake of his head. "How cunning these lunatics are!

I gathered up the self-command to protest. "To whom are you referring as a lunatic?" Sir Humphrey made no reply—to *me*.

"I expect to speak to my lawyer about lodging a permanent guardianship application as soon as this storm lets up. So you understand that Miss Dark is in no condition to assent to marriage."

"I'm perfectly in command of my wits," said I, now quite alarmed. No matter what the job required of me, I could not sit by in silence as they disposed of me as a madwoman. "And I don't mean to marry Mr Vandergriff! He and I would not suit each other at all!"

"Of course not," Sir Humphrey told me, in a humouring sort of voice. "No one shall force you to marry him, Miss Dark; you may put your mind at rest."

I swallowed hard. "What is going to happen to me?" My voice shook despite myself, for I did not like to let them know the fear which above all others had ever haunted my dreams. "Will you shut me up in a mad-house?"

"Not if you're a good girl, and let us give you all the peace and quiet you need," Sir Humphrey said. The man had the temerity to pat my hand. I felt nearly as sick as I had earlier that day, upon seeing the beach-comber with the axe. "Now, off you go with Mrs Lister, and take the dose the doctor left for you, so that you can sleep soundly."

Upstairs, Mrs Lister stood over me with such a steely look that I nearly had to swallow down the laudanum before she went away. She did eventually go, however, and I spat out the dose into my tooth-cup, making as little noise as possible. This done, I lay back in my chair, feeling trembly all over. I could see Sir Humphrey's game clearly enough now: he meant to keep me locked up, dosed with laudanum, as docile and quiescent as any opium-eater. If I *did* prove myself sane, there was Griff ready to march me to the altar.

And Sir Humphrey would do all this knowing full well— knowing as well as I did myself—that I was sane. *That*, I instinctively knew, was the significance of that gloating look he had given me at the dinner-table. Why else should he feel such a sense of triumph, unless this was his own revenge for the lost Noor-Jahan? I clapped a hand over my mouth, feeling once again sick with dread. *Think of the stakes*, I had told Vasily on the previous evening. Either I must ruin an innocent man, or he would have me locked up until I really did go mad. After that look, it was difficult even for me to believe in Sir Humphrey's innocence—but I closed my eyes and told myself that I might possibly be mistaken, all the same.

When I felt a little calmer, I conducted a swift search of the room. I found one of Griff's little bugs clinging to the underside of my bed, and another in the curtains. The transmitters scuttled about on eight tiny brass legs, for all the world like great clockwork spiders. I was distinctly tempted to open the window and hurl each of them into the darkness; but Griff would only replace them with more. On the other hand, if I allowed him to remain secure in the belief that he was listening in on me, he would, I hoped, leave me to my own

devices in other ways. If I was to carry our plan to fruition—
or at least if I was to escape the house—it would be best to lull
Griff into a sense of false security.

I let the bugs alone, therefore, and sat down at my writing-
desk, pulling a sheet of paper towards me. It was now
imperative to re-establish communications with the rest of
my crew. Sir Humphrey might have explained Mimi's absence,
but I did not think that she would relinquish me so tamely to
his care. With the storm abating, she would almost certainly
come to find me; and if that should happen, no word could
pass between us—not with Griff's bugs in the room.

For a moment, wistfully, I considered whether I ought to
take advantage of Mimi's coming to run away. But I had
already determined that *that* path ought to be closed to me;
and I had not yet investigated the chapel where my father
lay buried. Nijam would be disappointed in me if I did not.
Sighing, I searched the desk for paper and ink, and began
to write, telling my friends that I would try to be at the
chapel around midnight the next evening, weather permitting,
and on no account to try to rendezvous or speak with me
otherwise. This done, I punched a hole in the corner of the
envelope, attached it to a piece of thread from my sewing-
kit, and fixed it to the inside of the shutters that covered the
French door, where Mimi would be bound to see it if she
picked the lock. This done, I retired to my rest and slept very
badly all night, beset by the sounds of wind and water, and by
imprints or uneasy dreams. Once or twice I thought I heard
the shutters rattle; but I did not like to attract Griff's suspicion,
and so I did not rise from my bed.

Chapter XII.

In the morning, the clouds had cleared a little, and the wind had sunk at last to a languid breeze. I looked out upon a world streaming with murky rushing water. The Pok Fu Lum road had turned to a silvery ribbon, and every surface was scattered with debris—leaves, twigs, and one or two fallen trees. The lock on my shutters was open, the thread was snapped, and the letter was gone. I pushed open the doors and put out my nose, hoping for some other sign that my friends had been here in the night, and that I was not forgotten—perhaps even a transmitter which I could keep concealed in my room for use only at the utmost need—but there was none. There was only Mr Bone, the beachcomber, loitering outside my door. A damp, grubby-looking bandage was looped about his head, concealing one eye. Shuddering, I closed the shutters before he could see me and bolted the French doors from within.

Today I was released from my room for breakfast, which I took in the company of the gentlemen. Griff and Sir Humphrey made a laborious, infantile sort of conversation over the toast and kippers, as befitted a chat with a mad-woman. As the meal was drawing to its close I asked whether my room might be left unlocked today. This made Sir Humphrey and Griff exchange speaking looks.

"I don't see why not," said Griff.

Sir Humphrey pursed his lips, evidently ill pleased with the thought of letting me have any freedom at all. "What Miss Dark *needs*," he said, "is rest."

"Of course, but we can hardly keep her under lock and key like a criminal," said Griff. Sir Humphrey's brows rose as though for his part he thought this would be quite a reasonable course of action. "We don't want to provoke a turn for the worse, after all."

To this Sir Humphrey was reluctantly brought to agree, and I was, to my surprise, allowed the freedom of the house. My first object, of course, was to visit Lady Seton. The nurse, I conjectured, must take a few minutes each morning to visit the kitchen for a cup of tea, as she had upon the morning when Mimi and I had spoken with the unfortunate prisoner. My guess proved correct; and when I saw the nurse on her way to the kitchen, I crept in at the green-baize door, tiptoed into the sitting-room, and scratched upon Lady Seton's locked bedroom door.

"Lady Seton! It's me."

Within the room there was a scuffle, and the door rattled as she flung herself eagerly against it.

"Is that you, Miss Dark? Or is it a ghost?"

"I'm still not a ghost! See, I've brought you a newspaper." Although it was some days old due to the storm's disrupting the mail, it might nevertheless give her some hours of amusement, which would be better than being cooped up with nothing to do. She snatched it up and I added. "I'm sorry I couldn't bring you anything more interesting, but I can't get the door open myself. How are you?"

"I think I'm going mad in here," she said with a sob. "I keep seeing them all. All their faces…Say, are you sure you can't get word to Warren?"

"Perhaps I can do better than that," I told her. "Mr Vandergriff himself has returned to Hong Kong. But I'm afraid Sir Humphrey has him convinced that you are mad, and too excitable to be let out."

"But I'm not! I promise!"

"I don't think you are, either," said I. "Is there a message you would like me to give him?"

"Just tell him to come to see me," she said. "Sir Humphrey will try to prevent it, but I do not think he can bar the way to my own flesh and blood!"

I dared not stay longer, but I flatter myself that I left Lady Seton feeling more calm and hopeful than I had found her. Not wishing to leave by the main hall for fear of running into the nurse as she returned, I crept out by the doors which opened onto the loggia; and then, the coast being clear, I ventured down the stairs at the back of the house.

With a beating heart, I followed the wet, dripping path which led towards the chapel, which I had set as my *rendezvous* with my crew. I found it some way down the hill—a little white building in the same Tudor style as the main house, built next to the estate wall near a postern-gate leading onto the Pok Fu Lum road. It was overshadowed by the great banians, and but for the steaming tropical foliage, I might have thought myself a damsel in some mediaeval tale of knight-errantry. The gate towards the road was locked, but I did not think that this would present too great an obstacle to Mimi.

I next tested the knob of the chapel door itself: it turned, and the door opened a crack. My heart beat faster, making me feel a little dizzy—for despite the passing of the storm, the air was not much cooler and still very humid. I glanced around to see what my father's imprint was doing. To my surprise he was nowhere to be found, but there in the shadows beneath the trees was the same motionless, dreary figure I had first seen on the evening of my arrival. He was still barely visible in the deep shadows beneath the banian, but his body glistened with the blood of many wounds. My heart stuttered. For a long moment I only beheld the imprint in silent terror, feeling his agony and helpless wrath. Then footsteps beat upon my ears, and Mr Bone came down the path towards me.

"You're to return to the house," he told me, making a snatch for my arm. I wrenched it away—I thought my own limbs moved slowly, as though through honey, but I was quick enough to evade him. Turning my back, I hurried up the hill, towards the house.

Sir Humphrey may have permitted me to leave my room, but he had evidently set the beachcomber to prevent me wandering very far. At the foot of the steps leading up towards the house, I turned to see the man labouring after me, puffing like a bellows. I was short of breath myself, drenched in perspiration; and once again I had the uncomfortable feeling that the island, left with no other way to express its hostility, had decided to suffocate me.

Below, the beachcomber gazed up at me with one bloodshot eye, and another that was little more than a bloodstain on a bandage. That recalled me to the fact that he was also, now, a tool of Griff's, every bit as much as the gleaming little clockwork spiders in my bedroom. I shuddered. I did not wish to be spied upon—by Bone, by Griff, or by anyone. Nor did I wish to return to my room. Instead, perhaps fruitlessly, I turned aside and began to circle the house by way of the garden, which was still waterlogged and apparently determined to wreck my shoes. Recklessly, I allowed it.

Mr Bone followed me in dogged silence as I wove aimlessly between the flower-beds, cudgelling my wits for a means of shaking him off. As I came within sight of the front of the house, my heart leapt as I beheld a carriage waiting upon the gravelled circle before the great staircase. Sir Humphrey was receiving a visitor! Perhaps it was the doctor—or perhaps it was Schmidt, come to find me!

In the same moment I had a brain-wave. I knew now how to rid myself of my guardian. I roamed down to a lower terrace and doubled back by the way I had come. As I did so I began singing to myself the odd old folk song *Long A-Growing*. I stopped once or twice, moreover, to inspect the flowers, which were windblown and ruined. Mr Bone now followed me at a rather slower pace, as though he felt no pressing need to return me to the house. Perhaps he had only been warned to keep me away from the chapel? I thought of the bloodied imprint and shivered.

Presently, having set Mr Bone sufficiently off his guard, I dipped my hand into my pocket and came out with five silver shillings, which I allowed to jingle in my hand in time with my song. When I was certain that the beachcomber had caught the sound of money I took a stick and began to dibble in the earth, planting a shilling every six inches and continuing to sing my song of growing. When I had finished, I set my twig upright in the earth at the head of the row of silver, patted my muddy hands together to clean them, and then skipped away, still singing. In the loggia, a glance over my shoulder told me that Mr Bone had fallen for my bait: he was down on his knees in the garden-bed, pawing through the earth for the silver.

The sight was a pitiful one, and recalled to me certain days when I, too, might have sifted through the loam for a few odd shillings. Nevertheless, my gambit had bought me a moment's distraction in which to make good my escape, and I slipped around the corner of the loggia and hurried towards Sir Humphrey's study. A cautious glance through the window of that room dashed my hopes. Sir Humphrey was ensconced within, but not with Schmidt.

Nor was it the doctor, and I nearly went away again—until I imagined Nijam, like a rather acid Voice of Conscience, saying *Well, really, Dark—all that time in Seton Castle and you didn't manage to learn anything at all that might be useful!* Instead, therefore, I moved dutifully to the library and tried the French doors. To my delight, they were unlocked and admitted me at once. Creeping to the wall that stood between library and office, I found a place above the wainscoting to glue my ear to the wallpaper until I could quite clearly hear the voices in the next room.

"I really can't in good conscience allow it," Sir Humphrey was saying; which, coming from him, was a little rich. "You know, of course, that she has quite a sizeable fortune. You understand what a heavy responsibility *that* can be. It ought to be properly administered."

He could only be speaking of Lady Seton, who had brought a princely dowry when she married, and must have retained the right to administer it under the Married Women's Property Act.

"How sizeable, exactly?" his interlocutor asked. "You understand that it will look bad for you, if questions are asked, and if it turns out you have been keeping the property and the incomes thereof for your own use."

"Well, you understand that it has been appreciating for some decades, and I have only been drawing administrative costs—which, given my financial expertise, have not been insignificant."

He must already have been administering the fortune for some time, then—and paying himself a fat income for doing so! I restrained a sound of indignation. Evidently, Sir Humphrey had had his wife declared mad at least partly so that he could gain control of her fortune!

"Exactly how much?" the other gentleman pressed. "As your solicitor, you know that anything you tell me is strictly privileged. You may be perfectly honest with me."

"Well, the principal itself is worth about a million pounds by now," Sir Humphrey said, with great composure, "and my salary as trustee has been thirty thousand a year—only in recognition of my necessary work, you understand."

"Naturally," the solicitor said, with a dry note in his voice. I was speechless. This was a fortune indeed—and Sir Humphrey was taking an exceedingly comfortable annual income, simply for administering it! And having done so, he was quite prepared to boast of it to his solicitor! Had I been Lady Seton, I should have felt quite tempted to eat him alive for this behaviour!

"The difficulty in securing the guardianship of the unfortunate lady," said the solicitor, "is that the courts may wish to investigate these financial considerations, so as to be sure of a just and equitable arrangement. Then, too, I understand that the lady's sisters are shortly to come of age. Surely they are also entitled to shares in the trust."

That stopped everything I was thinking altogether in its

tracks. Surely they could not be speaking of Lady Seton! How could *she* have underage sisters? How could her dowry belong to them?

What—could Sir Humphrey could be speaking of *me?*

"In any case I would not have been entitled to touch the principal," Sir Humphrey said, as I grappled with the news that my sisters and I were the rightful owners of a million pounds. "I don't mind disbursing it to the other sisters—once they are of age, of course, and if all the legalities are observed. But Miss Dark's share must remain in trust, since she is unable to deal with it herself. It is likely that with careful management—and expert handling—her quarter of a million may continue to yield an income worth thirty thousand a year."

There was a moment's silence. All the indignation I had felt a moment ago on Lady Seton's behalf, I now felt upon my own. I had made no mistake upon the previous evening: Sir Humphrey meant to have me given over into his guardianship forever, because I was worth a small fortune to him. I now wished, most unbecomingly, to eat this man alive on my own account. But I had been raised to turn the other cheek and instructed—by Sir Humphrey—to revere him as a father. I struggled in silence.

"How fortunate, then, that you never disbursed Miss Dark's share of the trust when she reached her twenty-first birthday," said the solicitor, with that same note of dry mockery in his voice. "Will you be requesting the court to place her in your care, or in an asylum?"

"In my own care, of course. I wish to take the very best care of Miss Dark; one hears such horrible stories about asylums, and I would hate to endanger her health. If she was to die intestate, her property would naturally revert to her mother, and I'm afraid neither Dark nor his wife were ever very good at handling money. I shouldn't like so many shares of the company to be in the hands of such improvident people."

"It's a risk," the solicitor said. "There is—ah—shall we say, a *whiff* of self-interest about it, which the court is bound to notice."

"I don't think *that* need cause any trouble," Sir Humphrey replied, very satisfied with himself. "You haven't been in Hong Kong very long, have you? But I'm a magistrate myself, and well respected on this island. My friends know I'm an honest man."

"Then I'll lodge the required papers," the solicitor said, and I knew that would be the end of it. The solicitor might see precisely what Sir Humphrey was doing, and despise him for it, but he was a loyal dog and would do only as he was told.

Quite overwhelmed with this news, I staggered away from the wall and dropped into an armchair. Sir Humphrey, known to be an honest man! —Or winked at, because he was one of their own! The best that could be said for the situation, I thought, was that at least Sir Humphrey was willing to pay my sisters what they were due. But no—why should he, if the court did not outright demand it? Whether he did pay them, or not, *I* could make no objection: I would be locked up in a room of this castle, which I had already come to loathe.

Thirty thousand a year! —and just for *administering* the trust! Surely that income belonged rightfully to *us*. On thirty thousand a year, we might all have been living in luxury. I should not have had to leave my family. I should have escaped the hardship and backbiting of St Alphege's. I should never have wasted the best years of my life working as a governess, minding other people's children on a parsimonious income, welcome neither in the servants' hall nor the drawing-room.

I should not have adopted a life of crime, however nobly meant. I should not have been compelled to contemplate marriage to Griff. And I should have been able to spend my life doing other things, thinking other thoughts than simply of money and how I was to get it.

I had never in my life been so selfishly angry. I could not even justify my anger by thinking of my family: they were now supplied with all of life's necessities, and not in any pressing need of their lost fortune... That made no difference. For a time I gave myself up entirely to fury. Sir Humphrey's trap was closing about me, but I would foil him yet. For days I had been in a welter of nervousness because I could not bear the thought of ruining an innocent man. Now I knew for certain that Sir Humphrey was by no means innocent. I knew that he would lock me up and drive me to madness if he could, simply to get his hands on my money. I knew that he had me tied up in the habits of a lifetime, of deference and respect—but now the feathers had fallen from my eyes: those bonds had snapped. Did that man think he had me where he wanted me, like the villainous Percy Glyde, or the equally unprepossessing Mr Rochester? —inside a lonely cell, friendless and ill? If so, he was wrong! I refused to take part in any gothic romance, any more than I would take part in any improving fiction! In Molly Dark, Sir Humphrey had no ingenuous heroine, ripe for the plucking: he had a wily and manoeuvring female, a confidence-trickster seasoned in countless devious campaigns! In this lonely castle, closely swathed in cloud and wind, *I* was the monster who awaited the unwary.

Tonight, I would ransack the chapel and force it to divulge

all its secrets. And then I would set about the disgracing of Sir Humphrey Seton.

Chapter XIII.

That night, having seen me to my room, Mrs Lister duly locked the inner door as she departed. She was, of course, unaware that Mimi had unlocked the French doors on the previous night, thus giving me an easy mode of egress to the loggia. As tired as I was from the day's upheavals, I had no trouble remaining awake. As the grandfather clock downstairs tolled each passing hour and quarter-hour, I comforted myself that I should soon be in the chapel telling Mimi how desperately glad I was to see her.

By the time the clock struck three-quarters past eleven, I was ready, dressed in the same damp, mud-spattered white garments and waterlogged boots I had taken into the garden with me that morning. It seemed foolish to muddy a second set of petticoats, not to say likely to arouse suspicion with Mrs Lister and whoever handled the laundry. To this attire I considered adding a dark coat, the better to conceal me among the shadows; but this proved much too warm and I discarded it reluctantly. I must simply pray that I was not spotted; or that if I was I could pass myself off either as one of the house's many ghosts, or as the traditional mad heroine. If I was to be press-ganged into a gothic romance, I might as well turn it to my own advantage!

Carefully, thankful that the shutters did not creak, I opened my French doors and stepped outside. High above the house, ragged clouds blew past the moon, providing a fitful light. As I closed the doors with infinite care behind me, a patch of moonlight strengthened upon the loggia floor, and I beheld the prostrate form of a man at my feet!

My heart leapt into my mouth as I gazed down upon him—the beachcomber, I saw at once from the shape of his hat. For an endless moment I stood there, waiting for him to arise, and then—*what* then? I *must* get to the chapel—Mimi would be awaiting me there. But the man did not move, and after a moment, beneath the sighing of the wind, I began to detect his soft, steady breathing. Mr Bone was asleep.

I am not ashamed to admit that it took a moment or two to pull myself together after this shock. My heart was a drum-beat, labouring so hard in my breast that I pressed a hand against my mouth for fear of its disturbing the sleeper. At length, moving very softly and deliberately, I latched the shutters behind me, picked up my skirts, and stepped across Mr Bone's sleeping body. As I tiptoed away I congratulated myself upon my escape—but my ordeal was only beginning. When I stepped upon the cast-iron stair, the metal groaned beneath my foot. There was no other way down, and so I was compelled to take it anyway, as softly as I might; but the stair creaked, and I quivered, with every step. No doubt this was the way in which Mrs Lister had been alerted to my sleepwalking on that previous occasion. By the time I reached the lower level I was all in a welter of perspiration, expecting every moment to hear a shout of alarm—yet the house remained silent. I hastened towards the stairs that led to the garden, and my foot was yet upon the first of these steps when the moon went behind the clouds and I heard the spiral staircase groan again beneath the weight of another body!

Had I been seen? —or was Mr Bone merely investigating a sound he *thought* he might have heard? I did not remain to find out. Instead, I rushed down the steps, grateful for the sighing of the wind which covered the sounds of my footsteps. Even beneath the cover of the banian trees, whose broad leaves cast a Stygian shade across the hillside, I could breathe no easier. The closer I approached the chapel, the more frantic I became lest I might be halted before I could make good my escape! Yet at last I saw the gleam of its white walls rising pale in the shadows before me—found the door by touch—turned the knob, and slipped within.

Inside, it was absolutely dark. Just as earlier in the day when I made my first visit, there was no sign of my father's imprint. Although I had come to the castle at least partly in order to rid myself of that same imprint, yet for a moment I felt freshly resentful at having been once again abandoned. The carping little voice, which Sir Humphrey had instilled deep within me, observed that my father could not be relied upon even in death—but this time I recognised it at once for what it was, and trembled more with rage, than with fear.

"Mimi!" I whispered. "Mimi, are you there?" But my voice disturbed only the echoes.

Anxious not to miss her, I had set out a quarter of an hour before the time appointed for our meeting. Now I must await the hour of midnight, without falling into the clutches of the beachcomber. I wished to heaven I had not been so impatient. At that moment, had I not been so desperate to see my friends, I might have run back to the house simply to avoid being found alone in this place by my ghastly nursemaid! Instead

I felt my way to the pews which filled this dark and echoing space, took a candle and a box of matches from my pocket, and seated myself to wait. After counting to a thousand, I allowed myself to hope that the beachcomber had been unable to pick up my trail. In fear and trembling, I struck a match to light my candle.

The chapel, small as it was, had been built on traditional lines with a high roof beyond the reach of my candle's light and an octagonal nave behind the altar. As elegant and severely simple as it was, it was evidently intended to serve as a place of worship not merely for the family, but also for the hamlet of Pok Fu Lum. Lady Seton said my father had been buried here, but I saw no plaques or effigies that might signify a grave, not even in the pavement before the altar where one might expect to find them. It was as I bent over this pavement, searching desperately for a clue, that a flicker of movement caught my eye and my heart leapt into my throat for the third time that evening.

My father's imprint was behind me, looking solemn and a little anxious as he advanced towards the altar. Upon reaching the nave, however, he turned aside and led me towards a narrow stair set into the floor, which in the shadows by the wall I had missed seeing. Following him down those cramped steps, I found myself in a tiny but genuine crypt.

In the faint light of my candle the place was full of flickering shadows, so that the corner of my eye kept inventing ghosts or pursuers where there were none. The stone walls of the small chamber were lined with empty niches, empty save for one solitary coffin: my father's! I knew what I must do, of course. Bodies recall their spirits with a fiercer longing than any other object. If I wished to know how my father had died

I must open his coffin and reach inside. For a moment my heart failed me. I wanted nothing more than to flee the crypt, and the chapel too, and wait in solitary luxury to be saved.

Nevertheless I went on, fixing my candle to the edge of the niche with a few drops of melted wax. I do not know how to account for this to the reader, for I was nearly weeping with fear. I do not think that any sense of my duty to others could have made me do so. *I* had lost no one to the plague. But I recalled Sir Humphrey telling his solicitor, quite calmly, that he meant to keep me alive only because if I died my property might go to my mother—my mother who had almost died of consumption because we could not afford to send her to a sanatorium!

Anger, then—selfish anger, for my own injuries— overwhelmed every fear, and drove me on, trembling as I was. The coffin would need to be pried open, but I had prepared myself for this with my steel shoe-horn, which I ordinarily use to put on my boots. Gasping and sweating in the close, humid air, I managed to raise the coffin lid just enough to admit my hand, which is as small as most women's; I slid it in, shuddering at the awful smell of corruption, and *touched* the soft remains.

I knew that what I saw would be very shocking, and so it proved to be. In the blink of an eye I found myself and my father surrounded by men. So strong was the memory that it brought even one of the living with it: Sir Humphrey stood towards the end of the crypt with his hands in the pockets of his long dark coat, speaking soundlessly with a sneer on his lips. My father stood opposite him at the crypt's entrance, but when he tried to back away again, he was roughly seized by two of the other men. These were Chinese, with the hardened faces of ruffians the world over. Sir Humphrey gave an ironic bow and brushed past, leaving the crypt. My father, pale and trembling, said something to the ruffians, but they paid no attention. A third man drew a knife and plunged it seven or eight times, in quick succession, between his ribs; my father fell to the floor, and was bundled into the coffin that stood waiting in this very niche...

Mercifully, the vision faded as I recoiled from the coffin. With a sound like the crack of doom the lid fell shut. The puff of foul air it emitted blew out my candle. Absolute darkness flooded in on me, bright with afterimages. Again, I saw my father step into the crypt; again, I saw the flash of the knife as it sank into his body, and the spatter of blood as it was drawn out again.

As long as I remained in this place I would see the grisly scene play out, again, and again—

I was only conscious that I must get out. I do not know how I moved in that absolute darkness, thick with the reek of death and corruption. I know that it seemed the chapel itself had risen against me in the dark, hemming me in on every side with stone walls and bruising furniture and horrible, searing memories. Upstairs, I bashed my knee against one of the pews—but at length I found the chapel door. Beneath my frantic touch, it opened and released me into the free air—and into the arms of the man who stood there, waiting, it seemed, for me to emerge.

I drew breath to scream, and a hand clamped over my mouth; but the impulse had already left me. Instead, I let out a weak moan of relief into the hand, which smelled, as the sharp intake of my breath had done, of pine.

"Vasily," I sobbed, throwing my arms around him.

171

He removed his hand cautiously, as though he did not know whether I might yet scream. "It's me, little mouse. Do not weep."

"I know it's you; I could smell you," I murmured into his shirtfront. I must have been delirious with emotion: for a long time I only stood there, clinging to him in silent desperation. Vasily himself seemed uncertain of what to do: at first his body was stiff, and his hands fluttered about my shoulders, as though he was afraid to touch me. Later, I recalled the strictures I had laid upon him; but in that moment all I could think was that I had been alone and frightened, and Vasily had come to me, as he had always come before, each time he was wanted. At length his arms settled gently about me, and his voice sounded in my ear, murmuring comfort and endearment.

As my trembling subsided, my mind began to work again. —I knew, now, who the man had been, with the wounds in his body! I ought to have guessed it sooner: the possibility had always been in the back of my mind, too horrible to put into words.

"Vasily." I drew back to peer into the shadow of his face, though I kept my hands firmly fastened in the folds of his jacket. "Sir Humphrey had my father murdered."

"Yes," Vasily said, thoughtfully. "That doesn't surprise me. It's what I would have done in his position." Then he seemed really to hear what he had said, for he added, "If I were Sir Humphrey, I mean!—which I am not."

It is deplorable, I know; but I could not help laughing at that, and I badly needed something to laugh about. "Take me away from here, you villain," I begged; and arm-in-arm, we slipped through the postern-gate to where a little dog-cart was waiting in the road with a single somnolent horse in the traces. A moment later we were on our way back to Victoria: and all the worry and loneliness of the past two days, like a great storm hanging over my head, rolled away. The darkest secret of Castle Seton was laid bare, Vasily had come for me; and I was going home.

"Why are you so unsurprised?" I asked, picking up the thread of his previous comment.

"Ah," Vasily said. "Schmidt has not been idle the past two days. It has been a sore trial to him, but he has been lying manfully to Sir Humphrey, saying that he wishes to ship Indian opium to Canton via Hong Kong. In return we have induced notable confidences. In short, Sir Humphrey *has* been importing Yunnan opium, under the guise of those 'herbal remedies' you saw in the bills of lading. Most of it has been going to Canton, or to the Chinese market in Australia. He did not confess to selling any of it on the Hong Kong black market, of course, but that is what he is doing. Li Ling, the young clerk, has confirmed it."

I took a deep, slow breath. "If my father had discovered this, he would certainly have put a stop to it."

"A small quantity of opium is worth a very great amount, even on the black market," Vasily agreed. "As small as the volume of opium would be, in proportion to the tea and textiles, stopping the import of 'herbal remedies' would have destroyed a large proportion of the firm's income—at least until your father was able to find some other commodity equally valuable. That would explain the sharp loss of revenue."

"He must have been personally inspecting the ships as they came in," I murmured, "and that was how Sir Humphrey

173

was able to claim that he had caught the plague. But it wasn't the plague—it was a gang of hired blades! Being a magistrate, of course he would have been able to fudge the death-records, and to avoid an inquest." I pressed a hand to my mouth. "All my life, Sir Humphrey told me my father was improvident, with no more business sense than a baby. He wasn't improvident! He was *principled*. And Sir Humphrey m-murdered him…"

I had thought my mourning long completed—but had I ever truly begun to mourn at all? I had never known the truth about my father; and now I grieved the loss of the man I had never known: the man who had lost the world, but kept his own soul.

"Oh," I said softly, "how am I going to tell my mother?"

"In person," said Vasily firmly, "and once you are well out of Sir Humphrey's reach."

There was a note of foreboding in his voice. "Sir Humphrey is more likely to do my reason an injury than my life," I said. "If I die, my fortune goes to my mother, and then he will not be able to draw thirty thousand pounds a year for his own use."

"And if he comes to suspect that you intend to expose him?" Vasily asked. "Would he not consider your silence bought cheaply at the cost of thirty thousand a year?"

I shuddered, for the same thought had, I confess, occurred to me. "Let us hope that temptation will be removed, once I am no longer under his thumb at Castle Seton."

For some time the journey went on in silence, except that I asked after Mimi and was informed that she had found her way safely to the others in Victoria. The way was perilous, what with the dog-cart lamp flickering in the gusts of wind that swept the island from time to time, and the road still soft and eroded from the torrents of water which still poured over it. Yet I had no attention to spare for the road: all my thoughts were bent upon what I had learned in the chapel.

All this time, the anger I had felt for my father ought to have been directed towards Sir Humphrey Seton. It was he who had murdered my father to protect his ill-gotten fortune, and then kept my family and myself as long as possible in a state of helpless penury designed to prevent us ever learning the truth or reclaiming our share of those tainted millions. —I could no longer refer to it as our *rightful* share: for to amass it, Sir Humphrey must have been trading in opium all this time. Although the law had as yet not entirely forbidden the trade, I could not justify it upon moral grounds, considering the widespread plague it had become upon the Chinese people— no less pernicious than that of gin in Whitechapel; but the more noxious, because it affected so much more populous an empire.

It was not to be helped: I was once again helplessly angry with Sir Humphrey, and entirely upon my own account. I might have had a father. I might have been secure in his provision and proud of his diligence. Sir Humphrey had not only taken away my father in fact, but had poisoned my very memories of him. I laughed, and it sounded almost like a sob.

"Do you know," I said, "when Sir Humphrey sent the money for my first term at St Alphege's, he wrote to tell me that if I worked hard enough, I might be lucky enough not to end up as shiftless as my father? I thought I deserved it."

"I should say he owes you at least a hundred thousand pounds for that alone," Vasily said thoughtfully.

"I don't want his rotten money," I said.

175

"He owes you a *father*," Vasily replied, and I perceived that he was neither quite as abstracted, nor quite as calm, as he seemed. His voice sank. "Not everyone has one of those."

In due course we entered the city, which glowed with light. There were paper lanterns everywhere, and a festive air prevailed despite the damage still evident from the storm, and the streams of water still running through the gutters. Vasily returned the dog-cart to the stable from which he had hired it.

"Tell the man we'll need it again tonight," I told him. I had spent the latter part of the trip thinking furiously. Now, although my heart sank beneath the knowledge of what the plan might require of me, I would not relent. I could not give up my revenge on Sir Humphrey for all the wild horses in China.

"You can't mean to go *back* there," Vasily protested.

"I think I must," I told him. "I have a plan—but first, let's speak to the others."

He could make no objection to that. Our lodgings were a short walk away, up a narrow flight of stairs. I still remember the stifling darkness of that stairwell, and the overpowering aroma of boiled cabbage that hung about the place. Then the darkness was cleaved suddenly by a ray of golden light from a door. Mimi stood upon the threshold and said, "At last! Are you hungry?"

Chapter XIV.

I threw my arms around Mimi's neck. "How I've missed you!" I exclaimed, the tears springing to my eyes.

Mimi drew me into the room, and Vasily shut the door after. I found myself in a bare apartment which would have been cheerless to any other eye, but to mine was hallowed by the presence of my friends. Schmidt greeted me from the basin where he was washing dishes with his shirt-sleeves rolled up. At the other end of the rough kitchen table, scowling with absorption, Nijam sat tinkering with a machine consisting of a black box attached by wires and bands of metal to any number of unintelligible dooverlackies and thingamabobs— our long-distance radio-transmitter, no doubt.

In one other respect, too, the room was distinctly an improvement over Seton Castle: its huge windows were thrown open, allowing for proper ventilation. There was no scent of mildew here—only the damp, salty tang of the sea and the mingled scents and spices of the neighbourhood's evening meals. Breathing in those rich, pleasant aromas, I nearly wept with relief.

"The prodigal returns," Vasily announced.

Nijam tipped back her smoked-glass goggles and turned off her soldering-iron.

"It's about time," she said. "I understand that you destroyed *another* of my transmitters, Dark. Do you think I am made of them? Couldn't you simply have turned the thing off? And where is my book?"

There went through me a piercing shaft of what the doctors call nostalgia: not until I came home did I find just how terribly I had been longing for it. "Hullo, Nijam," I said fondly. "It's nice to see you, too. And where's Bill? I've been *dying* to meet him."

For a moment there was an awkward—nay, a guilty silence. Schmidt reddened and Nijam seemed suddenly absorbed in her gadgets. Mimi snorted.

"It seems that I am the only one who knows how to butcher a fowl," she said.

Vasily aimed a look of wicked amusement at Schmidt and Nijam. "Very delicious he was, too."

Schmidt's discomfort increased. Nijam pursed her lips defensively. "*Someone* has been spending all our food allowance on caviare and champagne, so of course we couldn't afford to let a perfectly good duck go to waste. Are you hungry?" she added.

"I was a moment ago," I said. I felt that if I was a duck I could never put any trust in Nijam at all, even if she *had* given me a name and fresh bedding. Yet the journey, after so many days shut up in that house, had restored my appetite. "I think I could demolish something that isn't duck."

Vasily assured me that this would be no difficulty. Given the smell upon the stairs, I expected cabbage. Instead, he set before me a cracked plate bearing two very tiny fowl all trussed up with string and very un-cabbage-like greenery. Supplementing this was a slab of coarse bread-and-jam.

"That's—er—*Cailles en feuilles de vigne,*" Vasily said, sounding suddenly very nervous. "I'm afraid they don't taste quite like the ones in Paris. I roasted them a little too long."

"Eat them, anyway," said Nijam in her most dictatorial tones. "We shall be lucky if we can afford anything but bread-and-jam for the rest of the week."

"They ought to be served with *pâté d'alouettes a la gelée,*" Vasily grumbled. "But no, *someone* keeps too tight a grip on the purse-strings."

Mimi snorted. "You were lucky to find quail and vine-leaves in Hong Kong at all, let alone larks' livers."

"They're delicious," I said, dutifully. In truth the quails were a little dry, but I felt that Vasily wanted all the encouragement he could get. "One day you will make some lucky young lady very happy."

Mimi snorted with laughter, but Vasily, who did not inhabit a sphere in which it was customary for either sex to cook, simply looked perplexed.

"If you've been cooking things like this, I'm surprised they let you out of the house at all," I added.

"It was dark and he insisted," said Nijam.

"Even prisoners must be allowed outside once a day, for the good of their health," Vasily said plaintively. "Besides, I must look after my figure. If I stay home and cook all day, I shall fatten. Stop clashing those dishes, Schmidt, and sit down. It's time we made plans."

We took our places at the table, and little by little traded all the information we had collected. Schmidt confirmed and enlarged upon what he had learned from Sir Humphrey regarding the latter's secret trade from Yunnan, and Nijam more fully related Li Ling's information that Sir Humphrey was supplying his dockhands with illegal opium.

"Mr Li says that he is very careful only to supply his own workers," Nijam said, readjusting her steel-rimmed *pince-nez* on the end of her nose. "If Sir Humphrey was known to be running opium from Yunnan to Canton, there could be a scandal—these days opium isn't what a white man should sully his hands with, of course—but none of it would actually be against the law. The Chinese authorities don't like opium, but they cannot very well prohibit it—not without British consent, given the two wars we fought to keep the trade going. And the British may not like to admit it, but Indian opium still keeps the Empire solvent. The only law Seton has actually broken, is supplying a limited amount of black-market opium to his own workers here in Hong Kong."

"What are you saying?" Mimi frowned. "Sir Humphey is able to trade opium to his heart's content, so long as he doesn't sell it *here?*"

Vasily grinned. "It's the scourge of the labouring classes, my dear Mimi. Of course it can't be allowed to wreak its havoc on British soil."

"Opium *is* legal here," Nijam added, "but only if it's sold under the government monopoly, which raises prices to prevent the poor from getting too much of it, and ensures that the Crown loses none of the profits from its sale. Of course Sir Humphrey holds no part of that monopoly; it isn't something a white man—"

"—should dirty his hands with," Mimi finished, nodding. "I know."

"But he *is* breaking the law here in Hong Kong, by supplying it to his workers," Schmidt put in. "Surely we can expose him *that* way."

"To a scandal," Nijam said, "and a fine. It would injure him, but not irreparably."

"Sir Humphrey is a magistrate," I put in. "He thinks he can get away with anything. Perhaps he really can."

And I told them everything I had learned that day myself, while listening in on the conversation with the solicitor and investigating the chapel. Vasily had only heard a part of the story, and as I explained Sir Humphrey's intentions for me, he paled.

"That man will stop at nothing to keep control of you and your money," he said at last. "You've been at Castle Seton long enough, Miss Dark. We have all the information we need to expose the man."

"This is precisely what we need—the right sort of victim," Nijam agreed. "Sir Humphrey murdered a white man and is trying to have his daughter committed as a lunatic. It's a journalist's field day."

"We may have all the information," I responded, "but what else? The evidence of my father's death is long rotted away, and ghostly testimony is not admissible in court. I shall have my work cut out for me as it is, just staying out of a strait-jacket!"

"You said you had a plan," Vasily reminded me.

I could no longer allow my fears to rule me. I drew a deep breath. "I've been looking at this all wrong," I said. "I didn't want to take Sir Humphrey's money; I only wanted to expose his evil deeds, but he's untouchable. That was foolish, and Mimi is right. We aren't magistrates; we can't really give justice. Stealing people's money is what we do best."

Mimi clapped her hands. "Yes! *I* want the aquamarine collar!"

"I didn't mean we should take it for ourselves," I protested, "Besides, the aquamarine collar belongs to Lady Seton, and by the time we're finished, she may be glad of it. What on earth do you want jewels for, anyway? I've never once seen you wear any of them."

Mimi scowled. "I like to hang them in my window," she said. "They catch the light."

"Then your window can do without Lady Seton's aquamarine," I said firmly. "As I said, I have a plan; only you won't like it, for it requires me to return to the house."

I had my work cut out to make Vasily keep silent long enough to hear me out; but in the end I succeeded, and a silence fell upon the table.

"It's a shame," Schmidt said, "that you cannot do something to make Sir Humphrey see the ghosts, the way you did with Vandergriff." He turned to Nijam. "Isn't there something we could do, to—to frighten him out of his wits and make him more receptive?"

Nijam looked very thoughtful, but I shook my head. "It's no use. The real diamond is goodness knows where, and even if Sir Humphrey were sufficiently receptive to see the ghosts, he's not tender-hearted enough to pay any heed to them if he did. Griff certainly is not. No—in the absence of a better plan, mine must suffice."

"I don't like it," Vasily protested. "Sir Humphrey is one thing, but Griff and this beachcomber are another. Not one, but *two* prosthetes to watch you? You would be entirely in their power. What if something was to go wrong? You could not speak to us. You could scarcely even steal away to meet us in the chapel."

"I should have to put the whole affair entirely in your hands,"

I said. Vasily blenched.

"You can't mean to do that," he said. "You could not possibly trust me so much."

Mimi tutted, holding up a finger. "No more of that, Vasya! We've spoken to you about this!"

Nijam sniffed. "You ought to know I'd never allow you to make a hash of things, Vasily."

"That's settled, then," I said, before he could renew his protests. I will not pretend to the reader that I was entirely pleased by the thought of putting myself once again in Sir Humphrey's power, but after what I had seen tonight, what else could I do? If I made good my escape, my enemy would be put upon his guard at once. "I will communicate with you by way of the chapel—if there's anything I must tell you, I will write it out and slip it into one of the Bibles, and leave it on the rear pew for you to find. And you must write back in the same manner."

"That isn't very secure," Nijam said with a frown.

"No," I admitted, "but it's safer than using transmitters, and I very much doubt whether anyone in that house has picked up a Bible in years, except the housekeeper, and she's obviously not Church of England… By the way, Nijam, do you have any medicine that might help a person sleep, without rendering them foolish and lethargic?"

Nijam read me a lecture about dosing myself without a doctor's oversight, but when I explained the circumstances, she fetched me some chloral, which she told me was far kinder than laudanum to the sufferer. Resigned, Vasily went away to fetch the dog-cart again, and by three o'clock in the morning he and I were well on our way back to Pok Fu Lum and my prison.

It was a silent journey, for I yawned mightily the whole way, and Vasily spent the entire journey deep in thought. "How will you find your way inside without stumbling over that damned beachcomber?" he asked, as we stole in at the postern-gate.

"I'll get into the house from below," I told him, "and use the internal stairs, which don't creak as horribly. Be careful *you* don't fall afoul of him when you return for my letters."

"Oh, I'll see to that," Vasily said with grim resolution. His words came back to me later, and I realised that this was when the thing must first have occurred to him—although I anticipate my story. We went up the path in silence. The wind had quieted since midnight, and the clouds had dissipated somewhat, leaving the moonlight stronger and clearer. In the silence, the garden was full of chirping insects and the gurgle of running water. We reached the edge of the shadows and saw Seton Castle itself looming over us, its white facade freshly washed by the storm. I shuddered, for I was irresistibly reminded of our Lord's words regarding whitewashed tombs, which within were filled with corruption and dead men's bones!

"I suppose this is good-bye," I whispered, but as I turned to go, Vasily's hand fastened about my wrist and I was compelled to turn and face him.

"Molly," he said hoarsely, as though releasing words long pent-up, "I mean it. You cannot trust me enough for this."

I wished he would stop telling me what I could or could not do. "What do you *mean,* Vasily? You keep saying it, and I keep telling you that I *do* trust you—just not enough to marry you!"

"But none of it is *real,*" he said. "I'd earn your trust honestly if I knew how—but I don't. Trust is a thing I've only ever stolen. You've begged me not to beguile you, but how can I do otherwise? Honest dealing is entirely foreign to me."

In the shadows I could not see his face, but I could hear the desperation in his whisper. I began to wonder if I had been misunderstanding all along—if perhaps he had some anxieties of his own.

"You think you've *beguiled* me into trusting you?"

"Didn't I?" he asked with a ragged laugh. "Can you look me in the eye and tell me it didn't work? How else could I make you care for me?"

This was a step too far, even for me, who had been thoroughly alive to Vasily's charms from the first moment we met in the little gold drawing-room at the Schloss Frohsdorf, and thoroughly suspicious of him in consequence. I scarcely knew whether to laugh or cry. "Do you mean to say that on the Königsberg voyage, when I was so sea-sick and you kept bringing me cups of tea—that you were beguiling me then?"

"I'm a spy and a traitor and a confidence-trickster, my dear! How else should I live, except by winning trust with loaded dice, and then betraying it?"

"And I should hope so," I said, stifling my laughter, "for how else am I to trick Sir Humphrey out of his fortune?"

"Oh, *bozhe moi*," he said despairingly. "I should never have aspired to your hand. I should have been content as a mere professional acquaintance. Why are you laughing? You trusted me once already, and I hurt you. I am false to my bones, and you laugh. Why must you continually put your head into the lion's mouth?"

"Vasily, Vasily," I said. I did not know whether I wanted to kiss his head or smack it. "When I said I didn't want to be beguiled, I meant I wanted you to stop trying to overwhelm my better judgement. Do you think me incapable of loving

185

anything but the perfect image of a man? I never meant I didn't want to be courted *honestly*."

"Oh," he said weakly, after a moment's silence.

"You were able to tell when Mimi was not being honest with you," I added. "What made you think—for a *moment*—that I could not tell the same? I could see your ghosts even when you tried to hide them from me; of course I knew your kisses were false. Why else should I spurn them? You may be a lion, but I am no foolish gazelle. I should have thought you knew me better than that by now."

There was a long silence. At last he said, "You *want* to be courted—by such a fool?"

I bit my lip. I did not know what to say. The words had escaped my lips unawares—and of course those were the ones he chose to hear!

"But *why?*" he demanded.

I wanted to laugh. "I suppose," I said, "that I am simply too fond of tea—and of disasters." Giving in to impulse, I took his poor silly head between my hands. "Believe this, if nothing else: the trust I have in you is real and true. That is why it hurts when you betray it. And as for the trust you've yet to earn—all I ask you to do, Vasya, is to answer me when I call, be there when I need you, and not betray me. You needn't be a lion, and I needn't be a gazelle."

He had gone very still when I called him *Vasya*. At length, he drew a tiny breath.

"What else can we be, if not beasts?"

It was dark, and no one was watching us but God. It is possible that a young lady forgot herself, then, so far as to lean up and kiss a former Grand Duke very softly upon the cheek.

"We might try simply being humans," I whispered, and with

that, I left him.

Chapter XV.

Perhaps it was a good thing that I, like Cinderella, must make my escape at that interesting moment. It must be nearly four o'clock in the morning, and the whole success of our plan depended upon my returning to my chamber before my absence was discovered. I could not remain in the moonlight with Vasily, a mess of emotion.

My heart could not help warming towards him. He was *so* willing to please, and *so* frightened of disappointing me! I found him impossibly endearing, and Mimi would be disgusted with me. All this time, when I reproached him for beguiling me, he thought I was telling him not to approach me at all—simply because I did not wish to be charmed into submission. Even now, I thought in an effort to moderate my feelings, I did not know whether he was capable of learning to charm at all without meaning to get something by it.

But I wanted him to try. I did not know quite when I had determined to let him court me; only that it had happened, and that just now in the garden I must have quite clearly communicated this desire to him. That was in itself a terrifying thought, and I stood in the shadowed verandah a moment, glancing over my shoulder at the shadows where Vasily must still be watching me. What if I allowed Vasily to court me, and then found that he was not for me, after all? Then all this trouble would be for nothing!

This was a depressing thought, and not one which I could well afford to dither over at that moment. Finding that the rear French doors were still unlocked, I let myself into the house. The first thing I noticed was that the shadows seemed a little less profound than they had at midnight: the first light of dawn had begun to creep through the windows. The second thing was that the door to Lady Seton's apartments stood wide open.

I glanced within to find the nurse sleeping soundly upon the sofa, and the door to the bedroom similarly open. This seemed a rather peculiar, if not disturbing, circumstance. Then a soft sound from the other end of the corridor drew my attention to the green-baize door which ordinarily sealed the rear of the house from the noble entrance-hall—but which now stood open.

That sound was very like a match being struck. My suspicions were confirmed the next moment, when the door was outlined with a soft glimmer of yellow light.

Heart beating, I approached the door and slipped sound-lessly into the entrance-hall. Lady Seton stood there in her night-gown with a flaring match between her fingers. Even as I watched, she slipped in at the door which led to Sir Humphrey's study. The match's fading glimmer burned out, leaving the house in darkness. I hastened to follow. Within the study a new match flared, outlining Lady Seton's figure before the great mahogany desk. Many of the papers which had been scattered across it a day or two previously had been tidied away; nevertheless, Lady Seton drew a ledger towards her—opened it up—and very deliberately touched the light to its pages.

I realised in a flash that my first presumption was incorrect. Lady Seton was not searching the study—she was setting fire to it!

"Lady Seton," I hissed. She turned towards me with a gasp, dropping her match. I hurried to the desk and slammed the ledger shut, snuffing out the flames at once.

"Go away," Lady Seton said, striking another match. In the flickering light, with her great staring eyes, and her hair streaming over her nightgown, she looked uncommonly suited to the part of the mad wife in *Jane Eyre*'s attic. "Go away or I'll make you."

Jane, in my position, had been able to call for assistance upon a man of low moral fibre. Mine now doubtless being some distance away, I was forced to deal with the matter myself. "How do you mean to do that?" I asked as calmly as possible. "By setting me on fire?"

She shook her head. "The house. If I burn the house, the ghosts will go away."

"Now, now," said I. "We've already settled that I am not a ghost."

She blinked at me. "You're still alive?"

If I stayed in this house much longer I was going to be irretrievably confused, what with Sir Humphrey telling me that I was mad, and his wife convinced that I was dead. "Very much so," I said with a sigh, "and I'd like to remain that way, if possible. Come along. I'm dying for a cup of tea, and I'm sure it will do you good, too."

So saying, I conducted her to the kitchen, added a little coal to the stove, and soon had a kettle put on to boil. It had occurred to me that Jane Eyre might have saved herself a nasty surprise and a great deal of trouble, had she only managed to have a nice cup of *tea* with the lunatic in the attic.

"How did you get out of your room?" I asked her.

Lady Seton shrugged. "Nurse forgot to lock the door. It happens, sometimes. How did you get out of yours?"

"In much the same way," I told her, spooning tea into the pot and filling it with hot water from the kettle. "What made you think of setting fire to the house? You might have killed everyone in it. I understand the desire to murder Sir Humphrey, but what about the servants?"

"Oh." She huddled a little, drawing her shoulders in, as though crushed by my severe tones. "I forgot about the servants—and Warren. There were ghosts everywhere. I couldn't sleep. I couldn't think." She raised her eyes hopefully. "They went away when you came."

Poor woman! she badly needed to get away from this house, and to have a little company and amusement. "Why did you marry him?" I asked, gently turning the teapot. "You must have known he was after your money."

"He was after Pa's money," she corrected me. "It wasn't Sir Humphrey I fell in love with, anyway—it was the Old World. London is so elegant, and Paris is more elegant still. I never wanted to go back to New York—and Sir Humphrey was a baronet's son and a perfect gentleman." I passed her a nice, hot cup of tea, together with the milk-jug; and she accepted them gratefully.

"And now where am I? Trapped in the colonies…Take my advice," she added, pouring an unreasonable amount of milk into the brew, and raising it with a sigh to her lips. "Don't marry a man who only wants you for selfish reasons."

That hit closer than she knew. I made myself smile. "How

can anyone want something unselfishly? Isn't desire itself selfish?"

She thought about that for a moment, and in the silence I reproached myself for taxing her with this at all. To what depths had I descended if I was asking *Lady Seton* for advice! Lady Seton, who had once asked her nephew to get her the Orlov Diamond!

"Marry a man who wants the same thing *you* want," she said after a moment, with a decided nod of her head. "It's the only safe way to go about it."

I could not help thinking of Vasily. "The last man who asked me to marry him," I said, "only seems to want things that will make him comfortable—like money, and power, and me."

Lady Seton's eyes narrowed with suspicion. "Does he think he'll get money if he marries you?"

"He thought he could buy me," I said dolefully. "But to do him justice, whenever he was forced to choose between me and money, he gave up the money."

She exclaimed as though I had said something impossibly endearing. "Oh! that's so sweet! Sir Humphrey would *never* have done such a thing for me."

Lady Seton's idea of a *beau geste* left something to be desired. I added, "Sometimes I wish that I *did* have money, for then I should be quite confident of keeping him, even after he was to tire of me. And then, sometimes I thank God I do not, for I should always wonder if it was me he truly wanted, or the money. It's horribly tiresome. I wish there was never such a thing invented."

"It's as the Good Book says," Lady Seton said with a staggering lack of self-awareness, "that the love of money is the root of every kind of evil! But you're a perfectly lovely girl, Miss Dark! Why should you need money to catch a man? Plenty of girls get married every day without it."

"Lovely?" I repeated with a laugh. In twenty-five years of life I had heard a great many old ladies tell me how lovely I was; a sentiment that was not, in my experience, commonly repeated—or even shared—by young men. "I'm no eyesore, I know, but a man like *him* could have any woman he liked, far richer or more beautiful. I'm half inclined to believe that he only wants *me* out of sheer contrariety, because he can't have me."

"Oh, I don't simply mean that you're pretty," Lady Seton said earnestly. "But you're lovely inside as well as out; and that's not a quality that anyone can take for granted in a spouse. I married a handsome man with handsome manners, and look where that got me!" She paused a moment, watching me through narrowed eyes. "I'll tell you what the matter is with you," she declared after a moment. "Somehow you have got the idea that you can only be valued in pounds and shillings. And because you don't have pounds or shillings, you presume that you must have driven this man mad with sheer animal longing, and therefore you don't trust him—even though he's given you such proof of devotion. Well, I'll tell you straight: if you keep thinking like that, you'll never find any man you *can* trust."

I opened my mouth to object. Everyone said that Vasily needed to earn my trust—even he agreed to that—but then, had not Nijam said something similar to this, on the Siberian train? Had it not recently occurred to me that I had been taught to consider myself worth only the money I could earn? And, had not Vasily very recently sworn to me that he wanted something more than the plaything of an idle hour?

Yet I now began to see that I had persisted in thinking of marriage as a kind of transaction, to which a woman might bring money or beauty; but whichever it was, she traded it for a man's strength and protection. In neither case could she be loved unselfishly, for herself, in the way that God loves. I heard myself worrying that I would be unable to keep Vasily once I had him, and it struck me that my fear had always been two fears—not just the fear that he could not faithfully love anyone, but also the fear that I could never merit such love.

Yet for all his faults, did I not love Vasily in this way? I loved him as he was, penniless and nameless. I would have loved him had he been married to Zlata, and forever beyond my reach. Why could I give others this regard, yet value myself so meanly? Was I not also a divine creature?

I had the horrible, creeping notion that in this, I had treated both myself and Vasily far worse than either of us deserved.

"Goodness gracious," I said blankly. "You are right."

"Of course I'm right," Lady Seton said, drinking off the last of her tea. "Lord knows I've made enough mistakes to learn *something*." She stifled a yawn. "Oh! I am so sleepy! I wish the ghosts would leave me alone long enough to sleep!"

That reminded me of the bottle Nijam had given me, and I fetched it out of my pocket. "This is for you," I told her. "It's chloral, and I'm told it will give you better sleep and leave you clearer in the head than laudanum will. The dosage is written on the bottle. I thought it might help."

Tears came to Lady Seton's eyes. "That's sweet of you," she said. "Must I go back to that room? You said you'd help me. You said you'd speak to Griff."

"I already have," I told her. I had managed to catch Griff alone as he was taking his post-prandial constitutional in the wet garden that afternoon. "Don't worry about my aunt," he told me, when I had passed on the message Lady Seton had entrusted to me. "I'm perfectly capable of taking care of her myself." From which I was left in grave doubt that he meant to do anything for her at all. I sighed. "I'll do more than speak to Griff, if I can. But that will need to wait until tomorrow, or even longer. The law is on Sir Humphrey's side, you know."

"I know," she said with a sigh of her own. "You don't suppose that if I set fire to the house during the *day*—"

"No," I said hastily. "The ghosts would still visit you; they don't care about the castle. Besides, if the doors and windows were opened more often, it wouldn't be so musty in here. Once we deal with Sir Humphrey you'll be sorry you burned down such a fine house."

If she wondered what this might mean, she gave no sign of it. "I guess I'll leave it alone, then," she said, and with that kissed me and departed. I went upstairs, making a circuitous route through a spare bedroom onto the loggia, and in again at the unlocked door to my bedroom. There was, for once, no sign of the beachcomber; a thing that worried me very greatly, for I did not know where he might have concealed himself. Venturing within my apartment, I lit a lantern to make a thorough search but found no evidence of an intruder. Wherever Mr Bone had got to, at least he was not lurking in my bedchamber... The dawn was now a strong rosy light in the east, but the shutters and curtains blotted it out; I might sleep a few hours until Mrs Lister bustled in to unlock the door and send me down to breakfast.

I was just drifting off when something struck me, and I sat bolt upright in my bed. I was absolutely alone in the room. My father's imprint, which had been my companion for years and had rarely left my side since that terrible morning in Moscow, was gone. Since that vision in the crypt, I had not seen him once.

Chapter XVI.

At first, my plan went as smoothly as clockwork. Schmidt arrived at the castle that morning a few minutes after I finished breakfast. I had settled in the library with volume two of *Can You Forgive Her?* as an excuse, if one should be required, and I heard him begin talking the moment Sir Humphrey met him in the entrance-hall. Although I could not make out any words, I did hear the feigned panic in his voice as Sir Humphrey shepherded him into the study and shut the door hastily behind.

Putting my book down, I pressed an ear against the wall with some of the same pleasant anticipation one feels as the curtain opens on the pantomime.

"Now, then, drink this and pull yourself together," Sir Humphrey said, making a decanter clink. "*What,* precisely, do you want me to do?"

"Lend me money," Schmidt said, breathless with what sounded like real nerves—no doubt the pressure of the performance was genuinely telling upon him. "I need a million pounds at once. Otherwise I'm a dead man."

There was a brief silence. "A *million pounds?*" Sir Humphrey repeated, sounding like a dowager who has heard a joke in poor taste. "Why the devil should I do that?"

"I tell you, I wouldn't ask for it if it wasn't a matter of life and death. I am an investor in your company—you told me yourself there is a fund worth one million at your sole disposal, should any emergency require it!"

"That money belongs to someone else," Sir Humphrey said in his most magisterial tones. So *now* he recognised the Dark fortune! "I cannot disburse it for an investor I scarcely know."

"*Gott in himmel!* Don't tell me you mean to refuse me!"

"You can hardly expect me to give up so much money to one who holds a mere twenty thousand pounds' worth of shares!"

"That was only an initial investment," Schmidt protested. "Listen to me! I owe that million pounds to someone who will kill me—and my wife and children—if I don't pay. That's why."

There was a silence before Sir Humphrey said, thickly, "Do you mean to tell me that you signed over a million pounds that was not even your own?"

"It *was* my own," Schmidt protested.

"Indeed! Are you being blackmailed?"

"No, it's nothing like that!"

"Then I'm very sorry for you, but that appears to be a problem for the police, not for me."

"No—not the police! Very well, I'll tell you plainly what the matter is! The matter is the Noor-Jahan diamond!"

I strained against the partition in a fever of anticipation.

"Good God," Sir Humphrey gasped, and I thought I heard a thud, as though he had dropped a brandy-bulb of his own upon the carpet. "What do you know of the Noor-Jahan?"

"Of the real stone?" Schmidt asked. "I've never laid my eyes on it, but I've never seen a more convincing imitation in all my life. It happened in Vladivostok, as I was about to take ship for Hong Kong. There was a young person—"

"Describe her," said Sir Humphrey, in a voice that quivered with anticipation.

"She was—ah—tall and fair, with blue eyes and a cleft chin-"

"Mary Dark!" he exclaimed in a tone of such venom that I shivered, once again feeling quite sure that he knew me to be as sane as himself.

"Yes, yes, that was her name," Schmidt replied. "She was out of money and desperate to flee Russia for Hong Kong, since her husband had been killed by the secret police in Moscow—some kind of political affair, I gather. She offered me the diamond for twenty thousand pounds—quite clearly a fraction of its real value. Since I did not have another diamond with me, I tested it using a pocket-knife."

"Allow me to hazard a guess," Sir Humphrey said in a voice into which the iron had entered. "It withstood the steel."

"Yes; and since the lady was desperate to sell the stone to the first comer, I did not wait until I might test it with one of my wife's diamonds—"

"In fact, you were taken in by a pretty face and a tale of woe," Sir Humphrey said grimly. "I'm afraid you wouldn't be the first to fall into my ward's clutches, Mr Schmidt. I am almost certain she is the one who first stole the diamond from *me!*"

"Your *ward?*"

"I can scarcely hope to conceal the fact," Sir Humphrey said, in a bleak tone that boded ill things to myself. "Go on."

"When I reached Hong Kong, I saw at once that Seton & Associates presented precisely the opportunity I had set out from Germany to find," Schmidt went on. "Anxious to secure a share in the company, I sought out one of the native businessmen, who valued the diamond at two million pounds on the open market. He was willing to offer me half of that sum, and since it represented a healthy return upon my original investment, I accepted." Perhaps here, he drew a deep breath. "At the time I was not aware that the gentleman was the representative of an organisation calling itself the Typhoon Gang."

"In fact, you sold an imitation diamond to the triad for a million pounds?" Sir Humphrey asked in unrelenting tones.

"You're a local magistrate," Schmidt blustered. "I don't see why such people are allowed such freedom to conduct their affairs! In Germany we run a tighter ship!"

"I have no sympathy for such folly," Sir Humphrey said coldly. "You had better just give them whatever remains of the million pounds they paid you; you can't possibly have squandered it in the past week!"

"But I can't get it," Schmidt said. "Not immediately. I've already dispatched it to Germany, and it's out of my hands for the next fortnight, at least. I'm only asking for a loan, of course! The moment the money reaches my bank in Germany I'll have it transferred back at once, and you won't be out of pocket a moment longer than I can help!"

"I tell you it's impossible! How should I explain it to my shareholders? You had better go to the authorities and ask their protection. I can't be held responsible for your actions."

"Why not?" Schmidt demanded. "Your ward is the one at fault in this! And now I find that the diamond belongs to you, too?"

"Now, listen here, young man—!"

"They've threatened my life if I go to the authorities." Schmidt overrode Sir Humphrey's stuttering outrage. "Don't refuse me, Seton. I don't want to tell anyone about the cargo you bring from Yunnan—but I am a desperate man. My whole family is in danger!"

There was a long, breathless silence, during which I bewailed the fact that I was not a fly on the wall of Sir Humphrey's study. I would have given almost anything to see the look on his face at that moment.

As for Schmidt, what excellent work he was doing! I was tremendously proud of him. And he had remembered the whole story, too—he must have been up half the night practising it!

The silence had become intolerable before Sir Humphrey answered. "Leave," he said thickly. "I see I have no choice but to help you escape the consequences of your own folly—very well! But I shall do it in my own way, not yours."

Schmidt began to say something about how little time he might have, but I was distracted from my eavesdropping by the sound of someone fumbling with the library doorknob. Glancing towards the French doors, I saw the outline of Mr Bone's conical hat in the loggia outside, obscured by the humidity which fogged the glass.

I had come to the library prepared to be discovered by one of the servants, with a book to explain my presence—but I could not bear to be trapped in this room alone with the beachcomber. Even as the door opened, I snatched up my book and sank behind the sofa.

I had thought myself safe from the man as long as I remained within the house. Having closed the door, however, he paused, and I heard a queer snuffling sound almost unbearably loud in the silence of that room. I held my breath, but my heart beat like that of a hunted animal. He was seeking me! —He had turned, and on soundless feet was stealing directly towards my hiding-place! Could he really scent me where I hid?

In an agony of fear, I pressed a hand against my mouth. Perhaps it would have been better, after all, to let him find me sitting in an armchair innocently reading my book! —Just as I had given myself up for lost, however, the door opened from the inside of the house, and beneath the sofa I watched as a pair of stiff, gentlemanly patent-leather boots entered.

"There you are, Bone. Good to find you so punctual," said Griff. I felt the perspiration break out afresh on my brow. "Let's have a look at that eye."

Seeing the patent-leather boots halt an arm's length from the rope-soled sandals of the beachcomber, I risked a glance around the corner of the sofa and watched as Griff pulled away the grimy bandage that wrapped the beachcomber's head, exposing a blinking, bloodshot eye to his scrutiny.

"Not bad," said Griff, pulling back a long, grimy curtain of hair to inspect the eye. "The healing is progressing faster than expected. Let's see if the thing works." He raised a hand to his temple and tapped against it with something like the gesture Nijam used in manipulating her own implanted prosthetics. I stifled a cry: within the depths of Bone's new eye there shone, briefly, a cold blue light.

Griff said very complacently, "Not bad at all. *You* will notice little difference, of course, Bone; but everything seen with that eye is now being transmitted directly to *me*. I guess you understand the purpose of this prosthetic?"

Bone hesitated, and then shrugged.

"This is to help me keep an eye on Sir Humphrey's ward," Griff said. "Your eye, in fact. Since you'll be inhabiting this fine house and keeping an eye on a pretty young lady, you'd best not forget yourself. I expect to see everything Miss Dark does unless she's actually indisposed; but I'll certainly see everything *you* do—and you had better not forget that the eye does other things, too, besides transmitting vision to me."

I was saved from the contemplation of this absolutely appalling prospect by the sound of a tap at the door. At Griff's assent, Mrs Lister entered.

"The master wants Miss Dark in his study," she said, sending such a piercing grey gaze about the library that I pulled my head behind the sofa again just in case she should spot me. "Have either of you seen her? She's not in her room."

"It appears I've installed the eye not a moment too soon," Griff said, unperturbed. "Come on, Bone. The hunt is afoot!"

He charged out of the room with the Blister and Bone trailing behind him, the very image of a steely-eyed, steely-hearted detective on the hunt for a missing jewel thief. Clutching my book, I arose from behind the sofa and retreated by way of the loggia. A minute or two later I was discovered by one of the Chinese parlour-maids on a damp bench-seat in the garden, who informed me in imperfect English of where I wanted, and by whom. With a sigh, I followed her into the house: I had, I knew, experienced my last moments of absolute privacy in some days.

I entered the study to find Sir Humphrey looking nearly as black as the storm-clouds from a few days ago. "I've just had a visit from a certain Mr Schmidt, one of your travelling-companions from Vladivostok," he began without preamble. "He tells me you accepted twenty thousand pounds from him in return for a very clever imitation of the Noor-Jahan diamond!"

Ordinarily, when compelled to tell people untruths, I find myself operating in a certain amount of trepidation, if not outright distress, which lends the fibs an air of authenticity. I was, however, feeling pretty much on top of the world at this moment; and it took a moment to summon the appropriately chastened look. "Oh, was he *too* angry with me? I *did* hope he would not lose by the transaction, for he and his wife were very kind to me! It was a *very* good imitation, and he ought to have been able to sell it for at least as much as he paid for it!"

"He *did* sell it," Sir Humphrey said, breathing heavily, "for a million pounds, to some people who will have his head now that they have discovered it is false!"

"Oh! Oh, *no!*"

"How dare you *oh-no* me!" Sir Humphrey roared, his face quite disfigured with rage. "You vowed you had not taken the diamond, madame! Now a man's life is in danger because of you—and worse still, *my* company is bound to suffer for it!"

I am not quite so conniving as to be able to summon tears on command; but I reminded myself that my life was worth a mere thirty thousand pounds-a-year to this man, and that assisted me to look pale and shudder at his thunderous outrage.

"Oh, Sir Humphrey," I cried, wringing my hands. "I didn't mean to make any trouble; truly I didn't!"

"Explain yourself," he demanded with a wave of his hand. "Where is the real Noor-Jahan? and where are all these imitations coming from?"

"I don't know," I wailed.

"Then you had better tell me what you *do* know, or you will find yourself confined to your room on bread and water!"

"Sir Humphrey, you could not be so cruel!"

"Speak!" he bellowed, and I disappeared behind my handkerchief for a moment, biting my lip to repress a peal of overwrought laughter. Do lion-tamers and bull-fighters feel the same sense of exhilaration while baiting the creatures that might so easily kill them? I did not like to be shouted at; but indeed I had concocted precisely the story that was most likely to rob him of all his wits. I had found Sir Humphrey Seton's weakness at last.

"It's perfectly true that I don't have the Noor-Jahan with me; nor did I take it!" I wailed, emerging from behind my handkerchief. "It was Grand Duke Vasily who took it in London, of course! And I hope you will not blame me, for I could not have stopped him—indeed I tried to help Griff to catch him!"

"And then you disappeared with the said Grand Duke, and married him?" Sir Humphrey retorted.

"What else could I possibly have done?" I cried, wringing my handkerchief. "Would you have forgiven my failure? or would the man I had promised to marry?"

"I suppose you are going to tell me that was the last you saw of the diamond?"

"I don't know," I repeated in a helpless whisper. "After Vasily died, I *thought* I was in possession of the diamond—that was why I came east, to Hong Kong! I always intended to return the diamond to you as a—a peace-offering! But it took all the money I had to reach Vladivostok, so then I took the diamond to raise a loan with it, and the man at the pawn-shop said that it was worthless! What else could I do? I was desperate—and there was Mr Schmidt, quite happy to purchase the stone at once. I never dreamed I might be putting him in *danger*."

"You evidently never dreamed of telling *me* all this," Sir Humphrey said.

I bit my lip. "How could I admit to having lost the Noor-

Jahan? Grand Duke Vasily must have sold it without telling me."

"*And* pocketed all the money!" Sir Humphrey added. "I presume that, since your marriage was not recognised by the Emperor, you have no claim to the estate."

"None whatever," I said dolefully. "I am afraid it has probably been confiscated. Perhaps," I added more brightly, "Nicky—the Tsar, that is—might reimburse us?"

"Are you quite mad?" Sir Humphrey demanded. "Me, approach the Russian Emperor to ask for two million pounds on the strength of an acquaintance with his cousin's mistress? I should be laughed to scorn—even if Mr Schmidt had not ruined me first!" He rubbed his chin. "What about the twenty thousand Schmidt paid you? As the proceeds of *my* stolen goods, I think it's the least you owe me!"

I repressed the urge to point out that this was merely a fraction of the sum he had stolen from *me*—and scarcely a drop in the bucket compared to the rest of his fortune. There is nothing so parsimonious as a certain kind of rich man. "It's gone," I whispered, hanging my head. "I'm sorry."

Sir Humphrey stared at me, his breast heaving like a bellows. He really was having a very trying morning. "It's *gone*? What happened to it? Did you lose it at cards?"

"Oh, no," I said, deploying the wide-open blue eyes, to which men were often so susceptible. "I used some of it to pay for my passage to Hong Kong, of course; and I was keeping the rest of it hidden in my cabin—in an envelope, you know, full of ten-pound notes—and when I went to get it at the end of the voyage it was—gone. Please don't distress yourself about it," I added kindly, as he turned to put a limp hand over his eyes. "It brought me to Hong Kong, after all; and that was the main thing!"

"Two million pounds' worth of diamond!" he exclaimed. "Gone forever!"

"A wise man," I quoted, *"should have money in his head, but not in his heart."* —Sir Humphrey gave me a look somewhere between bewilderment and disgust. "It is," I added, "one of the wise things you said to me when I was a girl. I have never forgotten it. —Oh, Sir Humphrey, I *do* hope you'll assist poor Mr Schmidt! I cannot help but feel that he is in trouble entirely on my account!"

"I don't see why I should!" Sir Humphrey exclaimed, sending me an ugly look. "The man is not *my* responsibility!"

"N-o, but I am," I pointed out. "And don't forget that he has a wife and children! I should hate for anything to happen to them! What a terror he must be in, only because he was kind to me!"

"Kind to you? He was probably the one who stole your money on the boat! Who else would have known that you had it? Don't you understand that on any vessel the captain keeps a safe for valuables?" He hurled this information at me as though unable to help himself, before pacing to and fro, muttering beneath his breath. I watched his face grow darker and darker as he did so; and in that moment my exhilaration began to fade, leaving only that dreadful premonition in its place. However much I had enjoyed baiting the bull, he would have no hesitation in killing me if I made myself too great an inconvenience.

"That man is blackmailing me," Sir Humphrey said after a turn or two. "If I do not hand over a fabulous sum of money, he means to ruin me. I refuse on principle to yield to such villainy!"

207

"But think how desperate he must be, to threaten such a thing!" I pleaded.

"His predicament is no fault of *mine.*" For a moment longer he paced, sending me such dark looks that I shuddered. "It isn't the first time a man has tried to ruin me," he muttered, speaking more to himself than to me. "I dealt with that once; I'm not afraid to deal with it again."

Had Sir Humphrey paid me any attention in the moments after this proclamation, he could not have failed to see that I understood the allusion perfectly, for I felt the colour flee my cheeks. Instead, he stepped towards the bell-pull and gave it an impatient tug; and I took advantage of this welcome opportunity to compose myself. I knew Sir Humphrey was not averse to violence. This was a known risk, albeit one that I had not expected to manifest so quickly, when money would have solved the problem just as easily.

I bit my lip: the moments passed in furious thinking, until Sir Humphrey's summons was answered by Mrs Lister.

"Where's Bone? Ah, there he is," Sir Humphrey said, beckoning the beachcomber from the hall. "Look here, my man—I want you to go into Victoria, to this address, and ask to speak either to the Vanguard or the Mountain of the Typhoon Gang. Tell them that Sir Humphrey Seton wants to discuss business that may be to their advantage, and ask them to send someone here. And I'll expect you home by noon, for I have other work for you to do." He turned once again to send me a deadly look. "As for you, Miss Dark, you are in disgrace! Mrs Lister will take you to your room. Since you are so evidently incapable of taking care of yourself, you are to remain in your quarters until this is all settled to *my* satisfaction, and if you wish to leave them you must call upon Bone or Mrs Lister to accompany you. No, I don't want to hear your complaints!" he added, as I opened my mouth to protest. "I must once again save myself from ruination at the hands of the Dark family! Take her away!"

Mrs Lister attached herself to my elbow with a pincerlike grasp, and thus manhandled me out of the room. We passed quite close to the man Bone; and I could not repress a gasp as I glanced up into his face. His gaze was fixed intently upon myself. One eye was brown; but the other—the one Griff had replaced with a prosthetic—was bloodshot and milky-pale. Shuddering at the way in which my self-proclaimed fiancé had so mutilated the man for his own inexorable purposes, I hastened from the room.

Chapter XVII.

I expected that the Blister would conduct me upstairs to the room I had hitherto occupied. Instead, as I turned towards the stairs, she gave my arm a wrenching tug. "You've been moved downstairs," she told me. "Master's orders."

"Downstairs?" I protested, resisting. "Then I should go up to pack my things."

"They've already been moved," Mrs Lister said. The two of us were still struggling at the foot of the stair when the front door opened and Griff entered in the company of a man nearly as tall, thin, and grey as himself, whose black bag marked him out as a medical man. At once the Blister released me, folded her hands, and stood at my elbow motionless and speechless—the model servant.

I myself was a prey to nerves. My plan had been to invoke the name of the Typhoon Gang as a sort of shadowy threat— but now Sir Humphrey had sent his myrmidon to summon them! That put us in a ticklish situation: for if Sir Humphrey asked the gang whether they were indeed owed a million pounds by Alphonse Schmidt, in all likelihood they would deny it, thereby exploding our hastily-constructed story. Alas! had we only been allowed the time to perfect our plans together! Now everything was in a shambles—and that was in the best possible result, if Sir Humphrey did not absolutely call upon the gang to defend him with violence. Nijam having related what Mr Li had told her about the triads, I felt no doubt at all that Sir Humphrey must have hired one of them to do away with my father. Perhaps even the Typhoon Gang itself!

Considering this, is it any wonder that Griff appeared to me in that moment as something of a delivering angel? Sir Humphrey knew no law but gold; acknowledged no deity but the market. Griff was a different proposition—a man whose highest ideal was the peculiar law of his own headstrong young country, no matter how incomplete, misguided, or malicious those laws might be. If Griff knew that Sir Humphrey was trading in opium, or was ready to deal with outlaws, there would be an end of their alliance at once. All I needed to do was to step forward and say a few words.

But would this be the wisest course of action? My rôle in our plan was perhaps the most difficult, for I must live in Sir Humphrey's house and report upon his actions, yet I had the most solemn instructions to do nothing else which might put me at risk. Now I was absolutely in Sir Humphrey's power, and the events of the morning, as necessary as they were, had caused him to tighten his fist around me. —I was to be a prisoner, and my quarters were to be moved, so that it would be more difficult for my friends to find me. I did not think that Sir Humphrey was ready to murder me; but if he believed me to be a danger to him, surely he would have no qualms in spiriting me away to some distant hidden location, in which my lively imagination could easily supply a nightmare picture of the ensuing decline...

I wavered. Natural timidity made me anxious to throw

myself upon the help of the first strong man who appeared before me, regardless of what had been agreed with the others. Yet there *were* those others to consider. They had asked nothing more of me, than to report on developments, and allow them to act. If I took matters into my own hands, I risked sabotaging my friends and alerting Sir Humphrey to my true designs.

No, I could not now alter the course we had charted. All the same, I turned towards the two gentlemen and cried out, "Oh, Griff! How glad I am to see you! This graven image is trying to put me into a room near Lady Seton's! Tell her I like my old room and won't be moved!"

"It's master's orders," Mrs Lister insisted.

"Now, now, Miss Molly," Griff said indulgently, taking my hand. "Why don't you like to be moved? I'm sure Sir Humphrey is only trying to take care of you as best he can."

I pointed towards the door which led to the rear of the house. "He wants to lock me up," I whispered, conscious even as I uttered the words how crazy they sounded—and yet, were they not entirely true? "All the windows down there have bars on them! I don't want to live in such a place!"

"It's for your own safety, you know."

Would nothing move him? Perhaps it was best not to confide in him, after all, if he was sufficiently naïve to believe anything Sir Humphrey told him. "Lady Seton shouts," I whispered—my final gambit. "She frightens me."

Griff sent the doctor a piercing look, the significance of which left me feeling somewhat puzzled. "I've brought a doctor to see Lady Seton; as her nephew, I thought it right to get a second opinion. I'm sure we'll set her right in no time. Now, Miss Molly, come along. You might as well do as Sir

Humphrey asks, just for now."

Mrs Lister's hand fastened once again about my arm—I was certain to have bruises the following day! —and the four of us ventured into the rear corridor, where for once Lady Seton was making no loud noises. The Blister opened the door opposite Lady Seton's, behind which Mimi and I had hidden a few days before. Obeying her signal to enter, my heart sank to see that bars had indeed been recently fitted to these windows. I was feeling more like a prisoner with each day that passed.

"Griff," I begged, as he paused at Lady Seton's sitting-room door, "please don't let Sir Humphrey lock me away here for good!"

"Don't worry," he told me, in the easy tones of a man who is not being shut up behind bars under suspicion of insanity. "Sir Humphrey means well."

Then the door closed upon me, and I heard the key turn in the lock.

This apartment was larger than the one which I had hitherto inhabited; indeed, like Lady Seton's, it consisted of several rooms. I had a sitting-room, a bedroom, and a small bathroom all to myself; and between these three rooms there was not a single window that had not been defaced with a large, immovable grille. Evidently the room had been prepared ahead of time for my coming—a sign that Sir Humphrey would have locked me away regardless of the morning's events.

Though large, the apartment was darker than my room upstairs and smelled as musty as Lady Seton's. It might have been a pleasant room if it had been properly ventilated. As it was, however, in more than one place, the paint had flaked away to reveal the rusty nails in the ceiling, while the cushions and bedding were nearly sodden in the damp. Nor did the additional comforts of sitting-room and bathroom do anything to allay my fears: they merely indicated that I could now be left immured for longer periods of time. As a final insult, someone—Mrs Lister, no doubt, for I now felt certain that I was being kept from any fraternisation with the Chinese servants—had gone through my room upstairs collecting my belongings. Now my white frocks were folded in the wardrobe, and my toothbrush was in the bathroom, and my valise was beneath the bed. I bitterly resented the thought of that gorgon of a woman going through my things, no doubt searching them for any damning evidence.

I must waste no time. Wishing that I had begged a new transmitter from Nijam after all, I went to the writing-desk and was disgusted to find that the fountain-pen one ordinarily expects to find in one's room at such a grand house was vanished, and had been replaced with a lead pencil. No doubt it was thought a pen was too sharp and dangerous for use by a madwoman. I drew out a sheet of paper, therefore, and began to scribble in a large, childish hand, disguising my report as a journal entry:

13 August, 189—

It is very dull in Castle Seton, so to pass the time I shall begin a diary, and write down everything that happens. Today Sir Humphrey is very upset with me for losing the Noor-Jahan. He has put me into a larger apartment downstairs, which I do not much like, for it is opposite Lady Seton's. I heard Sir Humphrey speaking about something called the Typhoon Gang. He sent Mr Bone to ask them to come and see him. I wonder why?

How I wish I had someone to talk to!

More than this I dared not say: I could write down nothing that could be allowed to fall into the hands of the enemy, such as that I had guessed Sir Humphrey was in the habit of employing the triads when he wished to carry out assassinations. Nevertheless, I felt certain that the others would understand the significance of this message: that Sir Humphrey was in communication with the gang for nefarious purposes, and my friends should apply to me for more information. Feeling helpless and a little sick, I folded the paper and slipped it where it would resist being found by any but the most rigorous personal search. Now I must get the message to the chapel without being seen; and that meant a weary wait, and any amount of nerve-wracking idleness.

In fact, something soon happened to break the monotony. I heard the door to Lady Seton's apartments open and close, and then hushed voices began to speak in the corridor. Hastening to my door, I planted an ear hopefully against the timber and was soon following the thread of the conversation.

"The evidence is not conclusive," the doctor was saying doubtfully. "Your aunt is certainly suffering from delusions of some kind, but otherwise she seems quite in possession of her wits. I should not say that she poses any danger to herself or others."

I felt glad for Lady Seton's sake that I was the only soul in the house who knew of her attempts to burn it down. But then, she had been sorely provoked!

"And do you think her a hopeless case?"

"Not at all—although if she is kept shut up like this she is likely to become so. This house evidently distresses her, and she is suspicious of her keepers. I should recommend a change of scenery and some lively company; then we might see whether or not she is indeed mad, or only melancholy."

There was a brief silence. "In fact," Griff said, "you'd say my uncle is treating her with absolute cruelty."

At that, the doctor began to stutter and correct himself. "Oh! Oh, no, I should not go so far. That might even be libellous! No doubt he is only doing as he has been advised—"

"I'm not accusing you of slander," Griff cut in coldly. "I've been away from Hong Kong barely a week, and now I return to find that Seton has made a prisoner of my aunt. Lady Seton isn't just anyone: she's Adelaide Vandergriff, of the Washington Square Vandergriffs. I can't let her go mad in a Hong Kong bungalow—think how it would reflect on the rest of the family! Would you be willing to stand up in a court of law and swear to what you've told me—that Lady Seton is *not* a helpless case, and simply requires a gentler course of treatment?"

"As to that—well, yes—but you understand that Sir Humphrey is a magistrate—"

"And I'm Warren H. Vandergriff," that gentleman said testily.

There was a moment's silence, and then the doctor said, "Yes—I'll swear to it, sir, if you're willing to stand by it. But it's not a sure thing, you understand. Sir Humphrey is quite capable of finding other doctors to swear to the opposite."

"You can let me take care of that," Griff said, and with that concluding statement the two of them got underway again, and soon passed beyond the green-baize door which separated the insane asylum from the rest of the house. I was left with a great deal of food for thought. I could not warm to Griff entirely, of course, given that his solicitude for his

216

aunt evidently did not extend as far as myself, in a similar predicament across the hall from her. Evidently it was the good name of the Washington Square Vandergriffs, not Lady Seton herself, that aroused his solicitude. But it seemed to me that both the great rich men of Castle Seton were keeping secrets from each other; and in that, it might be that there lay an opportunity for myself.

Chapter XVIII.

When the door opened that evening and Mrs Lister entered bearing my dinner, she found me awaiting her with my hands clasped in a posture of supplication.

"Oh, Mrs Lister," I begged. "I wonder if you would be kind enough to accompany me to the chapel after dinner."

"To the chapel? What do you want there?"

"I want to pray," I said plaintively.

Her lips thinned, and her pugnacious, Scottish accents broadened. "Surely the Lord can hear you just as well in your room as He can in the chapel."

I sighed. This sort of thing never happened to Jane Eyre. "No doubt He can," I said meekly, "but I have not been in a proper place of worship for ever so long, and besides, I need the exercise. I cannot leave this room without you; do say yes!"

She harrumphed, but returned in an hour to tell me to hurry because it was getting dark outside. I was aware of this; it was the reason I had postponed my expedition until the day's end. I emerged from my prison to find a man waiting in the dim corridor, and in that first moment, as the corner of my eye dragged over him, my heart leapt with hope and gladness. Then he moved, and the twilight illuminated the cold electric gleam of his unnatural eye, and the wild disarray of his hair and beard. My heart sank, and I turned away in disappointment. It was like the Ekaterinburg train station all over again. Oh, I *was* in a sorry state, if the *beachcomber* made me think of Vasily!

My two minders unlocked the French doors to the loggia and followed me into the warm twilight. Today, for the first time since my arrival in Hong Kong, the sky had cleared, allowing some rays of sunlight to reach through—although now this was only a fading memory in the west, and shadows now gathered beneath the banian trees that so thickly clad the slope between the house and the chapel. On the edge of the verandah my heart nearly failed me. All day, the silence of the house had been crushing, unrelieved by the pleasant chatter of my friends. Now I must venture into those shadows absolutely alone but for the watchful eyes of the two servants, neither of whom I trusted an inch. I could feel Bone's eyes fixed watchfully upon me, and I did not think the Blister would lift a finger or say a word to stop the man, should he take it into his head to disturb me in any way.

Still, I must get that slip of paper to the chapel, for my friends depended upon me for their news. I plunged down the steps with some of the same sensations I have had once or twice as a child, plunging into some dark stream or mirky pond for a forbidden summer swim. The air beneath the trees was still and stifling, and the chapel, when we reached it, was terribly dark. At the door, I begged them to give me a moment alone, but Mrs Lister refused to take the hint. Instead, she followed me doggedly into the gloomy interior, and lit a lamp with the evident intention of keeping a close eye on my actions. Mr Bone, of course, followed also.

In that gloomy stillness it was a constant struggle to get enough breath into my lungs. It was horribly unrestful sitting in that solitary place with my two minders twiddling their toes in the aisle. To make matters worse, my father's ghastly imprint had appeared and now hovered at my side, his wounds streaming with blood.

At first I tried to pray, but managed only nervous repetitions of a sort which Mrs Lister would no doubt have condemned as heathenish. Acutely conscious of the housekeeper's watchful eye, I took up a Bible and opened it at random. The words danced before my eyes, making no sense to me, but I must keep up appearances; so I stared at the page a while, and in time realised that I had opened to somewhere in Exodus. This is not a part of the Bible often selected by clergymen for an uplifting little homily, and was therefore somewhat less familiar to me than the other parts. It was too late to find some other text, however: I must pretend to read this one. I turned a page, and the words fairly seized me by the throat: *Ye shall not afflict any widow, or fatherless child. If thou afflict them in any wise, and they cry at all unto me, I will surely hear their cry; And my wrath shall wax hot, and I will kill you with the sword; and your wives shall be widows, and your children fatherless.*

I sat as though transfixed. Here was injustice, and fury, and vengeance! At that moment, the text seemed peculiarly apt to myself. *I* was fatherless, and my mother had been left a widow, and abandoned to die. Could it be, then, that the anger I felt against Sir Humphrey was something God Himself had felt on my behalf? What if I was to be the just instrument of His wrath? Indeed, I had never wished to *kill* Sir Humphrey, with a sword or without it—in this I was, if anything, gentler than the divine wrath.

Perhaps, after all, my selfish anger was not so selfish: perhaps it was something I had for a reason! Once again I stared, unseeing, at the page before me. I was conscious of a profound sense of relief. Once or twice over the course of the past few days, I had told myself that it was right to be angry with Vasily, because I was fighting at least as much for him as I was for myself. But in being angry with Sir Humphrey I was only fighting for myself, and not even for my family. Now I knew that was not true. If I was angry, it was on God's own behalf. I was meant to feel angry; I was right to feel angry. I was right to act on that anger.

In the aisle, Mrs Lister looked pointedly at her watch. I slipped my missive delicately from my sleeve to the Bible, laid the book on the pew beside me, and arose.

At that, the housekeeper had the nerve to say, "You were not very long at your prayers."

"I did not like to keep you waiting," I said mildly, making my way towards the door. Mrs Lister followed me; but scarcely had we emerged from the darkness when she took my arm again in that bruising grip and turned sharply towards the chapel.

"Bone!" she called. "What are you doing in there?"

I glanced over my shoulder, and what I saw absolutely congealed my heart in my bosom. The beachcomber stood in the pew I had just vacated. His face, half concealed by wild hair, was turned towards us; but in his hands was *the very Bible I had just laid down.*

He did not speak, but as he threw the Bible down and strode to join us, I wondered, with a feeling of absolute panic, whether I had only imagined the flutter of white in his hand, just before he thrust it into his trouser pocket.

"I *asked* what you were doing there," Mrs Lister snapped, but the beachcomber only shoved his way past us, setting off towards the house as though impatient to be back. With a snort of disgust, the Blister seized me again and hurried me along in his wake. As for me, I walked like an automaton. Outwardly I might have appeared calm, but inside I felt rather like the little Trojan boy who had to allow the fox to gnaw upon his innards. I knew without a doubt that my letter had been intercepted.

I scarcely recall the rest of our journey to the house; I was only trying to recall whether I might have said or done anything to betray my friends. I had done my best to disguise my report as a journal entry meant for my own eyes; but would Sir Humphrey be fooled? Surely he must guess that not even a lunatic begs a visit to the chapel merely to dispose of her journal—and I had reason to doubt that he truly believed me mad!

In a blink we had returned to the house. My quarters yawned before me, darker than ever in the gathering dusk, hot and stuffy. I had a sudden mad idea of trying to run away, but the housekeeper stood at my left elbow and the beachcomber at my right, both of them vigilant and no doubt eager for an excuse to lay violent hands upon me.

"Must you lock the door on me?" I begged, turning to the housekeeper.

"Master's orders," she said grimly, as ever.

"But what if there's a fire? I shall be trapped. *You* will not come to let me out."

"Take it up with the master," the Blister repeated, rather like an automaton herself. "Inside."

I felt inclined to protest that I could scarcely speak to

Sir Humphrey if I was locked into my room—but that was useless. If I did not obey I would be forced to do so. I went in, accordingly, and the key turned in the lock behind me. Hearing both my minders hasten away, I paced the room in distraction. No doubt Mr Bone was even now laying my letter before Sir Humphrey. —No, I must not lose my head. I must trust to my own carefulness. Even if he *knew* me to be in my right mind, he need not arrive at the conclusion that I was conspiring with others.

The real disaster was that I had failed to warn my friends of what Sir Humphrey meant to do. I could not try to use the chapel again as a post-office; not now that I had been discovered once already. But all was not lost. Schmidt, I knew, would almost certainly return to the castle tomorrow: I must try to attract his attention in some manner. But how?

I had just begun to cudgel my brain for an answer to this question, when I heard the beachcomber return to his post in the corridor. A moment later there was a queer, scraping sound at my door. My heart absolutely leapt into my mouth: for a moment I thought that he was fumbling at the lock, trying to enter.

The sound quickly ceased, however. For a long moment I stood straining my eyes through the shadows, trying to see what my guard had done to the door. It was useless… I lit a lamp and carried it nearer. Only quite close did I see what had changed.

A key lay upon the floor at my feet, evidently having been slid beneath the door.

For some time I beheld this miracle in utter incomprehension. A key? Surely not the key to my own door? But who would have done such a thing? Had one of the servants taken pity upon me? Had Mrs Lister had a change of heart?

Did I have a hidden friend in this house?

The thought swept over me with a sense of absolute euphoria. Snatching the key, I clasped it joyfully to my heart. My eye I applied eagerly to the keyhole, in hopes of identifying my saviour.

At once I met the gaze of another eye—a brown one, bloodshot and wild and half-concealed by ragged black hair. It pulled away from the keyhole in alarm and I saw that its mate was covered by a grimy hand—I was looking directly back at the beachcomber! Not only that, but he had by the simplest of means prevented Griff from observing what he had done!

I recoiled from the door, and the key dropped from my hand as all my jubilation turned in a moment to dust and ashes. A friend? Oh, how foolish of me, to think that anyone in this nightmare place could be my friend! Instead I was to be watched—and baited with false promises of escape!

With shaking hands, I drew my handkerchief from my pocket and made a wad of it into the keyhole. Then I fell back, pressing a hand to my swiftly-beating heart. Here was the key at my feet—a key that might or might not open the door between me and that horrible man! It could only have come from the beachcomber—but why? Had he meant to act upon his depraved intentions, would he not have used the thing himself? Or was this a gift with sinister intent? Did he think I would trust him because of this? Or did he make the gift on Griff's account, for some reason related to his designs on behalf of Lady Seton? Was it, after all, unnecessary to be a Vandergriff of Washington Square in order to merit his aid?

Or was it possible in the slightest that, having heard me

entreat Mrs Lister for the key, Mr Bone had taken pity upon me?

No answer to this conundrum presented itself, although I spared no effort in lying awake and fretting about it. The following morning, I determined to test the key at the first opportunity—but not until after breakfast, when Mr Bone had departed from his post in the corridor to smoke a cigarette in the loggia. It was most unsettling to see his outline before my window, particularly when I stole up to shut the curtains and found him gazing directly in at me. He turned away his head at once, but I pulled my curtains hurriedly shut all the same.

The key—oh, bliss!—did indeed turn in the lock. My heart was in my mouth as I crept into the corridor, for I did not know whether Mr Bone meant to swoop down upon me the moment I quit my room. Nevertheless, I locked the door carefully behind me, concealed the key within a garment that shall remain nameless, and peered into the entrance-hall to see a Chinese gentleman in Western-style garments being shown into Sir Humphrey's study. My heart sank. It was Schmidt I most wished to see, but instead the Typhoon Gang, it seemed, had already answered Sir Humphrey's summons!

Still, it was of the utmost importance that I should listen to their conference. On tiptoe, I made my cautious way across the empty hall and into the library, which was happily unoccupied. Ensconced in my old hiding-place between the sofa and the wall, I presented my ear to the plaster and found Sir Humphrey holding the floor:

"I can't offer you payment of the debt in full, of course," he was saying, and I felt my worries abate a little. Evidently, if nothing else, the Typhoon Gang was not going to tell Sir Humphrey that they were *not* owed a million pounds. "But it's possible that we may be able to do business worth at least that much. I'm told you've been doing a profitable line in the labour trade—bringing coolies, domestic servants, and entertainers from the mainland to Hong Kong. The problem is finding room on the island for all of them."

"Conditions on the mainland are bad," the triad man said, in a softly accented voice I must strain my ears to hear. "The authorities are harsh and disorder is growing. Many people are desperate to find better lives across the sea."

"If you want to trade in bodies, you'll need to find room for them," Sir Humphrey said. "That's where I can help you. My ships run to Singapore, London, Sydney, and soon to Mexico. I'll front you the money for your first shipment to Mexico; it won't cost you a thing. A million pounds? You could be making that every two years."

I shuddered, seeing what Sir Humphrey was about. The trade in indentures seemed scarcely less sinister to me than did the trade in opium. Entertainers! I did not think he meant a respectable sort of entertainment; I thought he meant something far more cruel and sordid. But of course, setting morals aside, the suggestion made decent business sense. Sir Humphrey had already made plans with Griff to ship Chinese labourers to Mexico, and the Typhoon Gang would be able to provide the materials, so to speak, of this trade. Doubtless the indentures would pay better than tea or textiles. Then, too, larger Chinese communities in Australia and Mexico would provide greater opportunities for selling opium in places where the laws against it were not so strict as they were in Hong Kong. In short, Sir Humphrey had found a way to keep his German investor, mollify the Typhoon Gang, and expand his trade; and the only people to suffer from this would be the hapless people who sought a better life elsewhere and were willing to endure something very like slavery in order to get it.

The Chinese gentleman, meanwhile, began to demur, saying that although the opportunity was an attractive one, he had no immediate plans to begin a trade across the Pacific. Although, perhaps if Sir Humphrey provided enough for the first *three* voyages the incentive might be greater? —I was distracted from this haggling by the sound of the front-door bell. When I put my nose through the library door and saw Alphonse Schmidt enter the entrance-hall, I could have wept in relief. Since the butler was taking Schmidt's hat and coat, I could not call out to him. Instead, I opened the library door a little further and began making frantic signs to attract his attention.

Before Schmidt could catch sight of these semaphores, footsteps echoed upon the marble staircase and Griff uttered a cheery greeting to the newcomer. I shrank back into the library. Schmidt, stammering a little at being thus cornered by a man he had last seen trying to throttle me in a Limehouse tenement, shook hands, pushed his poorly-fitted spectacles up his nose, and made monosyllabic replies to Griff's questions as regarded the German tea market. I gnawed at my nether lip, terrified lest Griff should recognise poor Schmidt, and beginning to despair of ever getting my information to my friends. It was Sir Humphrey who resolved my dilemma for me a minute or two later, when the study door opened and to Schmidt's palpable horror, he ushered the Typhoon Gang representative out into the hall.

"I think we will be able to deal very well together," Sir Humphrey told the Chinese gentleman, bidding him farewell with ceremonious bows. Griff, who said that he had been about to depart the castle for Victoria himself, also took his leave. When the door closed, Schmidt pointed a quivering finger after the Chinese gentleman.

"Was that—was that someone from the Typhoon Gang?"

"Their Mountain, in fact," Sir Humphrey said, mercifully communicating the most important part himself. "The leader of the clan. You may be pleased to hear, Mr Schmidt, that he has agreed to overlook your debt."

Schmidt stood gaping; at length he hitched up his sagging jaw and said, "What? Impossible. I owe them a *million* pounds—"

"Believe me, I've made it worth their while," Sir Humphrey said. "You and your family will be safe. The Mountain is quite satisfied with our settlement."

Schmidt became more agitated still. "But I am *not!* Why should they let something like this go? They might have made an agreement with *you,* but why should they forgive *me?*"

"Calm yourself," Sir Humphrey said, but Schmidt threw off his restraining hand.

"Don't you understand how these things work?" His voice sawed high in a panic. "I've still cheated them! How can they afford to let me go? They must make an example of me, for fear of others treating them the same way!"

"What do you expect *me* to do about it?" Sir Humphrey asked contemptuously. "Do you want me to go to war with them?"

Schmidt's bosom heaved, much like that of the Bride of Lammermoor in her mad scene. "I need you to pay them," he said. "It was *your* ward who got me into this mess; and you're legally responsible for her. If I must go to the authorities, I will—and I'll expose your trade in opium."

"I beg your pardon!" Sir Humphrey sounded outraged. "This is *blackmail!*"

By this time I was again gesturing wildly from the doorway, begging Schmidt for heaven's sake to stop talking, once again with no result. Was this truly the best he could do? Or had Nijam instructed him to employ this tactic lest Sir Humphrey proved obdurate? It *sounded* like a tactic Nijam might employ. Where was the finesse? Where was the careful attention to the psychology of the individual? Where was Vasily's defter touch in all this?

And there! Just as I could have predicted: Sir Humphrey was stomping to and fro, shouting for Mr Bone. The beachcomber at once appeared from the corridor at the back of the house, where he had no doubt been hard at work guarding my empty room. "Throw this man out!" Sir Humphrey cried, turning that distinctly unattractive shade of puce, with which he expressed any strong emotion. "I won't have damned blackmailers in my house—or in my company! Throw him out, I say!"

Mr Bone advanced upon Schmidt at once. The beachcomber was a shorter man, and slenderer than his opponent, who could quite easily have knocked him flat with one blow of a right arm which Achilles himself might have envied. Schmidt, however, only gave stammering protests as Bone attached himself to his collar and expelled him with some force by the front door.

The turfing completed, Sir Humphrey shot the bolt himself and stood breathing stertorously, absolutely gnashing his teeth. It struck me that now was an excellent opportunity for me to find Schmidt and shake some sense into him. I was about to leave my post in the library and slip out by the

French doors to catch my co-conspirator on his way home, when Sir Humphrey's next words drove all such thoughts from my head.

"Come here, Bone," he said in a low, hoarse voice. "Tell me: doesn't the Typhoon Gang deal in assassinations?"

My blood congealed within its veins. If Mr Bone replied, I did not hear the words.

"Go after the Mountain," Sir Humphrey said next. "Tell him I want his help ridding me of this hysterical German. I'm willing to pay whatever price he asks."

I made an involuntary movement; and that was my downfall. A marble bust of Lady Seton upon a wooden plinth stood just inside the library door. In my agitation, my elbow knocked against it. I snatched for the plinth and righted it, but a moment later the bust itself fell upon the rug with a sound like a thunderclap.

There was no time to hide. In three steps Sir Humphrey reached the door and threw it open, and I was revealed trying to dive behind the sofa!

"You! You minx!!" he bellowed, upon seeing me. He advanced upon me, his hands clenching and unclenching in a way that I found decidedly unsettling. "What have you heard?"

Chapter XIX.

"I don't know what you're talking about," I squeaked. "I only just came in from the loggia!" And then my legs gave way, and I collapsed upon the sofa.

Most of the time, feminine delicacy serves me well in the gentle art of deceiving people. Today, just when an air of innocent serenity would have been most useful, it worked against me: I was half fainting and evidently in a panic.

"You're lying," Sir Humphrey said at once. "Well, it doesn't matter! Who will trust the word of a madwoman? Bone! Come here, you villain, and explain to me how she escaped her room!"

The beachcomber shrugged. A sudden irrational terror took hold of me—that he might in fact tell Sir Humphrey I had a key. Then I should be absolutely helpless in the hands of a man who thought nothing of murdering people! Before the beachcomber could say anything, I let out a wild peal of laughter.

"You shouldn't trust your housekeeper overmuch," I said. "She's very clumsy with locks! And yes! I *did* hear what you said! I know you mean to murder that man to keep him quiet!"

This last statement quite distracted Sir Humphrey from the question of the key.

"That's nothing compared to what I'll do to *you,* if you keep shouting my affairs about the house!"

"Oh, what does it matter?" said I. I scarcely knew what I was doing; I had the feeling of being trapped in the arena with the bull again, evading its horns by the skin of my teeth and half convinced that each moment would be my last. "No one will believe a lunatic, after all! Or—are you sure that *you* aren't the lunatic?"

"What do you mean?" he asked.

"What can *you* mean by trying to kill a man, only because he has been deceived about a diamond?" I demanded. "Of course he is desperate enough to resort to blackmail! But he was kind to me when I needed a friend! For heaven's sake let me go and meet with him. I can make him see reason—I swear it."

"You're out of your wits," he said, contemptuously.

"No more than you are, for killing a man of his standing and connections." I tried not to allow the desperation I felt to show in my voice. I had failed to pass information in the chapel; I had failed to warn Schmidt this morning. Now Sir Humphrey was determined to commit murder, and I was incapable of issuing the warning on which my friends depended. Begging Sir Humphrey outright to let me meet with them was my one last hope.

Sir Humphrey laughed my request to scorn. "Do you think I'd really allow you to go and meet with that man? What, do you mean to set him upon his guard? If he does have blackmail material, he'll never give it up if he learns I mean to do away with him! Take her back to her room, Bone—and this time make sure she's locked in."

He tugged on the bell-pull, no doubt meaning to summon

Mrs Lister for a scolding. At once Mr Bone attached himself to my elbow and drew me with him to the part of the house I had come to think of as the lunatic asylum. The fear I might once have felt to be at this man's mercy was now entirely swallowed up by terror for my friends and myself. Having killed my father, Sir Humphrey was now preparing to kill Schmidt. Where would it all end? To whom could I turn?

The beachcomber took out a key, the twin of my own, and unlocked my room for me. I entered, but as he went to close the door behind me, desperation made me bold. Seizing his wrist, I tried to gaze into the face which he kept resolutely turned away from me.

"Why are you helping me?" I demanded.

He made no answer: he only shook me off and shut the door, and I heard his key turn in the lock. Gnawing at my nether lip, I returned to pacing my room. What did it mean? The longer I meditated upon the question, the more I suspected that I had Griff to thank for my one small freedom. Since the beachcomber was only willing to help me to a certain extent, he must therefore be under orders.

My choices at this moment were very few indeed. I might, it was true, let myself out of the castle under cover of night and flee to Victoria on foot. But that was risky. It would take me at least some hours to walk to the city, on a muddy road, in the dark. During all that time, I should be vulnerable to Sir Humphrey, if it was discovered that I had fled the castle. I might easily be followed and caught; and then Sir Humphrey would be especially careful never to let me escape again. I imagined the outcome then with horrible clarity: Schmidt dead, Vasily and Nijam shattered, and myself spirited away to some horrible dungeon, where I should pass the rest of my life as the helpless prisoner of Sir Humphrey Seton!

Or—I might appeal directly to Griff, who was already helping me and hindering Sir Humphrey for purposes of his own. To do so would be to throw myself upon the mercy of a man who had already treated me very badly, and to give up any hope of completing our mission in the way that we had planned it; but that was not to be helped. The others had got themselves into mortal danger, and I was not about to stand by and let Sir Humphrey murder any one of them.

It really was a crying shame. Had we only been able to communicate with each other, none of this might have happened! We might have developed a more robust plan, adaptable to the changing circumstances. But now—the game was too dangerous. We were confidence tricksters who preyed upon the hothouse flowers of royalty—princes and Grand Dukes whose fangs might elicit terror and obedience, but who had never had to face determined resistance. The Typhoon Gang, on the other hand, was populated with hardened assassins and street warriors before whom we would be little better than babies.

I came to this conclusion with a sense of overpowering relief. I need no longer to remain alone in this house, tormenting myself with terrors. I could escape with my life, and perhaps do a little harm to Sir Humphrey as I departed. The living were worth more than the dead: I ought to have known better than to succumb to the same temptation Vasily had fallen into, and to stick my neck out for the sake of a selfish desire. There: it was decided. I would tell Griff everything I knew, and I would ask him to let me go.

I had still a weary long wait before the dinner hour passed. Today I did not beg the housekeeper to escort me to the chapel;

from her hostile manner, caused (no doubt) by Sir Humphrey's having scolded her for letting me out of my room earlier, I did not think she would have helped me. Instead I kept a close watch at my grilled window until I beheld Griff in the garden—taking the stroll among the roses which he had once extolled to me as a better aid to the digestion than either port-wine or cigars, both of which he shunned as dangerous to the health and the morals. Having patted my pockets to ensure that the few belongings I could not bear to leave behind were still with me, I pinned on my hat, unlocked my door, hid the key beneath the soil of a potted palm just in case I should find myself immured there again; and stepped boldly out into the corridor.

Mr Bone sat there, ensconced in a chair with a newspaper and a mug of beer. He glanced up when I emerged and then leaped to his feet. He did not speak, but only stood there looking very foolish, as though he did not know what to make of this sudden reappearance. Marching up to him, I peered into that milky-pale mechanical eye.

"Griff," I said, shaping the word very clearly with my lips so that he should have no doubt of my meaning. "I want to speak to you. Wait for me."

A look of alarm came over Mr Bone's face as I addressed his master. He snatched at my arm, but I was too quick for him. Turning away, I sailed towards the French doors onto the loggia, and threw them open just as Griff himself came rushing up the steps from outside.

"Miss Molly, you can't be out here," he panted, seizing me by my much-abused arm. "Bone!" he added to the beachcomber, who had followed me into the loggia. "You were warned of what would happen if she was to escape again!"

With that Griff made a snap of his fingers. There was a soft fizzling sound, electrical in nature. The beachcomber made a peculiar sound of his own—a muffled groan of agony. I turned to behold him upon his knees, stuffing the ragged cuff of his shirt into his mouth as though to stifle his own cries. Griff snapped his fingers again. The beachcomber's eye glinted with a spark of blue light, and Mr Bone groaned again before slumping over, senseless, on the floor!

"Griff! What have you *done* to him?" I inquired in a voice high and breathless with terror.

"Don't worry," Griff said grimly. "He's not damaged. I've only taught him a lesson he won't soon forget. I warned him the eye would not merely transmit what he saw to me. Come, Miss Molly, how are you getting out of your room? This is the second time today, if Sir Humphrey is telling the truth."

Evidently Griff was *not* my helper: *he* could not have sent the key. I could not help but feel that I had made a horrible mistake in choosing to put myself into the hands of this monster. Still, I had committed myself to this course, and if I gave up now I might as well have signed Schmidt's death-warrant.

Instead of answering his question, therefore, I offered a different answer. "Your suspicions are correct," I told him. "Your aunt is not mad, and neither am I. Sir Humphrey is only keeping us locked up as a way to conceal his misdeeds."

"His misdeeds—do you mean the plague?" Griff said, almost contemptuously. "I know about that—my aunt told me. That's nothing. I can't hold him responsible for that."

"Not the plague—the opium," said I.

He was not expecting *that*. "The *opium?*" He cast a glance about the passage and then hurried me into another room—a music-room full of pianos and harps, ghostly and smelling of dust beneath the white draperies which protected them against it. "What opium, Miss Molly?"

Of course he did not know of the opium: he had never gone to speak with Sir Humphrey's Chinese employees. "Sir Humphrey is shipping cheap Chinese opium from Yunnan to Hong Kong under the guise of herbal remedies," I told him. "Some of it he imports to Hong Kong against the monopoly laws, which is how he keeps control of his workers. The rest of it goes to Sydney and Canton, at the very least. I've no doubt he plans to ship it to America, too, once you have your own ships making the China voyage. I can give you the name of a witness if you want it; but first I want you to return me to Victoria, to an address I shall give you, for I cannot stay in this house any longer."

Having for the moment run out of things to say, I looked up from my nervously twisting hands and found that Griff had crossed his arms and was watching me with rather a self-satisfied smile upon his face.

"Well," he drawled, "I didn't *think* you were mad."

I stared at him with parted lips.

"What?" he asked with a laugh. "I was only playing along with Sir Humphrey. It was evident that you were up to another of your little schemes, and playing mad only to further it."

"I *wasn't*," I protested. Apart from once having claimed to see ghosts when it would do me the most good, I hadn't played mad at all. It seemed that my sex had doomed me, rather than my behaviour.

"Don't try to play the innocent," Griff said, misunderstanding my protest. "You lost me two million pounds—why should I help you, after that? The least you could do was go mad and let Seton and Associates keep your fortune." He ruminated for a moment. "Of course, Sir Humphrey himself will need to go. Vandergriff and Son must be able to absorb the company. I can't do business with a man who's locked up my aunt for a madwoman."

I regarded him with disgust. He did not care about his aunt—only about the Vandergriff honour. It was the same with the Noor-Jahan. "Why, you aren't angry with me for breaking off the engagement at all, are you?" I conjectured. "Only for losing you all that money."

Griff smiled his thin, grey smile. "You're the kind of woman I'd expect to profit from anything, even an engagement," he said. "I can respect that; that's good business. In fact, if you can help me to ruin Seton, I'd be willing to marry you after all."

"On the contrary; I'm not that kind of woman at all," I said. Vasily, too, had accused me of being willing to marry Griff for his money, regardless of the sort of person he was. Perhaps I had been willing to do so *once,* but never again! "Besides, I can't marry anyone. I've been declared mad, remember?"

"Only by a doctor, and not by a court," Griff persisted. "You'd be happier with me than you would be in an asylum, you know."

I could not quite believe that after all that had happened, Griff was still willing to marry me. It was not that he trusted me; rather, he must feel confident in his ability to control me.

It was only later, of course, that I understood just how deadly serious he was, or how little my refusal would mean to him.

"I'm not going to marry you," I said, putting a quiver into my voice. "I'm still mourning my first husband. All I want is to leave this awful place and go home to my family in London."

"Well, then, help me bring down Sir Humphrey and I'll

arrange it."

"No, no," I protested again. "All I want you to arrange is a conveyance to Victoria."

"Is that all?" he asked, laughing. "Very well, I'll take you to Victoria. Give me a moment and I'll summon Bone."

He tapped against his temple, then, and his face darkened. He tapped again and gave an angry mutter of, "Nothing!"

"What's the matter?" I asked, nervously.

He took three steps to the music-room door, wrenched it open, and darted into the passage. I followed him. The beachcomber, who had been left lying flat upon the carpet, had vanished.

"He's gone," said Griff, in tones of outrage. "And he's done something to the eye; covered it or something. What can have possessed the man?

"Maybe you shouldn't have shocked him into insensibility," I said.

"You think this is his revenge?" Griff asked, sounding a little shocked himself. There was a silence. Griff ground his teeth together. "He's gone to find Sir Humphrey, I don't doubt. Come, Miss Molly; there's no time to lose."

Chapter XX.

Since ordering the carriage would alert Sir Humphrey to our unsanctioned departure, Griff conducted me a short way down the road by foot to the tiny hamlet of Pok Fu Lum, where the village's sole rickshaw-and-cart man was engaged to carry us the rest of the way to Victoria. As we took our seats, Griff removed his gloves and rolled up his sleeves, displaying a pair of mismatched forearms—one covered with, or perhaps made of, thinly overlapping brass plates; the other pale and slender and fitted with a narrow shunt. Bitter experience had taught me the use of both, for Griff's right arm contained a thin and lethal steel blade, while his left had a nasty habit of extending like a whip to catch and throttle his foes.

An hour since, consumed by fear of Sir Humphrey and the triad, Griff had seemed a lesser threat. Now, recalling that brazen hand about my throat, and his cruelty to the beachcomber, I repressed a shudder.

"You seem well-armed," I commented. This feeble attempt at levity made no impression upon him. "Are you expecting trouble, from Sir Humphrey or some other quarter?"

"When kidnapping a young lady, it's wise to be prepared," he declared, which left me no wiser than before as to whether he meant to threaten me, or my enemies with violence

In any case, Sir Humphrey did not bother us. As we approached the city past the crowded, odiferous slopes of Tai Ping Shan, I considered how I was to find my friends without alerting Mr Vandergriff to their hiding-place. Even if I asked Griff to let me down around the marketplace, would I undress that evening to find one of his horrible little bugs latched somewhere among my petticoats? Or how could I prevent him simply following me to the boarding-house if he took it into his head to do so? I could scarcely afford to let Griff catch sight of a supposedly dead Grand Duke.

I was still struggling with this dilemma when, to my great relief, I saw a familiar figure loitering at the entrance of the market with a gilt box under one arm.

"Tell the man to stop," I cried, seizing Griff's arm. Even in the sudden tropical twilight, I would have known that tall, broad-shouldered figure anywhere. "That's Herr Schmidt."

The rickshaw-man stopped anyway, which was gratifying. Too long in Seton Castle had ingrained the habit of asking my minders if I wanted anything. "Herr Schmidt! Herr Schmidt!" I cried, slipping from the vehicle before Griff could say anything else. As Nijam's Alphonse turned, I seized his arm with a grip like death, half afraid that if I let go he would once again evade me.

"Mr Vandergriff and I must speak to you," I said, meaning to warn him to switch off his transmitter. Schmidt patted his pocket to let me know it had already been taken off and stowed—why, I could not imagine. Did he know that Griff and I were coming? Then Griff himself caught up with us, and for a moment the three of us stood warily in the street. I watched Schmidt, and Schmidt watched Griff, and Griff watched me.

241

"There's a little café just here," Schmidt said at length. "Why don't we sit down and have tea while we talk?"

Some tables and chairs had been drawn up on the pavement, half in and half out of the warm yellow light streaming from within the great windows. Colourful paper lanterns made up any deficiency in the lighting. Schmidt ordered tea and opened the gilt box, producing what he told us were mooncakes for the coming Mid-Autumn Festival: sweet pastries filled with bean paste, with intricate designs embossed on top.

"This is the witness I told you about," I told Griff. "In the course of investing in the Seton & Associates company, Herr Schmidt discovered evidence that Sir Humphrey has been shipping opium to Hong Kong in defiance of the Crown monopoly. Isn't that so, Herr Schmidt?"

Schmidt sent me a look of surprise, nearly of panic. "Ye-es," he said cautiously, as his eyes begged me for some explanation of this sudden turn of events. "He's been shipping opium from Yunnan for ten years or more. Now he's interested in sourcing a higher class of the drug from India."

Griff gave a low whistle. "I guess that's why you and Sir Humphrey have been in such a fuss, the past day or two."

"I'm surprised you haven't been eavesdropping on Sir Humphrey yourself," said I.

"Miss Molly! Imagine how inconvenient it would be if he found me doing any such thing. I was going to meet with Herr Schmidt in any case." He turned back to Schmidt. "Hearsay won't convince anyone. What can you give me in the way of documentary evidence?"

"We found a ledger," Schmidt said reluctantly, "which quite clearly values the worth of the Yunnun 'remedies' at the price of opium over the past fifteen or twenty years." That, I thought, must be the book I had seen my father's imprint perusing with such attention; Mimi must have tracked it down in the course of her researches. "But Sir Humphrey was at some pains to convince me that shipping opium isn't strictly against the law."

"No, but I need to discredit Seton in the court of public opinion, just enough to give me a chance of winning a different lawsuit I mean to bring against him," Griff said, very readily. I saw his game then: Lady Seton might have a chance to make her voice heard, but only if Sir Humphrey's reputation had already been tarnished. "The evidence, if you please. I will, of course, pay you handsomely for it."

Schmidt sent me another look of mute panic. I supposed that I had felt the same protest and alarm when Vasily had insisted upon bringing Zlata into our confidences. Yet Schmidt could not know how very grave was the danger that threatened him, nor how pressing was my need for Griff's help. Relinquishing our evidence against Sir Humphrey might be the last thing we could now do before fleeing the island.

I was trying to communicate all this purely through the expression of my eyes when a new player appeared upon the scene—a willowy gentleman whose face was partially obscured by grey whiskers and eyeglasses. Slightly out of breath, he bustled up to our table, bowed, and greeted Schmidt before helping himself to a chair.

"Oh, si—Nicks," said Schmidt weakly. "I'm so glad you're here. This is Mr Basil Nicks," he added, to Griff. "My *charge d'affaires.* He will be able to provide what you need, I'm sure."

Griff and the newcomer shook hands. Neither of them spared a glance for me, which was just as well, for my aston-ishment must have shown upon my face. Basil Nicks, indeed! This *nom de guerre* was one which Vasily Nikolaevich had once ridiculed as the completion of his dreaded transformation into the ideal bourgeois husband. Indeed, had it not been for the name, and for Schmidt's slip of the tongue, I might never have recognised him. The transformation was remarkable! Vasily's piercing green eyes had been covered up with brown, rather than red, lenses, and his cultivated black beard had been turned into something grey and straggly by the application of false white hairs with, presumably, spirit-gum. It was not simply the obscuring of his features, however, which completed the illusion. Somehow he had altered his voice, his scent, his very walk, to those of another man. I might have passed him a hundred times in the street and never known him!

I had never known Vasily for such a fine actor! But of course he had never before *wished* to conceal himself behind false whiskers. Why should he, when it was so much more comfortable to proclaim himself a Grand Duke, and watch the world fall over itself to please him?

In fact, Griff had met both Schmidt and Vasily before. He could not have had more than a glimpse of Schmidt, who as a servant had not warranted much attention; but with Vasily he had become quite well acquainted. Yet the disguise fooled him, though there had been a time during those spring days in London when Griff had remarked upon the Grand Duke's habit of turning up like a bad sixpence every time he and I forgathered.

At the time, Vasily had excused this unaccountable behaviour by saying that he meant to assist me in my pursuit of Griff's fortune. *For creatures like us, my little mouse, there's no spur like jealousy.* —I bit my lip to hold back a sudden exclamation. No spur like jealousy, indeed! Had Vasily truly been speaking, not merely of Griff, but himself?

"And you must be Miss Dark," Vasily was saying in a prim voice, adjusting upon his nose what I now recognised, with another wild urge to laugh, as Nijam's *pince-nez*. "I didn't expect to see *you* here, young lady. The word is that Sir Humphrey has been besieging the courts for a guardianship order. He'll get it, too, if he isn't interrupted."

If this was a warning, it was quite an unnecessary one! I sent him what I hoped was a speaking look to ask whether anything was wrong, but of course with Griff at my elbow, what reply could he possibly make?

"Try a mooncake, Miss Dark," Vasily added, setting one before me. "I think you'll find it much to your liking."

I did not think so at all: I was not remotely hungry. But no—Vasily was sending me a speaking look of his own. I picked up the cake and quietly inspected it.

As Griff and Vasily exchanged polite nothings about the weather, I located a slit at the bottom of the cake, and very stealthily extracted the slip of paper within.

Slipping it beneath the table, I read the brief message printed thereon: *All well. Keep to the plan.*

I cast a glance at Schmidt, who looked distinctly uncomfortable. I bit my lip, unsure whether to believe the note. It would be just like Vasily to withhold information from me! I sent him a look of daggers and pressed my lips together, berating myself for my folly. I ought to have walked from Castle Seton, not thrown myself upon Griff's mercies. Now I could not speak openly to my friends without somehow detaching the prosthete—and he was in no hurry to leave.

"Now, about that evidence we were speaking of," Griff said, putting a definite end to the pleasantries.

"Mr Vandergriff is anxious that Sir Humphrey's involvement in the opium trade should be made general knowledge," Schmidt explained to Vasily. "It will assist Lady Seton."

"I see!" Vasily said, looking thoughtful. I hoped that he was now able to understand why I had seen in Griff a useful ally. "You understand the difficulty, however? My client is also in some difficulties with Sir Humphrey; if he lends *you* the evidence, he leaves himself without a defence."

I felt desperate. Mooncake or no mooncake, evidently Vasily did not understand how serious the situation was. Since I could enlighten him in no other way, I must enlighten him in Griff's presence. It could hardly injure *us,* and might do real harm to Sir Humphrey.

"I really think you should do as Mr Vandergriff asks," I said in a voice that had gone high and tight with worry. "Sir Humphrey knows that Herr Schmidt has the evidence, and in order to suppress it means to kill him."

In the absolute silence that followed, Schmidt's tea spilled into the saucer. Vasily concealed his surprise well, for I only saw a worried twitch of his eyebrows; but Griff responded with disbelieving laughter.

"What? Seton, a murderer? Miss Molly, you'll make me question your wits, after all."

"Don't laugh," Vasily said, with absolute gravity and a little of his old imperious manner. "It won't be the first time Seton has committed murder."

Griff, who had disbelieved me, became suddenly very serious now that Vasily had spoken. "Murder? What do you mean by *that?*"

For once I could waste no time indulging Griff. "It was foolish not to approach Sir Humphrey more gently," I told

Vasily and Schmidt, trying to communicate my desperation without alerting Griff to the full nature of my association with them. "You drove him straight into the arms of the triad. Now both of them have scented the opportunity to profit, but only after you are dead. You—and everyone you might be working with—ought to leave the island at once. The evidence can be left to Mr Vandergriff: he will know how to make use of it."

I could scarcely put it any more plainly than this: that in my opinion the game was up. But Vasily, to my chagrin, hardly seemed to take me seriously.

"Will he?" he murmured.

"The Vandergriffs won't stand for Aunt Adelaide being treated like this," Griff said, sounding a little offended. "Honour demands that I do everything within my power—"

"Nevertheless, your honour is no business of my client's," Vasily said with a flick of his kid-gloved hand. "Herr Schmidt means to use the evidence himself, and although we're grateful to Miss Dark for her warning, there's no reason he, *or* his associates, should stir a step from where they are."

My heart sank. After the loneliness, the terrible isolation of the past days, would he send me back once again to that horrible place—without even hearing me out?

Perhaps Vasily saw some of this upon my face, for he added, kindly, "Don't be nervous on our account, Miss Dark. Seton may *wish* us dead, but forewarned is forearmed, and he's likely to find it more difficult than he thinks."

Griff made a sound of disbelief. "I really cannot imagine that Seton would do such a foolish—"

He was interrupted by Schmidt, who leapt to his feet with such an explosive movement that his chair went over *bang* upon the pavement, a lady shrieked, and all the teacups upon the table jumped and rattled, spilling their contents. He threw his body before Vasily, who swiftly seized him in his arms and overturned both of them upon the ground. At the same moment, a shot went off somewhere behind me. There was now a cacophony of shrieks from the other patrons at the café. I sat motionless with terror. All about me was disarray. I had eyes only for Vasily and Schmidt, who sprawled upon the ground, a confused tangle of limbs. From that tangle a hand—I did not see whose—reached out wildly, and left a smear of blood upon the table-cloth.

A metallic sound from my other side drew my attention as Griff twisted in his seat. Even as another gunshot echoed through the crowd, sending people scrambling beneath their tables, Griff's gleaming brass arm shot out with awful speed. There came the sound of a blow and a groan behind me. At that moment my power of movement returned, and I turned in my seat to see—Mr Bone, the beachcomber!

It was he who, coming up behind me, had commenced firing in our direction. Now, having received the blow of Griff's mechanical fist to his jaw, he was in the act of staggering backwards, even as his revolver fell with a dull thud to the pavement. I expected the man to fall, for he looked as though a breath of wind could knock him down.

Yet he did not fall. Instead, he staggered out of range of Griff's arm, stared wildly about him, and then turned to run. The grimy bandage was again wrapped about his head, concealing the prosthetic eye. Griff snapped his fingers, evidently trying once again to activate the eye and deal out punishment; to no effect. Then Schmidt plunged past us, hot on the beachcomber's trail. Another moment, and both men were swallowed up in the crowds of people and the fading twilight.

I leapt from my seat and stumbled over fallen chairs to get to Vasily, who now pushed himself off the ground, clutching an oozing wound in his arm. One of the bullets had nicked him.

"Are you badly hurt?" I gasped, trying to steady his drooping head. "He's in shock—Griff, please—call a doctor—"

Griff's brass hand clasped around my wrist and drew me inexorably away from Vasily, who fell fainting upon the pavement.

"It's too dangerous for you here, Miss Molly," Griff said over my protests. "Come away!"

Chapter XXI.

"Let me go! Can't you see that he's hurt?" I shrieked, but Griff was inexorable. His steely grip tightened until the pain subdued me and I was forced, whimpering, to quiescence.

"What the devil is Bone about, shooting at me like that?" the American growled, hailing a passing rickshaw. "If we still had revenants, this sort of thing would never happen! Get in, Miss Molly; I must see you safely home. No, don't worry about the man Nicks! Couldn't you see he was barely grazed?"

"He was *bleeding*," I protested, attempting a look back over my shoulder. Vasily was now quite hidden from sight by a crowd of worried bystanders. He would get help from *them*, at least, if not me.

In the meanwhile—I must remember that this man was *not* my friend, and that I must not give him the slightest reason to think that my feelings for Mr Nicks were any stronger than mere acquaintanceship!

"What makes you think Bone was shooting at *you?*" I asked, once Griff had given the rickshaw-man the direction. It was Vasily, after all, who had been injured. It was Vasily whom Schmidt had leaped to save, when he saw the approaching peril!

"Obviously he was shooting at me!" said Griff. "It's quite

clear what happened—the fellow took a disliking to me, just because I would not tolerate his disobedience, and came after me to shoot me! He even covered his eye, so that I could not observe him... But I wish I knew why the dead-man mechanism was not working! He can't possibly have meddled with it himself. Can there be *another* prosthetician in this backwater?"

For my part, I should have liked to know where Mr Bone had found his revolver, and more than that, why he was trying to shoot at anybody! Just then, however, a horrible thought occurred to me.

"Do you think he did it on Sir Humphrey's orders?"

"Seton's orders!" Griff repeated, in some surprise. There was a long silence as he considered this. "You think that Seton could be trying to kill *me* now?"

"I know it sounds ridiculous," I began, defensively, "but I'm not mad."

"Holy Moses, I believe the little girl is right," said Griff in quite a new tone of voice. "Seton must have found a surgeon to meddle with the eye! Well, this *is* a stroke of luck! If Sir Humphrey *had* tried to kill me, the question of my aunt's sanity need not be mentioned in public at all. I might simply prosecute him for my own murder. Useful—this could be very useful!"

It would certainly be convenient for *me* if Sir Humphrey had been trying to kill Griff—but I was by no means sure that he was! What if Sir Humphrey had somehow learned that Vasily was still alive? What if he knew that I was still colluding with my old friends? Surely he would be absolutely livid, enough to cut out the triad and send his henchman to assassinate us at once!

The city crowded in upon us, hot and stifling despite the clearing of the storm. I touched the high lace collar at my neck, wishing that I was in the privacy of my own room and could strip it off and breathe a little more freely. Then, convulsively, my hand clutched at the fabric as I realised that the rickshaw was on the familiar road leading out of the city towards Pok Fu Lum and Seton Castle!

I must have made a sound, for Griff sent me an inquiring look. "Is something the matter?"

Something the matter! Indeed there was something the matter—for I had gone to all this trouble only to escape from Seton Castle; and now I was to be taken back there! Oh, yes: Vasily had quite distinctly begged me to remain there—-Vasily had told me that all was well—and Vasily had promised me that Sir Humphrey would find it difficult to kill them. Yet scarcely were the words spoken, than Sir Humphrey had indeed attempted murder!

Griff was still waiting for a reply, and something had to be said. "You are returning me to Seton Castle," I said in a stifled voice. "I wished to remain in Victoria."

"Alone?" Griff asked, raising an eyebrow. "You can't be serious—not when there are assassins roaming the street. Come back to Seton Castle; I'll be able to keep an eye on you there, and you can help me deal with Sir Humphrey."

I did not want any of Griff's eyes upon me. I bit my lip, considering my next steps. I wanted to defy him; but that would not merely be to defy Griff. It might not even simply be to defy Vasily—I did not know what he and Nijam might have been plotting together; I did not know whether one rash action now would spoil things for good. For a moment, an old voice awoke, whispering that Vasily could not be trusted;

but reason told me that this was the old irrational doubt once more rearing its ugly head...

My choice was quite a simple one, in the end: since I could not speak to Vasily or my friends, I must trust myself blindly to their plans. The only alternative was to run away on my own account, allowing ignorance and fear to govern me, and leaving Sir Humphrey to Griff, who might destroy the man but certainly would not concern himself with righting any of the wrongs he had committed, against anyone but perhaps Lady Seton.

Vasily had failed to follow the plan in Moscow, and it had nearly ruined everything. Now, as frantic as I felt with worry, I could only continue to follow the plan, trusting him—and all my friends—not to leave me in durance any longer than necessary. I had seen Vasily: I had received his assurance that all was well and that he wished me to remain where I was. Since that was all I had to go on, I must content myself to go on blindly a little longer. I was worthy of their care; I could trust them to provide it. I was not alone.

"Very well," I said, in a voice that was the merest thread of sound. "I'll trust you." Griff patted my hand, for he did not know that the person I addressed was far away.

I employed the remainder of the journey to Seton Castle fruitlessly racking my mind as to what Vasily might be planning. Really, it was too bad! I had made up my mind to remain in the castle, but I felt absolutely useless. I had not the slightest idea of what was going on. Both Vasily and Griff seemed determined to complete this job without me. Even Mr Bone, whom I had begun to view as a friend, had just attempted to murder my—Vasily.

The night was perfect, velvety darkness by the time we

returned to the castle, and my own heart was not much lighter. Griff insisted upon escorting me back to my room in the downstairs wing. "I take it you have a key," he conjectured as I opened the door to my dim, musty-smelling prison.

I refused to vouchsafe an answer. "What are you going to do now?" I asked instead, finding my way to a lamp and lighting it.

"Don't you worry your pretty head, Miss Molly," he told me with an ominous smile. "I'll take care of everything; and if you're wanted, I'll let you know. But don't worry: I'll bring Seton to grief, and if you help me I'll make sure you're released without any doubts as to your sanity."

I said very sweetly, "I'm terribly grateful to you, Griff. I know I can rely on you."

The words were an effort. What a nerve the man had, telling me to sit about twiddling my toes when he knew very well that I was an accomplished confidence-trickster!

Griff went on smiling. "There," he said, "was that so hard? I think you and I will do very well together." With that, he abandoned his lazy attitude, raising a hand to his temple. "It's Bone," he muttered just as the French doors opened at the end of the passage.

As Griff turned to confront the newcomer, I darted after him. I am uncertain whether I wished to lock my door between myself and the assassin, or to defend him from a clearly angry Griff—but in the end I did neither. In the uncertain light of my lamp, Mr Bone was only a dark shape at the end of the passage, hunched a little with pain or exhaustion. He looked pathetic and not at all threatening.

Griff confronted him with arms folded, like an emperor reproving an erring slave.

"You have a nerve, returning here after trying to kill us," he declared. "Who were you acting for?"

The beachcomber did not answer. Griff raised his hand, and the snap echoed through the passage. Again there came that faint glint of blue light from the prosthetic eye; and Mr Bone fell to his knees with a sob of pain. At the same moment, Griff's hand of brass snaked from his sleeve and caught the unfortunate beachcomber about the throat. I heard him choke, and saw him clutching feebly at the merciless hand.

"Listen carefully," Griff announced, in a voice so low that it seemed to emanate, not from any single place, but from the very shadows that surrounded him. "*I* gave you that eye; *I* see with it, and I can make you suffer with it, too. You work for me; you don't work for Seton." He paused, and then gave the unfortunate man a shake. "Do you understand?"

"Let go of him," I protested, although I did not dare to approach either of them, for I felt as though I was in a den of wild beasts. "How can he answer if you're choking him?"

"He can nod his head," Griff said, still in that terrible, calm voice. "Can't you, Bone?"

Mr Bone was about to have the life very softly crushed out of him—but he managed a feeble nod.

"*Who* do you work for?" Griff repeated, allowing his grip to relax a little.

"You, sir," the beachcomber rasped; and with a little metallic chatter the brass hand retracted into Griff's sleeve again. The beachcomber fell forward, supporting himself on one hand as he struggled to regain his breath. Griff smiled.

"Good," he said, pulling on the black glove, which he habitually wore to disguise the unnatural hand. "You will, of course, continue to make Sir Humphrey believe that you are his servant; but in reality you will report to me. Your duties remain the same. You will watch this passage and not allow Miss Dark to leave her room. She may need some reminding of it. I trust you will provide such reminders as necessary, or else I shall be obliged to deliver some of my own." He sent me a somewhat sarcastic smile. "Lock the door, Bone."

The man crept to his feet, fumbled within his pocket for the key, and approached my door. Warily I retreated, but the beachcomber did not raise his eyes to me. He drew the door shut, and I heard the rattle of the key in the lock. On the other side of the door, Griff said something inaudible but genial as his heavy footsteps departed. I heard the loggia doors open and close, and once again I was in my prison—this time, with less chance of escape than before!

Outside my door, I heard Mr Bone, whom I ought to fear, breathing in long, painful rasps. His chair creaked as he sank into it. I wondered how he had escaped Schmidt; I wondered how he had so quickly returned to the castle; I wondered whether Sir Humphrey had some hold over the man, to make him fire a revolver into a crowded street. I wondered what his true feelings were, and why he had given me a key and allowed me to use it.

The longer I pondered, the less sense it all made. On a sudden impulse I crept to the door, reached out a trembling hand, and tried the knob. *It turned.*

My heart felt as though it might be crawling up my throat. I stared wildly at the knob, which stood trembling in my hand. Open! Why was my door *open,* when it had been locked at Griff's command? Was I going mad, or was Mr Bone?

For another moment I stood there, trying and failing to understand; and then, very softly, I closed the door, stole to the potted palm in which I had hidden my own key, unearthed it and locked the door myself.

Chapter XXII.

That next morning I did not know what to do. My sense of injury had only grown. Surely Vasily need not leave me in such complete ignorance of his plans! Surely he might get word to me if he really wished to do so! But no: in the absence of any instructions, I must sit about and wait, for in throwing myself upon Griff's mercy I had only sabotaged myself.

Mr Bone spent the whole morning crouched like a wolf at my door, and at first I did not dare to venture past him. Whatever his true sentiments, I could not trust him to help me when both Sir Humphrey and Griff had him cowed into obedience. Perhaps this was a mistake. Had I ventured forth, I might have been a little better prepared for what followed.

At it was, I had no warning. Having found a deck of playing-cards in the escritoire, I was amusing myself with the morning's fifth game of Patience when footsteps echoed loudly in the passage and a booming voice could be heard ordering Mr Bone to open my door. I rose to my feet as Sir Humphrey entered, followed by a mystified-looking Griff.

Had I been uncertain of Sir Humphrey's mood, one glimpse of his reddened face would have banished all doubt. He was in a towering rage, and in his quivering hand was a sheaf of paper. "The game is up, Miss Dark," he announced, shaking these papers in my face. "Your little conspiracy is unmasked!"

With this he threw the papers down upon the table, scattering my cards and striking absolute terror into my heart. From four creased sheets of handmade paper, four faces looked back at me: Nijam, Mimi, Schmidt—and Vasily, in his disguise as Mr Nicks!

I was conscious of a great roaring in my ears. What could I say? How had this come about?

"I know you are in league with them," Sir Humphrey wheezed. "*This* one was masquerading as your maid. *This* one is the charlatan who sold me the false Noor-Jahan in London, claiming to be the Begum of Bihar. And *this* one, damn his eyes, actually invested twenty thousand pounds into my company and then had the gall to blackmail me!" His stubby finger pointed in turn to Mimi, Nijam, and Schmidt.

"I think you ought to sit down, Sir Humphrey," I said in a desperate attempt to buy myself the time to think. "You are not breathing very easily."

Rather than trying to compose himself, he became more agitated still. I don't suppose I had ever actually heard a grown man cluck like a chicken before. "Listen, you—!" he clucked. "Listen, you—!" and then words failed him altogether.

Griff walked calmly into the room, picked up the sketches, and took them over to the window. His face did not change, although it became a little paler, and his gloved hand clenched very tightly until the papers began to crumple between his brass fingers.

In time, Sir Humphrey recovered himself sufficiently to shake a fist in my direction—a violent motion that made me retreat an involuntary step. Where could I possibly seek refuge? Griff was at the window, which in any case was barred.

Sir Humphrey advanced upon me in a murderous rage; and Mr Bone stood in the door, his posture coiled and ready to spring. As for me, I could scarcely draw breath. Had thirty thousand pounds-a-year's worth of Sir Humphrey's patience come to an end at last? It seemed strange and not at all fair that after having survived melusines, werewolves and vampires, I should meet my fate at the hands of a perfectly ordinary shipping-magnate in the spare bedroom of Seton Castle.

"You've done this before, haven't you?" Sir Humphrey demanded hoarsely. "You and your little gang seem quite determined to ruin me—well, the game is up! I know who you are, and I know where your friends live! You will rue the day you thought to blackmail *me!* It may cost me a fortune, but I will put an end to your depredations!"

"What—are you going to kill us all," I asked in a voice that quivered, "the way that you killed my father?"

Sir Humphrey choked, and his hands twitched in a way I did not like. "How dare you!" he squawked. "Your father died because he defied quarantine, poking his nose where he shouldn't!"

"Don't be foolish, Miss Molly," Griff put in, turning from the window. "Sir Humphrey has no reason to kill you. In fact, it would be greatly to his disadvantage."

Perhaps Griff's words recalled Sir Humphrey to a sense of discretion, for he gulped and became a fraction calmer.

"Yes," I said bitterly, "because he would lose the shares that my father left to *me.*"

"He had no right to do that," Sir Humphrey said, "after having done his best to make sure they were worthless! Just as you had no right to steal the Noor-Jahan! I cannot comprehend why you and your father should have undertaken my ruin, but don't for a moment imagine that you will succeed! You will be kept locked away, where you can do no harm to yourself or others." His hands clenched and unclenched convulsively. "I *need* the command of those shares," he added in a low voice. "I have made over a great number of my own to the Mountain."

"For the assassinations, I take it?" Griff asked, as smooth as silk. "Not of Miss Molly, of course; I mean the others."

Sir Humphrey and I both sent him a startled look. I had not quite expected Griff to believe my accusations, and Sir Humphrey was of course unaware of what the American had learned from Vasily and myself upon the previous evening.

Sir Humphrey's tongue flickered out and dabbed at his lips. "They're trying to blackmail me by accusing me of importing opium from Yunnan! Ridiculous! Still, they will do me great damage if they are able to fabricate the evidence. I asked one of the triads to deal with Schmidt—but they've uncovered a whole conspiracy."

Sir Humphrey broke off for a moment and brooded. "This cannot be public knowledge, Vandergriff. You understand my position, don't you? A nest of snakes ought to be scotched without pity."

"I understand perfectly," Griff said. "When is it to happen?"

"Tonight. The natives are having some sort of festival; there will be enough commotion in the streets to cover up any sounds. Under ordinary circumstances I would go to the authorities, of course—"

"Of course," said Griff.

"—But that would be to play directly into the hands of these blackguards. No; this is the safest way by far. With the triad carrying out the work, no suspicion will attach to me; I'll merely have to dispose of the evidence they bring me that the job is done. Now, if you'll excuse me, I have an appointment in town."

Tonight! I pressed a hand to my mouth as Sir Humphrey turned and stalked from the room. All my nightmares breathed thickly down my neck—I was to live, yes, but alone and friendless, immured in some horrible prison without any hope of release, since Sir Humphrey was about to murder all my friends. I could not bear it. As Griff made to follow Sir Humphrey from the room, I clutched at his sleeve.

"Don't go," I whispered faintly. "I want to talk to you."

"Calm yourself, Miss Molly," he replied just as softly. "I told you I meant to handle everything myself, didn't I?"

With that he shook me off and closed the door behind him.

Steadying myself against the nearest piece of furniture, I took a moment merely to breathe—to calm my wildly beating heart. The faces of my friends watched me from the table, and in time I came to watch them back. They were done in pen-and-ink, and were quite good. Someone in the Typhoon Gang was rather an accomplished artist.

Perhaps *too* accomplished, I thought; and then I caught my breath.

Appearances are notoriously untrustworthy; yet after all this time I ought really to have developed a better habit of looking beneath the surface of things to what I really knew of people. I should always have known that my father was a good and kind man, since he had proved it so often to his wife and children. I should have known that Sir Humphrey, who had never said a kind thing to me in my life, was cruel and heartless. I should have known that Griff was only selfishly interested in his family honour, and that he saw me as a feeble creature incapable of helping him in his self-appointed task.

I knew that Vasily was nothing like Griff. I knew that if he had not communicated with me, it was out of no sense of superiority, but only the same kind of accident that had prevented my communicating with him. I knew that he and Nijam were very far from being fools. I knew that Vasily would never have ordered me to remain in this house had he known of any real danger that threatened me.

With that I knew, suddenly and beyond the faintest shadow of a doubt, what my friends must be planning—and what they needed from me.

There was a risk, of course. If I guessed wrongly in any particular, I might put myself in danger and upset all my friends' plans. I had once already taken a dreadful risk, and perhaps done some damage, by putting my trust in Griff. Now I must put my trust in myself and my friends, and perhaps the result would be better.

It must, in fact, be my task to handle Griff—not to look to him for protection, but to manoeuvre him into a place where he would be of most use to us, as a rich man whom Sir Humphrey could not safely offend. And this itself would require a certain amount of finesse, because although Griff ought to know full well that I was neither a madwoman nor a fool—although he knew me to be a practised swindler who had already given him material assistance—it still had not entered his mind to seek my help.

Sighing, I fetched my key and unlocked my door, hoping very much that the beachcomber would still be willing to help me. I took my time about it, and when I emerged into the hallway, I found Mr Bone standing with his back to the passage, looking out the French doors towards the sea.

I dared not speak, for I had found Griff's little bugs hiding within my new room, too. The beachcomber did not speak, either; but behind his back he flapped a hand at me, indicating that I ought to take the green-baize door leading to the front of the house. Without a word—without even the apology I so desperately wished to give him—I obeyed.

Griff was at the little writing-desk in the library, dashing off a number of brief notes. I noticed that at least one of them was directed to the gendarmerie. "Please don't be angry," I begged him by way of greeting.

Griff glanced up at me with those bleak grey eyes. "I warned Bone what would happen if he set you at large again."

"I think you ought to thank him rather than punish him," I said. "I explained to Mr Bone how very sorry you would be if you didn't hear me out, and he was clever enough to see that I was right."

Griff frowned slightly; but his hand, which was poised with the fingers ready to snap, lowered. "What's that supposed to mean?"

"It means that I don't think you ought to be cross with me," said I. "You wouldn't know anything against Sir Humphrey if not for me—not about the opium, and not about the triad, either. Why, you don't even know *which* triad you ought to be watching."

He raised an eyebrow. "And *you* do?"

"Of course I do; that's why I came."

"Let's hear it, then."

"First things first." I took my seat upon an ottoman at Griff's feet, looking earnestly up into his eyes. "What are you going to *do* about it?"

"I told you not to worry yourself about that."

"But my friends are in danger," I insisted.

"A fact of which they're well aware."

"And you don't mean to help them? I didn't come here to get them killed, you know!"

His eyes narrowed. "Then what *is* your game, Miss Molly? Don't try to tell me there's honour among thieves! What *really* brought you to Seton Castle?"

The art of confidence-trickery lies almost entirely in telling the subject what he *wishes* to hear. I touched the tip of my tongue to my lips and said, "I didn't come to Seton Castle for the good of my health. I came to get back the inheritance Sir Humphrey stole from me. *My* future rides on this, as well as yours. I'll give you the name of the triad if you'll cut me in on your plans."

Griff laughed.

"I see! Well, it's no more than I already meant to do by you, Miss Molly. It's as Sir Humphrey said: there's nothing to tie him to the crime. Nothing, that is, except the moment at which the assassins will hand over their proof." He smiled. "I don't need to do a thing; just sit pretty until they produce the evidence, and swoop in to catch them then."

I opened my eyes very wide. "But by the time that happens, my friends will be *dead!*"

"Indeed! Well, I'm afraid I'm reluctant to help your friends. For one thing, they stole from me two million pounds' worth of property; and for another, there's no easier way to bring Sir Humphrey down, than by making him an accessory to murder." Griff's eyes narrowed further, and I thought I detected a hint of cold amusement in their depths. "I wonder—is it really your friends you're worried about, or your inheritance? If you had to choose, which would it be?"

I touched my lips with the tip of my tongue, striving to achieve the appropriate air of indecision. I must go gently, making precisely enough protest that he would believe me. "Must I choose? There's still the fact that Sir Humphrey has been trading in opium."

"Which will create a nice little scandal and cost him some hundreds of thousands of pounds—perhaps even millions," Griff agreed. "But it won't release you from your prison."

"Griff!" I exclaimed. "You *promised*—"

"I promised that if you helped me, I'd see you freed. But you're determined to be difficult." He leaned forwards, his eyes alight with avarice. "If you refuse to help me, I shall have my work cut out to free my aunt; I can't be sure I will succeed in freeing her, let alone you as well. On the other hand, you might help me. Sir Humphrey will lose his liberty as well as his reputation; I will have you declared well, and you can be Mrs Vandergriff and the mistress of all Sir Humphrey's lost millions. Which is it to be?"

I strove not to allow my absolute repugnance to show upon my face. So this was the secret to his continued determination to marry me—an attachment, not to me, but to my fortune! I sighed. I *was* so tired of being treated as a thing to be had, instead of a person to be loved.

Griff spoke again: "You'll only get your fortune if you give up those criminals you call your friends, you know. So I ask again: which is it to be?"

"I think you're a brute," I said. A girl at school had once suggested this as the perfect insult to hurl at a man you wish to charm, since it flatters his masculine vanity.

Griff did not blush or look coy, but I did think the insult pleased him. "No one is going to help your friends," he said, "least of all me! So you might as well make up your mind to profit from Seton's downfall. You're a clever woman; you won't sacrifice yourself unnecessarily."

I bit my lip. I could not bring myself to promise to marry the man; but I thought that I could get him where he was wanted, and when.

"The triad is called the Typhoon Gang, and I'm sure that Sir Humphrey will meet them at the dockyard. It's on their territory, and the harbour will be handy for any evidence they wish to dispose of."

I prayed, as I said it, that this was true.

"Ah-h-h." Griff straightened with a look of satisfaction. "You're by no means as ill-informed as you seem, Miss Molly!"

"Let me come with you," I added, as his grey eyes narrowed in thought. "I want to be there when it all happens."

"Out of the question; the docks at night, when the Typhoon Gang are handing over the evidence, are no place for a young lady."

"I'm sure no harm will come to me in your company," I told him. "Besides, we have a bargain, and I wish to know that you'll hold up *your* end of it."

Griff smiled thinly, but agreed; and I returned to the green-baize door conscious of having won a great victory. A very pleasing day's work it was—apart from his determination to marry me!

I wondered whether this ought to give me pause—but at that moment I could scarcely summon the spirit to care. If anything went wrong tonight, likely we should all be dead. First we must complete the job, and then I could extricate myself from marriage to Griff.

As I entered the rear passage, I perceived with relief that

Mr Bone had endured this most recent escapade unscathed. As he opened my door and stood aside to let me enter, I could not help feeling grateful to him. I did not understand this man, but I knew that without his help I could scarcely have done anything today. On an impulse, I leaned up to him and whispered into his ear: "Thank you—I will ask nothing more of you now." I thought that he shivered at the words, but he made no answer: he only locked me into my room again.

I had yet a few hours to wait until we must depart on the evening's business. In the meantime, I heard brisk footsteps through the house and doors opening and closing as Griff hurried off to the city to set his own trap. He certainly paid a visit to Lady Seton, and I heard the Amazonian nurse making strident protests as she was shown firmly towards the entrance-hall.

Now that we were in the lull before the storm, I fell prey to some anxieties of my own. What if I had guessed Vasily's aim incorrectly? What if something went wrong—were my friends' lives, as well as my own freedom, at stake? To distract myself from my worries, I fixed my mind upon my father, and found with delight that I was still able to summon his imprint into being. He stood before me in the golden mid-afternoon light, no longer a terror, but a warm and beloved memory.

"I *am* sorry, Papa," I told him in a low voice, not caring whether Griff could overhear via his little bugs. "I am sorry for judging by appearances, and not by truth. I am sorry that I misjudged you, but I am sorry, too, for misjudging myself. The little girl you left behind deserved better than what Sir Humphrey was pleased to give her." How I pitied that child for all the times she was told how bad she and her family were, simply because they would not enrich themselves at any cost!

How I pitied her for being told that her only worth could be measured in money—for still feeling, even now, that she must be very wicked and depraved for defending herself!

The child that I was—the woman I had become—deserved better than to be reduced to a commodity: for Griff, for Vasily, or for anyone.

"From now on things will be different, Papa," I whispered. "I'm going to finish your work."

In my memory, he smiled through his tears, and bent down to press a kiss to my forehead.

"Be good," his lips said, and I smiled.

I would be good. I would hold Sir Humphrey to account for all the evil he had done—to me as well as to others.

Chapter XXIII.

I was so intent upon my own affairs that when Mr Bone conducted me into the city that evening to meet Griff, I was surprised to find the city glowing with festive lanterns and gaily-dressed holiday-makers. This, then, must be the Mid-Autumn Festival! The parts of the city reserved for Western residence now seemed dark and staid; but Tai Ping Shan and even much of the business district at the centre of the city fairly blazed with light. Lanterns hung everywhere, some in dazzling displays through which people strolled to admire the view. Others had been released into the sky, and drifted through the warm breezes like lesser moons. Music and drums played from every other street corner. The gates of the taverns stood open, and the streets were crowded not only with people, but with gaily decorated stalls selling fruit, wine, mooncakes, lanterns and many other pretty confections and ornaments which, if I had not been on a business of some urgency, would have tempted me to linger.

This was very far from being the grave, wise, and staid China of my nanny's stories: it was, on the contrary, something like a Christmas Eve at home, although much warmer. "I wonder what they're celebrating," said I, as our rickshaw passed a courtyard full of young ladies wreathed in smoke, amidst which a feminine voice seemed to be declaiming musically-inflected words like the tolling of a bell. My companion gave a shrug.

Griff was waiting for us at the same little café where Mr Bone had shot at Vasily—a fact for which I found I could not quite resent the beachcomber. Such a lot of people wanted to shoot at Vasily, after all! and it seemed quite incredible that after having sacrificed himself so often to help me, this man should have made his attack without some very pressing reason. Although I could not quite feel as friendly towards Mr Bone as I had before, on the whole I regarded him with pity, and not with fear.

We found Griff in the company of another elderly English gentleman, a little older and thinner than Sir Humphrey, and with more angular features, but otherwise very much of the same sort: prosperous, comfortable, and consequently in very good humour with himself and the world.

"Hullo!" said this gentleman as I approached. "What's this, Vandergriff? a lady?"

"The lady who is going to be my wife," Griff answered, very much against my will. "Allow me to present Miss Molly Dark, who knows something about this business. Miss Molly, this is Mr Blackmore, one of the magistrates here."

I gave Mr Blackmore an impeccable bow, for it was possible that he had heard of me—as a madwoman. The correctness of my greeting did nothing to temper his astonishment. "Surely this is no business for a young lady, Vandergriff."

"Oh, but Miss Molly is one of the New Women," Griff said, with a laugh. "Try to keep her away!"

"Is she indeed!" said Mr Blackmore, peering at me as though I was some exotic specimen. I have never claimed to be a New

271

Woman, but just at that moment I felt that I could, if only to stop them discussing me as though I was incapable of making any answer myself.

There were one or two small points the gentlemen wished to settle between themselves, such as the disposition of the policemen, and the means by which they were to be summoned (with a whistle, which Mr Blackmore had hanging about his neck). This done, they engaged rickshaws and the four of us were carried to the dockyard, where a single electric light was burning above the closed warehouse door. Here, a handsome young Chinese clerk met us and asked us to wait in the shadows of the great chests of merchandise, which had been stacked on the quay between the warehouse wall and the great black bulk of a steamer which had been anchored opposite.

For a time we waited. Under any other circumstances I might have found it a very pleasant evening, for the oppressive heat of day had given way to mild breezes and distant music, while the stars and lanterns floating overhead were reflected from the rippling waters of the harbour. The gentlemen certainly seemed to enjoy the evening, for they lit cigars and smoked while they waited, making small talk to pass the time. Griff must have removed his gloves, for from time to time, even in the shadows, a glint of light reflected from the cold metal of his hand. I and Mr Bone were absolutely silent. The young Chinese had taken his storm-lantern and gone away towards the gate. I wondered whether this was Nijam's Mr Li, and whether he might have told me anything about my friends. But of course, even if he had still been with us I could not have risked the question.

Not many minutes later, a little group entered by the

dockyard gate and approached the warehouse—a dozen or so men, all of them Chinese, most of them young and wiry-looking. In the shadows, the gentlemen put out their cigars and fell into silence. Griff's brass hand fastened upon me again and pulled me behind him—no doubt adding a new constellation of bruises to my arm. From the shadows of the merchandise, we watched in silence as the gang approached. One of them carried a blood-stained sack, the sight of which caused my heart to tremble—for if anything had gone wrong-!

At their head walked an older gentleman: the Mountain of the Typhoon Gang, whom I had last glimpsed paying a visit to Sir Humphrey. In almost the same moment a small door opened, and Sir Humphrey himself emerged from the warehouse. He was flanked by a pair of grim-looking white men who carried a small chest between them and kept their hands very near the grips of their revolvers.

The Mountain came forward to exchange bows with Sir Humphrey, and the small chest was placed upon the quay at his feet.

"A small gift," Sir Humphrey announced, "to thank you for your help and to show you what benefits might result from our partnership in the future."

"What is it?" the Mountain asked in his heavily-accented English.

"The finest of the Yunnan opium," Sir Humphrey proclaimed, in accents of pride. "Completely duty-free. Sell it or smoke it; whatever you like. There's plenty more where that came from."

Beside me, the magistrate gave a gasp of horror. "Vander-griff!" he hissed. "Did you know about this?'

Griff put a silencing finger to his lips, but even he could not resist giving a disapproving *tch.*

"I did not credit," the magistrate muttered more softly, beneath the sound of wind and water, and distant music, "that *Seton* should have involved himself in that filthy trade! And on the black market, no less!"

"You have his own word against him," Griff said meaningfully. "But listen!"

The Mountain, having signalled his men to retrieve the chest, now addressed Sir Humphrey in turn. "The gift is very generous," he said, "but not necessary. The Typhoon Gang keeps its word. We have finished your business." And he turned to signal the man who held that terrible sack!

Now, if ever, it was my turn to enter upon the scene.

What had been easy to believe in my dark little room at Seton Castle was somehow much more difficult now that a blood-spattered sack was being handed to Sir Humphrey by one of at least a dozen very hard-looking men. I closed my eyes first, breathing a fervent hope to my Maker that I had, indeed, guessed correctly. If I was wrong, all of us were undoubtedly dead. Then, with a preliminary gasp, I released a piercing sneeze upon the cool night air.

"Oh, dear! Oh, no!" I gasped, as Griff turned upon me with a grimace of rage. "Oh, I *am* sorry!"

"I'm very much afraid that you *will* be," Griff said, the long, gleaming steel blade appearing in a moment from his right hand.

"Don't—don't try to fight them," I begged. He must understand that his personal appendages could be no match for the firearms which now suddenly appeared in the hands, not merely of Sir Humphrey's henchmen, but also of the Typhoon Gang. Griff sent me a resentful look, but as the shouting ruffians surrounded us, his blade retracted as suddenly as it had appeared. The four of us put up our hands as directed and were dragged from our hiding-place to face Sir Humphrey and the Mountain.

Sir Humphrey, when he saw us, turned once again a shade which in pleasanter days might have filled me with concern for his health. As it was, I wondered whether the odds were good that he might fall dead upon the spot and save us all a great deal of trouble.

"Miss Dark!" he sputtered. "And you, Griff! —and Bone, and Blackmore! What the devil is this supposed to mean? Why are you allowing a lunatic to lead you around? I should have expected better from both of you!"

"I should have expected better from *you,* Seton," said Griff in a voice so calm as to be almost lifeless. "Do you really mean to run black-market opium to California? Is that why you were so eager for our partnership?"

"This is preposterous," Sir Humphrey said. "I've never had anything to do with opium in my life! Everybody knows that!"

"Give it up, Seton," Blackmore said, his whiskers quivering with emotion. His hand stole towards his breast, where the police-whistle was concealed. "We'll all swear to seeing you hand that chest of opium over to the Mountain just now."

"Keep your hands up!" Sir Humphrey said sharply. For a moment he gnawed at the ends of his moustache in silence, before seeming to come to a decision. "You won't swear to anything if you're floating in Victoria Harbour! Here, you— Mountain," he added to the triad leader. "Have your men shoot them."

The Mountain raised his eyebrows in polite disbelief. "The honourable gentleman is a magistrate," he said.

"If it's a matter of payment, we can arrange that later! Shoot them!" Sir Humphrey demanded, but the Mountain only bowed.

"He doesn't want to fall afoul of the Governor," Griff declared. "You'd best give yourself up, Seton."

"Not dashed likely!" Sir Humphrey cried—or words to that effect. "Very well—I'll do it myself if I must! Here—give me that revolver!" he panted, turning to one of the foremen who silently accompanied him.

I think the man was too startled to deny him. Griff did not move as Sir Humphrey possessed himself of the weapon.

"You're making a very great mistake," he said calmly, as the wicked little barrel was levelled at his heart. "Stop and think a moment. You'll never get away with this."

"I've got away with it before," Sir Humphrey hissed—and his lips tightened as he prepared himself to shoot.

Heaven only knows what might have happened next! But the light over the warehouse door, which alone illuminated the scene, dimmed and flickered. The next moment it went out!

For a moment, confusion reigned. In the darkness, I heard Sir Humphrey swearing for someone to bring a light. Griff seized hold of me, uttering some choice words of his own as he tried to find his way past the bales of merchandise piled upon the quay.

As for me, I kept my eyes fixed upon Sir Humphrey: and so I was the first to see the pale glimmer of light which appeared upon the warehouse wall beside him. Gradually at first, but then more swiftly, a shape took form. Thinking that I was seeing an imprint—which was curious, but unlikely to provide me with any advantage—I said nothing. Then one of the triad men gave a yell of fear. The hubbub upon the dock quieted as that cold grey light grew stronger, illuminating the distant shape of a Chinese dockhand. He seemed impossibly far away; but how could that be, when the warehouse door formed a barrier so near?

Sir Humphrey turned, with the rest, to gaze upon the uncanny sight. A distant, despairing wail rang in our ears. The figure—whether shade or imprint or ghost, it was like nothing I had experienced before—swept towards us, slowly at first, but then with increasing speed. Griff's hand gripped me with convulsive terror as the wail increased to an unbearable shriek. A distorted face was now quite clearly visible—blotched and blackened—a sufferer, it was clear, of the dreaded Black Death!

Still the apparition loomed nearer, now screaming like a freight-train—grew in an instant to gigantic proportions, raised on high a threatening hand—and swept darkness down upon us!

All sound and light ceased. Upon the quayside, chaos reigned. Mr Blackmore had fallen on his face. Nearly everyone was screaming or crying. Griff was shouting for someone to blow the damned whistle for the police. Sir Humphrey's voice rose above the rest, babbling like a madman.

"Begone, spirit, begone! It wasn't my fault! The plague would have come anyway!"

And in that moment, quite close to me, I *swear* that I heard Vasily speak, very light and exultant.

"*Now* he believes in ghosts. At him, my dear!"

I caught my breath and laughed; and then I summoned to my mind the imprints of all the sick and suffering whom I

277

had seen in the company of Lady Seton. At once they flooded upon me, together with all the dreadful sensations they had felt in life—the agony, the despair. I gasped, but I kept my head: I raised my hand and pointed towards Sir Humphrey.

"There he is," I panted. "There is the one who did you wrong."

They flooded past me and crowded in upon Sir Humphrey. I knew when he saw them, for then he began to scream. Never before had he been forced to *feel* as someone else felt. Until that moment he had passed all his days in comfort and self-satisfaction, his strongest emotion merely one of annoyance any time he failed to get his own way in something. Now he was being drowned in all the pain, the outrage—all the misery he had caused and laughed at!

I hesitated, thinking that this was enough—that after all, these people had suffered more than me and mine. But I had promised to stop despising myself. My wounds were as real, if not so deep, as theirs. I called upon my father's imprint.

Just as Sir Humphrey broke free of those who had died of the plague and staggered towards me, my father appeared from the darkness—my father as I had seen him in the crypt of the Seton chapel, gashed with many bleeding wounds. At the sight of the man he had murdered, Sir Humphrey recoiled with a shriek and threw up his hands to cover his face.

"Dark!" he howled. "Don't look at me like that—don't look at me! Oh—murder! Help!" and in his terror he lunged away from us and fled into the darkness.

"Not that way, you fool!" Griff shouted, but it was already too late. Blinded with fear, the man who had ordered our bodies to be thrown into the Victoria Harbour ran straight over the edge of the quay and with one last despairing cry plunged into the water.

At once the light over the warehouse door came on again, more fully illuminating the scene. From the direction of the gate, the young Li Ling and a small body of turbaned Indian policemen came running towards us. As the Typhoon Gang hurriedly concealed their weapons, Schmidt emerged from the shadows to shake hands with the broadly smiling Mountain. At my feet Mr Blackmore was recovering from hysterics, and Griff, still clinging like death to my elbow, gazed around him in pale, speechless amazement. I wondered whether the scene had reminded him of what happened when he held the Noor-Jahan in his ungloved hand.

"Hi, Schmidt!" Mimi called from somewhere behind us. "Come quickly! He's fallen in the water!"

Extracting himself from the Mountain's congratulations, Schmidt rushed past us, tearing off his jacket. There came a second splash a moment later.

"Ah, there you are, Dark," Nijam said, strolling into view. "Well done! I suppose you received our message?"

"Your *message?*" I gasped even as Griff made a choking sound—no doubt of recognition.

"Yes, the message we left in the chapel for you to find last night," Nijam answered, sending Griff a forbidding look. "What's the matter with *him?*"

"You're the woman who sold me an imitation diamond!" Griff cried, pointing at her. "Police! Arrest this woman!"

"They'll do nothing of the sort," Nijam snapped. "You've no evidence. How did you like my little sound-and-light show, Dark?"

I gaped at her. "That was *you?*"

"Of course," she said, managing to radiate satisfaction even through her habitual scowl. "It's a process of rapid-fire photography, which, when projected upon a wall by means of a strong light from the deck of that ship docked just yonder—oh, it doesn't matter! It worked, though—thanks to some very good acting by Mr Li. There's Science for you—just as good as ghosts, and a deal less trouble."

I pointed at the young Chinese man, who together with the Mountain, was engaged in an earnest discussion with the police. "That ghastly apparition was Mr Li?"

"Mimi made him up to look like a plague victim," Nijam said with ghoulish relish, "and she and Schmidt took photographs from the hospital for reference, to make it all look convincing."

"Who *are* these people?" Mr Blackmore gasped. Griff had helped him to his feet. "Are they part of the Typhoon Gang, too?"

Nijam snorted. "Nobody's part of the Typhoon Gang. Who would be so foolish? This is Li Ling, one of Sir Humphrey's clerks; and that older gentleman is his father, who is a well-known businessman on the board of the Tung Wah Hospital, and these are some friends of theirs from—a patriotic society." By this I supposed that she meant a revolutionary society; but as it turns out, these were tolerated in Hong Kong, since the government they wished to reform was not the one in Hong Kong.

"But what are you all doing *here?*"

"Well," Nijam said smugly, "I think that you'll find that Miss Dark and the elder Mr Li now own a controlling share in Seton & Associates, so this is, in a sense, *our* quay."

"That's impossible," Mr Blackmore protested. "Sir Humphrey would never sign over his company to the natives!"

"I can assure you he did," I put in. I was now able to piece together a little more of the story. Nijam and Vasily had indeed known what they were about, when they had Schmidt provoke Sir Humphrey into trying to murder them all! "He signed over a great many shares in order to hire them, under the mistaken idea that they were assassins."

Just then, Schmidt and Mimi returned from the waters, half-carrying, half-dragging Sir Humphrey between them. "But you're dead!" the waterlogged Sir Humphrey protested, glancing from his investor to my former lady's maid. "I paid the Mountain to kill you, and he did!"

"I'm afraid we're all very much alive," Nijam told him. Such was her evident satisfaction that I felt a pang of sorrow for Vasily, who was missing the opportunity of a lifetime. He *did* so love to gloat over his defeated foes, the poor man! and instead, he was required to hide himself from view!

"You—you—you're *that* woman!" Sir Humphrey gasped, making the same identification Griff had a moment ago. "Police! Police!" Tearing himself away from Schmidt and Mimi, he staggered over to the Indian gendarmes. "Arrest them all," he gasped, waving a hand. *"Those* people have cheated me out of two million pounds! And *this* is the notorious Typhoon Gang, who have received thousands' of pounds worth of shares in my business without the slightest notion of holding up their end of the bargain!"

"The bargain to do *murder,* you mean?" cried Mr Blackmore, who had now recovered his composure sufficiently to recall what had been about to happen before Nijam stepped in. "Including a magistrate of the peace?"

"I tell you they're the Typhoon Gang," Seton wailed. "They're criminals! Arrest them!"

"You're a criminal, Seton!" Mr Blackmore thundered. "We

can all swear that you were about to shoot us! And that's not even considering the smuggled opium! Take him away!"

"I'm not!" Sir Humphrey absolutely shrieked as the police descended upon him. "I haven't killed anyone! I didn't see any ghosts! I didn't even touch William Dark! Let me go!"

"Hopelessly insane," Griff said with a touch of amusement in his voice as they dragged Sir Humphrey away. "Don't you think so, Blackmore?"

"I shouldn't be surprised," the magistrate said thoughtfully. "Here, constable, don't forget to take that chest; that's smuggled Yunnan opium, I believe. And what's in this ghastly bag? Pig trotters? Take that, too. Mr Li, I trust you'll be answering a number of questions at the police station tonight. You too, Mr Schmidt, along with your friends. Well, well, well! Sir Humphrey Seton! Never in a hundred years would I have guessed! What's that, Vandergriff? No, I don't think we'll be needing you tonight. You might as well take Miss Dark home."

All this time Griff had not released me: he held my arm in a grip of steel—or more accurately, of brass. "Well, Miss Molly," he said now, "it's time for you to hold up *your* end of the bargain."

"What bargain?" I asked rather foolishly, for amidst the *dénouement* unfolding about me one piece of information had been burning in my thoughts. So, Vasily and Nijam *had* sent me a letter—and I had never received it! I had never even returned to the chapel! Oh! what a world of trouble and doubt I might have saved myself!

"What bargain?" I repeated more sharply, as Griff dragged me towards the gate. "Let me go! I never made a bargain with you!"

At my cry, Schmidt started after us. Griff turned on him, the blade whispering from his right arm, nearly catching Schmidt in the throat. He stilled; and Nijam caught onto his arm as though to hold him back.

"You people have been of great help to me tonight," Griff said very softly, "but from now on, if you interfere with me I'll have the lot of you arrested."

"Leave it, Schmidt," Nijam murmured.

I looked into their eyes. Perhaps a silent message flew between Nijam and myself. A conviction, which had now been growing upon me for some time, now solidified into something very near certainty. The first time the thing had occurred to me, it had seemed utterly preposterous; but thus far I had trusted my friends, and I thought I could trust them further.

"Don't do anything foolish," I said shakily. "I'll go with him, since he demands it."

Mimi gave a soft snort. "And she tells *me* not to sell myself!" she muttered, as Griff dragged me towards the gate. This was unjust: indeed I had no idea of doing so. I was pleased, at any rate, that they did not follow me. Only the silent Mr Bone, who had remained at our side the whole time, brought up the rear.

Chapter XXIV.

"I take it you remembered your promise at last," Griff remarked. Hurrying me through the gate, he conducted me into Sir Humphrey's carriage, which still waited in the street with a coachman who had managed to doze through the entire commotion. "On the whole, I think congratulations are in order," he added, taking his place beside me, as the beachcomber settled opposite. "My plan went off without a hitch."

"Allow me to congratulate you on your excellent management," said I, as drily as himself.

He darted me a self-satisfied smile. "I'm very impressed with you as well, Miss Molly. How did you manage to remain in communication with your friends? I never intercepted a single letter, signal, or messenger—and yet when the moment came, there you were, sneezing fit to burst. Why yes—I *do* believe that my plan to let you handle Sir Humphrey Seton has come off very nicely indeed."

Oh! so now it had been his plan to let us handle Sir Humphrey all along! I concealed my indignation. "If you are so happy with the result, can't you let me go? Why do I need to marry you?"

"Because of the very large number of shares you own," Griff

said. "My aunt will, of course, entrust the remainder of Sir Humphrey's shares to me, once he has been declared insane—and I think I can manage *that,* or my name's not Warren H. Vandergriff. With your shares and my aunt's within my possession I shall hold a controlling interest in the company. It won't matter if your Chinese friends *are* mad enough to think that they can run an international trading company."

"I don't see why they shouldn't. With the exception of a few executive officers, they've already been running it very successfully for some years," I pointed out. Griff only smiled. "What if I tell you I don't *want* to marry you?"

"You're much too clever to say a thing like that," Griff said, very confidently. "Not when a word from me could see your friends taken up for fraud."

I beheld him with growing detestation. "Are you threatening me?"

"Why should I need to do that? I'm only stating the truth: I can protect you, but only as my bride." —Because, no doubt, with Griff only the Vandergriff family name outweighed the claims of the law!

After a moment he continued. "You were eager to marry me three months ago in London. Why should that change? My own feelings have not; and neither have my prospects, except for the better. I've got money, brains, and looks; and I won't treat you badly. Someday you'll thank me for this."

If threatening my friends was his idea of treating me well, I shuddered to think how he might treat me should he believe me to have forfeited his care. Instead, I chose defiance. "My friends stole the Noor-Jahan out of the British Museum itself. I don't think they will have any trouble stealing me out of Seton Castle."

"Then they'd better hurry," Griff remarked, peering at his watch, "because I quite clearly asked the clergyman to be at the chapel by eleven, and it's now ten-thirty."

That quite took my breath away. "I—*tonight?*"

"I'm afraid time is pressing."

"But I haven't—I haven't prepared a trousseau," I said feebly. I had once again the uncomfortable feeling that I had blundered into the sort of book where young ladies are always being forced to marry scoundrels against their will. Only Griff was so extremely dull and respectable! If *I* had been allowed to pick the scoundrel to marry against my will, it would be the recklessly exciting sort of scoundrel who only does it because he's too terrified to admit that he is fond of you.

"You won't try to make trouble for me, will you, Miss Dark? As I said before, it would be very foolish."

I let out a sigh. Nothing I could say would move him. If I continued to defy him, then either he would hector me some more, or he would do something unspeakable to my friends. "All right," I said wearily. "I won't."

The beachcomber, all this time, held perfectly silent. I felt a moment's irrational resentment that he was not coming to my aid. Surely if I looked anywhere for help, it must be to him. I had not yet quite given myself up for lost: I had one or two tricks up my sleeve, and would not marry Griff if I could at all manage it. All the same, it was hard! I had spent so much time alone, cut off from every friendly or beloved face; and now at last, when all had gone so well—when Sir Humphrey had been carted off under suspicion of murder and smuggling and insanity and goodness knew what else—now I had a new battle to fight, with a foe both vigilant and unyielding, who had satisfied himself that I was objecting to him only under a momentary lapse of judgement!

Ruefully, I recognised this petulant mood for what it was. All my life I had depended upon other people for protection, in the belief that fighting for myself was selfish and wrong. Now that I was required to protect myself, I felt injured. I felt that by deferring to my judgement, my friends had abandoned me as worthless.

I knew that this was foolish. My friends would aid me when it was necessary, but they could not live my life for me. Had I not begged Vasily not to overwhelm my better judgement? And so he stood back, and was allowing me to use it. But I was weary. I wanted his help; I wished the time had already come that he could give it.

Too soon the journey was over: the carriage stopped at the little postern-gate in the Seton estate's wall, within which the chapel stood. Griff helped me down and the two of us went in by the little gate, with Mr Bone bringing up the rear. Candlelight streamed from within the chapel, but we entered to find the place quite deserted save for Lady Seton and a clergyman; who I later learned was responsible for the care of the Pok Fu Lum souls and a friend of Sir Humphrey's.

"Warren," Lady Seton cried, starting up. She looked very pale and was twisting a handkerchief as though the motion was the last thing keeping her nerves in check. "What has happened? Has Sir Humphrey returned?"

"Everything is right and tight," Griff said easily. "You're a free woman now, and Sir Humphrey is in the hands of the police."

"He is?" Lady Seton whispered. Despite the horrible way Griff was behaving to *me,* I was glad that I had done what I could to bring that look of hope into her eyes. "Oh, Warren!"

—and bursting into tears, she threw her arms around his neck.

"There now, don't strangle me! I couldn't tell you before; but that's the truth."

"But what's to become of me now?"

"You're not to worry about that," he said, disentangling himself from her embrace. "I shall take care of all that for you. I trust the servants gave you no trouble while I was away?"

"Only that Mrs Lister—but I did as you told me, and she ran away." Dabbing at her eyes with the much-abused handkerchief, Lady Seton turned to me. "Miss Dark, I suppose I have you to thank for all this! If you hadn't taken my message—"

"Now then, Aunt Adelaide," Griff said, "you know that we don't have the time to stand about chattering all day! We have a wedding to solemnise, and Miss Dark is very tired."

"A *wedding?*" Evidently Lady Seton had not quite grasped the reason for this midnight rendez-vous. She blinked from me to Griff, and then clasped her hands. "Oh, Miss Dark! Is *this* the gentleman you told me about?"

I did not quite know how to reply to this.

"Who else would it be?" Griff asked with a smile. "Come, Miss Molly, take my hand. Are you ready, Reverend?"

The clergyman, adjusting his steel-rimmed spectacles on the end of his nose, resembled one of those kindly old gentlemen in Mr Dickens. "I must say, this is all a little irregular. Ordinarily, the banns—"

"Forget the banns! We don't have them in the United States, anyway," Griff said. "I've got a special licence from the Governor himself—isn't that good enough?"

"Well—yes, I suppose…"

Griff had been busy, thought I, following him in a resigned sort of way to the altar. He must have been planning this for days—ever since he returned to the island. Why, he had never intended to help me get free of Sir Humphrey at all; from the very first, once he had arranged his uncle's downfall, he meant to get control of my fortune in this manner!

The clergyman opened his prayer-book and cleared his throat. "Dearly beloved, we are gathered here in the sight of God, and in the face of this—congregation." His voice faltered, evidently too keenly aware of the fact that this marriage was taking place in a chapel at the dead of night, with only Lady Seton and Mr Bone for witnesses.

"Continue," Griff said. "No, no, pick up where you left off," he added, as the clergyman made as if to turn the page. "No one shall say that I was not married properly."

Somewhat bewildered, but clearly unable to say for certain what troubled him, the old man continued with the charge. I stood there feeling that I was in a dream. I had never been married before, and I remember, as the familiar words washed over me, wondering whether it would be like this if I married Vasily, too—whether I would be able to hear a word of what was said, or whether all my being would be consumed with other thoughts. I glanced towards the pews. Lady Seton, in the front, gave me a fond smile. Mr Bone stood a little further back, a dark shape among the shadows. His shoulders were hunched a little, and his hands were a white gleam upon the back of the pew before him. I hoped—oh, I *hoped*—that I was right about him. In the other two people present I had no faith at all. The clergyman was too old, the lady too infirm, and both of them were feeble before Griff's force of will.

The clergyman read on. "I require and charge you both (as

ye will answer at the dreadful day of judgement, when the secrets of all hearts shall be disclosed) that if either of you know any impediment, why ye may not be lawfully joined together in matrimony, ye do now confess it."

This was the moment at which Jane Eyre had been saved from a bigamous marriage by the sudden appearance of a champion. I awaited mine in vain. There was no ringing step at the back of the chapel, no manly cry of "Halt!" or possibly "Nay!" —no Vasily, in fact, come to bear me away from this loathed nuptial.

There was only me.

"There is an impediment," I said, trying to hold my voice steady, and only partly succeeding.

"No, there isn't," Griff said.

"There is! I don't consent to this marriage," I added, turning to the clergyman, who stood gaping at us in impotent befuddlement "I have been brought here against my will, under threats that have been made against my friends, and I appeal to you to stand my protector."

"This is nonsense!" Griff protested. "You agreed to marry me in London not three months ago—"

"I changed my mind! It's a woman's prerogative!"

"You told me just now that you *did* consent."

"I stopped arguing, and only to get you to stop browbeating me! I'm supposed to be mad," I told the clergyman. "Sir Humphrey has already submitted his guardianship petition to the courts. I'm incapable of consenting to this marriage, even if I wanted to!"

"She's *not* mad," Griff said. "The petition is spurious and will be rejected."

"I am not two months a widow!"

"So you say; but your husband stole a diamond worth two million pounds from you; so don't try to get my sympathy in *that* way."

"Warren," Lady Seton objected weakly. "She says she doesn't want to!" Bless her for trying!

Meanwhile, the clergyman seemed absolutely speechless. Griff turned upon him. "Carry on with the service, reverend!"

"I won't!" I cried, nearly in tears.

Griff's forearm blade shot out with a flick of his arm: he placed the blade against my heart. "You will," he said in that passionless voice I had come to detest. "I warned you not to make trouble, my dear; I've determined to have you, and so I will."

This must have startled Mr Bone, for somewhere in the shadows there came a loud noise, as of a Bible being knocked to the floor.

I caught my breath on a sob, for I had learned a great many things from that sound.

"I won't!" I declared. "I'd sooner marry the beachcomber! I'd marry him this moment, if I could!"

There was another sound from the shadows, and Mr Bone advanced, as though ready to do me this service.

"What are *you* doing?" Griff demanded, sending the beach-comber a look of suspicion. "Don't make me snap my fingers!"

"Snap them all you like; see if I care," said the beachcomber in his hoarse voice; but he raised his hand, and in it was the revolver I had last seen putting holes in Vasily the previous evening. He levelled the weapon at Griff. "You heard the lady: she doesn't want to marry you. She wants to marry *me.*"

I gave another sob, but this one was half laughter. Griff's fingers snapped, but nothing happened. For a moment the blade at my breast wavered in disbelief—but when I thought to move away it found me again. I stayed where I was, but my eyes were brimming with tears.

"It's *you*," I whispered to the beachcomber. "It *is* you."

I saw now what for a long time I had not looked closely enough to see: the smooth skin, the straight nose, the glimmer of the false lens on his remaining good eye, changing green to brown. Vasily Nikolaevich gave the slightest bow. "It is I," he said, with exquisite grammar calculated to make the governess within me give a little sigh of happiness.

"What do you mean?" Griff demanded, seeming at last to lose his nerve. *"Who* the devil are you?"

"Aha!" Vasily cried, with something of his old manner. "You thought it was the poor old beachcomber, did you not? —when in fact—!" He caught himself. No doubt it had suddenly occurred to him that he could not really admit to being Vasily Nikolaevich, the dead Grand Duke.

Lady Seton leaped up like a jack-in-a-box. "Not the dead husband, surely?"

In the silence, one might have heard a pin drop. "No," said Vasily hoarsely, in the manner of the old beachcomber. What a struggle it must have cost him! "No, I'm just her henchman."

So demoralised was he that Griff was able to act. *"Now,* Aunt Adelaide," he cried, pressing the large, red button on a small widget that now suddenly appeared in his hand. Lady Seton gave a squeak of surprise. There was a whirring, creaking sound beneath the thin cape she wore. Then—a *thing,* black and mechanical and gleaming with oil, untucked itself from beneath, clamped onto her shoulder, and pointed its evil, dark little muzzle directly at Vasily.

"Good Lord!" I cried, revolted. "You *didn't!* Is that a—a—"

"It's a shoulder-mounted rifle," Griff said coolly, "with an automatic self-loading mechanism; so I would advise you not to make any foolish decisions."

"I must protest," said the clergyman faintly. "This is the house of God!"

"You prosthetised your *aunt?*" I shrieked.

"I gave her something with which to overawe the servants in my absence," Griff said testily. "It dismounts, naturally! Here, Aunt Adelaide, give me your trigger; I'll handle it from here."

I keenly felt the ridiculousness of the situation. Here was Griff holding me at sword-point, and Vasily holding him at gun-point; and then there was Lady Seton biting her lip in the pew, with her shoulder-cannon! If I wrote this down for my sisters, they would never believe me!

But there was no time to dwell in the moment. Lady Seton had taken out a little red-buttoned widget of her own and was regarding it doubtfully.

"Hand it over," Griff said, reaching out for it.

"Please don't let him have it, Lady Seton!" I begged. "I have a great deal of respect for your nephew, but I don't want to marry him! I'm in love with someone else!"

"Aunt Adelaide! Remember all I've done to help you!"

"Please, Lady Seton! If I've given you any comfort in your distress, hear me now!"

"Aunt Adelaide!" Griff thundered again, but it was too late. Lady Seton turned so that the muzzle of the rifle pointed at her nephew; and when he tried to correct its aim with one of the tiny levers that protruded from his widget, she used her own to override it.

"Don't shout at me, Warren," she said in a soft, unhappy

293

voice. "You didn't do anything to help *me*—not really. You only wanted to help yourself to Sir Humphrey's shipping company."

"You benefit from it, too," Griff declared.

"Yes; and I'm lucky that I do, or I might still be locked in that horrible room." She lifted her chin. "It's time I stood up for myself! You're *not* going to get control of Miss Dark's shares—and you're not going to get control of mine, either. From now on, *I'm* going to run Seton & Associates. Let them go!"

Griff did not move; he fixed his aunt with a baleful but impotent glare.

"You had better run, Miss Dark," Lady Seton added, to me. "Good-bye, and thank you! I look forward to doing business with you!"

I took an experimental step away from Griff, and he allowed it. In a moment I was at Vasily's side. Had it not been for the revolver he held, I might have thrown my arms about his neck; but instead I took his free hand in mine, and squeezed it with silent fervour.

"This company is doomed," Griff warned as we turned away. "Who owns it now? Two women and a gang of natives? None of you have any experience running a business—and if any of you presume that Vandergriff & Son will do business with you now, you're quite mistaken!"

I glanced back at him. "I think we'll do quite well without you," said I. "Tin is plentiful in Yunnan, I've heard, and might be nearly as profitable as opium. In the meanwhile, of course we shall hire someone to advise us—someone who knows a great deal more than *you* do about the Chinese trade. I think we'll do quite well, in fact."

"You'll have to find someone else to ship your workers,"

Vasily added, unable to forgo a taunt of his own. "And I suppose you'll have to get a wife the way the rest of us do—with your native charm. God help you." He bowed to Lady Seton, and we hurried from the chapel.

The postern-gate stood open, beckoning freedom. I made towards it, but Vasily had stopped dead, and pulled me to a stop as well.

"Molly," he said, "can you ever forgive me?"

I turned to him in a sort of frantic confusion. "Why—what have you done *now?*"

Vasily pointed towards the chapel. "He—Vandergriff—said he'd *have* you."

"I know, Vasily, but we must *go—*"

"And I could have bitten his throat out—but he doesn't *love* you—"

"Vasily, *really—*" I dragged him by main force through the gate. Oh, bliss! The night was clear, and in the light of the moon there was a tolerably good view of a carriage which was waiting there, with Schmidt holding the reins and Mimi and Nijam pacing about outside.

"Wait, Molly," Vasily begged. I turned to him, feeling a little more secure now within sight of our other friends. He caught both my hands in his and hurried on. "How can a man who *loves* you say such a thing? I see it now, and—how can you ever forgive me?"

I stared back at him for a long moment before all his incoherent words fitted together in my mind and I thought: *Oh.*

In one careless speech, Griff had held up a mirror to Vasily, and he had recoiled from it in some distress. And now he wished to waste precious time in flagellation! One scarcely knew whether to laugh or cry. But then we heard steps pelting out of the chapel.

"You might make a start by getting me *out of here!*" I hissed, dragging him again towards the carriage. Happily, Griff's footsteps turned away from us towards the house; but I knew better than to think he would give up his pursuit so easily.

"At last!" Nijam said as we hurried towards her. "Schmidt was just about to go in to fetch you! What kept you so long?"

"I've missed you too, Nijam," I said fondly.

Vasily, meanwhile, was critically surveying the carriage—another tiny dog-cart. "What's this? We'll never fit into this. Some of us will need to walk."

"I don't mind walking," Schmidt said at once.

"It's not to be thought of," Nijam retorted. "You're dead on your feet, and you haven't slept in two nights."

"Vasily and I will walk," I cut in, before Mimi, who had adopted a knowing smile, could say anything that would make both Nijam and Schmidt more uncomfortable than they already were. "It isn't far, and we have a great many things to discuss."

"Oh, *have* you?" Mimi asked. I divined that, distracted from making Nijam and Schmidt uncomfortable, she was now eager to do the same by Vasily and myself.

"Be off with you," Vasily said sharply. "If we haven't—"

He was interrupted by the sound of running horses, and we turned in alarm to see Sir Humphrey's carriage, with Griff beside the coachman on the box, come spinning towards us around the bend in the road.

"Off with you!" Vasily repeated, as he drew me into the shadows of the banian-trees.

Obligingly, the others leapt into the dog-cart and away

they pelted by the uncertain light of their lamps. In another moment Griff drew level with us. For a moment we heard him urging on the reluctant coachman, who protested that he was already driving as fast as was wise, given the darkness and the state of the road. Then that carriage, too, was swallowed up in the darkness. The sound of running horses persisted a little longer, and then silence returned to the world.

"So you'll forgive me?" Vasily asked, hopefully.

I sighed. Really, the man was incorrigible! But then after a moment I bit my lip with glee, for it struck me that he had come nearer than ever before to admitting that he loved me.

I linked my arm with his. "I'll consider it, but I make no promises."

There was nothing in the world but us and the moon, the flying lamps arising from the city, and the contented whirring of a thousand insects in the undergrowth around us. For a moment we walked along in silence, by degrees allowing the mild night to relieve the strain we had been under. Then Vasily said, "But I'm to understand that you've asked my hand in marriage?" and I dissolved into laughter.

Chapter XXV.

"I said I would marry the *beachcomber,*" I informed him. "I said nothing about Vasily Nikolaevich—nor about Basil Nicks, either!"

Vasily laughed. "Come, my dear! You won't escape your word so easily! You must have understood that it was me from the start—or at least, from the moment I gave you the key!"

"Not in the least! How was *I* to know that you were a master of disguise? The truth never even occurred to me until the moment you spoke in my ear on the quay tonight."

At first, Vasily laughed disbelievingly; but then he fell silent. "You *must* have known it was me," he protested. "Even if you never received my letter, you did everything nearly the precise way I asked for it."

"But I *didn't* know it was you—not really," I assured him. "I only knew that the beachcomber was on my side because he had given me the key, and allowed me to use it even when it cost him."

"But if you didn't receive the letter, how could you have known the triad wasn't?"

"From the sketches with which they betrayed us to Sir Humphrey, of course," I told him. "Only, they didn't betray us, did they? *You* provided the sketches, and they passed them on to Sir Humphrey at your instruction. I knew then that you must be in league with them; and with that I saw everything."

"But how did you know they were my sketches?"

"Oh," I said, "I recognised your style. I picked up your sketchbook by mistake when we were leaving Moscow."

"That was *private,*" he began, before falling silent—no doubt recalling the contents of that sketchbook!

To spare his delicate feelings, I changed the subject. "That must have been the real Mr Bone who shot you. Were you much hurt?"

"The merest scratch, I assure you."

"And do you really have a prosthetic eye?"

"Yes—I had Nijam transplant the wretched thing in place of my own, with a slight modification to allow me to control it. I could not have Griff always watching me, and making me dance to his tune. That happened on the night you came to visit us in the city, you know," he added. "I found the man creeping about outside the house, thinking that he had caught you where you oughtn't to be—but I caught *him,* and took him back to Victoria with me. Nijam is to be congratulated upon her knowledge of ocular surgery. Is there *anything* that woman can't do? —Don't answer that. She can make a radio out of two coacoa-nuts and a piece of string, but she can't tell Schmidt she loves him. Something will have to be done about those two!"

I did not know what was wrong with him, that he should be babbling on about Nijam and Schmidt at such a moment. "Oh, Vasily! She might have left your eye alone!"

"It healed quickly enough; the benefits of being bitten by my relatives, I suppose."

"Oh, *Vasily!*"

"If Bone had been going bald, now, *that* would have been a tragedy," he said, in a complacent tone that told me he rather enjoyed my protests.

I looked about for a beetle to drop down his neck. "You're more attached to your hair than you are to your *eye?* Can't Nijam put it back?"

"No, but this one is a deal more useful than the old one ever was—it can see in the dark and any number of things."

"But it transmits everything you see!" I shuddered. "How unspeakable!"

"Oh, of course I shall have Nijam disable *that* function. It was useful, anyway; if I hadn't been willing to lose an eye, I doubt she would have trusted me to watch you without giving myself away."

"Oh, *Vasily!*" I cried a third time.

"Modulate your bewailings, my dear, or I'll think you have developed a kindness for me."

I gave a laugh that was half a sob. All this time, I had thought myself so utterly alone; yet all the time, Vasily had been by my side—and in a way he had never been there before, so completely hidden that I had never dreamed it was he! On an impulse, I pulled him to a halt, seized his dear head in both my hands, and kissed first one eye, and then the other.

"I will treasure them both," I told him.

He went as still as death. "And my mouth?" he asked. "Don't let it become jealous of my eyes."

I pushed him away with a laugh. I was not ready to let Vasily begin overwhelming my better judgement again, but I was proud of myself for having the courage to kiss any part of him at all.

"I can still scarcely believe it," he added with a laugh of

his own. "You knew nothing—all this time—nothing of me, nothing of Li Ling and his people, nothing of the games we were playing with your life and freedom—and yet you took everything on faith."

"I hope this means you'll stop fussing about how I can never trust you," I said, with mock severity.

"My dear, my mouth is stopped forever—albeit, not in the way I prefer." He thought for a moment. "I suppose," he said slowly, "if you *didn't* know that I was the beachcomber, it would explain why you went to Vandergriff for help, and then hastened down to Victoria to tell me that the Typhoon Gang was out for my blood. That puzzled me a great deal; I had to run down to our lodgings and very quickly patch up a new disguise, with Schmidt stationed outside the market to catch you as you passed."

"So that was how he knew we were coming!"

"But why did you not leave a note in the chapel? I had collected the first one within a moment of your having left it."

"I saw that," I said ruefully. "I was convinced that it had fallen into the hands of the enemy—and that was why I believed I had nowhere to turn, but to Griff."

"It's my fault," he said. "I ought to have made doubly and triply sure that you knew it was I. Only I was afraid of so much as a whisper, for I knew that Vandergriff might be listening in. Little mouse, I'm covered in shame! You ought not to have believed yourself so utterly alone."

"All's well that ends well," I told him. "But what did you do with the original Mr Bone?"

"Oh, at first—once we had relieved him of the prosthetic eye—we put him on a ship to Singapore, with forged credentials and enough money in his pocket to see him into some

301

gainful employment. But he must have got ashore somehow before the ship sailed, and then he came after me. I think he had an idea that we had deprived him of a good thing, and wanted his revenge. But Schmidt caught up with him again after he shot me, and this time we saw him off for good."

I thought of the beachcomber with mixed feelings. It was now more than clear why he had at first repelled, and then comforted me. The real Mr Bone was a horrible man, after all; but for Vasily's sake, and because he had been rather heartlessly used by everybody, I hoped that he could find a way to better himself.

"Impersonating the man was a risk, I know," Vasily said at last, "but I was desperate to be by your side. I was going mad in that little room in Victoria, knowing that you were alone in that place, and that I was playing games with your life. But you didn't need me, after all."

"I did need you," I protested. "I think *I* might have run mad for sheer loneliness, had I not known that I had at least one friend with me."

He darted me a glance. "You're not going to run mad, Molly—no matter what anyone tells you!"

I could not help laughing. As I did so, a cloud which had lain on me half my life drifted away; for of one thing, at least, I was now quite certain. "Now that Sir Humphrey is no longer threatening to lock me up, I very much doubt that I will! Nor was I ever likely to! I see imprints, not delusions—and even they have been behaving themselves more politely in recent days."

Certainly, I would be surprised if I ever saw my father's imprint again. He certainly had not appeared, as was his invariable custom hitherto, at sunset.

Presently we passed between the hills and descended the road into the city. By now it was well past midnight, but the festivities were only just reaching their height. In the streets below there were more lanterns than ever, and the music drifted up to us until, despite my weariness, my feet almost itched to dance.

"In all this you trusted me better than I did you," Vasily said at length, musingly. "Can you forgive me for having so little faith in you?"

"That, as I hope to be forgiven, I will," I said primly. "But of course I knew I could trust you to *some* extent, Vasily. I have for some time. After all, you know all my secrets."

"I do?" For a while this struck him with silence. At last we passed beneath the last of the banian trees before the road plunged into the brightly-lit streets of the city. In these shadows, Vasily pulled me to a stop and turned me about to face him.

"Speaking of secrets, there's something I ought to tell you," he said. "Molly my dear! I love you to distraction. It's been creeping upon me for some time, but I knew it for certain that night at the British Museum, when the Noor-Jahan was in my hand and you looked so very certain that I was about to take it and abandon you. I ought to have known it sooner, when I found myself telling you to hand me over to the Okhrana for your own profit, because I could not bear to see you marry Vandergriff. But I have no excuse for afterward, when I made a modern play, as Mimi would call it, because I wanted to conceal my feelings until I was certain they were returned. My dear, I'm guilty of unforgivable cowardice—among other things. The truth is that I'm terrified by how much I want to be by your side. Not long ago I was terrified that you would

303

never return my feelings, and now I'm terrified that you do. I'm terrified that I might ruin you, I'm terrified that I might hurt you, and I'm terrified that I might lose you. I'm terrified of never being able to love you the way you ought to be loved." He paused; for a moment the spate of words which had carried him on so long, seemed to have dried up. At length he laughed uneasily. "Real things are costly. It was easier when I thought I could cheat you into a counterfeit of love."

"Oh," I said softly.

"I've been a very great fool, as well as a coward," he added. "I've never been so happy in my life as I was in those few short weeks between London and Petersburg—only I didn't see it. I thought I needed money in order to buy you. I thought that I could never be happy until I did. Only I threw it all away, because when happiness came for me at last it looked quite other than I thought—I was looking for something proud and decked in gold, but it was a soft, quiet, humble little thing; and I nearly destroyed it."

"I have regrets, too," I said, when he stopped to draw breath. "I valued myself by the money in my purse, and not as a human soul. And I presumed you valued me as little. That was an insult neither of us deserved."

"Perhaps not, but you are less to blame. I have never properly valued anything in my life, and you have always been far kinder to me than I deserve."

I gave him an impudent look. "I shall be as kind as I like to be, and you cannot stop me."

"I could kiss you," he said. His hands tightened upon my shoulders, and I felt a momentary thrill at the thought that he might carry out his threat: for something had cleared in the air between us, so that I would not have minded kissing him—nor did I think it would have been the sort of kiss it had been on the train, desperate and greedy and overpowering, being intended to take the place of something real.

But then, just as suddenly, he released me.

"I beg your pardon," Vasily said, abashed. "You told me not to try to sway you in that way."

"Besides which," I said, pulling myself together, "I think I would prefer not to kiss you in the guise of Mr Bone. Which is not to say that I *will* kiss you again, mind you!"

I stepped around him and continued down the road into the city, and the lights, and the music. But I moved in a secret kind of jubilation, after all. I had set out upon this venture in an attempt to see whether Vasily was able to learn from what I told him; and for the first time I had a hope that he could.

He fell into step again beside me. "Does this mean there's hope for me? Even if you *do* have a fortune now, to defend from plausible villains?"

"You are sorely mistaken if you think you were ever a *plausible* villain," I said. Mimi must be corrupting my good manners; either that, or I was a little light-headed with happiness. I sniffed. "I am not going to give away *my* fortune, just to make *you* feel better."

Vasily considered this a moment; and I thought I could *feel* his mood lightening. "What's your mother's address again?" he demanded after a moment. "I'm going to write to her."

I bit my lip; but I managed to keep my voice steady and guileless. "Whyever should you do that?"

"Because, Molly-my-dear, when a man wishes to employ all his wiles in convincing a woman...oh, you minx! I see that smile! *You* know why!"

"Why do you call me Molly all of a sudden?" I asked him.

"It used to be *my dear Mary.*"

"Oh! that!" There was another silence. "Everyone calls you Molly. I meant to create a special rapport by using a name no one else did." He darted me a glance that was half sheepish, half accusing. "I'll beg your pardon all you like, so long as you give me your mother's address!"

I sniffed: evidently he was not to be put off. "Well," I said, "I might have written to her already, myself."

"But I wish to write to her on a *very particular matter.*"

"So was my letter on a very particular matter." This was true; I had included my question with the third and most recent volume of my memoirs.

There was a silence as he considered this. "And?" he asked, in a voice dangerously calm.

"And," said I, "she said that she doesn't know Vasily Nikolaevich half as well as she should, and that in consequence of that, the rest of my friends who do, should consider themselves appointed to act *in loco parentis* for the occasion."

This time, the silence was longer.

"Do you mean to say," Grand Duke Vasily said, tearing distractedly at the long flyaway strands which had been gummed into his beard, "that if I wish to court you as my wife, I am going to have to ask the permission of *Mimi Laine?*"

I bit my lip, but there was no hiding my smile.

"And my *valet?*"

"I believe I made myself clear," I said.

We passed into streets alive with holiday-makers carrying red lanterns, and there was no more chance for conversation. Vasily tucked my hand into his arm and we walked together through a night full of lights and music and happiness. I do not suppose that I have ever known a better.

* * *

Here I shall pass over some of what happened in the next busy few days. How Griff took ship with the next tide; how Sir Humphrey's arrest became a nine-days'-wonder in Hong Kong; how all his crimes were uncovered, including many that we had never dreamed of; how I entered into the possession of my own inheritance and the guardianship of that belonging to my sisters; how Lady Seton was confirmed in the possession of her wits, her house, and her shares; how I was courted by the press as the younger and more interesting of Sir Humphrey's fair victims; how Lady Seton and the elder Mr Li and I discussed the ordering of the company that had so strangely fallen to our lot; how a mutual society was founded to aid the dockhands whom Sir Humphrey had kept for so long on little more pay than would keep them from starving; how Mimi most heartlessly charmed the young Li Ling, until I had to beg her not to make matters uncomfortable for me with his father, who had his hands sufficiently full trying to convince Lady Seton of his ability to manage a shipping company; how lawyers and magistrates, journalists and society ladies and even the Governor came and went and made a lion of me, until I was quite sick of roaring for their entertainment—all this the reader can well imagine.

There was a great deal of business to get through in a very short period of time, so that it was not until more than a week later, aboard the steamer to London, that any of us had a moment to draw breath. We were, for once, on rather a nice steamer, the sort fitted out with deck-chairs and fleet-footed stewards with cups of tea and deferential manners. The five of us, after a few days at sea during which I had and recovered from the usual bout of sea-sickness, now congregated in a secluded corner of the deck where no outsider was likely to disturb us as we opened the mail which had been awaiting us in Singapore, our latest port-of-call. There were newspapers and a pair of telegrams for me, and also a very sturdy-looking box for Nijam, accompanied by a letter.

"Open it up," I urged her, tossing my telegrams aside. *Those* could only be business, and I was nearly as tired of business as I was of this everlasting tropical humidity. The box looked far more interesting. I did not miss the covert glances which Schmidt was sending us from the rail where he was apparently receiving a ballet-lesson from Mimi, or the faint flush that had spread across his face when the box was handed to its recipient.

I sent Vasily a meaning look. He had not observed Schmidt's very interesting colour, however, being seated cross-legged upon the deck-chair beside me, hard at work upon a sketch which he steadfastly refused to show me.

"It's locked," Nijam said, rattling the combination-lock which held the box shut. She tore open the letter and gave a disgusted sigh. "Now it's asking me to solve an *algebraic equation?* Who has the time for that?"

"If you solve the equation, will that let you open the lock?" I asked. "Who's it from, anyway?"

"I don't know and I don't much care." Nijam sniffed, and tossed the box aside. At the rail, Schmidt looked downcast. "What's in that telegram?"

I handed them over, quite happy to let her deal with my business for me, and opened the Hong Kong newspaper. EMINENT BIONIC CHEMIST VISITS PLAGUE HOSPITAL, read a prominent headline; and beneath it, in smaller type,

Collects Bacterial Samples for Prosthetic Research.

I settled in happily to read more. My sea-sickness had left me feeling too tired and sleepy to try my hand at algebra, no matter how tempting the prize. But I thought the newspaper might contain some clues.

Beside me, Nijam gave a sound of satisfaction.

"It seems," she said, brandishing one of the telegrams, "that Seton is likely to escape all the consequences of his crimes on account of being declared mad, and locked up in an asylum!"

"Good heavens," I said. "There *is* justice in the world, thank God!"

"I shouldn't call it divine justice," said Nijam. "I should call it a very timely and well-judged application of cinematographic science, myself."

I was too tired, and too comfortable, to sit up and become indignant; but I turned my head to fix her with a look of stern displeasure. It was wasted upon her, of course—she was concealed behind a pair of smoked glasses. Perhaps these provided her with a vantage-point from which to observe Schmidt attempting a pirouette. There was certainly the faintest mischievous smile trembling upon her lips.

"What do you mean, cinematographic science?" I demanded. She must not be allowed to become too comfortable, after all. Not if she was going to say such fatuous things. "Sir Humphrey didn't go mad for a trifling sound-and-light show! It was the imprints summoned up by *me,* that swarmed upon him and sent him fleeing all the way into the Victoria harbour!"

Nijam's smile only became more provoking. Too late, I divined that it was directed at me, rather than Schmidt. "Would he have seen *your* ghosts at all, if not for mine?" She put up an elegant brown hand to conceal her yawn. "What do you think, Mimi—should Miss Dark retire, and allow *me* to handle the apparitions? I can produce as many as are needed, after all—and for a broader audience!"

"Throw a cushion at her, Schmidt," I begged. "You know you'd like to."

Nijam's Alphonse blushed.

"What a fetching colour, Schmidt," Vasily murmured, just loudly enough that none of us could miss it. I decided that it was high time Vasily had *his* share of the fun.

"My friends," I announced, clapping my hands for attention, "there's something Vasily has been *dying* to ask you, on a very serious matter that will affect all of us. Indeed, I'm surprised he didn't broach the topic *days* ago."

He sent me a look of outrage. "My dear Mary Angelica, I was only waiting for the proper moment."

"And now I've prepared you one," said I, placidly. "Fire ahead, Vaska."

He knew that I was teasing him with the pet name he said ought to belong to a cat—but he drew a deep breath anyway and said, "I am given to understand that I must ask *you,* in place of Miss Dark's parents, for permission to pay her my respects."

Nijam dragged her eyebrows up and her smoked glasses down, gazing upon us with quiet but unmistakable glee. Schmidt's mouth dropped open, and he gestured questioningly to himself. Mimi straightened, blinking. "What's this? Pay her? Pay her what?"

"Respects, Mimi," Vasily said in a long-suffering kind of way. "I wish for your permission to court Miss Dark."

"Is this true?" Mimi demanded, turning upon me. "It isn't

another of Vasily's little jokes?"

"No, Mimi; it's quite true. That's what my mother said."

A glee of her own, quite unholy, lit up Mimi's face. She turned upon Vasily with an outstretched hand. "A hundred pounds," she declared, "and you shall have my blessing."

"I fear Mrs Dark has misplaced her confidence," Vasily said drily, to me.

Nijam arose majestically from her deck-chair, setting down the telegrams. "For shame, Mimi. Have you no sense of your responsibility—to Miss Dark and her family, as well as to this venture? Come, Schmidt! I should like to discuss this with a person of sense and judgement."

"As would I," he said, contriving not to change colour too much. The two of them walked down the deck together a way before stopping to put their heads together. Vasily and I watched them in an agony of expectation. Mimi watched them, too; but I do not think *she* was in any agonies about it. Nijam had left a peppermint on her deck-chair, and Mimi let out a gurgle of satisfaction as she pounced upon it.

"Sometimes," said Vasily with a conscious laugh, "I have the strangest feeling that Nijam and Schmidt are the parents I never had. Quite an unpleasant thing to discover at my age!"

I opened my mouth to say that I was quite well equipped with parents of my own, thank you. But then it struck me how Schmidt was gentle and stubborn, as my father had been; while Nijam, who was tall and beautiful and forbidding, and always right about everything, was uncannily like my own mother.

"Oh, dear," I said in fascination. "It's *true*."

Already the two had finished their consultation and turned back to us. I found that despite my lassitude, I was sitting up, straight and expectant, in my deck-chair.

Schmidt spoke first, clearing his throat. "We have agreed to allow it."

"*Under* the conditions laid down by Miss Dark aboard the Siberian train," Nijam added, sitting down and picking up her box again. "No pity-mongering. No confidence tricks. No unsolicited kissing. The arrangement to be terminated at any time on Miss Dark's sole discretion, and *no wheedling.*"

"But on that understanding," Schmidt added more kindly, "we're delighted to see it. Mimi is delighted too, I'm sure."

Mimi raised her eyes to the heavens and heaved a sigh. "Oh, *very* well, since Dark seems to wish it! But I'll expect a pearl from you, Vasily, next time we're in Paris. The sort that looks like melting candle-wax."

"The finest of baroque pearls shall be yours, Mimi, the moment I can in good conscience steal it." Vasily threw Nijam and Schmidt a glance, and for a moment I thought that there was real gratitude and relief upon his face: a raw, unpracticed expression, which I could not recall ever having seen there before. "Nijam and Schmidt shall have one each, too, if they want one."

Schmidt cleared his throat. "Miss Nijam doesn't like pearls, but—"

His words were interrupted by a squeal of girlish delight. For a moment I supposed that a sixth person had, unbeknownst to the rest, added herself to our party. Then I realised that *Nijam,* of all people, had thrown up her hands and uttered a second squeal.

"*Yersinia pestis!*" she cried.

Had she grown a second head I might have been less startled. Sounds of girlish enthusiasm seemed utterly ill-suited to her.

"Bless you!" said Vasily, no less startled. "I hope it isn't catching!"

"Oh, it is—horribly!" Nijam cooed, extracting a vial from its nest of cotton-wool within the box. It was filled with a clear liquid and decorated, not very reassuringly, with skull and crossbones. "Someone sent me *Yersinia pestis!* Look, Dark! In the fourteenth century, this very bacillus wiped out half the world's population! …But *who?*"

Schmidt looked pink and gratified, but of course Nijam never looked in *that* direction. I glanced at my newspaper, and smiled. What an able confidence-man Schmidt *was* becoming, to be sure!

As Nijam went about excitedly menacing each of us in turn with her deadly bacillus, I picked up my second telegram and opened it. It was from Vienna, and I smiled. Mimi might be getting her baroque pearl sooner, rather than later. Herr Haber congratulated us upon a job well done, and informed us that he had a new venture already waiting for us—in Paris.

S. D. G.

Miss Dark will return in
A Stab in the Dark

Unhistorical Note

I've never liked to put *too* much history into my *Bête Époque* stories, but in writing this book I felt particularly annoyed by the constraints that fasten upon every author of historical fiction. Time, opportunity, and propriety all made it wiser for me not to delve too deeply into the magnificent, unique and endlessly fascinating backdrop of 1890s Hong Kong.

But what a setting it is! In the 1890s Hong Kong was a burgeoning metropolis, home to thousands of adventurers from around the globe: wealthy English businessmen who built themselves grandiose mansions such as the "Douglas Castle" (now the University Hall of Hong Kong at Pok Fu Lam which I have stolen for Sir Humphrey Seton); Portuguese, Arab, Jewish, and Eurasian merchants; and vast numbers of Chinese labourers, businessmen, students, refugees and revolutionaries. Triads trafficked in people and drugs; the Revive China Society held training for insurgents and planned uprisings and assassinations; conglomerates of Chinese businessmen banded together to bid on the lucrative opium monopoly; and when the bubonic plague tore through the city in 1894, the Japanese bacteriologist Kitasato Shibasaburo became the first to identify the deadly bacillus responsible. (The bacillus itself was for some mysterious reason ultimately named in honour of Alexandre Yersin, the French-Swiss bacteriologist who, working independently on cadavers set

314

aside for Kitasato, identified the bacillus later the same month).

Of course, the whole history is deeply overshadowed by opium. The First Opium War of 1839-44 did not merely force the Chinese government to cede the island of Hong Kong to the British as a colony: it also set the stage for nearly a century of British imperial reliance on the export of Indian opium to Chinese communities around the globe. The trade was of such vital importance in keeping the imperial ledgers in the black, that no less an authority than Carl Trocki suggests that the British empire can best be understood as a global drug cartel. British public opinion began turning against the trade in the 1870s, when the effects of opium abuse began to be more widely publicised, and the Hong Kong-based English merchants began to distance themselves from the trade. But even in the hands of non-English merchants it continued to keep the empire afloat well into the twentieth century: in 1905 it was still important enough to warrant serious attention from the Quaker reformer, Joshua Rowntree, in works such as *The Imperial Drug Trade: A Re-Statement of the Opium Question.* By the 1880s, as much as 70% of the opium refined in Hong Kong itself was being exported to the Chinese diasporas in Australia and California. If opium tends to feature in most stories set in the nineteenth-century Orient, it's only a reflection of historical reality.

I had my work cut out to acquaint myself with the basics of this fascinating history, and consulted a number of resources—but I'd recommend two books in particular to the casual reader hoping to learn more: Steve Tsang's *A Modern History of Hong Kong* and Carl Trocki's *Opium, Empire and the Global Political Economy: A Study of the Asian Opium Trade*

1750-1950. On the other hand, if you have questions about my depiction of insanity in the nineteenth century, I can recommend reading Nellie Bly's 1888 exposé, *Ten Days in a Mad-House.* Much of the way Miss Dark is treated in this book is lifted, rather uncreatively, from that shocking real-life account.

Thanks are due once again to my wonderful beta and sensitivity readers for their help—Christina Baehr, W.R. Gingell, Schuyler McConkey, Claire Trella Hill, and above all Amanda Tong, who brought the eye of a native Hong Konger to this story. Any errors that remain are of course my own. I would also like to apologise to *Jane Eyre.* I love you, Jane - I promise.

Suzannah Rowntree
March 2024

About the Author

Suzannah Rowntree lives in a big house in rural Australia with her awesome parents and siblings, drinking fancy tea and writing historical fantasy fiction that blends real-world history with legend, adventure, and a dash of romance.

You can connect with me on:
🌐 https://suzannahrowntree.site

Subscribe to my newsletter:
✉ https://subscribepage.io/srauthor

Also by Suzannah Rowntree

The Miss Sharp's Monsters Series
The Werewolf of Whitechapel
Anarchist on the Orient Express
A Vampire in Bavaria

The Miss Dark's Apparitions Series
Tall & Dark
Dark Clouds
Dark & Stormy
Dark & Dawn
A Stab in the Dark

The Watchers of Outremer Series
A Wind from the Wilderness
The Lady of Kingdoms
Children of the Desolate
A Day of Darkness
A Conspiracy of Prophets
The House of Mourning

The Pendragon's Heir Trilogy
The Door to Camelot
The Quest for Carbonek
The Heir of Logres

The Fairy Tale Retold Series
The Rakshasa's Bride
The Prince of Fishes